PENGUIN BOOKS

The Sword of the Te~

Ducking under the swi~ ~nged forward, shoulder dropping, and caught th~ ~ in the chest, knocking him backward, half up the embankment. The thief swung the sword again, the blade slashing toward his head in a whistling arc. Holliday threw himself to one side as the sword came close to decapitating him.

The man turned, tossing the sword away, and scrambled up the bank, using both hands to haul himself upward. Holliday lunged again, managing to grip his attacker's ankle. The man kicked back furiously, this time connecting, catching Holliday in the chin. Holliday fell away, stunned, then tumbled back down the embankment. By the time he got to his feet again the man who'd burned down Uncle Henry's house and tried to steal the mysterious sword had vanished into the night.

The Sword of the Templars

PAUL CHRISTOPHER

PENGUIN BOOKS

PENGUIN BOOKS

Published by the Penguin Group
Penguin Books Ltd, 80 Strand, London WC2R ORL, England
Penguin Group (USA) Inc., 375 Hudson Street, New York, New York 10014, USA
Penguin Group (Canada), 90 Eglinton Avenue East, Suite 700, Toronto, Ontario, Canada M4P 2Y3
(a division of Pearson Penguin Canada Inc.)
Penguin Ireland, 25 St Stephen's Green, Dublin 2, Ireland (a division of Penguin Books Ltd)
Penguin Group (Australia), 250 Camberwell Road, Camberwell, Victoria 3124, Australia
(a division of Pearson Australia Group Pty Ltd)
Penguin Books India Pvt Ltd, 11 Community Centre, Panchsheel Park, New Delhi – 110 017, India
Penguin Group (NZ), 67 Apollo Drive, Rosedale, Auckland 0632, New Zealand
(a division of Pearson New Zealand Ltd)
Penguin Books (South Africa) (Pty) Ltd, 24 Sturdee Avenue, Rosebank,
Johannesburg 2196, South Africa

Penguin Books Ltd, Registered Offices: 80 Strand, London WC2R ORL, England

www.penguin.com

First published in the USA by Signet, an imprint of New American Library,
a division of Penguin Group (USA) Inc. 2009
First published in Great Britain by Michael Joseph 2011
Published in Penguin Books 2011

1

This is a work of fiction. Names, characters, places and incidents are either the product of
the author's imagination or are used fictitiously, and any resemblance to actual persons,
living or dead, or to actual events or locales is entirely coincidental.

Set in 13/15.25 pt Garamond MT Std
Typeset by Palimpsest Book Production Limited, Falkirk, Stirlingshire
Printed in England by Clays Ltd, St Ives plc

ISBN: 978-0-241-95115-6

www.greenpenguin.co.uk

To Mariea, Noah, Chelsea & Gabe with all my love.

Acknowledgments

I would like to thank Brent Howard and Claire Zion at NAL for giving me the idea, the entrancing and spiffy-looking Leora, the best nurse in the world, and her fiancé, the real Raffi Wanounou, for letting me steal his wonderful name. Mazel tov to both of you.

Where is the grave of Sir Arthur O'Kellyn?
Where may the grave of that good man be? –
By the side of a spring, on the breast of Helvellyn,
Under the twigs of a young birch tree!
The oak that in summer was sweet to hear,
And rustled its leaves in the fall of the year,
And whistled and roared in the winter alone,
Is gone, – and the birch in its stead is grown. –
The Knight's bones are dust,
And his good sword rust; –
His soul is with the saints, I trust.

– Samuel Taylor Coleridge,
'The Knight's Tomb'

Hic iacet Arthurus, rex quondam rexque futurus.
Here lies Arthur, the Once and Future King.

– Sir Thomas Malory,
Le Morte d'Arthur

Glory to God Who did take His servant for a Journey by night from the Sacred Mosque to the farthest Mosque, whose precincts We did bless, in order that We might show him some of Our Signs: for He is the One Who heareth and seeth all things.

– The Koran, The Night Journey, Chapter 17, Verse 1, in which the Prophet is shown the great wonders in the ruins of Solomon's Temple

And he will stretch out his hand against the north, and destroy Assyria; and will make Nineveh a desolation, and dry like a wilderness.

– Zephaniah 2:13
The Holy Bible, King James Version

The Sword of the Templars

I

'In *The Da Vinci Code*, Dan Brown depicted the Knights Templar as being the sacred keepers of the secret of Christ's bloodline. In *Indiana Jones and the Last Crusade* they were portrayed as immortal guardians of the Holy Grail. In the movie *National Treasure*, Nicolas Cage described them as being the caretakers of a vast fortune buried under Trinity Church in downtown Manhattan. According to various religious scholars they were gatekeepers of the Temple of Solomon in Jerusalem after the successful conclusion of the First Crusade as well as protectors of pilgrims on their way to the Holy Land.

'Bull. The truth is the Knights Templar, this self-described Army of God, was nothing more than a gang of extortionists and thugs. As a group they were certainly the world's first example of organized crime, complete with secret rituals and a code not unlike that of the Sicilian Cosa Nostra – the Mafia.'

Lieutenant Colonel John 'Doc' Holliday, a dark-haired, middle-aged man in an Army Ranger uniform wearing a black patch over his left eye, looked out over the classroom, checking for some sort of response from his students, or failing that at least an indication of interest. What he saw were eighteen 'firsties,' fourth-year students, all male, all wearing the same 'as-to-class' short-sleeved blue uniform blouses with a neat triangle of snow-white T-shirt showing at the neck, all wearing the same gray trousers with a single stripe, all with the same high-and-tight haircut, all with the same sleepy, glassy-eyed expression of young men attending the last class of an academic day that had started almost ten hours before. Incredibly, this was the cream of the West Point graduating class, most of them single-minded ring thumpers who'd already branched Artillery, Infantry, or Armor, and none of whom had the slightest interest in medieval history in general or the Knights Templar in particular. Future Warriors of America. *Huah!*

Holliday continued.

'The big problem with the First Crusade of 1095 was the fact that the crusaders won it. By 1099 they'd captured Jerusalem and they were an army without an enemy. No more godless Saracens to slaughter. Knights of the time were professional soldiers, swords for hire bought and paid for by wealthy noblemen, most of them French,

Italian, or German. They were *chevaliers*, literally men who could afford to ride a horse; chivalry and fair damsels in distress didn't factor in the equation. They were killers, plain and simple.'

'Warriors, sir.' The observation came from Whitey Tarvanin, a tough-looking Finn from Nebraska whose pale skin and even paler hair had given him his nickname. He was obviously Infantry, the crossed idiot sticks on his uniform blouse proud proof of that. When he'd posted a few weeks ago he'd actually chosen Fort Polk, Alabama, the least attractive choice on the roster, just to prove how down and dirty he was.

'No, not warriors, Cadet, mercenaries. These guys were in it for the money, nothing more. No Honor, Duty, Country. Maybe a little raping and pillaging on the side; after all, according to the rules of engagement in the eleventh century non-Christians were going to Hell anyway, so they didn't count. The nobles had promised them all sorts of plunder in the Holy Land, but as it turned out there wasn't enough to go around and thousands of these *chevaliers* came back penniless and a lot of the nobles were close to bankruptcy, as well. Many of them returned home to find that their lands, castles, and everything else had been stolen by scheming relatives or simply forfeited by one king or another for taxes.'

Holliday paused.

'So what does an unemployed soldier whose only real skills involve hacking, butchering, and otherwise committing acts of extreme violence on the godless enemy do with himself once that enemy has been vanquished?'

Holliday shrugged.

'He does what men in that situation have done since the days of Alexander the Great. He turns to crime.'

'Like Robin Hood?' This was from 'Zitz' Mitchell, skinny, pimples, wire-rimmed glasses, and a hairline already edging backwards into baldness. After watching Mitchell go through four years at the Point, Holliday was still amazed by his stamina. He'd expected the beanpole cadet to wash out after Beast Barracks, if not before. But he'd stuck it out. Holliday smiled. Mitchell's pimples would go away eventually.

'Robin Hood was a romantic fantasy invented by songwriters who came along a few hundred years after the fact. The people I'm talking about, the *routiers*, as these vagabond highwaymen were called, were more like Tony Montana in *Scarface* – products of their environment; an unskilled ex-con Marielito washed up on the shores of Key West doesn't have much choice if he wants to get ahead in his new home: he deals cocaine. A *routier* in medieval France joins a gang of like-minded ex-soldiers and starts plundering the countryside or offering villages and towns "protection" for a price.

'One of these men was Hugues de Payens, a French knight in the service of the Duke of Champagne. The duke ran short of money and Sir Hugues switched allegiance, fighting with the army of Godfrey of Bouillon until Jerusalem was overthrown.

'Godfrey was installed as king of Jerusalem, and using his prior connection Sir Hugues along with half a dozen other *routiers* petitioned King Godfrey for the job of guarding the new pilgrim routes through the recently captured Holy Land, along with the right to establish their headquarters in the ruins of the old Temple of Solomon.

'Pilgrims were big business back then, and tolls from the pilgrims formed the basis for economy of the newly "liberated" Holy Land. Godfrey agreed, and Sir Hugues took things one step further, ratifying his position by having Pope Urban II grant him the status of a holy order, thus freeing the newly formed Knights Templar from the obligations of any sort of taxation, not to mention making them answerable only to the Pope.'

'He made them an offer they couldn't refuse.' Zitz Mitchell grinned. 'Godfather style.'

'Something like that.' Holliday nodded. 'Sir Hugues and his fellow *routiers* controlled a lot of military might. Godfrey had upset a bunch of his colleagues by accepting the title of king. At the very least Godfrey was buying protection for himself in the fragile little kingdom.'

'So what happened?' Whitey Tarvanin asked, suddenly getting interested.

'There had always been rumors about some sort of treasure hidden in the Temple of Solomon, maybe even the Ark of the Covenant, the box that supposedly held the second set of the Ten Commandments brought down from Mount Sinai by Moses.'

'Second set?' Tarvanin asked.

'Moses broke the first tablets,' said Granger, a football jock with the nickname Bullet, which probably had something to do with the shape of his head. He was also the class's biggest über-Christian. The hefty point guard had been scowling at Holliday since he'd mentioned Dan Brown and *The Da Vinci Code*. A sensitive topic for a lot of people, although Holliday wasn't quite sure why; after all, it was a novel, a work of fiction, not a campaign platform or a sermon. Granger cleared his throat as though he was embarrassed about displaying too much knowledge in front of a teacher. 'God wrote them down a second time and Moses put them in the Ark. It's in the Bible.'

'It's also in the Koran,' said Holliday mildly. 'It has a deep significance for Muslims as well as Christians.'

Granger's scowl darkened and his big head turtle-tucked down into his beef-slab shoulders.

'Did these guys find it?' Tarvanin asked.

'Nobody's quite sure. They found something, we know that much. Some say it was gold from King Solomon's Mines; others say it was the Ark of the Covenant; others say it was the secret wisdom of Atlantis. Whatever they found, within a year the Knights Templar were loaded. They financed their pilgrim escort service, built castles up and down the pilgrim routes to Jerusalem, and sold their muscle to anyone who could pay.

'Because of the distances involved between Europe and the Holy Land, they borrowed an idea from their Saracen enemies and introduced an encrypted note of transfer – a deposit of money in one place could be transferred on paper for thousands of miles. Wire transfers before they had wires.

'The Templars also began making loans at interest, although this was specifically forbidden in the Bible. As time went on the Templars even began financing entire wars. Land and other

7

assets were regularly used as collateral and often wound up being forfeited, expanding the Templars' power and wealth even more.

'Within a hundred years the Templars were into everything: loan-sharking, real estate, the protection rackets, shipping, smuggling, bribery, you name it. By the end of the next century they were the next best thing to a multinational conglomerate, and there's no doubt that much of it came from illicit sources.

'In most major cities of the time, from Rome to Jerusalem, Paris and London to Frankfurt and Prague, you didn't make a major move without consulting the local Templar authority. They controlled politics and banks, and owned entire fleets of ships. They were their own army, and by the beginning of the fourteenth century they had an unsurpassed intelligence network that spanned the known world. By then, of course, Jerusalem was back in the hands of the infidel, and the Holy Land was a battleground once again, but by then it didn't matter anymore.'

'So what happened then, sir?' Zitz Mitchell asked.

'They got a little too big for their britches,' explained Holliday. 'King Philip of France had just fought a long war with England. He was broke and he owed the Templar banks a lot of money. They were on the verge of taking over the entire country. The Pope was getting a little nervous, too; the Templars had far too much power within the church and were easily capable of putting their own man on the papal throne if they chose to.

'Something had to be done. Pope Clement and King Philip concocted a plan, laid charges against the Order for various crimes, some real and some false, and on Friday the thirteenth, 1307, most of the Templar leaders in France were arrested. They were tried for heresy, convicted, tortured, and burned at the stake. Eventually the Pope ordered every Catholic king in Europe to seize Templar assets under threat of excommunication, and by 1312 the Knights Templar had ceased to exist. Some say that the Templar fleet took the Order's treasure to Scotland for safekeeping, and other people think that they managed to flee to America, although there's no proof of that.'

'I don't see the point,' said Whitey Tarvanin. 'It's like most of this historic stuff. What's it got to do with right now? With us?'

'Quite a bit actually,' replied Holliday. It was an argument he'd heard a thousand times, usually from the mouths of gung-ho kids exactly like Whitey Tarvanin. 'Have you ever heard the expression "Those who forget history are condemned to repeat it"?' There were a lot of blank looks. Holliday nodded. He wasn't surprised.

'The quote is generally attributed to a man named George Santayana, a Spanish-born American philosopher of the early twentieth century. In the way that Adolf Hitler forgot the lessons of history and tried to invade Russia in the winter. If he'd remembered Napoleon's disastrous attempt he might have consolidated the Western Front instead and won the war in Europe. If we'd paid attention to history and remembered the decades-long failure of the French in Vietnam, maybe we wouldn't have tried to prosecute that war in the same way they did and maybe we wouldn't have lost it.'

'So what does that have to do with these Templar guys?' Zitz Mitchell asked.

'They got too powerful and they forgot who their friends were,' said Holliday. 'Just like we did. The United States came out of the Second World War with a per capita casualty rate that was lower than Canada's, and we suffered none of the catastrophic damage done to Europe and Great Britain. We also had made enormous industrial wartime loans that put us into the world's economic forefront. We dominated the world, just like the Templars. People got jealous. People got pissed off.'

'9/11,' said Tarvanin.

'Among other things,' said Holliday. 'And to make things worse we started mixing religion with politics. An old argument just like the Crusades. Our God is better than your god. "*God Is with Us*" on the Nazi belt buckles. Holy Wars against women and children, Catholics killing Protestants in Belfast. We went into Iraq for the wrong reasons and we left our friends behind. More people have been killed in the name of God and so-called "faith-based values" than for any other reason.

'You can bully people into being your allies, but when things get bad don't expect them to stand beside you, especially when you put God into the mix. The separation of Church and State. That's what the Constitution is for, although we seem to have forgotten that, as well. And as for the relevance of history you can probably trace the troubles in the Middle East directly back to Moses.'

'Don't you believe in God?' Bullet Granger asked.

'My personal beliefs have nothing to do with it,' said Holliday quietly. He'd been here before, as well – shaky ground, the kind of thing that could get you into trouble.

'You're always knocking Christians and the Bible. Moses, and like that,' Granger argued.

'Moses was a Jew,' said Holliday, sighing. 'So was Christ as a matter of fact.'

'Yeah, well,' grumbled the big football player, brooding. The bell rang.

Saved.

2

Lieutenant Colonel John Holliday stepped out of
Bartlett Hall and paused for a moment, enjoying
the early-evening sunlight that bathed the gray
stones of the United States Military Academy at
West Point. Directly in front of him was the
broad expanse of the Plain, the celebrated parade
ground that had felt the heels of ranks of marching cadets for more than two hundred years. All
the greats had been here, ghosts in cadence from
George Armstrong Custer to Dwight D. Eisenhower. To Holliday's left were a score of other
stone buildings rising like the protective bastions
of some crusader's castle. To the right, beyond
the baseball diamond on Doubleday Field, were
the bluffs that stood above the wide silver brush-
stroke of the Hudson River as it flowed the last
fifty miles down to New York City and the sea.

There were monuments scattered everywhere
on the grounds, commemorating battles, brave
deeds, brave men, and most of all the dead, grad-
uates of this place who'd given their best, their all
and their lives for one cause or another, the causes

now long forgotten, found only between the dusty pages of the history books that Holliday loved so well. That was the problem of course; all wars became meaningless in time. The Battle of Antietam was the bloodiest single conflict in American history with 23,000 dead in a single September day, and now it was a plaque on the side of an old building and a picnic ground for tourists toting cameras.

Holliday had fought his own war, of course, more than one in fact, from Vietnam to Iraq and Afghanistan, with half a dozen others in between. Had his fighting made any difference, or the lives of the men who died beside him in those terrible, lonely places? He knew that the simple answer was no. They kept on growing poppies in Afghanistan, oil still flowed in Iraq, rice still grew in the paddies around Da Nang, babies still starved to death in Mogadishu.

That wasn't the point, of course. Soldiers didn't think that way – they were trained not to. That's what places like West Point were for: to ensure that the next generation of officers in the United States Army would follow the orders of their superiors without question, because if you stopped or even hesitated long enough to ask that question the other guy would probably put a bullet in your head.

Holliday smiled to himself and went down the steps. All those wars, all those battles and the only injury he'd ever sustained was a blind eye caused by a sharp stone thrown up from the wheel of his Humvee on a back road outside Kabul. The eye had cost him his combat posting and had eventually led him here. The fortunes of war.

He crossed Thayer Road and started down the footpath that cut across the Plain at an angle. A pair of cadets rushed by, pausing just long enough to throw Holliday a rigid salute as they passed. Cows, by the look of the stripes on their tunics – third-year cadets. Firstie year to get through and then they'd be off to their own far-flung outposts of democracy. A long time ago in a galaxy far, far away. Holliday shook his head. Did George Lucas ever wonder just how many West Point Luke Skywalkers he had inspired? A cool gust of wind spun across the parade ground like a shiver. It wasn't even summer yet, but the breeze felt like fall. The leaves rattled in the trees that stood along the path for a few seconds, and then the strange feeling was gone. Goose just walked across his grave. One of his mother's favorite spooky sayings from long, long ago.

Holliday reached the far side of the Plain and the Thayer Statue, then crossed Jefferson Road and walked past Quarters 100, the superintendent's white-brick house, with its twin cannon guarding the front walk. He continued on to Professors Row with its neat cluster of late-Victorian houses and finally reached his own quarters at the end of the block, a little two-bedroom Craftsman bungalow built in the 1920s and the smallest accommodations on the Row.

Stepping into the cozy house was like going back in time. Warm oak, stained glass, and built-in cabinets were everywhere. There was even an original slatted Morris chair and matching ottoman in the living room beside the tiled fireplace, as well as plain painted cabinets and a huge porcelain sink in the simple kitchen at the back. He'd turned the larger of the two bedrooms into a study, the walls lined with his books. The smaller bedroom held nothing but a bed, a chest of drawers, and a bedside table. There was a single photograph on the table: Amy on their wedding day, with flowers in her hair, standing on a beach in Hawaii. Amy when she was young, eyes bright and flashing, before the cancer that swept through her like the cold wind that had rushed across the Plain a few minutes ago. It took her in the springtime, killing her before summer's end. It had been ten years ago now, but he still remembered her as she was in the fading picture on the bedside table, and mourned her and her vanished smile.

Mourned their decision to put off having children for a little while longer, because a little while never came and there was nothing left of her in the world.

Holliday went into the bedroom, stripped off his uniform and changed into jeans and an old USMA sweatshirt. He went to the built-in bar in the living room, poured himself a good belt of Grant's Ale Cask, and headed into his study, bringing the drink along with him. He put a Ben Harper and the Blind Boys of Alabama CD into the stereo and sat down at his old, scarred partners desk. He booted up his PC, did a quick check of his e-mail, then opened up the file for his work in progress, a half-serious, relatively scholarly work he had tentatively titled *The Well Dressed Knight*, a history of arms and armor from the time of the Greeks and Romans to the present day.

The book had originally been the subject of his doctoral thesis at Georgetown University back when he'd been at the Pentagon more than a decade ago, but with the passage of time it had turned into the massive, doorstopper epic that he used as both a hobby and a way to occupy his mind when it started to turn into the dark corners of memory that sometimes haunted him. At nine hundred pages he'd just finished with John Ericsson and the construction of the Union Navy vessel *Monitor*, the first American ironclad, and he still had a long way to go.

He'd been interested in the subject of armor since he was a kid playing with his Uncle Henry's antique lead soldiers in the big Victorian house up in Fredonia where the old man still lived. Henry had been a teacher at the State University of New York in Fredonia for years and before that something vaguely sinister and hush-hush during the Cold War. It had been Uncle Henry who'd interested him in history in the first place, and it was Uncle Henry who'd managed to wangle him the congressional recommendation that got him into West Point and out of the intellectual desert of Oswego, New York. Not to mention freeing him from a life of stormy alcoholic desperation with his widower father, a railroad engineer on the old Erie Lackawanna Line until he was laid off in the early seventies.

By then Holliday was already off to West Point, and a few years later, gone to war in Indochina. When his father died of liver failure in the spring of 1975, a twenty-four-year-old Holliday, now a field-promoted captain in the 75th Ranger Regiment, was helping the last evacuees board helicopters during the fall of Saigon.

Holliday sat at his desk working until taps sounded at ten o'clock. He got up, made himself a cup of tea, and then went back to his computer and spent another hour checking over what he'd just written. Satisfied, he switched off the computer and leaned back in his battered leather office chair. He intended to spend a few minutes reading the latest Bernard Cornwell book and then head to bed. His telephone rang. He stared at it, listening to it ring a second time. He felt a little lurch in the pit of his stomach and a clench in his throat. Nobody called with good news at eleven o'clock at night. It rang a third time. No use putting off the inevitable. He picked up the receiver.

'Yes?'

'Doc? It's Peggy. Grandpa Henry's at Brooks Memorial in Dunkirk. I'm there now. You'd better get here quick; they don't think he's going to make it.'

'I'll be there as fast as I can.' It was three hundred and fifty miles to Fredonia, seven hours if he drove straight through. He'd be there by dawn. Peggy was weeping now; he could hear the tears in her voice. 'Hurry, Doc. I need you.'

3

'You were the late Mr. Granger's nephew?'

Holliday nodded. 'He was my mother's older brother.'

'And he was your grandfather?' the lawyer asked, turning to Peggy Blackstock, the attractive dark-haired woman sitting beside Holliday on the other side of the gleaming glass-topped desk.

'That's right. On my mother's side.'

'So Colonel Holliday is in fact your second cousin and not your uncle,' said the lawyer. The mild reproof in his tone seemed to suggest that there was something inappropriate about their relationship. A pretty, thirty-something not-quite-niece with a roguish-looking not-quite-uncle who could have been her father. The lawyer was exactly the kind of small-town holier-than-thou, self-important pencil-necked jerk that Holliday had hated since he could remember. Another few years and he'd be running for mayor.

'I guess so,' the young woman replied with a shrug. 'He's always been Uncle John to me, or just Doc. What does it matter?'

'Just getting things straight in my mind,' said the lawyer airily. 'My father's notes in Mr. Granger's file are a little ... disjointed, you might say.'

The lawyer had the head of a much thinner man on a pudgy body that no amount of pinstripe tailoring could disguise. His hair was slicked back with some kind of gel, and he had a blue-black sheen of five o'clock shadow across his cheeks and jaw. Behind him on the wall was a prominently displayed Juris Doctor diploma from Yale Law School. The lawyer was the younger Broadbent of Broadbent, Broadbent, Hammersmith, and Howe, the firm that represented Holliday's Uncle Henry. As the lawyer had explained to them earlier, his father had recently retired with Alzheimer's and Broadbent the younger was taking up the slack. He'd made it sound like some kind of sacred duty rather than a job.

'If the interrogation is over maybe we could get on with the matter at hand,' said Holliday.

'Certainly,' answered Broadbent a little stiffly. He cleared his throat and flipped open the file on his desk with one perfectly manicured finger. 'Mr. Granger left a surprisingly substantial estate for a university professor.'

Holliday wasn't really interested in the greasy

little lawyer's opinions about his uncle, but he kept his mouth shut. He just wanted to get the whole thing over with.

'Please.'

'Yes, well,' said the lawyer. He went on. 'There is a pension fund amounting to something more than three quarters of a million dollars, various stocks and bonds of an equal amount, a life insurance policy fully paid up valued at half a million dollars, and then of course there is the Hart Street house and its contents.' Hart Street was a short cul-de-sac a little way from the center of town. Uncle Henry's house was a massive, Shingle Style Queen Anne mansion at the end of the tree-lined block, backing onto Canadaway Creek. The creek was where Uncle Henry had taught Holliday to fly-fish for steelhead trout when he was a little boy.

Broadbent cleared his throat again. 'According to the will everything is to be divided equally between you and Miss Blackstock.'

'Who is the executor of the will?' Holliday asked, sending up a silent prayer in hopes that it wasn't the lawyer.

'You and Miss Blackstock are coexecutors,' said Broadbent, his voice prim. 'Equally.' He glanced at Peggy, smirking.

'Good,' said Holliday. 'Then we won't be

needing your services any longer. Do you have the keys to the house?'

'Yes, but . . .'

'I'd like them please,' said Holliday.

'But . . .' Broadbent looked at Peggy for support. He got none. She just smiled pleasantly.

'The keys,' repeated Holliday. Broadbent unlocked a drawer in his desk, rummaged around for a moment, and brought out a heavy ring of keys with a string and paper tag attached. He leaned forward and dropped the key ring on the desk in front of Holliday and then sat back. Holliday scooped up the keys and stood up. 'If there's any paperwork to sign, send it to us at the house. We'll be staying there for the time being.'

'Is that the case?' Broadbent said to Peggy coldly.

She stood up and threaded her arm through Holliday's. She leaned her cheek on his shoulder affectionately, batting her eyelashes and smiling at the lawyer. 'Anything Doc says is just fine by me,' she said. They started to leave the office. Broadbent's voice stopped them.

'Colonel Holliday?'

He turned. 'Yes?'

'My father's notes referred to an item that might have been in your uncle's possession. Part of his collection.'

'My uncle collected a lot of things,' said Holliday. 'Anything that interested him.'

'The item in question had a special significance to my father.' Broadbent paused for a moment, frowning. 'They knew each other, you know,' he said finally. 'They were in the same outfit during the war.'

'Really,' answered Holliday. 'I didn't know that.'

'Yes.'

'So what was this object?' Holliday asked. 'And why was it significant?'

'They found it together,' said Broadbent quietly. 'In Bavaria. In Germany.'

'I know where Bavaria is, Mr. Broadbent.'

'They found it in Obersalzberg. At Berchtesgaden.'

'Really,' said Holliday. Berchtesgaden was the location of Adolf Hitler's summer house. Uncle Henry had never mentioned being there, at least not to Holliday. If he remembered correctly Berchtesgaden had been captured by the 3rd Infantry Division.

'Just what was this object that they found together, your father and my Uncle Henry?'

'A sword, Colonel Holliday. A sword.'

'What kind of sword?' Holliday asked.

'I have no idea,' answered Broadbent. 'I only

know that my father thought it was extremely important.'

'Important, Mr. Broadbent, or valuable?'

'Important.'

'I'll let you know if I find it,' said Holliday.

'I'd be happy to purchase it from you at any price you thought appropriate,' said Broadbent.

'I might not be happy to sell it to you, though,' answered Holliday.

They left the office and went downstairs to the street. It was early afternoon, the summer sun shining brightly from an almost cloudless sky.

'You were mean to him,' said Peggy, laughing. It was the first time she'd laughed since Uncle Henry's funeral two days before. Holliday squeezed her arm in his. Peggy was a Pulitzer Prize–winning photojournalist, and her work took her around the world and back again. He hadn't seen her for more than a year this time. He wished their reunion could have come under better circumstances.

'He deserved it,' said Holliday.

'What was all that about a sword?' Peggy asked.

'I have no idea,' answered Holliday, 'but I do know that Uncle Henry wasn't in the Third Infantry Division, and they were the guys that took Berchtesgaden in 1945.'

'So what now?' Peggy asked.

'Lunch,' said Holliday. 'Something fancy at the White Inn?'

'Cheeseburgers and fries at Gary's Diner,' answered Peggy.

'Even better,' said Holliday.

4

As usual the old diner around the corner on Eagle Street was packed with SUNY students, but eventually Peggy and Holliday got a booth next to a window and spent a long lunch hour catching up and going over old times. Apparently Peggy had been on assignment covering the most recent G8 summit being held in Niagara Falls when the call came in about Uncle Henry, which put her only a two-hour drive away from the old man's deathbed. At least he hadn't died alone. In that way, at least, she'd been lucky. Before that she'd been in Nepal, and before that she'd been in the new African war zone in the Jwaneng district of Botswana, documenting yet another potential genocide.

'How's your love life?' Holliday asked, changing the subject. There had been boyfriends in Peggy's life since the third grade, and she was notoriously either falling in love or out of it. She had the combination of good looks and flashing, energetic personality that drew men to her like a magnet.

She shrugged her shoulders absently and speared a French fry with her fork. 'A little fling with a guy named Olivier the last time I was in Rwanda but nothing serious since then.'

'Maybe you should get together with our friend Broadbent the lawyer. He seemed pretty interested.'

'*Ee-uw,*' said Peggy in her best Lisa Simpson voice, wrinkling her nose. 'Birth control in a pin-striped suit.' She swirled another French fry in a pool of ketchup on the edge of her plate and popped it into her mouth. 'I'd rather die first.'

'Maybe you should start thinking about settling down,' said Holliday.

'Why?' Peggy asked. 'I like things the way they are, at least right now.'

They spent some time talking about her work and a book she'd been working on about modern photojournalism and about Holliday's endless treatise on arms and armor and about the past and the future for both of them. Finally they talked about Henry and the present and what they should do about it.

'What about the house?' Peggy asked. A waitress came and cleared away their plates and brought them coffee. The diner was clearing out; the students were leaving and the afternoon was fading away. Clouds were sweeping in off Lake Erie, and the sky was turning gray.

'I've been trying not to think about it,' answered Holliday. He suddenly had a frighteningly strong urge for a cigarette. He hadn't smoked since Amy died. 'Sometimes I think I spent the best days of my childhood there.'

'Me, too,' said Peggy. Holliday could see tears welling in the corners of her eyes and could hear them beginning to clog in her throat. 'He gave me my first camera, you know,' she continued. She blinked the tears away at least for the moment. 'It was a Kodak Baby Brownie from the forties. I think he picked it up when he was in England. I used to take pictures of bugs and things down by the creek. I got so frustrated that what I saw in the viewfinder was never what showed up in the pictures; then Grandpa Henry explained it to me. I was the only kid in grade three who knew what parallax was.'

'He taught me the same lesson, except it was about trout fishing and the Cattaraugus Indians,' Holliday said with a laugh. 'The fish wasn't quite where you thought it was even when you could see it in the water.' He shook his head sadly. 'There was a time in my life when I thought Uncle Henry knew everything worth knowing. I still think that way sometimes.'

'I'm going to miss him so much,' whispered Peggy.

'Me, too,' said Holliday. 'But that's not answering your question about the house, is it?'

'No,' the young woman agreed.

'Maybe it's time we confronted the inevitable,' sighed Holliday.

'Maybe you're right,' answered Peggy.

Twenty-six Hart Street was like a Walt Disney version of a haunted house, complete with a spooky turret and a widow's walk with a wrought iron railing on the flat peak of the steeply sloping mansard roof. The house was set back on the property, enclosed by a low brick wall and surrounded by plantings of ancient elms, birch and gnarled black walnut trees, their limbs goitered and twisted like the arthritic crones found in fairy tales. Nobody had cut the grass in a while.

A sloping gravel path led down between the trees to the bank of Canadaway Creek, the burbling shallow stream hidden behind the long drooping branches of a dozen weeping willows, the far bank much higher than the near one and dense with undergrowth. Approaching the tottering Shingle Style Queen Anne monstrosity at the end of the street was like the opening pages of one of C. S. Lewis's Narnia tales; there was a sense that entering the house might take you anywhere and not necessarily to places you'd like to go, a vaguely sinister call to adventure.

John Holliday and Peggy Blackstock went up five worn wooden steps to the covered piazza-style front porch. Holliday brought out the fat bunch of keys the lawyer had grudgingly handed over and tried them one at a time. Finally he found one that fit into the old Yale lock and turned it. He grasped the faceted crystal door-knob and opened the door. Holliday stepped inside, Peggy close behind him.

Instantly they were assailed by a cloying, familiar scent. 'He's riding high,' said Holliday.

Peggy smiled. 'He has P.A.'

'Pipe Appeal and Prince Albert,' they said together, finishing the old advertisement that Uncle Henry would quote every time he took his ancient briar out of his jacket pocket, polishing the bowl against the satin fabric of the waistcoat he always wore before clamping the smelly pipe between his teeth, smoke fuming up and staining his white mustache a permanent nicotine yellow.

In the center of the wide hall a stairway spiraled up to the second floor. To their left was the library; to the right was the old-fashioned parlor. Behind the stairway was the dining room with its imposing fireplace, and at the end of the hall were the pantry and the kitchen. A glass-enclosed conservatory had been added at the rear of the house, and for many years Henry had bred roses there.

The floors throughout were heavily varnished pine, covered with a collection of worn Persian carpets and runners of every age and description. The walls were wainscoted in black walnut, with plain plaster above, painted white once but faded to a neutral beige after so much time. The furniture was all dark late-Victorian with heavy, deep brown velvet drapes to match. Small landscapes in plain gold frames lined the walls in the hallway, each with its own brass-sconced light. Against the wall opposite an old elephant's foot coatrack and umbrella stand was a giant longcase grandfather clock, the brass face enclosed in an oak case inlaid with mahogany and satinwood. It ticked heavily, the steady sound echoing a little, making the empty silence in the rest of the house even more oppressive.

'It sure feels empty,' whispered Peggy sadly.

'Yeah,' agreed Holliday. 'It sure does.'

They did a quick tour of the house. Every horizontal surface was covered with knickknacks and collectibles: shelves full of antique bottles, tables covered with stacks of old magazines, collections of minerals and fossils in glass-fronted display cases. A mantelpiece filled with ships in bottles, some of the bottles so old the glass was clouding.

There were four bedrooms on the second floor, a bathroom with a separate water closet, stairs leading up to the widow's walk and the turret room. Everything was equally cluttered. Located conveniently beside the toilet was a stack of *Life* magazines dating back to the 1930s. Once upon a time the turret room had been a children's play area, but now it was only a repository for broken furniture awaiting repairs that would never come and old luggage and boxes that would have been stored in the attic or garage of most houses.

Only one of the bedrooms had been occupied, the smallest, which had its own fireplace. Like everywhere else in the house it didn't look as though anyone had dusted in decades, and soot from the fireplace and smoke from Henry's inevitable pipe had made the window that looked out over the rear yard and the creek almost opaque.

'Never the greatest housekeeper, was he?' Peggy commented. She fluffed up the down-filled pillow and smoothed out the pale blue chenille comforter on the big four-poster bed that took up most of the room, her fingers running sadly across the old fabric.

'No,' murmured Holliday. They made their way downstairs again, going through to the kitchen. The furniture here was Early American – a pine table in the middle of the room with four plain matching chairs, ladder-backed with woven rush seats. The cupboards were painted wood inset with pale blue Delft tiles. The floor was gray-green linoleum.

The old Kelvinator refrigerator was filled with bits and pieces of past meals – a dried-out piece of steak badly wrapped in wax paper, a chunk of orange-colored cheese, an open half-used can of Campbell's Chunky Chicken soup, some limp celery; an enormous jar of Cheez Whiz squatted on one of the racks.

'Uncle Henry's secret vice,' said Holliday. 'Cheez Whiz on toasted Wonder Bread.'

'Grandpa Henry once wrote an article for *Smithsonian* magazine about Edwin Traisman,' said Peggy. 'I did the photo research and layout for him.'

'Who?'

'Edwin Traisman. A Latvian from Wisconsin. The guy who invented Cheez Whiz.'

'Figures he'd be from Wisconsin,' said Holliday.

'Turns out he also invented the McDonald's French fry,' continued Peggy. 'He was ninety-one when he died.'

'Guess he kept away from his own creations,' grunted Holliday. They went through the pantry and into the dining room. The darkly paneled room was dominated by an enormous display cabinet that took up one entire wall from floor to ceiling. The glass-fronted cabinet was filled with tier upon tier of stuffed birds and animals, from a tiny sparrow to an enormous horned owl, from a glass-eyed chipmunk forever climbing an amputated length of tree limb to a snarling bobcat riding a papier-mâché and chicken wire boulder. The rest of the room was filled with a long, highly polished dining room table flanked by eight high-backed chairs upholstered in blue morocco leather. There was an ornate morini bowl of wax fruit as a centerpiece that was as dusty as everything else in the house.

'It always made me nervous eating in here,' said Peggy. 'All those glass eyes watching me.'

'He bought the whole thing from a small-town natural history museum that was closing its doors,' said Holliday. 'He was never into birds or animals really. He told me he'd picked it up at an auction for next to nothing. It was the bargain that attracted him.'

'Was he working on anything?' Peggy asked. 'I've been out of touch.'

'Me, too,' said Holliday. 'I hadn't talked to him in quite a while. The last time we spoke he'd just come back from some sort of research jaunt to

Oxford. I think it was just an excuse to see some of his old friends from before the war. That was more than a year ago. I really don't know what he was up to. He always had some sort of project going.'

They moved into the library. It was a magnificent room, the walls lined with arch-topped fruitwood bookcases, the spaces in between hung with fantastic oil paintings of medieval battle scenes done by long-forgotten artists. There was a wrought iron chandelier hanging from the dark oak coffered ceiling, and the floor was covered with a gigantic tree-of-life pattern Persian carpet done in shades of rose and deep blue.

There was a functional desk set at an angle in one corner, several comfortable old fan-backed club chairs upholstered in faded velvet that had once been red but that had worn down through the years to a faded pink, a small couch, and Henry's personal chair, a giant green leather monstrosity that looked as though it had been spirited out of a nineteenth-century English men's club. There was a conveniently placed pole lamp with a fringed shade and a side table at the chair's right hand, just the perfect size for a book and a late-night tipple of sherry, or perhaps a small tumbler of Henry's favorite single malt.

The chair stood just beyond the hearth of the

plain, practical fireplace. Above the fireplace was a signed mezzotint by the apocalyptic British artist John Martin, showing the fall of Babylon in desperate, murderous detail, complete with a tiny Assyrian priest being scorched by bolts of divine lightning descending from boiling, wrathful thunderheads above the ancient temple. There was a quotation in Italian printed within the frame. Holliday quoted it from memory; it had been Uncle Henry's credo:

> *Ognuno sta solo sul cuor della terra*
> *traffito da un raggio di sole:*
> *ed è subito sera.*

'Which means?' Peggy asked.

> *Every one of us stands alone on the heart of the earth,*
> *Transfixed by a beam of sun;*
> *And suddenly it is evening.*

'Easy for you to say,' quipped Peggy.

'It's from a poem called "It Is Now Evening" by Salvatore Quasimodo.'

'The hunchback?'

'The Italian poet. He won the Nobel Prize, if I remember correctly. Henry met him in Rome after the war.'

'Sad,' said Peggy, staring up at the print above the fireplace.

'Not to Uncle Henry.' Holliday shrugged. 'To him it was a caution: your time on earth is brief, don't waste it. Death comes to us all. Every day is a gift.'

'And it came to Grandpa in the end,' sighed Peggy, slumping down into the big green chair.

Holliday went to the desk and sat down in Uncle Henry's old-fashioned wooden swivel chair. The desk was a massive oak rectangle, the twin pedestals roughly carved with trails of ivy and shapes of birds and small forest animals. There was a large, leather-edged blotter on the top surface and a green-shaded brass banker's lamp to light it.

The wood was dark, worm-eaten, and polished by time, the edges of the pedestals worn and chipped. Holliday had always assumed that the desk had been made from the remains of a ship-wreck, although he'd never asked about it and now regretted not doing so. The desk looked Spanish, perhaps fifteenth century. He had no idea how it had come to be in a house on the shores of Lake Erie, but like many things in Uncle Henry's life there was almost certainly a story behind it.

There were three drawers in each pedestal

and another drawer in between. Holliday went through each drawer carefully and methodically. The drawers on the left were filled with personal files relating to Uncle Henry's bills, banking, old tax returns, receipts, and the general maintenance of the house. The drawers on the right were filled with more files, these mostly relating to his years at the university and his professional correspondence.

There was one marble-sided cardboard accordion file filled with incomprehensible notes on scraps of paper, written in at least three languages that Holliday could decipher, including what appeared to be Hebrew. He also found several maps, including one of La Rochelle on the Bay of Biscay coast of France.

The map was small, the paper fragile and yellowed. It looked as though it had been torn out of an old Michelin guidebook. There were several faint notes on it in faded pencil: Huguenot? Ireland? Which Rock? Holliday put the map back in the cardboard file.

He looked in the center drawer. There was nothing in it but stationery and an old, blunt-bladed, ebony-handled dagger that looked as though Uncle Henry might have used it as a letter opener. Holliday had never seen it before, but he immediately recognized it for what it was. He flipped it over to check the inscription engraved on the tarnished blade just to be sure: *Meine Ehre Heisst Treue – My Honor Is Loyalty*. It was a Nazi SS dagger.

'What was he doing with one of these?' Holliday said aloud.

'What?' Peggy asked. Holliday explained.

'I guess it was a souvenir,' Holliday said finally, holding it up for her to see.

'Was he ever in Germany during the war?' Peggy asked, frowning. 'I thought he was in intelligence, like Ian Fleming and all those guys who sat around smoking pipes and thinking up ways to irritate the Gestapo. I never thought he actually *did* anything. I mean, you know, anything dangerous.'

'Neither did I,' said Holliday.

'Maybe it's a fake, a reproduction,' suggested Peggy.

'I don't think so,' answered Holliday, hefting the old edged weapon. It had the cold weight of something used in a dark time for dark deeds. History was fused in the dagger, the sensuously shaped blade tempered in spilled blood. Or maybe he was reading too much into it. The lighting runes and swastika could still cast a nasty spell. He tipped the dagger back into the drawer and pushed it closed.

'Maybe that's what Broadbent was talking about,' said Peggy, getting up out of the chair and going to the wall of bookcases on the other side of the room.

'You could call that dagger a lot of things,' answered Holliday. 'But no one's going to mistake it for a sword.'

'I wonder why it was so important to his father?' Peggy said. She smiled suddenly. 'Look at this!' she said excitedly. 'All the old kids' books he introduced me to. They're all here.' She started reading titles. 'All the Narnia books, *Five Children and It*, *Swallows and Amazons*, *The Wouldbegoods*, *The Famous Five* by Enid Blyton; they're all here!'

Holliday joined her, his eyes scanning the shelves and finally finding what he'd been searching for: a single heavy hardcover volume, still in its pale green and cream colored dust jacket, a first edition of T. H. White's Arthurian epic, *The Once and Future King*.

Uncle Henry had read the entire four-part story to him when he was a young boy, and later Holliday had read it again by himself many times over. If ever there'd been a story for a boy on a rainy day in upstate New York, that was it. He smiled at the memory; the kind of book that Harry Potter would have read and treasured. He flipped open the book to the title page and a small piece of paper fluttered out and drifted down onto the carpet. Holliday slid the book back into place and bent to retrieve the folded scrap. There was writing on it done in Uncle Henry's unmistakable copperplate script with a fountain pen, the black ink faded to a sepia.

'"*Hic iacet Arthurus rex quondam rexque futuris*: Here lies Arthur, the Once and Future King. Seek through the storied years to find the treasure down below: thus it is for you to seek and thus it is for me to know."'

'What's that all about?' Peggy asked.

'The first part of it is supposed to be the Latin inscription on King Arthur's grave in Avalon. It's the last sentence in the T. H. White book.'

'What about the rest of it?'

'Some kind of riddle.'

'Who for?'

'Me presumably,' said Holliday. 'It was my favorite book. He knew that eventually I'd come back for it.' He paused, then added softly: 'After he died.'

'Any idea what it means?'

Holliday whispered the riddle to himself again, then stepped back from the bookcase, looking at the collection of children's stories as a whole. 'The storied years: all these books. Your childhood and mine.'

'Treasure down below?' Peggy queried.

'There's nothing down below,' said Holliday. 'Just more books.'

'Down in the basement, under the floorboards?'

'I never saw Henry hammer a nail in his life, let alone tear up floorboards,' snorted Holliday. 'Not his style.'

Holliday stared at the bookcases. They had obviously been custom made, fitted into the house as it was being built, which predated Uncle Henry's occupation by decades. They were like a row of narrow Gothic arches, the kind of exotic cabinetry the late Victorians were so fond of, especially in a town like Fredonia which was full of houses like Henry's. Each bookcase had eight shelves, floor to ceiling except for the points of the arches and the ornately scrolled kick plates at the bottom.

Holliday looked down at the riddle again. 'Thus it is for you to seek and thus it is for me to know.'

Peggy saw it first.

'The kick plate,' she said, dropping down on her hands and knees. She ran her fingers along the four-inch-high strip of wood, pressing lightly every few inches. At the center of the kick plate the pressure resulted in an audible clicking sound and the wood jumped forward an inch or so on some kind of spring mechanism.

'A secret drawer,' said Holliday.

'Grandpa Henry's stash?' Peggy said, smiling up at Holliday.

'Open it,' he said.

She did. The drawer was the same depth as the bookcase, about eight inches, running from one side to the other. It was lined with very old and very worn satin that might have been purple a hundred years ago but which was now faded to a pale eggplant shade. There was a single object in the drawer. It was wrapped in a red, gold, black, and white silk pennant that was as unmistakable as the dagger in the desk.

'What the hell is *that*?' Peggy asked, horrified.

'It's the *Standarte des Führers und Obersten Befehlshabers der Wehrmacht*,' said Holliday, wrapping his tongue around the German. 'Adolf Hitler's personal standard. His battle flag.' He paused. 'Let's see what "treasure" is hidden underneath it.' Peggy tentatively unwrapped the silk covering.

'Amazing,' she whispered.

'A sword,' said Holliday, looking at the object nestled in the secret compartment. 'A crusader's sword.'

5

The sword was three feet long with a simple cross guard and a flat, circular pommel. The hilt looked as though it had been covered in some sort of ancient varnished leather, now almost completely rotted away by time to show the wire wrapping underneath. The blade was roughly thirty inches long, double-edged with a shallow fuller, the so-called blood channel running down the center and gently ridged from the center.

'Crusader's sword?' Peggy said. 'It doesn't look like much to me.'

'It was called an arming sword, or a short sword,' said Holliday. 'It was the equivalent of a Wild West six-shooter – a working weapon for everyday use. Cops carry pistols, knights carried these. It must be the one Broadbent mentioned.'

'I thought swords were fancier.'

Holliday bent down and picked up the weapon, World War II standard and all. There was a small label on the flag: *'Kuhn & Hupnau – München.'* He turned and brought the sword back to Uncle Henry's desk, laying it carefully down with both hands. It looked almost obscenely beautiful in its ghastly silk nest. A gleaming device meant only for killing. A thousand years old and as deadly now as it had ever been.

'It's a rich man's sword, fancy or not,' he said, examining it closely under the light.

'How can you tell?' Peggy asked.

'It's Damascus steel,' he answered.

'What's that?'

'See the watery texture in the blade?' Holliday said, pointing out the rippling patterns that ran through the metal, like oiled moiré silk. 'Damascus steel was made with a special kind of iron imported from India and later from Persia. Only a few of the greatest swordsmiths knew how to use it. They were almost a secret society. During the forging the metal was folded over again and again, sometimes fifty or a hundred times like a Japanese katana. The end result was a blade so strong and sharp it could cut through any kind of armor or chainmail. Use it the right way and you could literally cut a man in half if you knew what you were doing. They say it was strong enough to cut through solid rock.'

'The Sword in the Stone?'

'That's probably the origin of the story.'

'Damascus is the capital of Syria. How would a crusader get hold of a sword made by the other guys?'

Holliday laughed. 'Don't kid yourself. There was as much trading with the enemy back then as there is today. War has always been about money. Standard Oil of New Jersey was refueling Nazi submarines in the Atlantic right up until Pearl Harbor.' He shook his head. 'The real question is how Uncle Henry got the sword and why he was keeping it a secret.'

'Maybe we should ask someone.'

'Who?' Holliday asked. 'It's not as though he had a lot of friends. Ones that are still alive anyway.'

'How about the university?' Peggy suggested. 'Maybe somebody there.'

'He was a professor emeritus. He didn't lecture anymore. I think he was thesis advisor to a few grad students, but that's about it.'

'Still . . .' Peggy said.

Holliday glanced at his watch. It was five o'clock. Probably too late for anyone at the school. He stared at the sword. He knew well enough that an artifact of such good quality and condition would normally have pride of place in the collection of any museum. It was a collector's dream. In the hands of an expert there was even a good chance that the actual swordsmith could be identified; most smiths had a private 'chop' or hallmark that they stamped somewhere on their work. Why had Henry decided to keep it hidden from prying eyes? Curiosity got the better of him.

'We can give it a shot.' Leaving the sword where it was, they left the house, Holliday carefully locking the front door behind them.

'Your ride or mine?' Peggy asked. She had a Hertz rental from Niagara Falls while Holliday was using a Crown Victoria tan sedan from the West Point Motor Pool. It had the suspension of a tank, no radio, and no cup holders.

'Yours,' said Holliday.

The SUNY main campus was less than a mile north of the Hart Street house. The grounds were pleasant, treed, and mostly modern, a lot of the buildings bearing the unmistakable mark of the architect I. M. Pei, the Chinese-American designer who seemed to favor flat, featureless cubes and rectangles that often looked like three-dimensional studies in geometry rather than buildings. Someone had once called it 'fortress architecture.' To Holliday it seemed more like simple random shapes made from a child's wooden blocks.

The History Department was located in Thompson Hall, a squat firebrick rectangle with a jutting wing at each end. Holliday and Peggy began navigating a series of windowless, dimly lit corridors.

'I remember studying places like this in Sociology,' muttered Peggy as they trailed down yet another bleak hallway. 'They were meant to be riot proof. Narrow stairwells, bad lighting, slow elevators.' She snorted. 'Who riots in universities these days? They're all business students now. No more sex, no more drugs, and no more rock and roll. Just beer and football.'

'Don't kid yourself.' Holliday grinned. 'There's still a lot of sex, drugs, and rock and roll, even at West Point.'

'Be still my heart,' gasped Peggy in mock horror. 'You mean the Army of One smokes pot?'

'That's the least of it,' replied Holliday. 'Think of all the places the Army sends its soldiers: Vietnam, Panama, Iraq, Afghanistan; drug paradises, each and every one.'

'You're too cynical.'

'Heroin use in America increased by almost two hundred percent during Vietnam,' said Holliday. 'Of course I'm cynical.'

They found the Medieval Studies Department on the third floor. The offices stood around a central reception area guarded by a secretary. The nameplate on the secretary's desk identified her as Ms. Caroline Branch. The name was apt; she was thin as a twig. She appeared to be in her late fifties or early sixties. Once upon a time she'd probably been quite beautiful, even model pretty, but the years had taken their toll. The high cheekbones now stood out like ax blades, her neck was thinning, the wrinkling hidden behind a colorful scarf, the small breasts impossibly symmetrical in a padded bra. Her hairstyle was a flipped-under look from the seventies, streaks of gray overtaking what once might have been chestnut but which was now merely brown.

Her hands had long, elegant fingers, unadorned, and a few gnarled raised veins, and a few more age spots. There were no bangles on her wrists. She looked as though she'd been a secretary forever. Holliday introduced himself and Peggy. Ms. Branch seemed unimpressed; there wasn't even a token expression of sympathy at Uncle Henry's passing. Holliday could smell the faint, sour scent of tobacco in the woman's hair and some kind of sweet alcohol on her breath. A secret smoker and a sherry drunk, perhaps.

'We were wondering if we could get into Professor Granger's office,' said Holliday.

'We'd like to get some of his personal things,' added Peggy.

'It's very late,' the secretary complained. She gave an obvious glance at the large-faced men's-style watch on her right wrist. 'I was just about to leave.'

'We won't be very long,' said Holliday.

'We could lock up if you wanted us to,' offered Peggy.

Ms. Branch looked insulted.

'I couldn't allow that, I'm afraid,' she said.

'How long were you the professor's secretary?' Holliday said.

'Administrative assistant,' she corrected curtly.

'Administrative assistant,' repeated Holliday.

'I've been with the university for forty-three years. I came here directly from the Albany Academy,' said Ms. Branch primly.

Forty-three years. Late sixties, early seventies, which fit the hairstyle. The Albany Academy was almost as old as West Point, a place to keep the daughters of New York State's rich and powerful until it was safe to let them out on their own. She'd turned to stone here, petrified like an insect in amber. Odd that the woman had come to work at SUNY rather than take classes; there was more to Ms. Branch than met the eye.

'You were with Grandpa Henry all that time?' Peggy asked.

'I wasn't *with* your grandfather, Miss Blackstock. I worked for him.' There wasn't the slightest deference in her voice; after forty-three years she probably had more dirt on more people than anyone else in the university. She didn't need job security – she had gossip instead. Holliday smiled to himself. Good intelligence could take you anywhere.

'Could we get into the office?' Holliday pressed gently. Ms. Branch gave him a long, steady look.

'If you must,' she said, relenting. She opened the center drawer in her desk, took out a ring of keys, and stood up. Holliday and Peggy followed her to a closed office door on the far side of the room. A small plastic sign read simply: DR. HENRY GRANGER. Ms. Branch unlocked the door, opened it, and stepped aside.

'We'll be quick,' promised Peggy.

'Please,' said Ms. Branch. Did she have cats to feed? Was it laundry day? Holliday offered her a diplomatic smile as he passed.

They stepped into the office. It was large and airy, one wall lined with pale oak bookcases, another with framed photographs, and a third with a cluttered bulletin board. Surprisingly the fourth wall had a window.

The office looked out across the SUNY ring road to Maytum Hall, one of the I. M. Pei buildings, the geometry in this case being a concrete semicircle with narrow glass slits at regular intervals. To Holliday it looked like an outsized version of one of the concrete bunkers Rommel had erected on the Normandy beachhead.

The ground between Thompson Hall and the concrete semicircle consisted of neatly manicured lawn, the occasional curving path, and trees planted here and there in case the symmetry became too overpowering.

Peggy checked out the trophy wall of pictures, and Holliday sat down behind the modern desk. It even had a computer terminal. He tried to boot it up, but it was password protected. He opened the center drawer and found an address book, which he began to flip through.

'Weird picture,' murmured Peggy, leaning into the wall for a closer look.

'Weird how?' Holliday asked, still flipping through the old address book.

'It's a photograph of three guys, with Grandpa Henry at one end in civilian clothes and the other two guys in uniform. Army, I think. British. From the background I'd say it was taken somewhere in North Africa. Cairo maybe. Could be Alexandria.'

'So? What's weird about that? Henry was a medieval scholar. He's traveled all over the world.'

'The inscription says: "Derek Carr-Harris, Leonard Guise, Donald Mitchie, April 1941." Then the word "Postmaster" with a capital P.'

Holliday flipped through the address book. There was a U.K. listing for a D. Carr-Harris but nothing for Guise or Mitchie.

'Interesting. Postmaster sounds like it might have been a code name. But we weren't at war in April '41. What's Henry doing hanging around in Egypt with a couple of Brits in uniform eight months before Pearl Harbor? He started off in the OSS, the Office of Strategic Services. The OSS wasn't even organized until 1942 – June or July.'

'"Curiouser and curiouser" as Alice said down the rabbit hole,' Peggy murmured, looking at the next picture on the wall. 'Here's another one with Carr-Harris and Grandpa Henry in it. Neither one of them is in uniform.'

'What is it?' Holliday asked, continuing to rummage through the drawer. He found Uncle Henry's passport and checked the dates. It was still valid. There were four stamps on the last page: one going into Canada at Niagara Falls, an entry stamp from Heathrow Airport in London two days later, and another entry stamp into Frankfurt dated a week after that. The last stamp showed his reentry into the U.S. three weeks following his entry into Germany. All the stamps were from three months ago.

'They're standing in this huge room with a gigantic open window you could fly an airplane through. There are mountains in the background,' said Peggy, describing the photograph.

'Is there an inscription?'

'Yes. It says "Berghof 1945."'

'You're kidding me!' Holliday stood and went to the wall of photographs. He gazed over Peggy's shoulder and looked at the picture. Uncle Henry and Carr-Harris were little more than silhouettes, insignificant against the grotesquely out-of-scale room they were standing in. It really was enormous. The snowy peaks of the Salzburg Alps were clearly etched in the distance.

'Remind me where Berghof is again?' Peggy asked.

'Not where, what,' explained Holliday. 'The Berghof was Adolf Hitler's name for the summer house in Bavaria that Broadbent mentioned. The Führer was trying to be a man of the people. It means "Mountain Farm."'

'Which explains the flag the sword was wrapped up in,' said Peggy. 'But what was Grandpa doing there with that Englishman? What was he doing there at all?' She paused. 'I thought the lawyer said his father was with Grandpa when he found the sword.'

Holliday nodded. 'So did I.'

'So where is he?'

'A lot of questions about Henry today and not enough answers.'

'So what do we do now?'

'Ask more questions,' said Holliday.

6

Holliday stepped out of the office. Ms. Branch, the secretary, was sitting at her desk. A large purse stood waiting beside her computer screen, now shrouded with a plastic cover. She was reading a pale green hardcover book. It looked very old; Holliday couldn't see the title. Ms. Branch looked up, closing the volume, her index finger inserted to keep her place.

Holliday saw the cover. There was a picture of a beautiful young woman with long auburn hair inset into the fabric. The title was stamped beneath it in faded gold: *Anne of Green Gables* by L. M. Montgomery. Surprise, surprise; it seemed there was still a romantic little girl hidden inside the secretary's arid soul. The book looked as though it might have come straight off Uncle Henry's shelf of children's books.

'Yes?' Ms. Branch said.

'According to his passport my uncle traveled to Canada a few months ago.'

'That's right, in March.'

She didn't even have to consult a day book. Interesting.

'Do you know where he went?'

'Toronto.'

'Do you know why?'

'Yes,' said Ms. Branch. 'He went to see a colleague at the Centre for Medieval Studies. The University of Toronto. Dr. Braintree.'

'And then he went on to England and Frankfurt?'

'Yes.'

'Any particular reason?'

'Certainly,' said Ms. Branch, her tone crisp. 'The Master's Lunch.'

'The Master's Lunch?'

'Balliol College, Oxford. They have a lunch for the senior Old Members every two or three years.'

'He went to England to have lunch?' Holliday asked.

'He had a great many friends at Oxford,' said Ms. Branch.

'Any in particular?'

'I wouldn't know.' Icy.

'What about Frankfurt?'

'Are you asking me if I know why the professor went to Germany?'

'Yes.'

'I have no idea,' said Ms. Branch. She stiffened in her ergonomically designed chair. 'And I'm not sure I like being interrogated.'

'I'm sorry,' said Holliday. 'I didn't mean it to sound that way.'

'I'm afraid it did.'

Holliday paused. Something was nibbling at his subconscious. More than a year ago Henry had been diagnosed with early-stage macular degeneration: his eyes were failing. He'd voluntarily stopped driving. He tried to visualize his uncle riding the Greyhound. Somehow it didn't compute.

'How did he get to Toronto?'

'I drove him to Buffalo,' said Ms. Branch. 'He caught the afternoon train.'

A little bit of color flushed her cheeks. Her eyelashes fluttered slightly. She clutched the book in her lap like a drowning sailor. She looked almost demure – Bambi caught in the headlights of an oncoming car. Years peeled away in an instant. Suddenly, Holliday got it. Curtains parted, the fog lifted, the veil dropped from before his eyes, and all was revealed.

Of course.

The old copy of *Anne of Green Gables* probably *had* come from Uncle Henry's shelves. They were lovers, or had been once upon a time.

It seemed strange now – and maybe high on Peggy's *ee-uw* scale – but not so strange if you went back forty-three years to young Caroline Branch's arrival in Fredonia, hormones freshly released from the all-girl confines of the Albany Academy.

Holliday did the math: the mid-sixties, the Playboy Philosophy, the Summer of Love, and all that malarkey; she would have been nineteen or twenty and fresh as a daisy. Uncle Henry would have been in his forties, very much the pipe-smoking debonair professor, maybe even a little bit of distinguished gray at the temples. Hugh Hefner with an education.

Teacher and student for as long as it lasted and maybe longer than that. It wouldn't be the first time in academia that a professor had bedded a coed. Henry had never married and, according to the nameplate on her desk, neither had Ms. Branch. Maybe it really was an old-fashioned love story. He stared at the secretary with fresh eyes.

'Do you have any other questions?' Ms. Branch asked stiffly, perhaps reading his mind a little.

'Not right now.'

'It really is getting quite late,' she prompted baldly.

'We won't be much longer.'

Holliday turned on his heel and went back into

the office, shutting the door behind him. Peggy was sitting in front of Henry's computer, trying passwords.

'Try Caroline,' said Holliday, keeping his voice low.

'What?' Peggy asked, brow wrinkling.

'The password. Try Caroline.'

'But . . .'

'Later. Just try it.'

Peggy gave him a look, but she typed the name into the slot and hit return.

'Nothing,' she said. She sounded almost relieved.

'Try Caroline Branch, all one word,' he instructed. She typed. She stared at the screen.

'I'll be damned,' she whispered. 'It worked.'

'I think they were lovers back in the day,' explained Holliday quietly.

Peggy snorted. 'Grandpa, you old dog!'

'What kind of files do you see?'

'The usual stuff. Looks like a lot of old lectures in his "My Documents" files. One called "Letters," another labeled "Expenses." "Graduate students." "Tutorials." Nothing out of the ordinary. Nothing about a sword anyway.' She glanced up at Holliday. 'Presumably that's what we're looking for.'

'Is there an e-mail account?'

'Grandpa Henry using e-mail? Come on, now.'

'Grandpa Henry having a love affair with Ms. Branch?' Holliday grinned.

'Point taken,' said Peggy. 'I'll check.' She tapped a few keys. 'You're right. There's a Hotmail account: medievalscholar99@hotmail.com.'

'What's the last message he sent?'

'It's to medievalscholar123@hotmail.com,' said Peggy. 'Sent a week ago.'

'What's the subject line?'

'It's a thank-you for a reply from the 123 person. The subject line for the original message is "QUERY."'

'What does it say?'

'It says: "Dear Henry, as I suggested to you on your visit it looks like you have some early combination of a Book/Masonic-Pigpen/Elian problem going on, but without the key I'm afraid it's probably indecipherable. There's no mention of it anywhere in the literature that I can find. There's a fellow in Jerusalem named Raffi Wanounou who knows a lot about crusader castles; maybe he can point you in the right direction. He works at the Institute. Sorry I can't be more help. It was nice seeing you in March. Hope things went well with Donald. Keep in touch." It's signed Steven Braintree.' Peggy made a face. 'There's such a name as Braintree?'

'It's part of Metropolitan Boston. John Quincy Adams was born there,' said Holliday. 'Apparently this particular Braintree is a professor at the University of Toronto.'

'What's all this "Book/Masonic-Pigpen/Elian" stuff?' Peggy frowned. 'It's all gobbledygook.'

'I think he's talking about codes,' answered Holliday. 'You ever read a book called *The Key to Rebecca* by Ken Follett? They did a TV movie of it back in the eighties with Cliff Robertson.'

'Not my era.'

'It was about a code based on a Daphne du Maurier novel called *Rebecca*.'

'Laurence Olivier and Joan Fontaine. 1940. Alfred Hitchcock.'

'The forties *is* your era?'

'Absolutely.' She grinned. 'All that noir stuff. Great lighting, everybody smoking cigarettes.'

'I thought you quit.'

'I did. Sort of.'

Holliday sighed. Peggy was going off on one of her tangents. He headed her off at the pass.

'*Anyway*, the book was used as the key for the code. I think that's what the e-mail means when Braintree refers to "book." Pigpen is sometimes called the Masonic Code, which sort of fits in with the sword. I have no idea what "Elian" refers to.'

'Did Grandpa have some particular interest in codes?'

'Not that I knew of,' said Holliday, shaking his head.

They spent another few minutes browsing through Uncle Henry's files without success, then gave it up, retreating under the barrages of psychic artillery coming through the closed door from Ms. Branch's direction. They drove back to the Hart Street house and spent the next two hours going through Uncle Henry's study and anywhere else they could think of, looking for anything else that might shed some light on the sword wrapped in the flag and Henry's reasons for hiding it away so carefully, including a close look at the file of correspondence in the old man's desk. The only thing they came up with of any interest at all was Henry's invitation to the Balliol College Old Master's Lunch with an obscure message scrawled on the back:

Oxford 4:20 Abingdon Express-40 bus/Reading train/Reading toward Carmarthen change Newport toward Arriva Trains Wales - Holyhead to Leominster. Will pick up. No cabs. L'Espoir, Lyonshall, Kingston, Herts. 44-1567-240-363

'Directions from Oxford to Leominster, in Herefordshire,' said Peggy, pronouncing it

'Lemster.' 'I know it's pronounced that way because a Welshman once corrected me.'

'There's a place in Massachusetts with the same name,' said Holliday, 'They pronounce it "Lemon-Stir," home of Foster Grant sunglasses and the original plastic pink flamingo.'

'Your brain must be a very strange place,' said Peggy, laughing.

'In my business your head tends to get clogged with a lot of irrelevancies. Take horses. Did you know Adolf Hitler had a thoroughbred named Nordlicht, or North Light, and that it died on a plantation in Louisiana in 1968? Or that George Armstrong Custer was riding a horse named Victory at the Little Big Horn, not Comanche for instance? Or the fact that Teddy Roosevelt was the only one of his Rough Riders at San Juan Hill who had a horse at all?'

'And I'll bet you know its name,' said Peggy.

'Of course.' Holliday grinned. 'It was called Little Texas. By the time they got to San Juan Hill the horse was exhausted, so Roosevelt had to dismount and lead the charge on foot.' He laughed. 'Although I think it probably had more to do with public relations; didn't look good in the papers to be the only one in the saddle.'

'That's enough history,' said Peggy, holding up her hands in defeat. 'Let's go eat.'

'Gary's Diner again?' Holliday said.

'Let's try something more upscale,' suggested Peggy.

Upscale in Fredonia, New York, meant the White Inn, an outsized mid-nineteenth century clapboard farmhouse with an overdone columned portico and a wrought iron fence that made it look like an imitation of its namesake in Washington, D.C. According to Peggy they served a mean chocolate martini in the lounge and great prime rib in the dining room. Holliday let Peggy have the prime rib while he ordered the baby spinach and shrimp.

'You sure you don't want the prime rib?' Peggy asked. 'That thing on your plate looks like an appetizer.'

Holliday looked at the immense slab of meat Peggy was happily carving her way through. It looked like enough to feed a small army and came complete with a giant baked potato swimming in butter and sour cream, butter beans, and a side salad besides. She popped a forkful of meat into her mouth, then tore up a dinner roll and used it to swab up a small puddle of au jus that was wending its way dangerously close to the baked potato and its sour cream and dripping butter pat summit.

Holliday speared a shrimp.

'You're young. I'm old. Gotta watch my figure.'

'I'm like a hummingbird,' said Peggy, scooping up some baked potato. 'I have to eat my own weight every day or I fade away.' She ate some butter beans. 'And you're not old, Doc, you're distinguished.'

Holliday looked at her fondly. In jeans and a T-shirt Peggy could probably pass for a freshman at the university. He, on the other hand, had salt-and-pepper hair that was now considerably more salt than pepper, used reading glasses, wore Dr. Scholl's in his shoes, and occasionally felt twinges of arthritis in his joints. She was still climbing uphill in the morning of her life, and he was sliding slowly down in the early evening; a world of difference.

'Easy for you to say,' he said wistfully. *Who was it who said that youth was wasted on the young?*

'George Bernard Shaw,' he said.

'Huh?' Peggy asked.

'Nothing,' said Holliday.

Peggy sliced off another chunk from the slab on her plate.

'Speaking of old, what are we supposed to make of Grandpa Henry and the secretary?'

'He wasn't always old.'

'He didn't mention her in the will.'

'I'm not surprised. Wills are public documents,

and discretion is clearly important to her,' he shrugged. 'Besides, he may have already given her his bequest.'

'What do you mean?'

'She was reading a copy of *Anne of Green Gables* when we came into the office.'

'So?'

'It was a first edition.'

'You think Grandpa gave it to her?'

'Probably,' he nodded. 'You still have that BlackBerry machine?'

'I'll have you know it's called a personal digital assistant,' said Peggy airily, swabbing a piece of prime rib in a generous blob of horseradish. 'Or sometimes "CrackBerry" for its addictive qualities.'

'You have it with you?'

'Always,' nodded Peggy. She put down her fork, rummaged around in the old denim messenger bag she used as a purse, and eventually pulled out the flat little rectangle of black plastic.

'See if you can find out what a first edition of *Anne of Green Gables* is worth.'

Peggy tapped away briefly, using thumbs instead of fingers. The device reminded Holliday of the all-knowing featureless black slabs in the epic space movie *2001*. Except, he thought, *2001* the year was long gone, the slab fit into one hand, and this time *we* are the monkeys.

Peggy's eyes widened.

'Twelve thousand five hundred dollars,' she said, awed.

'What did I tell you?' said Holliday. He ate another shrimp. 'The Anne book probably isn't the only thing he gave her.'

'That sounds like the punch line to a Marx Brothers joke.'

'I'm serious.'

'He must have cared for her,' she said. 'I wonder why he never made it formal.'

'Maybe she didn't want to get married. Maybe he liked the status quo.' Holliday shrugged. 'We'll probably never know. Children never really know their parents; that goes double for nephews and grandfathers.'

'So what do we do now? About the sword and all that, I mean?'

'I'm not sure. The sword belongs in a museum, I know that much. Or we can sell it if you want. It'll be worth more than the *Anne of Green Gables*, that's for sure.'

'I don't need the money.'

'Neither do I,' said Holliday.

'Why don't we donate it to a museum in Grandpa's name?' Peggy suggested.

'Good idea,' agreed Holliday.

'And the house?'

'Selling it, you mean?'

'I've got a three-room apartment in New York that I'm barely ever in. You live at the Point. We're the only heirs. I don't have any room for half that stuff.'

'Ditto.'

'Why not an auction?'

'Sounds good to me,' said Holliday, although he hated the idea of having to sort through his uncle's possessions; history was one thing, but personal history was a different thing altogether. He wondered if they should quietly tell Miss Branch that she was welcome to a memento from the house if she wanted it. Maybe better to let sleeping dogs lie.

'Buy me one of those chocolate martinis in the lounge for dessert, and then we'll go back to the house and start figuring out what we want to keep and what we want to let go. How's that?'

'Deal,' agreed Holliday. Two of the frothy, too-sweet cocktails and a long-necked Heineken later they headed back to Hart Street, a few blocks away on the other side of Canadaway Creek.

It was almost fully dark by the time they turned off Forest Place and steered into the short cul-de-sac. Lights were on in the few houses on the tree-lined street, and a soft breeze was blowing, taking some of the edge off the early-summer heat.

'I love that smell,' murmured Peggy happily as they left her rental car at the curb. 'Somebody's burning leaves.'

That wasn't right.

'In July?' Holliday said. They reached the stone wall in front of Uncle Henry's house and turned up the walk.

Peggy squinted ahead into the gloom.

'What's that in . . .'

The concussion from the explosion lifted them both off their feet, throwing them backward onto the ground, flaming debris and broken glass blossoming into the air as they fell. Holliday rolled with it, holding his arms up across his face. He got to his hands and knees just in time to see the giant fireball swallowing up the entire front of the house in an all-consuming whirlwind. A moment later Peggy groggily began struggling to her feet.

'Down!' Holliday yelled. Concussion, then blast, then fire: the first axiom of the thermochemistry of explosives. He lurched forward and bowled Peggy off her feet, tumbling them downward as the firestorm roared briefly overhead.

Out of the corner of his eye Holliday caught a flicker of shadowy motion and turned his head to follow it – a figure, hunched, carrying something, racing away from the house, heading through the trees. Peggy must have seen the man, as well.

'Get him!'

'Are you all right?'

'Yes! Yes! Just get him!'

Holliday scrambled to his feet again and ran forward, skirting the angry fire spitting out of the burning house in long fiery tongues. The blazing heat was already beginning to shrivel the young leaves on the surrounding trees. A bank of rose-bushes planted on the protective flank of the old house burst into flames; the first early-summer flush of blooms turned to black ash in an instant. The upstairs windows began to explode like gun-shots, and the first searching fingers of fire crept out through the tinder-dry shingles of the roof.

The shadow figure appeared again, outlined in the light. The figure turned, and for a split second Holliday had a glimpse of a startled face, pale and narrow, some sort of hood or cowl disguising the rest of his head. The eyes were wide and glisten-ing. Then the man turned away, running hard toward the creek.

For a moment Holliday thought that the man might have a boat in the water, but at this time of the year the creek was too low for that, and besides, where would he go? The creek wound its way through the town and into the suburbs, finally emptying into Lake Erie; not the smartest escape route. Could he have a car waiting at one of the bridges along the route? It seemed too elaborate.

The man fell; Holliday heard the dull explosive grunt as he hit the earth. He picked himself up, but Holliday had gained valuable ground. For the first time he saw what the man was carrying: Uncle Henry's sword, still in its ghoulish silken shroud. Burn down a house to cover his crime? Crazy. What was going on?

Broadbent the lawyer?

No; this man was tall and lean, legs pounding like a long-distance runner. Broadbent was built like a Teletubby. The purple one, Tinky-Winky or whatever the hell his name was. The one with the purse.

'Stop!' Holliday yelled, feeling like an idiot even as the word burst out of his mouth. The man was a thief and an arsonist; why would he stop? Holliday sprinted after his quarry, one eye on the ground in front of him looking for obstacles, the other on the runner.

He was breathing hard now, but he forced himself to go even faster. The thief had stolen Uncle Henry's sword and burnt down a house full of memories – Holliday's memories, the best ones from a childhood where they were few and far between. In the distance Holliday heard sirens.

The man fell again, tripping on a branch,

almost losing the sword, and Holliday gained a few more yards. He twisted around one of the willows at the embankment and then jumped down onto the narrow strip of stony beach below. Holliday was hard behind him, close enough to see the reflective swoosh on the heel of the runner's New Balance shoes.

The fugitive splashed into the water, pushing himself toward the opposite bank. The creek was no more than two feet deep at the foot of Uncle Henry's property, but the rocks were slippery, covered with weed and algae. The man slipped, regained his balance, then slipped again. The breath was tearing out of Holliday's lungs in angry gasps, but he was gaining. He slammed into the water. Ten, maybe fifteen feet away now, so close he could hear the other man's ragged breathing as well as his own.

The running thief reached the far bank of the creek. There were only two ways to go. To the left, the bank was shallower, and led up to the football field where the Fredonia Hillbillies played. The right side was steep and wooded. He'd go left. Holliday swung that way, trying to cut him off. The runner reached the far bank then turned suddenly, throwing the silk pennant to one side and brandishing the sword.

Holliday pulled up short, arching back from

the swinging blade. The man was no swordsman, but thirty inches of sharpened steel was daunting in anybody's hand. He caught a better glimpse of his antagonist; not as young as he'd first thought, maybe late thirties, clean shaven, hair hidden under the hood of a black sweatshirt.

Ducking under the swing, Holliday lunged forward, shoulder dropping, and caught the thief in the chest, knocking him backward, half up the embankment. The thief swung the sword again, the blade slashing toward his head in a whistling arc. Holliday threw himself to one side as the sword came close to decapitating him.

The man turned, tossing the sword away, and scrambled up the bank, using both hands to haul himself upward. Holliday lunged again, managing to grip his attacker's ankle. The man kicked back furiously, this time connecting, catching Holliday in the chin. Holliday fell away, stunned, then tumbled back down the embankment. By the time he got to his feet again the man who'd burned down Uncle Henry's house and tried to steal the mysterious sword had vanished into the night.

7

Doc Holliday and Peggy Blackstock showed up at the Main Street offices of Broadbent, Broadbent, Hammersmith, and Howe at nine the following morning after spending a few brief hours sleeping in adjoining rooms at the White Inn. They'd watched as the Fredonia Volunteer Fire Department desperately tried to quench the flames consuming Uncle Henry's house, but in the end all they could really do was contain the blaze and keep it from spreading to other houses on the street. By three o'clock in the morning the old Queen Anne mansion was nothing more than cinders and ashes.

According to the fire chief, a man named Hoskins, admittedly no expert, the fire was almost certainly arson, originating at the gas stove in the kitchen of the house. To the chief it looked as though someone had blown out the pilot lights, switched the gas on full, and left some sort of timing device attached to a small initiating device, perhaps something as simple as a cardboard tube filled with match heads.

There was no way of telling if the arson was professional or amateur; you could find out anything on the Internet these days, including detailed instructions on how to build a time bomb or burn down a building.

'Miss Blackstock, Colonel Holliday,' said Broadbent, standing up behind his desk as they were ushered into the lawyer's office by his secretary. 'Nice to see you again. So soon.' He didn't look pleased at all. He extended his hand across the desk. Peggy and Holliday ignored it. 'What can I do for you today?'

'My uncle's house burned down last night.'

They sat down; so did Broadbent.

'Yes,' said the lawyer, affecting a solemn tone. He sounded like an undertaker. 'A terrible thing.'

'The fire chief thinks it was arson,' said Holliday.

'Really?' Broadbent said. 'Do you have some sort of experience with that kind of thing?'

'Somebody burned down my uncle's house last night, then ran away. I almost caught him.'

'Really?'

'Really.' Holliday paused. 'He was stealing something from the house.'

'What would that be?'

'You know exactly what he was stealing,' said Holliday.

'I do?'

'A sword, Mr. Broadbent. The sword you were so interested in yesterday.'

'So it really does exist then?'

'You know it does.'

'What exactly are you inferring?' Broadbent asked mildly.

'I'm not inferring anything,' snapped Holliday. 'I'm telling you straight out: you hired someone to steal the sword and burn down my uncle's house.'

'I wouldn't go around saying that sort of thing in public,' the lawyer advised. 'You might find yourself staring a lawsuit in the face.'

'So you're denying it?' Peggy asked angrily.

Broadbent smiled.

'Of course I'm denying it, Miss Blackstock. I'd be a fool not to, even if by some bizarre stretch of the imagination your allegation had any substance or foundation, which it does not.' The lawyer turned to Holliday. 'Besides, Colonel, as we are both aware, you have no proof.'

'You were asking about the sword yesterday.'

'Piffle,' said Broadbent, flicking the fingers of one hand into the air. 'Coincidence.'

'My uncle found the sword in 1945. He kept his possession of it a secret for more than sixty years. Why would he do that?'

'I have no idea,' answered Broadbent.

'And your father never mentioned it to you.'

'No. As I mentioned to you yesterday, I only discovered its existence when I reviewed the notes my father had made in your uncle's file when I took over his practice.'

'Why would your father have kept the sword's existence a secret?'

'I have no idea,' said Broadbent, sighing. 'I only know it was very important to him.'

'Yet he never made any attempt to get it back.'

'No. Perhaps he didn't know that your uncle still had the sword in his possession.'

'He could have asked.'

'Apparently he didn't, or at least I have no knowledge that he did.'

'You said your father was with my uncle when the sword was found.'

'That's right.'

'Are you saying he has some degree of ownership?'

'Your uncle stole it from him.'

'So you decided to steal it back?'

'Don't be silly.'

'What was your father doing at Berchtesgaden?'

'He was a major in the Third Infantry Division, "Rock of the Marne." He was an adjutant to Major General John W. O'Daniel, the commanding officer.'

'My uncle wasn't in the Third Division,' argued Holliday. 'He wasn't in the military at all.'

'No,' replied Broadbent. 'His cover portrayed him as a civilian consultant to the Monuments, Fine Arts, and Archives Branch. In actual fact he was a spook, a member of Donovan's Office of Strategic Services, the precursor to the CIA.' Broadbent paused. 'Presumably he was more interested in protecting or discovering sources of intelligence than he was in recovering stolen artwork.'

'You seem to know a great deal about my uncle.'

'I made it my business to.'

'Why?'

'For one thing he was my father's client.'

'I don't get this,' said Peggy. 'If my grandfather stole the sword from your father, why would Grandpa have made your father his lawyer?'

'They were friends,' said Broadbent. 'From what I understand they had a great deal of shared history.'

'I never heard him mentioned in any other context except being Uncle Henry's lawyer,' said Holliday. 'There was nothing in his correspondence that would lead me to believe that they were friends either.'

'Then I guess you didn't know your uncle very

well,' replied Broadbent with a shrug. 'The fact remains that you have something in your possession that rightfully belongs to my family.'

'Prove it,' said Holliday, standing. Peggy followed suit. Broadbent remained in his chair.

'You could make this very simple,' said the lawyer, sighing again. 'You could simply sell the sword to me; it can't have anything but a monetary value to you anyway. It would mean a great deal to my father.'

'I thought he was non compos mentis,' said Peggy. 'Alzheimer's. What would he care?'

'It would mean a great deal to me,' said Broadbent.

'That's the whole point,' said Holliday, smiling down at the lawyer. 'I want to find out exactly *why* it would mean so much to you. Why you'd burn down somebody's house to get it.' He turned on his heel and left Broadbent's office, Peggy right behind him.

They went back to the White Inn and ordered breakfast. Holliday had Eggbeaters and dry toast. Peggy had blueberry waffles topped with whipped cream, bacon, and home fries. They both drank coffee.

Holliday watched her eat, awed by the young woman's capacity for food.

'You never gain an ounce, do you?'

'Nope,' she answered, putting a piece of bacon slice atop a square of syrup-soaked waffle.

'I hate you,' said Holliday fondly.

'I'm your niece,' answered Peggy blithely, popping the food into her mouth and chewing happily. 'You're not allowed to hate me; it's against the rules.'

'You're actually my second cousin. They have different rules for that.'

'Only in the Ozarks,' said Peggy. She scooped up some home fries.

'I once had an insurance actuary tell me that there's a freight train and a level crossing out there for all of us. One way or the other, it's just a matter of time,' said Holliday. 'Maybe you'd better ease off on the cholesterol.'

'I can't,' said Peggy. 'I'm foolish youth, remember? I have a reputation to protect.'

'You have whipped cream on your upper lip.'

She wiped it off with her napkin.

'What do we do about Broadbent?'

'Right now?' Holliday said. 'Nothing. He's right. We don't have any proof that he was involved with the fire.'

'What about the guy you chased?'

'Fredonia's police force has one investigative sergeant. I'm not holding out a lot of hope.'

'So we let it drop?'

'No, we do what I said. We find out why Broadbent wants a thousand-year-old sword so badly.'

After breakfast they went up to Holliday's room and retrieved the sword, which he'd hidden under the mattress of his bed. He laid it out on the table beneath the window.

'Okay,' said Peggy. 'It's an old sword wrapped up in an old flag. Other than the fact that Grandpa found it in Adolf's living room, what significance could it have?'

'Let's begin at the beginning,' said Holliday, staring down at the sword. 'Uncle Henry's had the sword for more than half a century – why all the sudden interest now?'

'Something he found out?'

'Like what?' Holliday said. 'It's an old sword, just like you said. It was clearly owned by a wealthy man, probably a knight or even a lord.'

'What's the country of origin?' Peggy asked.

'There's no way to tell. It's not like a painting, it has no provenance, and I doubt if there's anything in the record to tell us how it got into Hitler's hands. It's undoubtedly some kind of plunder, looted by the *Einsatzstab Reichsleiter Rosenberg*, the Reichsleiter Rosenberg Institute for the Occupied Territories. Either that or Hermann Göring's people. They had a thing for going after

Masonic relics; it played into the whole Aryan thing.'

'The Masons had swords?' Peggy asked.

'No, but the Templars did; the Templar mythology and the Masons' started getting mixed up in the early 1800s.'

'So it could be a Templar sword then.'

'Sure.'

'How can you tell?'

'You can't.'

'I thought you said the really good swordsmiths left their signatures on their swords.'

'That's right. Their chop. They engraved it or embossed it.'

'But this sword doesn't have one.'

'You'd have to take off the wire wrapped around the tang to find out.'

'So?'

Holliday looked at the sword. The leather wrapping that had once covered the wire was virtually nonexistent, and it looked as though the wire was already loose.

'Any good archaeologist would scream blue murder,' he muttered.

'Indiana Jones has left the building,' urged Peggy. 'Do it.'

'Foolish youth is right,' he said, but he began to carefully unwrap the wire. By the time he reached the second level down he knew that the wire was gold; the top layer had been stained by the disintegration of the leather covering.

It was a single length made up of at least a dozen shorter pieces welded together. He also realized that someone had done this before now – the wire was too loosely wound to have maintained its integrity for a millennium. It took him the better part of half an hour, but he finally removed the last of it.

'What is that?' Peggy said as the tang was revealed.

'A chop,' said Holliday. 'Two of them, as a matter of fact.' One was in the shape of a bee, stamped into the steel. The second was delicately engraved: two knights in armor riding a single horse, the official symbol of the Knights Templar. Below the symbol were the letters D.L.N.M.

'The two knights on the horse is the symbol of the Templar Order. I don't know about the bee.'

'The initials there,' said Peggy, pointing to the four letters. 'The initials of the guy who made it?'

'I doubt it.'

Holliday flipped the blade over.

'Amazing.'

Stamped into the steel were the words: ALBERIC IN PELERIN FECIT.

'You're the scholar, Doc. What does it mean?'

'"Alberic made this in Pelerin."'

'What's a Pelerin and who is Alberic?'

'Pelerin was a crusader castle in the Holy Land, what we know as Israel now. It was the only castle that was never taken by the Mameluk sultans. Alberic was a dwarf, supposedly a creature who made magical swords. The Hitler connection is a little clearer now.'

'You really do know everything, don't you?'

'I told you, I read a lot.'

'A mythical dwarf who made magical swords. This isn't *The Lord of the Rings*, Doc, this is real.'

'Tell that to Adolf. Alberic was the mythical dwarf who guarded the treasure of the Nibelungen in Wagner's opera, Hitler's favorite.'

'Okay. It's a Templar sword made by a mythical dwarf that wound up being owned by an opera-loving German megalomaniac dictator mass murderer. Where does that get us?'

'He wasn't German actually,' corrected Holliday. 'Hitler was Austrian.'

'I repeat, where does that get us?'

Holliday didn't answer. He picked up the spiraled length of wire and examined it closely, running the edge of his thumb along its length. He smiled.

'Canada,' he said. 'That's where it gets us.'

8

Driving Peggy's rental, they crossed the border at Niagara Falls and turned northeast, roughly following the shore of Lake Ontario under cloudless summer skies, reaching the city of Toronto ninety minutes later. Neither Peggy nor Holliday had ever been there, and both were surprised at the city's size. In fact Toronto was the fifth-largest metropolitan area in North America, with a population of something over six million, spread out along twenty-nine miles of Lake Ontario and occupying 229 square miles of territory that had once belonged to the Algonquin Indians.

To Peggy Blackstock and Doc Holliday it looked like a cleaner version of Chicago, with a modern subway system rather than the antiquated El train. There was an enormous, soaring concrete structure on the waterfront that reminded Holliday of the Seattle Space Needle on steroids and a domed stadium that Peggy thought looked like a gigantic vanilla cupcake. They booked into the Park Hyatt two blocks from the center of the city, the intersection of

Bloor and Yonge where east became west and uptown became down.

The hotel was directly across Bloor Street from the pseudo-Norman pile of the Royal Ontario Museum, complete with turrets and a grand columned entrance that made it look more like a courthouse than a place of learning. Recently some museum committee in its infinite wisdom had decided that the building needed to be modernized, and an architect had been hired. The result was a giant glass and steel, sharply pointed crystalline extension that looked like some science-fiction starship that had fallen to earth and fused itself to the old building.

Kitty-corner to the hotel was another large building of the same vintage but with more columns. Like a lot of the property in the city center the building was part of the University of Toronto. The top floor was home to the university's Centre for Medieval Studies, a rabbit warren of offices that might have come out of a novel by Charles Dickens, all dust and echoing corridors and creaking wooden floors.

Steven Braintree's office fit the profile of a Medieval History professor: stacks of books, files, and papers on every flat surface, sagging bookcases, overflowing files, cabinets, and cardboard boxes on the floor, and a dying aspidistra plant on the radiator with a single wilting purple flower straining toward the narrow grimy window. Braintree himself was something else again. He looked to be in his mid-thirties with shoulder-length dark hair, dark intelligent eyes behind a pair of fashionable Prada glasses. He was dressed in jeans and a white T covered by an expensive-looking short sleeve, green silk shirt.

Braintree had only known Uncle Henry by reputation and a few telephone calls before their meeting in March, but he was shocked by the news of his death. According to Braintree, Henry had never discussed an actual sword on his visit in the spring, but he had seemed quite intrigued when Braintree told him of some recent discoveries in the Vatican Archives that suggested there was a complex encoding system that had first been used during the early Crusades that involved 'common decryptors.' The decryptors were usually well-known passages of scripture that were common to both the sender and the receiver of the coded message. The encryptors were usually variations on the Ancient Greek '*skytale*' system.

The *skytale* was a baton or wand of a particular length and diameter on which a strip of parchment would be wound, like paper on a roll. The message, sometimes in plaintext and sometimes numerically or alphabetically shifted, would be written out along the length of the baton. When it was unwound it would be incomprehensible gibberish and would only make sense again if it was wrapped around another, identical *skytale*. What the documents in the Vatican had described was a combination of this method, the Caesar Shift. Thriller fans might recognize it as the same 'book' code in Ken Follett's spy novel *The Key to Rebecca*.

'The gold wire wrapping on the hilt of a sword,' Holliday said with a nod.

Braintree smiled broadly, then clapped his hands together.

'Exactly!' the young man said. 'That was your uncle's hypothesis. If you somehow marked the length of wire at the appropriate points to coincide with the text on a common document, the wire would take the place of the parchment wrapped around the *skytale*. Even if the sword fell into the wrong hands it would be useless unless you knew the key! How did you figure it out?'

Holliday reached into the pocket of his jacket and took out the coil of gold wire that had been wrapped around the steel tang. He handed it to Braintree. The young man tipped his glasses up onto his forehead and examined the wire closely, running his thumb and forefinger down its length.

'Bumps,' he murmured. 'Like little beads.'

'Gold solder,' agreed Holliday. 'Unevenly

spaced, but repeating. A total of seventy-eight beads as you call them.'

'Not a very complex message,' said Peggy.

'The beads aren't the message.' Braintree smiled. 'They're like the rotors on the German Enigma machine from the Second World War. If you lay the beads on the wire along the key text it will give you the appropriate transpositions to use.'

'I'm lost,' said Peggy, frowning.

'I think I see it,' said Holliday. 'If you repeat the spaces between the beads throughout the text, that will give you the message.'

'That's it,' nodded Braintree.

'I'm still lost,' muttered Peggy.

The professor shrugged.

'It doesn't really matter unless you've got the key.' He paused. 'Where's the sword now?' he asked. 'You didn't bring it with you by any chance, did you?'

'Not the kind of thing you want to carry across borders these days,' said Holliday. 'It's safely tucked away.' In fact they'd taken the sword to Miss Branch, who'd tucked the weapon away in the university's security vault.

'Too bad,' said Braintree, 'I would have loved to have seen it.'

Peggy reached into her bag and took out a

handful of digital prints she'd made of the sword. Braintree looked at each of them carefully.

'An arming sword,' the professor said, nodding. 'Early thirteenth century if the Templar seal is any indication.' He looked up at Holliday. 'You're sure it's authentic?'

'I might be fooled by a good reproduction,' he said, 'but not Uncle Henry. Besides, who would go to all the trouble?'

'If it's real it would be worth an enormous amount of money. I've got a few rivals across the road at the Royal Ontario Museum who'd probably sell their own mothers to get a sword like that in their collection. It would be worth faking just for the financial reward let alone anything else.'

'Grandpa wouldn't have gone to so much trouble over a fake,' said Peggy.

'The inscription is a little bit over the top though, don't you think? Alberic in Pelerin? Do you know the provenance? Whose collection was it in?'

'Adolf Hitler's,' said Holliday flatly, enjoying the startled expression on the Canadian professor's face.

'You're sure?'

'Positive.'

Braintree looked through the pictures again, then nodded slowly.

'It makes sense, historically. Hitler was intrigued by all that pseudo-scientific garbage Nietzschean stuff about the Aryan race. Blood and Soil, the Ring of the Nibelungen. Valkyries. Dwarf swordsmiths, Templars, Masonic rituals. He would have loved it.' Braintree gave a short, sour laugh. 'Who knows, maybe he thought it was *Tirfing.*'

'What's that?' Peggy asked.

'The sword of Odin,' said Braintree. 'If you like Wagnerian opera.'

Peggy snorted. 'Only what I heard on the soundtrack of *Apocalypse Now*,' she answered.

'Then again . . .' mused the professor. 'Maybe it's not that Alberic at all.'

'There's more than one?' Peggy said.

'Yes, actually,' said Braintree. He got up from behind his desk and began going through piles of books stacked up on the floor. Not finding what he wanted, he moved to the bookcases that lined one wall, humming to himself and occasionally pulling a book halfway out to examine it.

'Aha!' he said at last. 'Got you.'

'Who?' Holliday asked.

'Him,' said Braintree, handing him the thick hardcover book. Holliday read the title: *The Templar Saint, Alberic of Cîteaux and the Rise of the*

Cistercian Order. He looked below the title. The author was somebody named Sir Derek Carr-Harris with a lot of letters after his name, including 'D. Litt. Oxon' and 'KCBE.' A knight commander of the British Empire, one better than Paul McCartney, and a doctorate from Oxford, to boot. Impressive. And the name was vaguely familiar, as well.

'You think this is the Alberic inscribed on the sword?'

'It would make sense, especially since the word "*fecit*" in Latin can mean "made for" as well as "made by."'

'Made for Alberic in Pelerin,' said Peggy.

'It could easily be a play on words,' suggested Braintree, taking the book back from Holliday and flipping through it to the index. 'The message was intended *for* Alberic, and the sword was manufactured *in* Pelerin for the express purpose of getting the message to him, probably at the monastery in Cîteaux.'

'Where's that?' Peggy asked.

'France,' replied Braintree. 'Just south of Dijon.' He nodded to himself, running his finger down a page in the index then stopping. 'Here it is,' he said, a note of triumph in his voice. He went back to his desk and picked up one of Peggy's photographs. He glanced at it, then handed the picture to Holliday. It was a close-up of the chops on the tang of the sword and the inscription.

'*De laudibus novae militiae*, addressed to Hugues de Payens, first Grand Master of the Templars and Prior of Jerusalem.'

'I don't understand,' said Holliday.

'The initials D.L.N.M. D*e Laudibus Novae Militiae*. It was a famous letter written to Payens, the founder of the Templar Order. It's the code key.' He paused. 'And there's one more thing, the clincher.'

'What?' Holliday asked, feeling a surge of excitement as faint clues from the past began drifting up to the present day like whispering ghosts as the mystery was unraveled.

'Bees,' said Braintree, pointing to the stamped design in the photograph. 'In France Alberic of Cîteaux is the patron saint of bees and beekeepers.'

Peggy picked the book up off the professor's desk.

'I know this name,' she said, thinking hard. Finally she got it. 'The photograph in Grandpa Henry's office. The one taken in Cairo or Alexandria in 1941. One of the men in the photograph was Derek Carr-Harris.'

'Who went to Oxford,' said Holliday, staring at the cover of the book in her hand.

'Who wrote down the directions to his country house in Leominster on the Old Members invitation,' finished Peggy, grinning.

Braintree looked confused.

'Did I miss something?'

9

After spending less than twenty-four hours in Toronto, Peggy Blackstock and John Holliday took a late-night British Airways flight from Pearson International to Heathrow, arriving at nine o'clock the following morning. Calling ahead to Derek Carr-Harris's office in Oxford informed them that the professor was on summer holidays at his country house and could not be contacted there since his office politely but categorically declined to give out either his address or his private telephone number. The phone number in Uncle Henry's address book rang unanswered when they called, so presumably it was his home number in Oxford.

Arriving at Heathrow, they took the Underground to Paddington station and paused in the station restaurant for a horrible breakfast that advertised itself as sausages and eggs, but wasn't, and an equally terrible cup of coffee. Breakfast eaten, they climbed aboard the train to Wales and three hours later found themselves in the country town of Leominster.

'Lemster,' as Peggy pronounced it, had achieved some notoriety in the Middle Ages as a thriving market town where you could buy the best lamb's wool in the world – 'Leominster Oro' as it was called. Since then it had become a quaint backwater on the ancient and often disputed border between England and Wales. To Holliday it seemed to have the same faintly over-varnished look of tourist towns in the States that often survived on their questionable history, their tourist appeal, and the quality of their French fries, or in the case of Leominster, its Mousetrap Cheese and its endless variety of antique shops.

'Just a little "twee,"' as Peggy put it, strolling down the High Street toward something called 'The Buttercross' looking for a place to rent a car. She settled on a squat-looking little Toyota Altis from Avis, and after getting some complicated directions from a pimply young attendant named Billy who kept on referring to Peggy and Holliday as 'Yanks' they set off, heading west on the Monkland Road. Switching to the even narrower A44 after a few miles, Peggy gripped the wheel tightly as she piloted the car between the bracketing hedgerows on both sides of the road. Every now and again they'd reach the top of a hill and, for a second or two, they'd catch a glimpse of the pastoral patchwork of fields they were driving through.

'Its like going down a bobsled run,' she muttered, praying that they wouldn't meet someone driving in the opposite direction; the road was barely wide enough for the compact Altis, let alone a full-sized car, truck, or God help them, some lumbering piece of farm machinery – or even worse, a flock of the wooly sheep the area had once been so famous for.

'Okay,' Peggy said to Holliday, keeping her eyes peeled for jaywalking sheep. 'Reality check time. You're giving up a month of trout fishing in Patagonia, and I turned down a choice assignment in New Zealand, a place I've never been, I might add. So once again, why are we doing this?'

'Because that son of a bitch Broadbent had Uncle Henry's house burnt down,' said Holliday.

'That doesn't explain why we caught the red-eye to Heathrow and had to eat British Airways cheese rolls,' said Peggy.

'Presumably he burned down the house in an effort to hide the fact that he'd stolen the sword,' answered Holliday. 'The sword was that important to him.'

'It's just a sword, Doc. An artifact from the Middle Ages, like Leominster back there. What does it have to do with us?'

'A thousand years ago somebody in the Knights Templar sent a message to one of the Templar founders in France. It was so important that the message was sent in code, wrapped around the hilt of the sword that Uncle Henry found in Hitler's country house in the Bavarian Alps. Uncle Henry thought it was important enough to have hidden it away and never mentioned it for more than half a century. In fact he was making sure that no one got hold of the sword until after he was dead – that's why he put the clue in that copy of *The Once and Future King*. It was important to the Knights Templar a thousand years ago – it was so important that your grandfather went to great lengths to hide it away, and it was important enough for Broadbent to commit a crime for it. That means the message encoded on the sword is *still* important. *That's* why we're doing this.'

Following young Billy's directions they took the second right turn after the A44 intersection and headed down a narrow unnamed road for a hundred yards or so, then turned onto a wooded country lane with a small sign that read L'ESPOIR in faded white letters painted on a rusted milk can perched precariously on a pile of stones.

'The Hope,' translated Holliday, reading the sign. They drove down the lane, the dense scrub of witch elm and lime trees on either side of them almost brushing against the car. An old steel farm gate yawned open on the right. Peggy turned the car into the scruffy front yard of *L'Espoir*.

There were half a dozen buildings scattered about in a loose cluster around the main farmhouse including a pair of sagging, half-timbered barns, something that might have once been a stone granary, and a more recent Dutch-style open structure with a very old-looking curved, corrugated, and rust-stained iron roof. Instead of hay under the roof there was an eighteen-foot coble dinghy overturned on sawhorses desperately in need of paint. Holliday could read the name on the transom: *Dawn Treader.* Clumps of grasses grew waist high everywhere in the yard except on a gravel-strewn patch where the oil leaks of cars and farm machinery had stained the soil.

There were two ancient-looking Volkswagen campers beside the Dutch barn, an even older Morris Minor estate wagon up on blocks beside the granary, and a relatively new-looking but extremely muddy Land Rover parked beside the farmhouse. Off to one side there was a weed-choked pond surrounded by a bank of dried-out bulrushes. All of this was enclosed by a shielding fortress ring of hedges, trees, and shrubbery run amok.

'Not much hope here,' said Peggy, pulling up beside the Land Rover. They climbed out of the car and stood looking at the farmhouse in the early-afternoon sunlight. The house was as much a hodgepodge as the rest of the property: a central building of thatched-roof stone with a sagging half-timbered extension that could easily have been sixteenth or seventeenth century and finally a 'modern' brick extension that looked like early Victorian, all of it cobbled together with struts, timbers, and unsuccessful patchworks of stucco and plaster. At first glance there didn't seem to be a window or doorframe still hanging true.

There were three doors on the near side of the farmhouse to choose from. Holliday knocked on the most substantial, an oak-planked slab with iron strap hinges, the wood stained almost black with the passage of time.

A moment later they heard shuffling footsteps and then the drawing of a heavy bolt. The door opened. The man who answered the knock was tall and a little stooped, with thinning hair that looked as though it might have once been blond but that was now a peculiar color of nicotine gray. He appeared to be in his eighties, and once upon a time he would have been called handsome. He wore bright red half-framed reading glasses on a long aquiline nose, a tatty green cardigan that was missing a button or two over a striped white shirt and wrinkled cotton trousers that were splattered with paint. There were expensive-looking slippers on his feet, and a tumbler with an inch of amber liquid in his left hand.

'Yes?' he said.

'Sir Derek Carr-Harris?'

'Mr. Carr-Harris will do,' he answered, almost sheepishly. 'The "Sir" makes me feel too much like a country squire out of a P. G. Wodehouse novel. Sir Watkyn Bassett in *The Code of the Woosters* or something. And you are?'

'John Holliday and Peggy Blackstock.'

The man standing in the doorway beamed.

'From America. Henry Granger's nephew and his granddaughter, yes?'

'That's right,' nodded Holliday.

'How wonderful!' Carr-Harris said. 'Do come in!' He stood aside and waved them in with his whiskey glass. They stepped into a short hallway lined with bookshelves, and Carr-Harris closed the door, bolting it behind him. He led them into a large, high-ceilinged living room; the rafters were made of hand-hewn beams two feet thick.

There were framed paintings on the walls, all oils and all from the British Romantic School of the early nineteenth century: bucolic country scenes with buxom milkmaids and Turneresque sailboats setting out on stormy seas. Where there weren't paintings there were roughly made bookcases. Between two of the bookcases there was a tall, Victorian walnut gun case with a glass door. There was a vaguely musty smell that came either from the books or the moldy thatch in the roof. There wasn't the faintest sign of a woman's touch anywhere in the room.

Peggy wrinkled her nose.

The furniture was old, worn, and unpretentious, club chairs and a couch or two drawn up in a vague circle around an oval hearth rug that stood in front of an enormous stone fireplace. There was a large utilitarian desk off to one side with an old IBM Selectric typewriter on it surrounded by piles of books and papers. Carr-Harris folded himself into one of the club chairs and waved Peggy and Holliday to a couch. They sat.

'So how is dear old Henry?' Carr-Harris asked. 'Well, I hope, although one mustn't expect too much at our age of course.'

'He's passed away,' said Holliday.

'Oh, dear,' murmured Carr-Harris. He took a long swallow of his drink and sighed. 'He was very old,' he said philosophically. 'Like me.' He took another sip of whiskey and looked lost in thought for a few moments. 'I saw him quite recently,' he said finally. 'The Old Members Lunch at the College, you know.'

'In March,' said Holliday.

'That's right,' said the elderly man.

'That's why we're here,' said Holliday.

'Ah,' nodded the old man. 'You found the sword then. Well done, young fellow. Henry said you would, you know!'

It was a long time since Holliday had been referred to as 'young fellow.' He smiled.

'You knew about the sword?' Peggy asked, surprised.

'Of course I knew about the sword, young lady. I've known about it since Postmaster. Nineteen forty-one or thereabouts.'

'Postmaster,' said Holliday, making the connection. 'The photograph of you and Henry on the wall of his office.'

'That's right,' said Carr-Harris. 'It was no great secret. Henry and I were working with that young Fleming lad in Naval Intelligence, the one who wrote all those dreadful penny dreadfuls.'

'James Bond,' supplied Peggy.

'Umm,' nodded Carr-Harris, polishing off his drink. He set the glass down on a small table beside his chair, then fumbled around in the pocket of his sweater and brought out a package of unfiltered cigarettes and a lighter. He lit one and took a deep drag, easing himself back into his chair.

It was an odd sight; Holliday was used to seeing smokers in craven little huddles in their narrow ghettos outside of office buildings, not in mixed company, and he certainly wasn't used to seeing smokers in their eighties. Carr-Harris was clearly a man from a different age and time.

'What was Postmaster?' Peggy asked.

'Like something from a Hornblower novel,' said Carr-Harris, chortling happily. 'A cutting-out expedition.'

Peggy frowned. 'Cutting out what?'

'A ship,' answered the old man. 'An Italian liner called the *Duchess of Aosta*. We suspected her of being used as a mother ship for German U-boats. She was based on the island of Fernando Póo off the coast of Guinea in West Africa. I believe they call the island Bioko or some such now.'

Holliday wondered what any of this had to do with the sword, but he kept silent and let the old man rummage in his memories.

'The name Postmaster was something of a joke,' said Carr-Harris, puffing on his cigarette. 'It's what they call an undergraduate student at Merton College, and all of us were from Balliol. Silly. They were the ones who'd organized the whole thing, including *Maid of Honour*.'

'*Maid of Honour*?' Peggy asked.

'A Brixham trawler,' explained Carr-Harris. 'Part of the Small Scale Raiding Force. Special Operations Executive, and all that lot. The sort of thing that Fleming and his sort thrived on, at least in the planning if not the execution.'

'Leonard Guise and Donald Mitchie,' said Holliday, 'the two other men with you and Uncle Henry in that photograph.'

'That's right.' Carr-Harris nodded. 'At any rate the *Duchess of Aosta* was in Fernando Póo. Malabo, I believe the port is called. Filthy place. A swamp really. Anyway, the ship was there as well as a pair of German trawlers that were supposedly interned for the duration.

'The main job was to take *Maid of Honour* into the port, put a line on the *Duchess*, and tow her off to Lagos down the coast. Henry and I went into the town to get the captain and the crew drunk while the rest of the crew hauled the ship away. What we were after were the codes of course, not the ship itself; that was a bonus.'

'Codes?' Holliday asked.

'*Kurzsignalheft*,' said Carr-Harris, 'the German code books. We already had the Enigma by then, but the German *Kriegsmarine* had any number of codebooks and they kept on switching them. Cheeky lot. The *Kurzsignalheft* we managed to filch off the *Duchess of Aosta* were the first ones they had at Bletchley Park.'

'The British cryptanalysis headquarters,' said Holliday, nodding.

'That's right,' said Carr-Harris. 'They both worked there eventually, Guise and Mitchie. Ended up doing something frighteningly scientific with computers, I think.'

'I really don't see what this has to do with Grandpa Henry's sword,' commented Peggy, clearly a little frustrated by the old professor's roundabout tale.

'Ah,' said Carr-Harris. 'The letter.'

'The letter?'

'The *Duchess of Aosta*'s regular route was from Genoa to Argentina and back. It was in the mid-Atlantic on its return journey when war was declared and the shipping line ordered its vessels into neutral ports. In the case of the liner, that was Fernando Póo. One of the passengers on board was a man named Edmund Kiss, purportedly an archaeologist and a crony of Hitler's. Kiss had been in Buenos Aires on behalf of the Nazis discussing some silliness about an Aryan race in Antarctica. We found the letter in one of the staterooms on the Boat Deck; Herr Kiss must have overlooked it when he disembarked.

'He was a South American specialist, I believe,

or described himself that way. The letter was from Hans Reinerth, Himmler's so-called Director of German Prehistoric Studies, and mentioned another archaeologist, an Italian colleague named Amedeo Maiuri, and a sword he'd found during his excavations in Pompeii. Maiuri was convinced the sword was of Templar origins. Apparently Maiuri had talked about the sword with Mussolini himself, suggesting that it would be an ideal gift for Hitler on their next meeting. Henry was very excited by that bit.'

'What was so exciting?' Holliday interjected.

'I'm not entirely sure. The propaganda value, perhaps. Like Hitler's supposed reliance on astrologers, or that utterly apocryphal story about his lack of testicles. There was some folderol in the letter that mentioned that the sword could well have been forged from the Spear of Destiny, the spear that pierced Christ's side at the Crucifixion, and might have occult powers like the granting of eternal life.'

Carr-Harris made a sound that might have been a laugh. 'Clearly it didn't work for Mr. Hitler.' The professor shrugged. 'That was the first we ever heard of the sword. There were other rumors about it throughout the war, and then of course Henry and I discovered it when we were sent to Berchtesgaden.'

'Did you ever meet a man named Broadbent when you were there?' Holliday asked, still searching for a connection between the two men.

'Not that I recall,' said Carr-Harris.

'Why would Grandpa keep the sword's existence a secret?' Peggy asked.

'And why all the sudden interest now?' Holliday added.

'I'm not entirely sure,' mused Carr-Harris. 'I do remember him swearing me to secrecy when we discovered it. Order of the New Templars. Black Shields and White Shields or some silliness like that. He seemed very serious about it.'

The old man clambered to his feet and picked up his empty glass.

'Drink?' he said, gesturing toward a simple wet bar on a table beneath one of the big lopsided windows to one side of the fireplace. There were half a dozen bottles of various liquors, a seltzer bottle, and several glasses.

Holliday and Peggy both declined. Carr-Harris shuffled across the room and poured himself another whiskey, adding a noisy spritz of soda. He turned and headed back to his seat, the ash on his cigarette now dangerously long.

The high-powered rifle bullet took the old man between the shoulder blades, exploding through his spine and bursting out of the center of his chest, blood spraying. His arms spread and the whiskey glass flew from his hand, his eyes already sightless as he fell. A heartbeat later the sound of the window breaking filled the room in a sudden, tinkling clatter, and then there was only silence.

They threw themselves onto the floor. In front of them the body of the old professor bled into the oval rug. A second shot entered through the already shattered window and thumped into the back of the couch. There was no other sound.

Suppressor, thought Holliday. Maybe an M4A1 like they'd used in Iraq. Mean suckers. A big-bore rifle for special operations, dead silent, dead accurate, and just plain deadly.

'Holliday?' Peggy said. Her voice was quiet and controlled. No panic. She'd taken her cameras into firefights before. She was waiting for some direction. There was a crash as another bullet smashed into the gun case on the far side of the room and another window blew out. A second shooter.

'Stay down,' said Holliday. He crabbed to the left, pulling himself around to the far side of the couch. A steady flurry of shots stitched their way across the bookcases, shredding the spines of books and sending a confetti storm of paper into the air. Bullets struck the side of one of the picture frames on the wall, splintering it and sending the painting spinning into the air. The bottles on the bar suddenly exploded, and the smell of liquor filled the air. The room was being steadily and inexorably eviscerated in absolute silence. It was terrifying. It was meant to be. Holliday stared at the gun case.

A bullet had hammered through the doorframe, exploding the lock and striking the stock of one of the standing rifles. It looked like an old Grulla Armas over and under shotgun from Spain. Several other weapons were still intact, including a Martini-Henry lever action dating back to World War I and a Lee-Enfield carbine.

There was one pistol, a Broomhandle Mauser with a heavy box magazine and the lumpy-looking polished wood grip that gave the weapon its name. On the shelf beneath the semiautomatic there was a blue and gold box of Serbian Prvi Partizan custom 9-mm parabellum ammunition. The same stuff the bad guys used in Kosovo. From the illustration on the box it looked as though the bullets were preloaded onto stripper clips. Another flurry of shots and the crashing of another window, this time on his right. Firing from three sides now.

'What are you doing?' Peggy whispered, nervous now.

'Thinking,' said Holliday. 'Hang on.'

'Doc? What's going on?'

He didn't bother answering. Instead he closed his eyes and tried to visualize the property. The fireplace was behind him: south. There was an open flower garden and patio on that side separating the house from the screening trees. He could see the patio through the shattered window.

The hallway they'd entered through was on his right: northeast. The oak-plank door, the side yard, and the car. Beyond the vehicles was the Dutch barn. No cover there, so that meant the shooter was in the trees. The window they'd fired through to hit the gun cabinet was on his left: west. The densest part of the windbreak and the closest to the house. Directly ahead of him there was an open archway leading into the old country kitchen. No windows that he could see, so no shot. Maybe a side door.

He opened his eyes and lifted his head an inch or two. They were shooting from the trees and not from the roofs of any of the outbuildings. No possible high ground. The terrain dropped slightly toward the north, but not appreciably. The ballistics decreed that the trajectories of the bullets would be flat unless they were up in the trees, which he doubted.

Holliday gritted his teeth in frustration. It had

been a long time since he'd done this kind of thing for real. Too long. Old soldiers didn't just fade away – they got rusty, as well.

He forced himself to stay calm and concentrate. He was boxed in on three sides. The two shooters east and south would keep them pinned down in a crossfire while the guy in the northeast would come in and take the oak-plank entrance. They wouldn't wait too long. Another minute or two and they'd be coming in the windows, blasting away.

'Go to your right,' he called out. 'Keep down. When you get beyond the couch, head for the archway and see if you can get into the kitchen. Wait for me.'

'What then?'

'Just do it.'

He heard her begin to move. There was another barrage of silent shooting that tore into the walls and smashed into furniture. Holliday rolled sideways across the floor and finally banged into the gun cabinet. Out of the corner of his eye he saw Peggy scoot by.

'Keep going!' he urged.

He watched her go past through the archway into the kitchen, and then he reached up blindly until his fingers closed on the cold metal of the old Mauser. He pulled the gun down and then reached up and fumbled for the box of ammunition. He tore it open and pulled out one of the twenty-round clips.

He retracted the bolt and felt it lock into place, then pushed in the clip from the top, loading the pistol like an old M1 Garand. The bullets clicked down against the magazine spring until the clip had fully loaded. He pulled out the empty strip and tossed it aside, then eased back the bolt. The gun was ready to fire. He jammed a couple of stripper clips into the pocket of his jacket, then lifted his head again, the Mauser gripped firmly in his right hand.

'I'm in the kitchen!' Peggy called.

'Coming,' said Holliday. He pushed up onto his hands and knees then sprinted for the archway into the kitchen. Too late. The oak-plank door at the end of the short hallway was thrown open on his right. A figure in hiking boots, jeans, and a dark green pullover surged into the hallway, a long-barreled weapon in his hand. Russian, a Bizon submachine gun with all the bells and whistles including a suppressor, a POSP sniper scope on the upper rail, and a sixty-four-round helical feed magazine slung under the barrel. Enough to start his own private war but clumsy to handle in the confines of the hallway.

The man wasn't wearing a vest. He raised the

big assault rifle as he jumped forward, but the extra-long suppressor snagged a bookcase on his left, losing him half a second of response time. And his life. Holliday aimed center of mass and started squeezing the trigger on the old Mauser again and again at a range of about ten feet.

The bullets punched into the man's chest, the Mauser barking loudly. Six rounds, six hits, four more in the magazine. The man with the big assault rifle made a brief sighing noise and then toppled over. Holliday stepped forward and caught him, dropping the Mauser and taking the rifle out of the dead man's unresponsive hands, feeling the corpse's last rattling breath on his cheek. There was a tattoo on the inside of the dead man's right wrist: a sword, its blade enclosed by a ribbonlike loop and surrounded by a band of runic letters.

Holliday eased the body to the floor, then stepped forward and kicked the door shut. He walked backward, stepping over the dead man, the assault rifle locked and loaded in his arms. He bent down and picked up the Mauser, dropping it into his jacket pocket, then backed out of the hall and crouched down.

Still three shooters, or only two now? There wasn't a sound. However many men were still out there, they would have heard the unexpected, harsh report of the Mauser and they'd know that something was wrong. Holliday hefted the Bizon in his hands and smiled grimly to himself. Something *was* wrong, but not with him. Rusty maybe, but an old soldier armed to the teeth.

'You okay?' he called to Peggy.

'Yes,' she replied.

He listened. Silence. 'I'm coming in.'

He scuttled forward in a crab walk and went through the wide, oak-truss archway. The kitchen was obviously very old. There was a huge fireplace of hand-cut stone and ballast bricks with a beehive oven to one side against the back wall. A massive maple cutting block stood on hand-hewn peg legs in the center of the room, with pots and implements hanging overhead as well as a forest of garlic and drying herbs.

The ceiling was some dark wood, blackened with age, and the floor was made of pine planks, pegged, at least a foot wide. There was one small, deeply inset window to the left of the fireplace and very high on the wall, and a row of Victorian kitchen cabinets against one wall.

Only the appliances were vaguely modern: a white-enameled refrigerator with a drum top from the forties and an older Aga gas cooker and range. No dishwasher. The counters were tarnished zinc. The sinks were galvanized metal.

There was an oddly placed narrow door between the sinks and the window. It faced north, toward the trees that lined the lane leading to *L'Espoir*. There was a heavy ring of keys suspended from a spike hammered into the frame. Peggy was standing with a meat cleaver raised in her hand beside the maple chopping block. She stared at the assault rifle in Holliday's hands.

'Where'd you get that?'

'Never mind.'

'The old man is dead, isn't he?' Peggy said. 'I didn't really look too closely, but he's dead, isn't he?'

'Yes, he's dead,' nodded Holliday.

'This is crazy,' said Peggy. She was breathing hard, eyes wide.

'It's the sword,' said Holliday. 'It's got to be, it can't be anything else.'

'They killed him,' said Peggy weakly. Her chest was rising and falling too quickly; she was hyperventilating, the adrenaline running through her hard. He knew the feeling. It could carry you away, make you want to *do* something, to make a move, any move, rather than hold your position and figure the odds.

'There are at least two of them out there, maybe three. Someone must have followed us here from the airport. They were ready for us.'

'You think Broadbent set this up?' Peggy asked, unbelievingly.

'There's some connection. Now's not the time to try and figure it out. We've got to get out of here alive.'

'Amen to that,' said Peggy. 'How?'

Holliday pointed the barrel of the assault rifle at the narrow door in the kitchen wall.

'That leads to the vegetable garden. I saw it on the way in. The garden's between that stone granary and the side of the house.'

The building was square, twelve feet on a side with a conical thatched roof and raised on 'straddle stones' to keep out vermin and the damp. There were no windows, only a wide plank door on one side. The space between the ground and the floor was too narrow and too constricted to be a sniper position; their attackers were effectively blind on that side. Coming out the kitchen door, the granary would be in front of them beyond the vegetable garden with a line of trees twenty yards to the west on their left, separating *L'Espoir* from the main road.

The rental car and Carr-Harris's Land Rover would be ten yards to their right, the Land Rover screening the little Toyota. The Land Rover was a four-door with right-hand drive. The Toyota was a two door; to get somebody into the passenger seat would require going around to the open side of the vehicle, exposing them to killing fire.

'Where are the keys to the rental?' Holliday asked.

'In my bag,' said Peggy. The bag, miraculously, was still slung over her shoulder. The Toyota key had an electronic buzzer. He looked over Peggy's shoulder at the spike on the doorframe. There was no plastic buzzer key. He closed his eyes for a second, visualizing the moment when they rolled into Carr-Harris's farmyard.

Was the window of the Rover rolled down or was it closed? Would someone like Carr-Harris lock up his vehicle or leave it open? Hard to say. It didn't really matter; they didn't have too many options, and they were running out of time. He had kept the door to his house bolted; he'd heard the old man throwing it open when he answered the knock.

But maybe he never used that door. Maybe he came into the house through the kitchen. Lots of people did that; the country version of coming in through the garage. Holliday glanced at the door. No bolt. He frowned. Too much to think about; he was getting a headache. His own adrenaline was still pumping. He took a deep breath and let it out slowly. The bad guys would be regrouping. Now or never.

'Do exactly what I tell you,' said Holliday.

He explained the plan to Peggy, and less than two minutes later, keeping low, he cracked open the kitchen door and listened. Nothing but the cascade rustle of wind in the trees and the rattling shiver of it blowing the bulrushes around the little pond like dry bones.

He felt a sharp tug of old memory: a sinister moment in a dark movie theatre long ago, watching a film called *Blowup* as the actor David Hemmings stands in a strange, silent parkland, listening to that same ghost wind sound, wondering if he has just witnessed a murder. All of that with the grassy knoll in Dallas still relatively fresh in everyone's mind. Knowing what it's going to feel like a split second later when everything is suddenly about to go terribly wrong and your life is about to change forever. He blinked in the afternoon sunlight and tried to shake off the sudden sense of ominous dread. And failed.

Holliday listened, muscles tense. Nothing at all. He took a deep breath and held it, then threw open the door, rising to his feet and running into the open, screening Peggy, who was on his heels.

'Now!' Holliday yelled. Peggy lifted the rental keys, squeezing the plastic tab. There was a loud beeping sound as the doors unlocked on the far side of the Land Rover.

Their aim distracted by the beeper, the invisible shooters concentrated on the Toyota, stitching the side panels and the windows with rapid, silent fire. Peggy peeled left behind him, and they threw themselves into the Rover, him behind the wheel, her into the back.

Holliday jammed the ignition key into its slot and hauled the automatic-shift lever into reverse. Bent far over to the right, he kept his head down and rammed his foot down on the accelerator.

The Rover rocketed backward, and Holliday slewed the wheel around blindly, shifting slightly in his seat to catch a glimpse out through the windshield, gauging the moment, then dragging the shift lever down into drive and hammering the gas again, sending them flying toward the open gate as bullets snapped and banged into the rear of the vehicle.

A round shattered the rearview mirror six inches from his head, but it was too late. He dragged the wheel left, and the Rover swayed wildly, brushing into the trees on the opposite side of the lane for a few seconds, almost careening into the unseen ditch. They burst out onto the roadway and into the light. Holliday swung them left, heading down to the main road a hundred yards away. He risked a quick look over his shoulder. No one behind them.

Peggy rose up nervously from the backseat and looked warily around.

'I think we're okay for now,' said Holliday.

He looked to the left. He could just make out the chimneys and the dark thatched roof of *L'Espoir* beyond the trees as they sped away. There were dead bodies to deal with, evidence to remove. It would take them a little while. Maybe they'd even burn the place down like Uncle Henry's. He swung out onto the wider main road and turned toward Leominster. They were all right for the moment, but for how long?

They left the Land Rover in the car park of the Leominster Sainsbury's supermarket and walked to the British Rail station. Twenty minutes later they boarded a train bound for the main junction city of Crewe, in Cheshire, then quickly caught a connecting train to the ferry terminus in Holyhead, Wales.

After a cursory run through Her Majesty's Customs they went on board the high-speed Stena ferry, a catamaran powered by twin Rolls Royce jet engines that looked more like a giant blue and white shoebox on monster skate blades than an oceangoing vessel.

On the inside the ship was fitted out like a cut-rate Las Vegas casino, complete with video poker, slot machines glowing neon, and a constant tinkling background track of European-style Muzak playing against the overpowering throbbing roar of the jet turbines deep down within the hull of the ship.

Snot-nosed Irish kids trolled the lounges begging their mothers and fathers for euros to play the slots while the weary parents sagged in the padded vinyl airline-style seats, staring out at the rushing, steel-blue Irish Sea, exhausted from a day's shopping for running shoes and school clothes for the fall at the discount outlet stores in Holyhead.

Sixty miles of open sea and ninety minutes later they reached the Ireland side at Dun Laoghaire, pronounced 'Dun Leery,' the ancient port once used by Viking raiders as a base from which to raid the English coast. The name was changed to Kingstown in 1821 in honor of a visit by George IV, then promptly changed back to Dun Laoghaire exactly a hundred years later on the heels of Irish independence.

Dead tired, Holliday and Peggy dragged themselves off the ferry in the fading evening light, took the footbridge across Harbour Road, then staggered down the long flight of steps to the Dublin Area Rapid Transit platform. They caught the short-run commuter train to Connelly Station in Dublin, six miles to the north, lined up for a taxi, then drove into the center of the city.

Taking the cabdriver's advice they booked into Staunton's, a trio of elegant Georgian town houses that had been turned into a hotel overlooking the large, lush, iron-fenced rectangle of St. Stephen's Green. It was just past ten o'clock.

They locked the door to their room, flopped down onto the twin beds, still fully dressed, and were both asleep in seconds.

When Holliday woke up the following morning Peggy's bed was empty. Twenty minutes later she was back carrying a green and gold Dunnes Stores bag and two large paper cups full of Seattle's Best Coffee. She went into the adjoining bathroom to unpack the toiletries while Holliday gratefully slurped at the coffee.

'There's a big shopping center on the far side of the park,' she called out. 'We should go there later and stock up.'

'Good idea,' said Holliday. Everything they'd brought with them had been in the trunk of the rental car parked in Carr-Harris's yard. All they had now were their passports and their wallets.

Peggy popped her head around the bathroom door.

'I'm going to have a quick shower. Why don't you go down and order us breakfast?'

'All right,' said Holliday. She went back into the bathroom and shut the door. A few seconds later he heard the hiss of the shower. He finished his coffee, then left the room, locking the door behind him. He went down the elegant winding staircase to the main floor, then threaded his way through several connecting corridors to the dining area.

The room was smallish and relentlessly red. Red walls, red carpet, and red leather upholstered chairs. Several curtained windows looked out onto the roaring morning traffic heading around the park.

It was almost eleven, and the room was empty except for an elderly priest in the far corner reading *The Catholic Weekly* and drinking coffee. Holliday seated himself at a table beside one of the windows, his joints still aching from the previous day and a night spent on a too-soft mattress.

A waitress appeared idiotically overdressed in the Irish interpretation of a French maid's uniform, complete with a frilly apron and a frilly little hat to match. Her nametag read NADINE. She had a long, rodent-like face and graying hair bizarrely done up in overtight, African-style cornrows that acted like a Botox injection, viciously pulling up the skin of her forehead and painfully arching heavy, dark eyebrows that ran together over the bridge of her long nose. She appeared to be in her late fifties and looked extremely bored. She had a thermos jug of coffee in her hand that she was holding like a weapon.

'Are you still serving breakfast?' Holliday asked.
'Full Irish or Continental,' she answered.

'There's no grapefruit this morning,' she warned. Her vaguely sinister Dublin drawl made the question of the grapefruit sound like a bomb threat.

'Full Irish,' said Holliday. 'Two, please. My cousin will be down in a few minutes.'

'Your cousin, is it?' the woman said skeptically.

'That's right,' said Holliday

'American, are you?' Nadine said.

'That's right,' said Holliday, trying to keep a polite smile on his face; it wasn't easy. He'd had drill sergeants who were more polite.

'Thought so,' grunted the waitress. She turned on her heel and left the room, pausing to refill the priest's cup of coffee. She'd never offered the coffee to Holliday.

Peggy appeared a few minutes later, her dark hair tousled and wet from the shower. She saw Holliday, veered between several tables, and sat down across from him.

'I'm famished,' she said. 'You realize the last time we ate was on the plane?'

'I ordered for us,' said Holliday. 'The waitress didn't give us much choice, so it's full Irish for both of us.'

'In England that would be egg and chips,' said Peggy.

'I think full Irish is a little more extreme,' said Holliday.

The waitress appeared a few minutes later, an enormous plate in each hand. She set them down in front of Holliday and Peggy.

'Holy crap,' murmured Peggy, looking down at the plate. On it were two fried eggs, sunny-side up, swimming in iridescent grease, their undersides a burnt-crisp web of charred whites, the yolks staring wetly up at her like deep orange eyes.

Beside the eggs there was a lump of baked beans in the shape of an ice cream scoop, two wrinkled rashers of pale pink bacon, a raft of link sausages, a small crop of fried mushrooms next to a dissolving slice of fried tomato, a mountainous pile of fried potatoes, and two fried circular objects each the size of a silver dollar, one black, one white.

'What are those?' Peggy asked, indicating the coin-shaped objects on the plate.

'Black pudding and white pudding, miss,' explained the waitress.

'What's black pudding?' Peggy asked.

'Pig's blood and oatmeal, miss,' said the waitress. She pronounced the word 'blood' as 'blud.'

'And white pudding?' Peggy said.

'Pork meat and suet,' said the woman in the maid's outfit. 'They used to use sheep's brains, but they're too afraid of the scrapie since mad cow. Best part of twenty years past,' she added, as

129

though the lack of scrapie-infected sheep's brains was somehow a terrible culinary loss.

'Ah,' said Peggy.

'Will that be all?' asked the waitress, turning to Holliday. He nodded. The waitress turned and left the room.

'I've lost my appetite,' said Peggy, looking down at the plate.

'When I ate with Uncle Henry he used to scold me if I didn't eat everything on my plate. "Think about the starving children in China," he'd say.'

'With me it was the starving kids in Africa,' Peggy answered. She started to eat, carefully avoiding the black and white puddings. The waitress reappeared with a vintage toast rack filled with half a dozen thick-cut slices and a plate of butter.

'I wonder what the rate of heart attacks is in Ireland,' said Peggy. She picked up a slice of toast and used it to mop up a sea of leaking egg yoke. Holliday didn't answer, concentrating on his own breakfast for a little while. As he ate he found himself thinking about the firefight at Carr-Harris's the day before, the old professor, his arms spread wide as he died, the man with the Russian submachine gun in the narrow hall, the bark of the Mauser.

Almost twenty-four hours ago now. Soon

someone would come by the old man's house, the mailman or the milkman or a neighbor, and everything would begin to come crashing down on their heads. Two dead bodies in the house, their rental left behind in the yard. They'd left a trail of bread crumbs a blind man could follow, let alone the police. Except for fleeing, they'd done nothing illegal, but if they fell into the bureaucratic horror show that was bound to surround Carr-Harris's death it would take days if not weeks to escape.

'This is getting out of hand,' he said finally.

'The breakfast?' Peggy said.

'No. What we're doing. Tracking down an old sword that Hitler might or might not have owned is a long way from murdering people. We're way out of our depth here,' said Holliday.

Peggy put down her fork. She turned her head and looked out through the filmy sheer curtains. A bright yellow double-decker open tour bus rumbled by, its side panels covered in manic advertising slogans, the seats on the upper decks crammed with stunned-looking tourists in bright clothing trying to cram Dublin into a day trip.

'I think it's too late to back out now,' the young woman said finally. 'You said it yourself: those guys shooting at us yesterday must have followed us to Carr-Harris's place. They knew exactly what they were doing.' She paused. 'I don't think people who are willing to kill to get what they want are going to back down. Even if we did bail out and head for the hills, I think they'd just track us down and try it again. We have to keep going.'

'I can't put your life in danger,' said Holliday. 'It's too dangerous.'

'Do I detect a note of sexism here?' Peggy said. 'A bit of patronizing from my overprotective cousin?'

'Maybe,' he admitted. 'It's hard enough in the kind of situation we were in yesterday without . . .' He let it dangle, afraid of putting his foot in his mouth. Peggy did it for him.

'Without a woman along?' she said, finishing the unspoken sentiment.

'I didn't say that.'

'But you were going to,' grinned Peggy. 'Admit it.'

'Never,' said Holliday, grinning back.

'Believe me, Doc, the people who were shooting at us yesterday aren't sexist; they'll kill anyone who gets in their way or has something they want.'

'Who are *they*?' Holliday asked. 'Some kind of neo-Nazi group? I thought that kind of idiocy went out with the whole skinhead thing.'

'Old Nazis never die,' said Peggy, picking up her fork again and prodding a sausage on her plate. 'They just change their names.' She put the fork down again and pushed the plate away from her slightly. 'There's lots of them around. The British Nationalist Party, Combat 18, the BNP's armed division, the Nationalist Party of Canada, Aryan Nations back home. France, Belgium, Italy, Spain, even Germany.'

'What about the Russians?' Holliday suggested, remembering the Bizon submachine gun.

'There used to be a bunch called *Pamyat* back in the early nineties, and there's been an upsurge of Russian neo-Nazis in Israel,' said Peggy. 'The Russian National Socialist Party is an offshoot of *Pamyat*. They released a video a while back showing somebody being beheaded in a forest.'

'You can't be serious,' said Holliday.

'Dead serious,' said Peggy. She shrugged. 'They run a newspaper called *Pravoye Soprotivleniye* or *Right Resistance* with a circulation of at least a hundred thousand. The paper used to be called *The Stormtrooper*.'

'Are they big enough to have organized the attack on Carr-Harris?'

'Almost certainly,' answered Peggy. 'The neos these days are very computer savvy; they've even got an electronic clearinghouse on the Internet called "Blood and Honour" and their own version of Wikipedia called "Metapedia." Spooky stuff.'

'You seem to know an awful lot about it,' said Holliday.

'I did the pix on a series of articles for *Vanity Fair* last year,' she answered.

'So what do we do now?'

Peggy glanced down at the various remnants of fried food congealing on her plate.

'Buy the Irish version of a roll of Tums and figure out our next step.'

'Carefully,' said Holliday.

'Very carefully,' agreed Peggy.

Doc Holliday and Peggy Blackstock stood on the upper deck of the small car ferry and peered out across the broad lake as they neared the German side of the water. Here the lake was called the Bodensee; on the Swiss side it was called Lake Constance.

They were within a mile or so of the dock at Friedrichshafen, but there was nothing to be seen ahead except a gray wall of fog, the horizon stolen and the sun invisible. Every few seconds the ferry's foghorn would moan, the sound repeated back to them out of the featureless gloom like the unrequited mating calls of vanished sea creatures. Barely visible, the inky waters of the ancient alpine lake broke thickly against the sides of the ferry.

'The Twilight Zone,' said Peggy, the sound of her voice flattened by the heavy mist. There were other people nearby on the deck, but they were as invisible as everything else, no more than shadows appearing and disappearing as they went by. When people spoke it was in murmurs and low whispers, like children afraid of the dark unknown.

Six days had passed since the firefight at *L'Espoir* and the murder of Carr-Harris. They'd stayed in Dublin for most of that time, waiting to see what the fallout would be from the death of the old Oxford professor at his country home.

There seemed to have been no consequences at all; it was as though the whole thing had never happened. Nothing in any of the newspapers that Holliday looked through and nothing on the radio or television. No hue and cry, no be-on-the-look-out-for-these-fugitives, no policeman hammering on their hotel room door, no ringing of the tele-phone. Nothing.

In the end the only conclusion that Holliday and Peggy could make of it all was that their opponents, whoever they were, had carefully cleaned up after themselves either to keep the police off their tails or to ensure that they would find the two Americans before the authorities. One way or another they were only buying themselves a little bit of time; eventually the crime would be discovered.

Peggy and Holliday hadn't been idle during their brief hiatus in Dublin. Peggy had spent some time re-outfitting themselves from stores at the St. Stephen's Green Shopping Centre while

Holliday followed the few frail leads they had, researching the names Carr-Harris had mentioned at an Internet café at the foot of bustling Grafton Street, a crowded pedestrian mall that ran between the corner of St. Stephen's Green and the entrance to Trinity College on Nassau Street.

Holliday concentrated on tracking down the three names involved with Carr-Harris's Postmaster escapade off the coast of West Africa during the early days of the war: Edmund Kiss, Hans Reinerth, and the Italian, Amedeo Maiuri.

Several things quickly became apparent, linking the men above and beyond the letter Uncle Henry had discovered on the captured ocean liner: all three men were somehow involved with archaeology, and all three men were deeply involved in mysticism, Kiss and Reinerth with the Nordic roots of the German race and culture, Amedeo Maiuri with the essence of the Ancient Roman military ethic.

Kiss and Reinerth had both become SS officers during World War II, and Maiuri had held equivalent rank in the Fascist Black Brigades. Maiuri had been one of the founding members of the School of Fascist Mysticism in Milan and both Reinerth and Kiss had been high-ranking and important members of the 'Study society for primordial intellectual science "German Ancestral Heritage,"' commonly referred to as the *Ahnenerbe*, the fundamental source and rationalization for Hitler's race laws and the annihilation of the Jews.

All three men survived the war and escaped serious prosecution. Kiss faded from view without a ripple, while Reinerth had been intimately involved with the creation of a museum of Stone Age culture still thriving today and located not far from where they were right now on the Bodensee. But eventually he, too, slipped into obscurity. Maiuri, his reputation carefully sanitized soon after Italy's capitulation in 1943, continued in his previous occupation as director of the archaeological dig at Pompeii until his death in 1960.

Digging even deeper as he ricocheted across the Internet from one linking Web site to another, Holliday eventually found the common thread that bound all three: they had all been members of a secret society formed by a man named Jörg Lanz von Liebenfels, a former Cistercian monk. The name of the society, organized in 1907 in Burg Werfenstein, Austria, was 'The Order of the New Templars.' Originally adopting a right-facing red swastika as its symbol, the Order used the same icon later adopted by the officially recognized *Ahnenerbe*: a sword, its blade enclosed by a loop of gold and surrounded by a band of runic letters; exactly the same design Holliday had seen on the wrist of the dead man in Carr-Harris's hallway.

Seeing the image on the screen brought him up short. Was it possible that some arcane bit of old folklore still existed? More likely that the symbol was being used again for some other twisted purpose.

The Order of the New Templars apparently went underground after the war but reemerged in Vienna during the fifties with an ex-SS officer named Rudolf Mund as Prior of the Order. Mund spent almost twenty years trying to resurrect his version of the organization but failed. Nazism was a forgotten enterprise; Communism had replaced it as the world's enemy.

Digging deeper still, Holliday followed the faint trail left by Mund, eventually connecting him to another SS officer, the man who had in fact been Mund's superior during the war, SS-Gruppenführer General Lutz Kellerman. Kellerman had also been a member of the Order of the New Templars as well as being a close friend of Heinrich Himmler, chief of the SS and the Gestapo who was in turn the sponsor of both Edmund Kiss and Hans Reinerth. Wheels within wheels.

Kellerman vanished after 1945, presumably escaping through the Vatican 'ratlines' and with the help of the near-mythical ODESSA, the *Organisation der ehemaligen SS-Angehörigen*, the Organization of Former SS Officers.

Kellerman's family enshrined his memory and rose to some wealth and notoriety as exporters of farm machinery to Brazil and Argentina. For years there had been rumors that the SS officer had escaped to South America with a fortune in looted gold and jewelry, but no one had ever found any hard evidence.

Kellerman's son, Axel, had tried unsuccessfully to purchase himself a career in postwar German politics, but even the ultra-right-wing *Republikaner* party refused to endorse him. Axel Kellerman, now in his fifties and using the name 'von Kellerman,' ran the family enterprises from the ancestral castle estate just outside of Friedrichshafen.

Friedrichshafen was a small city of roughly sixty thousand, its main industries being the revitalized Zeppelin works and Friedrichshafen AG, a manufacturer of transmissions for farm machinery and heavy equipment. On the surface the town appeared to be a bright, modern tourist-oriented location far from the bustling industrial centers of Munich, Stuttgart, and the Rhine–Ruhr industrial area, but the city by the lake had a much darker past.

During the war the Zeppelin works manufactured components for the v2 rocket with labor provided by slaves from a satellite of Dachau concentration camp located on the outskirts of the town. Most of the old city center had been completely destroyed during the Operation Bellicose bombing raid of June 20, 1943.

'Do you really think this man Kellerman is going to have any useful information?' Peggy asked as they stood together on the upper deck of the ferry. 'And more importantly, if he *does* have any information is he going to give it to us?'

Holliday shrugged. His brain was getting tired, stumbling over names, dates, events, possibilities. History for him was usually clear, a set of absolutes, set in stone. Now it was something different, vague and without a coherent order. He'd spent a lifetime in the military, where goals were achieved by direct action; there was nothing direct at all about the problem of Uncle Henry's sword.

'He's all we've got,' said Holliday finally. 'Kellerman's father knew all the parties involved, and he was close to Himmler. He would have known about the sword, I'm almost certain of that. Lutz Kellerman is the link to it all, not to mention the tattoo on that guy's wrist.'

'But so what?' Peggy said. 'How does that help us?'

'What we need to find out is the location, if it still exists, of the right copy of the letter written by Alberic to Hugues de Payens, the founder of the Templars. Without the letter the code on the gold wire is useless, like Braintree told us in Toronto.'

'D.L.N.M. *De laudibus novae militiae*,' said Peggy.

'Your Latin is improving,' smiled Holliday.

'And the fog is lifting,' answered Peggy.

Ahead of them, a few hundred yards away across the water, the harbor front of Friedrichshafen appeared through the thinning mist. On the right there was a large, modern-looking marina; a forest of sailboat masts rose like sharp splinters cutting through the shredding fog.

There was a heavy stand of trees coming down to the shore on the far left, the twin onion-domed towers of a church rising up through the greenery. In the center was the harbor itself, with the ferry dock and the updated Bauhaus-style glass and steel Medienhaus, the town library, directly behind it. Strung along the old seawall Holliday could see an assortment of older, red-roofed buildings that had survived the bombings. Rising behind it all were the steep, lushly forested hills and valleys of the Bavarian Alps.

'Postcard time,' said Peggy.

'We'll see,' said Holliday. Baghdad had been a Disney location before it turned into a war zone.

The ferry nosed between the jutting arms of the harbor breakwater and moved toward the docks. People around them began heading down to the main deck and their automobiles. The engines on the ferry reversed in a growling throb, the sound vibrating up through the hull. The fog was quickly disappearing and the sun was shining down on the town. Peggy was right; it was a post-card.

'We'd better go,' she said. The ferry had almost reached the pier.

'All right,' nodded Holliday. They turned away from the rail and headed for the companionway stairs behind them. Perhaps now they'd find out why Uncle Henry's house had been put to the torch and why his friend Derek Carr-Harris had been murdered. First they'd find a cheap hotel in town, and then they'd lay siege to Axel von Kellerman in his castle.

13

According to the brochure Holliday and Peggy picked up at their Friedrichshafen hotel, the original Schloss Kellerman had been built in A.D. 1150 by the Grafen von Kellerman-Pinzgau, feudal lords of the area. The castle was destroyed during a peasants' revolt in 1526 and had lain in ruins ever since.

The 'new' Schloss Kellerman, an exquisite manor house in the Baroque style of the times built at the foot of the hill on which the ruins still stood, had been constructed in 1760 by Count Anton von Öttingen-Kellerman, a reigning Bavarian prince of Pinzgau and a descendant of the original owners.

The Schloss had been in the possession of the Kellerman family ever since, and as well as still being the family residence it was also a museum and occasional venue for seminars dealing with European Stone Age and Bronze Age studies.

The Kellerman estate was located four miles north of Friedrichshafen, set at the foot of a steep, heavily wooded hillside and reached by a twisting road that wound between the trees, eventually opening up into a broad meadow, part of which was a planted orchard while the other part had been laid out as a formal ornamental garden complete with animal topiary and a high hedge maze. Beside the maze there was a pea gravel parking lot.

'Creepy,' said Peggy, climbing out of the Peugeot they'd rented two days before in Zurich.

The weather was sunny and warm, without a hint of the gloomy fog that had greeted them on their arrival the day before. Holliday locked the car, and he and Peggy walked up the path toward the house.

The manor was a sprawling series of two-story buildings arranged in an elongated L shape, the red tile rooflines broken here and there with turrets and towers, all of it done in whitewash over stucco, some of the walls overgrown with ivy. The windows were arched and recessed, outlined in strips of fancy brickwork, and the towers were finished with Lego-like stepped fretwork.

The lawns surrounding the estate were golf course groomed, the flowerbeds neatly edged with six-inch-high retaining walls, the beds themselves ablaze with flowers and dense with perfectly manicured shrubbery. It was all like a giant dollhouse owned by a dainty princess, an unflawed dream you only saw in *Architectural Digest*.

'No littering around here,' commented Peggy. 'Someone's a bit of a neat freak.'

They went up a broad series of granite steps and reached the main entrance. The capstone in the arch over the open doorway had been carved into an armorial shield: a single upright sword, bound by a twisted ribbon.

'Isn't *that* interesting?' murmured Holliday, looking upward.

They stepped through the broad entrance and into the manor house. A female uniformed attendant took their money, handing them each a yellow plastic squeeze badge and a pamphlet in return. The pamphlet was trilingual: English, French, and German. They walked down a long entrance hallway, their feet echoing on the black and white tiles of the marble floor.

A few people were wandering in and out of rooms, all wearing the same expression of bored expectation common to tourists already overburdened with more information than they needed. Judging by the minimal crowds, it didn't look as though Schloss Kellerman was very high on anyone's 'must-do' list.

According to the brochure, two large rooms on the left contained models of both Stone Age and Bronze Age villages that had once occupied the grounds of the Schloss, while the smaller room on the right, once the manor's dining hall, was now given over to relics and artifacts relating to the Kellerman family.

'I'm still not sure what this is going to accomplish,' said Peggy. 'We don't even know if Kellerman is here.'

'Recon,' said Holliday quietly. 'Getting the lay of the land.' He turned right into the old dining hall.

The room was immense, ceilings soaring twenty feet overhead, coffered in exotic woods. The plaster squares between the thick crossed beams were inset with sculptured plaster medallions of cupids and angels cavorting around the cables supporting a dozen dangling crystal chandeliers.

The far wall was set with three tall windows sheeting sunlight into the room and across the dark blue patterned carpeting that lay across the dark oak floor. The nearer wall was hung with portraits of Kellermans long past. Where there were no portraits in oils there were photographs in silver frames, and between all of the hanging art and photographs there were eight full suits of armor, evenly spaced, running the length of the room like knights waiting for their king.

On the end walls were the broad hearths and wide mantels of matching fireplaces. The fireplaces were both cold and empty, scrubbed clean of any evidence of use. Above them tapestries had been strung. Between the fireplaces, where there once would have been a dining table capable of seating sixty guests or more, there was now a row of glass and wood display cases, each one containing items from a distinct period in the history of the Kellerman family.

A Viking 'bearded' iron broadax blade discovered during a nineteenth-century archaeological dig on the grounds; a chalice and candlesticks used in the family chapel of the original castle; an enameled brooch portraying Christ, once worn by Countess Gertrude, the wife of Count Anton von Öttingen-Kellerman, the builder of the most recent Schloss. An ornate Kleigenthal naval saber presented to a Kellerman who'd joined the German Navy in the 1800s. A *Pickelhaube* spiked Prussian Army helmet worn by yet another Kellerman general, this one during the First World War.

Evidence of Kellermans everywhere, but not a sign of SS-Gruppenführer General Lutz Kellerman anywhere at all.

'So World War Two never happened,' Peggy murmured.

Beside the open doorway leading to the inner hall there was a tall glass case given over to the present-day Kellerman family. There were several scale models of farm machinery manufactured by Kellerman AG, a cutaway model of a patented device for sowing grain, and at least a dozen photographs of Axel Kellerman: Axel at a charity banquet on the arm of a blond television actress, Axel at a child's hospital bed, Axel with a famous grinning Hollywood star on a film set, Axel wearing scuba tanks and levering himself into a boat in the Caribbean.

He was tall, athletically slim, and darkly handsome. His face was long and sharp-jawed, his hair black, sweeping back in a widow's peak. He had a long aristocratic nose, deep-set piercing eyes and a full mouth with lips that were down-drawn and just a little too feminine for such high cheekbones. There was something faintly reminiscent of the vampire about him that was simultaneously both attractive and repellent.

There was no classic family portrait; no wife, no children. One photograph showed Axel Kellerman in hunting clothes with a shotgun in his hands and an elegant liver-ticked German gun dog at his side. Behind him, slightly out of focus, was the building in which they now stood.

'He's written his father out of the family history,' commented Holliday.

'Schwarzenegger did it – why not Axel Kellerman?' Peggy responded.

They left the room and crossed in front of a wide, curving staircase that led up to the second floor.

'I don't believe it,' said Holliday, turning back toward the main hallway. He folded up the brochure and slid it into the side pocket of his jacket. 'From everything I read on the Net he sounds like his old man reincarnated: same political convictions, same military aspirations. I would have expected a place like this to be a shrine.'

'I guess he figures you can't have a Nazi past and sell farm machinery at the same time,' said Peggy as they stepped out into the sunlight again. 'Your basic ruthless German efficiency.'

'I still don't believe it,' repeated Holliday. They walked back down the path toward the parking lot. 'It's a cover-up. The whole place is a stage set. That's not the real Axel Kellerman. He's got a Batcave somewhere, I guarantee it.'

'I wonder where?' Peggy said. Holliday shrugged. He took out the keys and beeped open the car doors.

'I don't have the faintest idea,' said Holliday. They climbed into the Peugeot. Peggy did up her seatbelt and smiled.

'Time for me to show my skills,' she said.

*

The Gaststätte Barin-Bar was an old-fashioned rathskeller, or basement bar, in an older building next to the Friedrichshafen railway station and only a short block from the waterfront. Peggy had discovered the place after a brief conversation with the desk clerk at their hotel and a fat tip to an elderly and gloomy-looking baggage handler at the train station.

The cavernous old restaurant and bar was dimly lit, wood-paneled, and decorated with the mounted heads of stuffed game animals, mostly toothy, glassy-eyed wild boars and blank-faced deer with enormous racks of antlers. There was a pair of bearded mountain goats with curling horns at the far end of the room, and the immense, dusty, and snarling brown she-bear that gave the restaurant its name looked angrily out from over the bar. Holliday smiled; he'd be angry, too, if someone mounted his head over a basement bar. The whole place smelled of beer, cooked cabbage, and frying meat.

It was the middle of the afternoon, and the rathskeller was almost empty. A family of Japanese tourists was sitting at a table close to the cellar stairs working their way through plates of fried potatoes and bratwurst, whispering to each other and surreptitiously taking photographs with a shiny little digital camera. A fat man with white hair was crouched at the dimly lit bar, his thick fingers wrapped possessively around a large mug of beer.

'Nice place,' commented Holliday as they found a table and sat down. 'You sure know how to pick 'em, Peg.'

'You travel around as much as I do you find out the best place for anything – guns, crooks, hookers, information most of all – is at the bar that's closest to the local train station. Where the old geezers hang out and drink. Tunbridge Wells to Timbuktu, it's always the same.'

'There's a train station in Timbuktu?' Holliday teased.

Peggy sighed. 'You know what I mean,' she said. 'If you want information on our friend Kellerman, this is the place to get it.'

A waitress with teased blond hair dressed in a folksy dirndl came out of the kitchen, spotted Holliday and Peggy, and came over to their table. She didn't even hesitate, speaking English automatically.

'Can I get you anything today?' she said pleasantly.

'Two Augustiner Bräu,' responded Peggy.

'Anything else, madam?'

'Rudolph Drabeck?' Peggy asked. It was the name given to her by the old baggage man at the station.

'What do you want with Rudy?' the waitress asked cautiously.

Peggy took out a rust-colored fifty euro note and laid it on the table.

'Local color,' said Peggy.

'*Was?*' asked the waitress, frowning.

'Information only,' explained Peggy.

The waitress gave them an appraising look, then turned and went to the bar. She said something to the man hunched over his beer. The man turned and looked at Holliday and Peggy. Peggy nodded and picked up the fifty euro note, waving it.

The white-haired old man picked up his beer mug and crossed the room to their table. A few feet away the Japanese family shrank away from him as he passed. Reaching their table, he took a long pull from his beer mug and waited, his bleary eyes fixed on the money in Peggy's hand.

'*Ja?*' he asked. His voice was scratchy and hoarse, thick with too much booze for too many years.

'*Sprechen Sie Englisch?*'

'Sure, of course,' said the man, weaving a little. He made a little snorting sound. 'Doesn't everybody now? I have Russian, too, a little. Italian, some.' He shrugged.

'Why don't you sit down, Herr Drabeck?' Holliday offered.

'Herr Drabeck was my *Scheisskopf* of a father, the schoolteacher of *rotznasigen* little children. Call me Rudy,' the old man said sourly. 'Everyone else does.' He shrugged again and sat down.

Holliday studied him briefly. He was short and fat with an untrimmed, gray beard shot through here and there with streaks of black. His hair was unkempt and unwashed, thinning back to the middle of his pink skull. His face was round, the cheeks pouched and sagging, the pale blue eyes vague behind plastic-framed glasses.

His bulbous nose was broken with booze veins, and he had the flushed, ruddy complexion of someone with uncontrolled high blood pressure. He wore a wrinkled old brown suit, and he'd obviously been wearing it too long. His white shirt had been washed a thousand times, and the collar was permanently gray. At close range he smelled of cigarettes and fried onions. He appeared to be in his eighties, which would have made him twenty or so during the war.

The waitress appeared again, bringing Peggy and Holliday their beer in tall pilsner glasses.

'Give him one of these, as well,' said Peggy, lifting her beer glass and nodding toward the old man.

'*Nein,*' said Drabeck quickly, speaking to the

waitress. *'Kulmbacher Eisbock. Ein Masskrug, bitte, und ein Betonbuddel Steinhäger.'*

'Pardon?' Peggy said. Her high school German had been exhausted back at *'Sprechen Sie Englisch.'*

'Ein Masskrug is what you call a liter,' explained the waitress, grinning. 'Steinhäger is a kind of gin. He wishes a whole bottle.'

'A whole bottle?'

'That is what he says,' replied the waitress.

'Und ein Strammer Max,' added the old man, blinking earnestly.

Peggy turned to the waitress.

'He is asking now for a sandwich. *Leberkäse* – liver cheese, I think you say, with a fried egg on top, sun part up and toasted in the pan.'

Peggy stared at Drabeck.

He shrugged again and smiled. His teeth were small, yellow, and uneven.

'All right,' said Peggy. The waitress went away. She turned back to Drabeck. 'You've lived in Friedrichshafen for a long time?'

The old man stared at the fifty euro note in front of Peggy on the table. She slid it across to him. He grabbed it and slipped it quickly into the sagging pocket of his jacket. He drained the last of the beer from his mug and set it aside, placing his hands flat on the table. The fingers were long and surprisingly small and delicate. Veins twisted across the skin like worms underneath the wrinkled flesh. The nails were broken and cracked, dark with dirt, thick and yellow.

'Old hands,' he said.

Peggy said nothing. The man continued to look mournfully down at his hands. 'Old,' he repeated.

'They look like they might have played the piano once,' ventured Holliday.

'Violin,' murmured Drabeck. 'I once played the violin, in Vienna, a very long time ago. The *Wiener Symphoniker*, the Vienna Symphony.'

'You were a violinist?' Peggy said, wondering for a moment where this was leading.

'I was a boy, very young. I was at the *Universität für Musik und darstellende Kunst Wien*, the music school in Vienna, yes? I had a job; I was to be with the *Symphoniker*, my dream since I was very small. Then came the Anschluss, and we were all Nazis whether we liked to be or not; it made no matter.'

'That would have been 1938, then,' said Holliday. Hitler's relatively peaceful annexation of Austria.

'Ja,' said Drabeck. The waitress returned, carrying a tray. On it were an array of bottles, plates, and glasses, including an enormous glass mug of foaming beer as dark and opaque as Guinness. She set it all down in front of the old man.

His eyes gleamed. He slathered the Strammer Max sandwich with horseradish and dark mustard then took an enormous bite. Egg yolk squirted out of the sides of the sandwich and dripped into his beard. Hand shaking a little, he picked up the big glass mug and quaffed an enormous slug of the black, foaming beer to wash down the food. He sat back in his chair, sighing, his breath coming in hard little puffs as though he'd just been in a footrace.

'What happened then?' Holliday said.

Drabeck wiped the sleeve of his jacket across his mouth, taking the foam out of his drooping mustache.

'My *Schwuchtl* father knew the big cheese here, yes? The boss, Herr von Kellerman, the Count up in his big Schloss there by the ruins. He and my father were together in a . . .' He paused, his bushy eyebrows lowering as he frowned, looking for the right words. '*Ein Geheimbund . . .*'

'Secret group?' Holliday said. 'Secret society?'

'*Ja*, that is it,' nodded Drabeck. He took another bite of the sandwich and more egg yolk dripped. He put the sandwich down and licked his fingers, then took another long swallow of beer.

'Do you remember the name of the secret society?' Peggy asked.

'*Ja*, sure,' said the old man. He took another

bite and spoke through the mouthful of food. *'Die Thule Gesellschaft. Der Germanenorden.'* He swallowed and drank more beer.

'The Thule Society,' nodded Holliday. 'The Teutonic Order of the Holy Grail. They were formed just after World War One.' The Germans had been looking for some grouping mythology to make themselves feel more important, much like 'The Star-Spangled Banner' being written as a morale booster after the British burned Washington to the ground and captured Detroit. Except that the song that became the national anthem was no more than a patriotic song that bound the nation together and boosted an overtaxed country's sense of itself a little. The urge for Germanic mysticism had given birth to the rise of Adolf Hitler, the seed of his anti-Semitic screed planted in the rise of Aryan fundamentalism, his first converts among members of groups like the Thule Society.

'Ja,' said Drabeck. 'That's it.' He unscrewed the top from the clay bottle of Steinhäger and poured himself an oily couple of ounces into the inverted cone of the glass brought by the waitress. He drank it off neat and smacked his lips. *'Mein Vater*, my father, thought it was a sign from the heavens, the symbol of Thule and the . . .' He paused again. *'Das Wappen, das schildförmiges,'* he struggled.

Holliday got it.

'The shield, the coat of arms.'

'Ja,' said Drabeck, relieved. 'The, how you said, coat of arms of the Thule and the family of the Kellermans was so much the same.' He poured another glass of the clear gin and drank it off again, then reached into the breast pocket of his jacket and dug out an inch-long stub of pencil. He picked up a napkin and drew on it quickly. A simple sword in front of a slightly curving swastika. *'Thule Gesellschaft,'* he said, showing them. He added the sword and ribbon crest they'd seen carved in the stone above the front entrance to Schloss Kellerman. *'Das Wappen auf das geschlecht Kellerman, gelt, ja?'*

'The sword again,' said Peggy.

Drabeck tapped at the drawing with his pencil stub.

'Ja, der Schwert.' He nodded emphatically.

'So,' said Holliday slowly. 'Your father and Herr Kellerman were in the Thule Society together . . .' He let it dangle.

Drabeck poked the last of the sandwich into his mouth and chewed reflectively.

'Kellerman was *ein Obergruppenführer*, a general in the *Schutzstaffel*, the SS. He knew people in the Party, so my father also. Little Heini – Himmler, Goebbels, and *der Dicke*, the Fat One, Göring, he knew all of them, so they had my father become *Stellvertreter-Gauleiter . . .*'

'Deputy gauleiter, district boss?' Holliday supplied.

'*Ja*, as you say, boss of the district, the town here.'

'And you?' Peggy asked.

'I played the violin.' Drabeck shrugged, pouring another glass of Steinhäger. He drank, then wiped his lips with the back of his thumb. 'What could I do? My eyesight was poor, I could not shoot, or kill, or anything like that, so Kellerman made me his *Putzer.*'

'Putzer?' Peggy said.

'*Der Hausdiener,*' said the old man, struggling.

'Orderly, I think,' said Holliday. 'An aide-de-camp.'

'*Ja,*' said Drabeck. 'His servant. I polished his boots and ran his bath, just so, *ja*? I went with him everywhere, polishing his *verdammte Stiefel*. Russia, Stalingrad, Italy, Normandy, always polishing the boots.'

'The Berghof?' Holliday asked. Was that the connection with the sword?

'*Ja*, sure, there, too, a few times. There I am having the privilege to pick up the *Hundkacke* of Blondi, Hitler's dog, from the rugs and fetch *die Nutte* Eva's little cakes from the town. And polish the boots.'

'And then?' Peggy said.

Drabeck poured more Steinhäger.

'You know Dachau?' Drabeck asked.

'The concentration camp?' Holliday said.

'Ja, das Konzentrationslager,' nodded the old man. 'They had a camp here for the workers at Dornier and Maybach. Making *Raketen, ja?'*

'v2 rockets,' supplied Holliday.

'Vergeltungswaffe Zwei, ja,' nodded Drabeck. 'They had to have people to work. Italians and Poles mostly. *Juden,* of course. Jews. My father took women from the camp and . . . used them.' The old man paused, looking down into his empty glass. His hand was on the clay bottle, but he made no move to pour from it. He looked up and stared Holliday in the eye. 'When the war was over and the Americans released the prisoners, some came to the town looking for my father. He was hiding at Schloss Kellerman. You know it?'

'We were there this morning,' said Holliday.

'They found him in the old ruins. They brought him back here to the town square and hung him from a lamppost with *dem Kabel,* the electrical wire. He kicked and jerked for five minutes, and his face turned black. His tongue was like a fat sausage sticking from his mouth. I was his son. They made me watch.'

'Holy crap,' whispered Peggy.

'*Ja,*' agreed Drabeck. 'It was unpleasant for me.'

'By then Lutz Kellerman had disappeared?' Holliday asked.

'*Natürlich,*' grunted the old man. 'No more boots for Rudy.' He poured himself another glass of Steinhäger. His forehead and cheeks were shiny with sweat. He belched quietly, and a hiss of gin fumes laced with horseradish and hot mustard spread across the table.

'And Axel?' Holliday said.

'Switzerland,' said Drabeck. 'A refugee, with his mother and his older sister. He was young, three, four maybe.'

'When did they come back?'

'Nineteen forty-six. Things were bad here then. No work for anyone. Everyone was *Geld brauchen*, penniless; the Kellermans were *in Geld schwimmen*: they had money. Lots of it. They went into business. *Die Zugmaschinen*. Tractors. People loved the Kellermans again.' He drank more Steinhäger. '*Dem Geld verfallen sein,*' he said philosophically and sighed.

'And you?'

The old man laughed and belched again. Behind the bar the waitress looked up at the sound.

'Frau Kellerman hired me to polish *her* boots,' said Drabeck. 'Forty years I work for the family and then one day, *phhft*! Rudy is no good any more. Too old. Too much drink. Forty years, no pension. Nothing; *der Kotzbrocken*.'

'When we were there today we saw no evidence that Lutz Kellerman had ever existed. There was no mention of him at the museum, no pictures, nothing.'

Drabeck laughed again.

'*Keineswegs!*' he snorted. 'Of course not! Hitler was a bad dream for Germany, a nightmare they would sooner forget; a nightmare I would forget if it was possible.' Drabeck poured more Steinhäger and drank it.

His nose was running now, and he wiped it on the sleeve of his jacket. His eyes were wet and filled with tears.

'Friedrichshafen made the Hindenburg only. Zeppelins, not death *Raketen*. Boys who yodel and play the alpenhorn. Girls who make *Apfelstrudel* and fat babies. It is a different world now; there is no room in history for *Konzentrationslager* or men like Obergruppenführer Lutz Kellerman.'

'Surely the son has not forgotten his father,' said Holliday.

'No,' Drabeck said. 'He remembers him well enough. He hides it.'

'Hides what?' Peggy said.

'His father's things, *Gegenstände mit Nostalgiewert* – I don't know the word in English for this.'

Nostalgiewert. Nostalgia?

'Memorabilia?'

Drabeck shrugged.

'*Egal welche,*' he grunted. Whatever.

'Medals, uniforms, that kind of thing,' prompted Holliday.

'*Ja*, sure,' answered Drabeck. His eyes were shifting, and he was beginning to look uncomfortable. Talking about himself and the past was fine; talking about the master's secrets was something else.

'So he has a shrine to his father somewhere?' Peggy said, pushing. Drabeck looked down into his empty glass, his lips pursing.

'*Ja,*' he said slowly.

Holliday caught Peggy's eye. He made a little gesture with his thumb and forefinger, rubbing them back and forth. She nodded and dug into her bag. She pulled out a pale green hundred euro note.

She folded it in half and slid it across the table, nudging Drabeck's glass. There was a second of hesitation, and then the old man's fingers delicately pulled the bill toward the edge of the table and it disappeared into his pocket.

'Where?' Holliday said flatly.

There was another second's hesitation. Drabeck licked his lips, and then he spoke.

'He has a place . . .' the old man began.

14

'We should have brought a gun,' said Peggy. They were lying on the edge of the bluff that stood over Schloss Kellerman on the broad, sweeping meadow below. It was dusk, and the first security lights were coming on around the complex of buildings. Through his newly purchased binoculars Holliday could see the distinctive pink glow of high pressure mercury vapor lamps; in full dark the Schloss would be lit up as brightly as a Hollywood premiere.

'Guns are stupid,' said Holliday, putting down the binoculars. 'You wind up getting shot.'

'Funny sentiment coming from an old soldier.'

'Old soldiers don't get to be old by overestimating the value of firepower,' answered Holliday. 'Don't carry a gun unless you're willing to kill someone with it, which I am not willing to do at the moment.'

Peggy frowned.

'I'm not one of your first-year students at the Point, Doc. I don't need a lecture. I just thought it might be nice to have some backup if this guy

Kellerman was responsible for murdering Professor Carr-Harris and burning down Grandpa's house.'

'We don't know that for sure,' said Holliday.

'It's a pretty good assumption. We wouldn't be here otherwise.'

'Assumptions without evidence are the kind of things that start wars,' said Holliday. 'I repeat, guns are stupid.'

'You're lecturing again, Doc.'

'Comes with the territory.'

He scanned the grounds of the Schloss again. Nothing was moving. An hour ago a van had pulled up with the evening shift of guards. Eight armed, uniformed men, all tall, fit, young, and definitely Aryan. Axel Kellerman was clearly not an equal opportunity employer. The van had picked up the eight men from the earlier shift and driven off.

Twenty minutes later a tall, dark-haired man in an expensive suit, wearing a green Tyrolean hat complete with boar's brush decoration, had climbed into a big, black Mercedes sedan and driven off toward Friedrichshafen. It could have been Axel Kellerman, but it was hard to tell for sure. The parking lot of the Schloss was empty.

Holliday swung the glasses to the left. At the far end of the bluff, two hundred yards away and partially screened by a stand of pine trees, the ruins of the old castle rose in the gathering darkness like an ancient megalith. The promontory was barred by the original curtain wall, or what was left of it: a twelve-foot-high mound of crumbling stone and rubble.

Behind the wall, standing like an immense broken tooth, were the remains of the keep, the stone fortress that had once stood in the center of the castle, protected by a moat and drawbridge, the last line of defense for the old Count Kellerman-Pinzgau.

Peggy took a shiny camera the size of a cigarette pack out of her bag and took a few quick exposures of the ruins.

'What are you doing?' Holliday asked.

'Taking establishing shots.'

'We're snooping, not making a documentary.'

'Snooping, documentary, what do I care? I'm taking pictures, that's what I do, Doc.'

She aimed the camera at Holliday and clicked off a shot.

'No flash,' he said. 'Nothing will come out,' he said.

'Don't be silly,' answered Peggy. 'This thing will take pictures by starlight. Welcome to the digital age, old man.'

Holliday picked up the binoculars again and

turned them toward the Schloss. Still no movement. The only sound was the light, warm wind sifting through the surrounding trees.

'All right,' he said quietly. 'It's all clear. Keep low so your silhouette doesn't break the horizon; we wouldn't want some guard on a smoke break seeing you. Head for the barbican.'

'The what?'

'The gatehouse in the wall, that big square thing.'

'Gotcha.'

'Go.'

She went. Thirty seconds later he followed, running hard, crouching low.

They reached the old gatehouse in the wall, then paused. The courtyard beyond was dark and empty. Nothing moved. In the far distance Holliday could hear the moaning rumble of a passing train.

'Maybe Drabeck was feeding us a load of bull,' said Peggy. 'Maybe this is all a waste of time.'

'Nervous?' Holliday asked.

'I'm feeling just a wee bit criminal.'

'Barely that,' said Holliday. 'Trespassing maybe.'

'So far.'

'So far.'

They waited for a moment more, catching their breath.

'Now what?' Peggy asked, bent low, panting, hands on knees.

'More running,' said Holliday. 'The second barbican in front of the moat. From there we cross the bridge into the keep.'

'You first this time,' said Peggy. 'Age before beauty.'

'You wish,' said Holliday. He eased himself forward for a few feet and looked out into the courtyard. A few yards away he could see a regular outline of stonework that was all that remained of the original Great Hall, the lord of the manor's residence in peacetime. A little beyond that was a circular pile of stones that had probably once been the castle well, and beyond that, thirty feet on a side and rising eighty feet or more into the night sky, was the keep.

The rest of the courtyard was rubble weeds and tall grass. No evidence of guards or even casual visitors. No litter, no cigarette butts or pop cans on the ground. Kellerman ran a tight ship. Holliday took a deep breath, let it out slowly, and then sprinted across the courtyard, not pausing until he'd reached the shadowed safety of the keep's gatehouse. He waited, watching as Peggy followed, cloth bag over her shoulder, long legs pumping, bringing her across the courtyard a few seconds later.

'Okay,' she said. 'Now what?'

Holliday glanced upward. He could see the pattern of holes drilled in the stone roof of the gateway. 'Murder holes' used for pouring boiling oil down on the besieging enemy.

Beyond that was the narrow earth bridge that crossed the moat. In centuries past the bridge would have been wood and the moat would have been filled with water or sharp stakes, the medieval version of tank traps meant to slow the work of approaching siege engines or sappers intent on undermining the walls.

Holliday suddenly found himself wondering who had been here before him. Places like this *were* history. They were steeped in it, bathed in its blood, and eventually ruined and forgotten by it. What armored knights on horseback had come through this gateway, what princes and what kings?

'Having a history moment, are we?' Peggy said, grinning at him in the gloom.

'Oh, shut up,' he said fondly, grinning back. 'You know me too well. Come on.'

They ran across the narrow earth bridge, the moat no more than a shallow curving ditch on either side of them, thick with grass and weeds. They reached the arched entrance to the keep and stepped inside. Castles had their individual characteristics, but their architecture was as predictable as Big Macs from Nashville to Novgorod. He'd taken a class of seniors to Russia on a goodwill tour the summer before and he'd actually *eaten* a burger in Novgorod, so he knew what he was talking about.

Inevitably the keep would have had five levels rising from ground level. Stores, an administrative level, the keep's version of the Great Hall, a residential level, and an armorers' level. Above that would be the tile-covered wooden roof and an open fighting platform for archers. There would be garderobes – medieval toilets – jutting out at every level and emptying down into the moat.

Below ground level were the cells used for prisoners and below that the keep's well and the cistern used for filling the moat and as a catchment for rain, giving the keep a secondary supply of water for cooking and cleaning. All in all a very effective and self-contained environment for a castle under siege, its curtain wall already breached. All of this would have been connected by a series of stone stairways built between the inner and outer walls of the keep. If Drabeck had been telling them the truth, their destination would be one of those old stairways that led down to the dungeons and the water supply.

Holliday peered into the gloom. There was the darker shadow of a doorway on the right. He pointed.

'There.' He touched Peggy's elbow, and they pelted across the open paving stones that had once been the foundation of the keep. They reached the doorway. Inside the small arch and to the left there was a narrow stone stairway leading downward. The steps were worn by centuries of use. Few princes and even fewer kings had used these steps. This was a stairway for servants and jailers.

Holliday took a small Maglite from the pocket of his jacket. He went down two steps and turned it on. The steps were no more than a foot wide and very steep.

'Careful,' he said, looking back over his shoulder. 'Take it slow.'

He went down the steps, holding the light high, the palm of his free hand against the stone wall for balance as he descended. Peggy followed cautiously. At the bottom of the steps there was a small vaulted vestibule and a formidable iron door. The door had four immense strap hinges on the left, secured with thumb-sized rivets, and an old-fashioned ward lock on the right with a latch above it. Peggy tried the door.

'Locked.'

'Nobody carries a key that big around with them,' said Holliday. He swept the beam of light around the small area. There was nothing. No potted plant, no convenient rock or welcome mat, no chink in the mortar of the close-set stones.

'No key here,' said Peggy. 'We're out of luck.'

'Maybe not.'

'Explain please.'

'Benedict Arnold,' Holliday said suddenly, snapping his fingers.

'Pardon?'

Holliday stepped forward, using the Maglite to scan the hinges. They were set apart equally on the door, each hinge a good five inches wide, each with four giant rivets securing it. Except for the middle hinge, which had five rivets. An oversight? A later repair? Maybe. Then again.

He poked each one of the rivets with the ball of his thumb. Nothing, but he felt the third rivet move slightly. Instead of pushing, he pulled. The rivet popped out an inch, and there was a satisfying clicking sound from inside the door.

'Try it now,' said Holliday. Peggy tried the latch. The door opened.

'Shazam. How'd you figure that out?'

'Benedict Arnold commanded West Point before he turned traitor. After he fled they went through his residence and found a secret panel in the attic with a lock like this one.'

'Crafty devil.'

'Let's not stand around too long,' said Holliday. 'It's gone beyond simple trespass now.'

Peggy pulled open the door, and they stepped inside.

Holliday swung the flashlight, and the beam picked up an old-fashioned metal toggle switch screwed to the wall beside the door. He flipped it to the ON position. The room lit up.

'Holy Batcave, Doc! You weren't kidding!'

The cistern was a curved-roof chamber fifty feet long and twenty wide with a single horseshoe archway at the midpoint. The ceiling, walls, and floor were made with rectangular blocks of limestone so closely set that there was no need for mortar. Industrial pan lights dangled down from heavy electrical flex stapled to the roof stones. Four immense ceremonial banners were hung like tapestries on the wall at the end of the room. The designs of all four were remarkably similar.

On the far left was the rune circle and sword insignia of the *Ahnenerbe*, the Nazi ancestral heritage organization. Beside it was the sword and ribbon symbol that Holliday had seen tattooed on the dead man's wrist at Carr-Harris's farm and cut into the stone above the doorway of the Schloss

Kellerman. The third design showed another circle of runes containing a sword wreathed with heraldic dragons, and the fourth banner was stitched with the sword and a right-facing, curved-arm swastika of the Thule Society, the so-called Teutonic Order of the Holy Grail. All the banners were done in red, white, and black, the Nazi palette.

'This guy Kellerman has a real thing about swords, doesn't he?' Peggy commented, staring at the garish tapestries.

'One sword in particular, I'm afraid,' said Holliday.

The rest of the cavernous chamber was filled with displays like the museum in the Schloss. A case of weaponry included a boxed, gold-plated Mauser .32-caliber presentation automatic pistol marked '*Meister Schieben*' – Master Shooter – with the same sword and ribbon insignia carved into the grips, as well as a battered MP18 submachine gun with a wooden stock and even a *Panzerfaust*, the German version of the American bazooka.

There were several uniforms on mannequins from SS General to the plain dress of a World War I *Kaiserjäger* infantryman with the rank of *Gefreiter*, or lance corporal, presumably meant to indicate Lutz Kellerman's rise from the trenches to the Nazi General Staff.

There were pictures of Lutz Kellerman everywhere. Lutz Kellerman with Rommel in North Africa, leaning on a massive Panzer 1 tank. Lutz Kellerman with Adolf Hitler and Albert Speer during the Führer's whirlwind three-hour tour of the French capital. Lutz Kellerman in a candid shot at the Vatican with Vice-Chancellor Franz von Papen and Cardinal Eugenio Pacelli, the man who would become known as 'Hitler's Pope,' probably taken in 1933 just before or just after the signing of the *Reichskonkordat* between the Nazis and the Roman Catholic Church. Lutz Kellerman standing with SS-Obersturmbannführer Martin Weiss, commandant of Dachau concentration camp, beneath the infamous ARBEIT MACHT FREI – 'Work will give you freedom' – gateway.

Most interesting of all, a much older Lutz Kellerman standing with his son on a hill across from the gigantic statue of Christ the Redeemer atop Corcovado Mountain overlooking the city of Rio de Janeiro in Brazil. In the photograph Axel Kellerman looked to be about eighteen. The car behind them was a 1959 Chevy Impala, with its classic sweeping fins and cat's-eye taillights. Proof that Lutz Kellerman had survived the war and lived at least that long afterward.

Father and son were remarkably alike. Same long aristocratic nose, same fox-like face and widow's peak, and same slightly feminine lips. The biggest difference between the two was the long, disfiguring *Renommierschmiss* or 'bragging scar' that ran from just beneath Lutz Kellerman's left eye down to his chin, earned in some long-ago saber duel where the object was not to inflict a wound but to receive one. The most perverted courage Holliday could think of, displayed not on a battlefield but in a fencing salon with celebratory champagne to follow.

'Look at this,' said Peggy, from the far side of the room. She was standing in front of a large desk. On the wall above it was a framed photograph of Hitler, and on the desk itself was a family portrait in a silver frame – a handsome woman in a forties-style dress standing with a young girl, six or seven, and a baby in her arms. Behind them, as distinctive as the statue of Christ the Redeemer in Rio, was the rough claw shape of the snow-capped Matterhorn. The Kellerman family safe in Switzerland for the duration. On the desk was a leather-bound book. Embossed on its cover was the death's-head insignia of the *Totenkopf*, the 33rd SS Division in charge of concentration camps.

'A diary?' Holliday asked.

Peggy flipped it open. Dates at the top of the page, inked entries in neat, small handwriting.

Lutz Kellerman's journal. It appeared to be for the year 1943.

'Does that camera of yours take close-ups?'

'Sure.'

'As many pages as you can.'

'Done.'

Peggy took the camera out of her bag, opened up the journal to the first page, and got started. It took her the better part of twenty minutes. Holliday was wandering through the room, looking through the exhibits, trying to find some connection between Lutz Kellerman and the Templar sword Uncle Henry had hidden in his house.

The only faintly relevant thing he could find was a picture of Himmler, Goebbels, and Lutz Kellerman standing on the balcony at the Berghof, coffee cups in hand, at least corroborating Drabeck's story that Kellerman had actually been at Hitler's summer house in the Bavarian Alps.

'Finished,' said Peggy, joining him. 'About two hundred pages. It'll be fuzzy, but give me a decent computer and we'll be able to read it.'

There was the sound of a wooden match striking across rough stone. Holliday and Peggy turned.

'Herr Doktor Holliday, Fräulein Blackstock,' said Axel Kellerman, standing in the doorway to the chamber. Two blond, uniformed men stood behind him. Both of them were armed with very modern looking Heckler & Koch G36 assault rifles. Kellerman lit his cigarette then blew out the match. He exhaled twin plumes of smoke through his nostrils and smiled. 'How good of you to drop by.'

'I told you we should have brought a gun,' muttered Peggy.

15

Handcuffed, Holliday and Peggy Blackstock were taken back down to the Schloss in a security golf cart. Peggy had been relieved of her camera and bag, and Holliday had the Maglite taken away from him. Arriving at the estate, Holliday saw that the big Mercedes sedan he'd seen leaving the property earlier was back in the parking lot. The guards pulled him and Peggy out of the golf cart and pushed them toward the car.

Two more security guards came out of the service entrance, the hunched and handcuffed form of Rudolph Drabeck sagging between them. The first pair of men disappeared back inside the Schloss, taking Holliday's Maglite and Peggy's camera and shoulder bag with them. The guards with Drabeck were wearing sidearms. From where Holliday was standing they looked like bulky HK45 automatic pistols.

Kellerman stood beside the open driver's-side door of the big sedan.

'We are, as the saying goes, taking you for a

ride,' he said. 'You will please get in the backseat, both of you.'

'I don't think so,' said Holliday. One of the guards separated himself from Drabeck and grabbed Holliday by the arm, dragging him toward the rear door of the vehicle. Holliday tried to jerk out of his grip, then stumbled, barging into Drabeck and almost knocking him over. The old man grunted with surprise. Holliday saw that Drabeck's face had been beaten raw, his nose broken, the nostrils crusted with blood.

'Please, Doctor, I would rather not resort to violence,' chided Kellerman. 'Yet.'

The guard pulled Holliday upright. Kellerman gestured with his chin.

'Take off their handcuffs,' he ordered. The guard did as he was told. Peggy and Holliday rubbed their wrists.

'*Ich flehe dich an!*' groaned the old man, pleading, '*Bitte, ich flehe dich an!*'

'What's he saying?' Peggy asked, turning to Holliday.

'He's begging for his life,' translated Kellerman, his voice flat, without emotion. 'Now, please, get in the car. We're already behind schedule.'

'Where are you taking us?' Peggy asked.

Kellerman sighed.

'To a place where no one will hear you screaming and where bloodstains will not mar my expensive carpeting,' responded Kellerman. '*Ein schweinbetrieb*, a pig abattoir I own a short distance from here. Eminently suitable, I think. You will be tortured while Doctor Holliday watches. When he tells me where he has hidden the sword that your grandfather stole the torture will stop.'

'Uncle Henry didn't steal the sword and you know it,' said Holliday.

'I don't have time to argue semantics with you, Doctor. Get in the car.'

'And if I don't?'

Kellerman sighed theatrically again.

'Then I'll have no choice but to ask Stefan to break Miss Blackstock's fingers, one by one,' said Kellerman. There was no arguing with that; the logic was impeccable.

'All right,' said Holliday. He ducked into the backseat of the car with Peggy right behind him, prodded by Stefan. The door slammed. Kellerman got behind the wheel. Outside there was a sound like a sharp, barking cough. Turning, Holliday saw Drabeck drop to the gravel surface of the parking lot.

Stefan the security guard unscrewed the fat suppressor from his pistol, reholstered the weapon, and picked up Drabeck's feet while the other man lifted his shoulders. They carried the dead man to the back of the car, and Kellerman popped the trunk. The two security guards hoisted the body of the old man up and in, and then slammed the trunk lid. Stefan got into the backseat beside Peggy, and the other man climbed into the front seat beside Kellerman. Stefan unholstered the squat, heavy-looking automatic again and held it in his lap, his thick index finger curled around the trigger.

'You didn't have to kill him,' said Peggy, her teeth gritted and her eyes wet with tears.

Kellerman glanced at her in the rearview mirror. His face was expressionless.

'He was of no further use to me.'

Kellerman turned to the guard in the seat beside him.

'*Zeit in die Heia zu gehen, jawohl?*'

'*Dein Wunsch ist mir Befehl, Mein Herr,*' the guard said and laughed. Kellerman turned the key in the ignition and dropped the transmission into reverse. They backed and filled, then headed off down the winding tree-lined driveway to the main road. The car turned right, away from Friedrich-shafen, and Kellerman drove into the darkness, north toward the nearby mountains.

'Maybe you should tell me why the sword is so important to you,' said Holliday from the backseat. He tried the door handle. Kellerman had locked it remotely. 'I know you're crazy, but even a crazy man doesn't kill over a piece of memorabilia.'

'I assume you're trying to irritate me,' said Kellerman as he drove the big car along the dark road. 'A rather juvenile tactic. Frankly, I had expected more from a man like you.'

'I'm stressed at the moment,' answered Holliday dryly.

'The sword belongs to me,' said Kellerman. 'It is my family legacy.'

'It's just a sword. Not even a very good one,' responded Holliday. 'They're not hard to come by. Try eBay next time instead of murdering innocent people.'

'Derek Carr-Harris was hardly innocent,' laughed Kellerman, the sound hollow and utterly without humor. 'He was a cold-blooded murderer, as was your uncle.'

'That's a lie!' Peggy said hotly.

'My uncle was a medieval historian,' said Holliday. 'During World War Two he was attached to the Monuments, Fine Arts, and Archives Branch. It was an extension of the Roberts Commission set up by FDR. Their job was to protect objects of cultural value from plundering and destruction. Even German ones.'

'True,' said Kellerman, 'but the MFAA was also a cover for a variety of independent, intelligence-related actions by the British and the Americans at the end of the war.' Kellerman paused. A truck swept by in a rush of sound, washing the interior of the car for a moment with the beams from its headlights. 'You're something of a military historian, Doctor. Have you ever heard of something called Operation Werewolf by any chance?'

'Sure,' said Holliday. 'It was a last-ditch defense plan organized by Himmler and run by an SS-*Obergruppenführer* named Prutzmann. It was a left-behind partisan organization.'

'Oddly, very much like the so-called Tribulation Force described in a series of popular Christian novels in your country,' nodded Kellerman. 'But the Operation Werewolf I am referring to was a joint operation devised by a number of high-ranking intelligence officials in both America and the United Kingdom. It was jokingly referred to by Winston Churchill as the *Kammerjäger* Brigade. Do you know what a *Kammerjäger* is, Doctor?'

'I can guess.'

'It means vermin exterminator, Doctor Holliday. The *Kammerjäger* Brigade's mandate was to find, hunt down, or otherwise discover the locations of names on a list of various high-ranking SS officers and other important members of the Reich, and having found them their further instructions were to assassinate them.' Kellerman paused, and then spoke again. '"What we do in life will echo in eternity,"' he quoted. 'You know those words, Herr Doktor Holliday?'

Who *was* this guy?

'Russell Crowe in the movie *Gladiator*.'

'Good words, Doctor, and true ones. Your uncle and his English friend wrote them in blood in the spring and summer of 1945. My father was one of the names on Churchill's death list, Doctor, and both your uncle and Derek Carr-Harris were killers in the *Kammerjäger* Brigade. To my sure knowledge they were responsible for the assassinations of more than two dozen good men in Germany, Austria, and in Rome. They very nearly caught my father, and if they had, they would have killed him on the spot.'

'You're a liar!' Peggy snarled. 'Grandpa never killed anyone!'

The road ahead was completely dark. There was forest on either side of them. No traffic, not even distant headlights. There was no way to tell how long it would be before they reached their destination.

Now or never.

Holliday leaned forward slightly. The guard in the front seat tensed, his hand going toward his holstered weapon.

'Kellerman?'

'Yes?'

Holliday whispered in his ear.

'Fick' dich selber, du Arschloch.'

He let the pencil he'd palmed from Drabeck's pocket in the parking lot drop down his sleeve and into his right hand. He swept his arm up backhanded across Peggy's front, plunging the sharpened point of the pencil into Stefan's right eye and deep into the frontal portion of his brain, killing him instantly. A single shriek died half-stillborn in Stefan's throat. Fluid from the burst eyeball drained down his cheek.

Leaving the pencil in place, Holliday dropped his hand into the dead man's lap, prying the big automatic from his nerveless fingers. He thumbed down the safety, and, twisting his body while leaning over Peggy, covering her, he fired repeatedly into the rear of the front seat.

Upholstery exploded and the bullets took the security guard in the groin and belly, the concussions from each shot filling the interior of the car with a sound like raging thunder. The man twisted and jerked, screaming as he flopped back against the dashboard. Lifting the heavy pistol above the back of the seat, Holliday fired twice more, hitting the security guard in the throat and face. There was a humpty-dumpty instant as the man's head burst open, spraying the front seat and the windshield with blood, brains, and bone chips. Kellerman swerved, tires squealing as the car almost went off the road. Holliday jammed the muzzle of the pistol under Kellerman's collar.

'Pull over,' he ordered. 'Now.'

Silently, Kellerman did as he was told, guiding the big car onto the gravel shoulder. The inside of the car smelled like blood and gunpowder. Holliday worked his jaw back and forth; his ears were ringing. Adrenaline was rushing through his system, and his stomach was roiling. Most other times and places he would have been sick. He swallowed bile.

'Unlock the doors,' he ordered. 'Reach for some kind of weapon and I won't even think about it.' Kellerman nodded, his head barely moving. He reached down and touched a button on his door. There was a dull clicking sound. Holliday glanced out the window. Dark woods on either side. They were in the middle of a forest.

'You okay, Peg?' Holliday asked.

'Yeah,' she answered, her voice choked. Stefan's body was sagging against her like a sleeping lover.

'Open the door and push out the body,' ordered Holliday.

'I don't want to touch him.'

'Just do it, we don't have much time.'

'Okay.'

She leaned over the dead man and tugged the door open. Pushing and straining, she toppled him outward. The corpse flopped half out of the car, legs and feet still inside. Peggy kicked and struggled, finally managing to get the rest of the body out. Holliday looked out through the blood-sprayed windshield. Still no traffic.

'Get the guy out of the front seat,' he said to Peggy.

'Aw, come on!'

'Do it, Peg!'

She climbed out of the car, stepped over Stefan's body and opened the front passenger-side door. Grimacing, she grabbed the nearly headless body by the arm and hauled it out of the car.

'Now what?' Peggy called from the side of the road.

'Get the gun out of his holster. There's a little lever with an S on it on the left-hand side. Push it down. Aim it at Kellerman. If he does anything that makes you nervous, squeeze the trigger and keep on squeezing until you don't feel nervous anymore.'

'Okay,' she answered. She crouched down over the guard's body and retrieved his weapon, taking off the safety and aiming the pistol back into the car.

Holliday turned his attention back to Kellerman.

'I'm getting out of the car and so are you. Make any kind of stupid move and I will kill you, understand?'

'Yes.'

'Do it. Slowly.'

The two men climbed out of the car. The open air smelled like pine needles. A breeze sighed through the trees. The moon was rising. The forest looked like something from a fairy tale.

'Walk around the front of the car and stand on the shoulder,' ordered Holliday. Kellerman did as he was told. So far he had barely spoken. Less than five minutes had passed since the tables had abruptly turned. Holliday followed Kellerman around the big car, the .45 aimed squarely at the small of the man's back. Kellerman glanced down at the crumpled bodies of his security guards.

'Stefan has a two-year-old son. Hans was about to be married.'

'Spare the sentiment,' said Holliday. 'It doesn't suit you.'

'I will kill you for this,' pledged Kellerman.

'So what?' Holliday said. 'You were going to kill us anyway.' He turned to Peggy. 'Search him. Weapons and cell phones.'

'Do I have to?'

'Yes. Give me the gun.' She handed him the weapon. He popped out the magazine and put both pistol and magazine into the pocket of his jacket. Peggy searched Kellerman. She came up with a Deutsche Telekom iPhone and a palm-sized Beretta Tomcat .32-caliber automatic. Holliday put both into his other pocket.

He turned back to Kellerman. 'Roll your friends into the ditch.'

The German gave Holliday a long appraising look but said nothing. He dragged the bodies to the edge of the ditch that ran beside the shoulder of the road and pushed them over.

'And now?' Kellerman asked sourly.

'And now we go,' said Holliday. 'When the next *Autobahnpolizei* patrol comes by you can explain how your two dead employees got that way.'

Peggy stepped forward, looked into the front seat at the mess, and then got into the back. Keeping the big automatic trained on Kellerman, Holliday got behind the wheel and switched on the ignition.

'I think I'm going to be sick,' said Peggy weakly. 'Please get me out of here.'

Holliday spun the wheel, making a U-turn and heading them back toward Friedrichshafen. He stepped down on the gas. In the rearview mirror the tall figure of Axel Kellerman receded and then was swallowed up by the darkness.

'We lost the pictures,' said Holliday.

'No, we didn't,' said Peggy from the backseat. She poked her hand into the back pocket of her jeans. She pulled out a slim piece of plastic a little bigger than a piece of Juicy Fruit gum and held it up for Holliday to see. The word 'Sony' was imprinted on the side.

'What's that?' Holliday asked.

'A flash memory stick,' she answered. 'I down-loaded the pictures while we were still in Keller-man's Batcave. We've got them all. Like I said, Doc, welcome to the digital age.'

16

'How are you doing?' Holliday asked. It was shortly after the lunch-hour rush, and they were sitting in an outdoor café just off the Piazza del Gesù Nuovo in the coastal city of Naples, Italy. Peggy was drinking from a green bottle of ice-cold Nastro Azzuro, and Holliday was on his second cappuccino. The crusty remains of an excellent margherita pizza lay between them on a serving platter. It was hot, bright sunlight shining down out of a brilliant blue sky. Traffic roared loudly around the square. Two days had passed since their gruesome adventure in Friedrich-shafen.

'How am I?' Peggy said. 'I'm still trying to figure out how we got from there to here.'

'By train.' Holliday smiled.

'I didn't mean that,' she said.

'I know,' he said quietly. He glanced out across the piazza. In the center of the slightly tilted cobblestone square loomed the soaring, ornate, rococo Guglia dell'Immacolata obelisk, erected by the Jesuits in the seventeenth century to commemorate the Immaculate Conception and to consecrate their new basilica, after which the piazza was named.

The piazza was the historic center of the old city by the sea, but its importance had faded long ago, and now, instead of praying priests and monks from holy orders, the streets were lined with bars and clubs and by-the-slice pizza shops, the sidewalks thronged with tourists, the roadway jammed with trucks and cars and rushing scooters, their sewing machine engines whining like enraged mosquitoes as they threaded their way dangerously in and out of the rushing traffic that circled endlessly around the enormous spire. It was a long way from the lonely roadside in the Bavarian Alps.

After leaving Kellerman in the darkness, they'd driven back toward the Schloss, retrieving their rental from where they'd parked it on the far side of the bluff that held the castle ruins. There they abandoned the Mercedes with Drabeck's body in the trunk.

Holliday drove them into Friedrichshafen, just managing to catch the 10:40 ferry, the last one of the day. They reached the Swiss side of the lake forty-five minutes later and arrived in Zurich two hours after that. Peggy found a twenty-four hour Internet café where they accessed the memory stick and printed out the diary photographs in ninety-four double-page entries.

They checked the sheets one by one, looking for a familiar word or name. They found what they were looking for in the entry for Monday, September 27, 1943: the word 'Naples' and a name – Amedeo Maiuri, the Italian archaeologist who'd originally discovered the sword during his excavations in Pompeii, a few miles south of the city in the shadow of Vesuvius, the towering volcano that loomed over the Neapolitan landscape.

It was enough for Holliday. They boarded the morning high-speed train to Milan, and then took the slower overnight train to Florence, once the home of Leonardo da Vinci, Michelangelo, and, much later, Salvatore Ferragamo, shoemaker to the stars. In Florence they took the requisite pages from Lutz Kellerman's wartime diary to the people at the local Berlitz office and had them translated. Translations done, they continued on to Naples.

Peggy nursed her beer and stared blankly out at the whirling traffic and the chattering crowds on the sidewalks. Her time in Friedrichshafen had taken its toll. She looked worn, tired, and depressed. Holliday wasn't surprised; he wasn't faring much better. Since the beginning of their pell-mell escapade he'd seen five men die and had been directly responsible for the violent deaths of three of them. Whether they deserved it or not was irrelevant; he'd been the one who'd snuffed out their lives. Their blood was on his hands, and the responsibility for that weighed heavily on him.

'Do you want to quit?' Holliday said.

Peggy turned to him, startled. 'What?'

'Do you want to quit?' he repeated. 'We can stop right now, you know. Get on a plane and be back home in time for breakfast tomorrow.'

She frowned and took a little sip of beer. She put the bottle down, picking at the paper label with her thumbnail.

'I'm not like you,' said Peggy finally. 'I'm not a soldier. I see bad things in a viewfinder, not for real.'

'Believe me, kiddo, I don't feel any different than you do,' responded Holliday.

'I want the bad stuff to be over,' she said. 'Is it?'

Holliday shrugged.

'There's an old saying that dates back to the Bourbon kings – *"Vedi Napoli e poi muori."* "See Naples and die."' He paused and shrugged again. 'Bad stuff begets bad stuff, battles breed more battles, and one war leads to the next. There's no guarantee that it's all going to be clear sailing from here on out.'

'What about Kellerman?'

'What about him?' Holliday replied.

'Is he going to quit now?'

'He knows what's in his father's diary. He's connected. It wouldn't be hard for him to track us down.' Holliday shook his head. 'No, he won't quit.'

'Then neither should we.'

They drove the bright red Fiat 500 rental inland from the Bay of Naples, skirting the brooding base of a sleeping Mount Vesuvius, then headed into the rolling countryside beyond. All around them were neat vineyards and stands of walnut trees, hazelnut trees, apricots, and centuries-old groves of olives. The entire area was supposedly controlled by the Camorra, a homegrown Neapolitan version of the Mafia, but there was no sign of it here.

It was hard to imagine such a pastoral and beautiful landscape as a war zone, but on the ninth of September, 1943, the Allies landed on the beaches of Salerno, fifty miles south, and by the middle of the month they were pressing inland and up the coast to Naples while the German Army under Albert Kesselring slowly withdrew to the north.

According to his diary, on September 28 Lutz Kellerman, leading a small company of crack soldiers from the 1st SS Division Leibstandarte SS Adolf Hitler, arrived in the town of Nola, approximately thirty kilometers northeast of Naples. They were equipped with a number of half-track armored personnel carriers mounted with heavy machine guns, some *Kettenrad* tracked motorcycles, half a dozen Panzer IV tanks, and a Kübelwagen command car for Kellerman. Their official mission was to harass the enemy wherever possible, gather intelligence and forage for supplies, sending out three man '*brandschatzen*' pillage and burn patrols into the countryside. Kellerman, however, had his own agenda.

Having met with Amedeo Maiuri at a private rendezvous at the archaeologist's villa in the suburbs of Naples two days before, Kellerman left the bulk of his men to secure and pacify the town while he and a handpicked platoon of men went to the place Maiuri had discussed with him at their meeting.

The location in question was a large, seventeenth-century Palladian palazzo on a hilltop just outside the tiny village of San Paolo Bel Sito a mile or so to the south. The Villa Montesano, as it was called, had a long and illustrious heritage going back to the Cistercian Order of the Knights of Calatrava, who were closely allied with their Cistercian brothers, the Templars.

The villa, built more like an abbey than a private home, had been passed down through a number of families over the centuries and was now owned by Signora Luisa Santamaria Nicolini, widow of Henry Contieri, whose uncle Nicola had been Archbishop of Gaeta. The ties with the Church and the Templars were clear, but more importantly, the entire Naples Archives were now being stored for safekeeping in the villa; 866 cases in all, containing more than thirty thousand precious volumes and fifty thousand parchment documents dating back to the twelfth century and the time of the Crusades.

According to Amedeo Maiuri, among those documents were the Angevin Templar Archive and a volume once possessed by the famous Templar navigator Roger de Flor, the near-mythical seaman knight who was said to have somehow spirited the Templar treasure out of the Holy Land and hidden it for safekeeping.

Maiuri had once seen the book and read the Latin inscription on its cover that said the words within the volume could only be understood by the man who owned the True Sword of Pelerin. The book was a copy of *De laudibus novae militiae*, the letter written by Bernard of Clairvaux to Hugues de Payens, first Grand Master of the Templars and Prior of Jerusalem.

Once again, according to the diary, Lutz Kellerman had gone to the villa, met with Signora Nicolini, the owner, and also with the resident director of the displaced Archives, a man named Antonio Capograssi. On being questioned by Kellerman, even under the threat of burning the villa and the contents of the Archives, neither the woman nor Capograssi admitted anything.

Capograssi insisted that no such book was in the Archives, and to prove it he showed the entire inventory to Kellerman. There was no mention of Roger de Flor or any copy of *De laudibus novae militiae*. Not satisfied, Kellerman began to pry open crates, helped by his men, including a young Rudy Drabeck.

After several hours they had found absolutely nothing. In the diary Kellerman mentioned that while they tore open crates they could hear the sounds of artillery in the distance. Allied artillery, coming up and inland from Salerno, on the way to Rome and eventually, as the SS general confided to his diary, to certain victory. Italy had fallen, the Reich would soon follow; it was only a matter of time. Finally, frustrated with the sound of artillery growing with every passing hour, he gave the order to his men: *'Alles einaschern'* – 'Burn it all.'

Which is exactly what they proceeded to do.

The members of his platoon piled paper, straw, and gunpowder in the four corners of each room, and then set it alight. Within minutes the Archives was enveloped in flames. In less than an hour the entire villa was an inferno. By the following morning the Villa Montesano was a smoking ruin, never to be occupied again, and Lutz Kellerman was gone.

Following the map directions they'd been given by the rental company in Naples, Holliday drove the little red car to the outskirts of the town of Nola, then turned onto the via Castel Cicala and headed into the open countryside again. They went around a high, circular hill crowned with the ruins of an ancient castle and into a small wooded and steep-sided valley. They turned onto an even narrower road then rose up out of the valley on the winding strada Comunale Nola-Visciano, then slowed.

'It should be somewhere on the left,' said Holliday, peering through the windshield. 'Two big pillars on either side of a long driveway.'

'If Lutz Kellerman burned the Archives, why are we bothering with this place anyway?' Peggy asked.

'Because it's the only thing we have to go on right now,' said Holliday. 'Quit being a wet blanket.'

'I'm trying to be a realist, Doc.' She punched

him affectionately on the shoulder. 'Someone's got to hold my romantically inclined uncle in check.'

Holliday caught something on the edge of his peripheral vision and slowed the car even more.

'There,' he said, spotting what he'd been looking for: two crumbling, turret-like pillars guarding the entrance to an overgrown, rutted driveway, both sides of the road guarded by groves of ancient, twisted olive trees. He turned the car, and they bounced down the driveway, the tall weeds in the center of the ruts brushing against the bottom of the chassis. Loose stones clattered against the side panels. A hundred yards farther on, they reached the weed-clotted remains of what had once been the Villa Montesano.

They parked the Fiat and wandered through the scattered stones of the once-proud estate. Even in ruins it was impressive. The palazzo had been oriented to the east, looking down the wooded hillside. From the crest of the hill, the view swept out over the town a few miles away and farther to the city and the Bay of Naples, a sublime azure dream melding with the bright blue sky in the distance.

Once there had been a lavish terraced garden below a series of columned balconies where now there were only weeds, broken stone, and heavy undergrowth. The floors of the palazzo, once a rich display of mosaic, lay shattered and stained by over sixty years of exposure to the elements. Room after room lay roofless and open to the sun and rain, their frescoed walls faded and blotted with mold.

Roof beams rotted on the ground like scattered bones. Wrens made nests in the lintels of empty windows. A gold and brown, delicately checkered Marsh Fritillary butterfly drank nectar from the purple trumpets of a Dragonmouth nettle in the shelter of a doorway. Somewhere a cicada sang its droning, high-pitched song. There was no wind at all; the air was perfectly still. A frozen country landscape painted by Canaletto.

Behind the ruins on the plateau of the hill there were the remains of several outbuildings, the abandoned ornamental gardens, long forgotten, overgrown, and choked with weeds. The only building that looked intact and at all maintained was a small gardener's potting shed at the edge of the neglected flowerbeds. At the far side of the estate there was a screening stand of walnut trees. Beyond that, in the middle distance, were more verdant hills, and then the first rugged mountains of the Apennines.

Holliday stood in the middle of what once had been the oratory, or chapel, of the villa. The walls were no more than a few stones high, and part of the charred floor had sagged and tipped into the cellar below.

Often when he stood in places like this Holliday could almost hear the voices calling to him out of the past. A long time ago, standing on Burnside's Bridge at Antietam, he'd felt the vibration of men's feet and the thunder of horses' hooves as Union and Confederate soldiers fought in the bloodiest battle of the Civil War. Walking down the broad boulevard of the avenue des Champs-Élysées in Paris, it was the deep-throated rumble of German tanks that haunted him, history come alive in his imagination. But this was a dead place; even the ghosts had gone.

'You were right,' he said to Peggy. 'It was a waste of time. There's nothing here.'

'Look,' she answered, pointing.

Holliday followed her pointing hand. A short, somewhat stooped man was approaching them from the direction of the stand of bushy walnut trees. He was carrying a wicker basket and wore the distinctive white habit and black scapular apron of a Cistercian monk: the order founded by St. Alberic of Cîteaux, the spiritual father of the Knights Templar and the author of *De laudibus novae militiae*, the text embedded with the coded message of the Templar sword.

17

They walked out of the ruined oratory and met the monk as he came across the open field. From the white hair peeping out from beneath his wide straw sun hat, his spectacles, and his wrinkled face, the monk looked to be in his mid-seventies, but still too young to have been anything more than a very small child when Lutz Kellerman gave his destructive order.

When he spoke the monk's voice was soft and evenly modulated. The basket in his hand was full of walnuts.

'*Il mio nome è Fratello Timothy. Lo posso aiutare?*' My name is Brother Timothy, may I help you?

'*Parla inglese?*' Holliday asked. His Italian was fluent, but Peggy barely knew enough phrases to order a meal.

'Yes, of course,' answered Brother Timothy. The accent was cultured and intelligent.

Holliday decided not to beat around the bush.

'This is the Villa Montesano where the Archives were destroyed in 1943?'

'Yes,' said Brother Timothy.

'By an SS officer named Lutz Kellerman?'

'He did not leave his name, Mr . . .?'

'Holliday. Doctor, as a matter of fact.'

Better to use whatever ammunition you had.

'Ah,' said Brother Timothy. 'And your companion?'

'My name is Peggy,' she replied. 'Blackstock.'

'Ah,' said Brother Timothy once again. 'An interesting name. Black stockings were an article of formal dress in seventeenth-century England, rather than the more informal blue stockings worn by the masses. Perhaps that is the origin of your name.' He gestured toward the basket at his feet. 'I have been gathering walnuts for some experiments I am doing regarding the use of walnut extract as a high blood pressure supplement. Perhaps you'd like to tell me what you are doing here.' It wasn't a question.

An etymologist and a research scientist in a monk's habit. An interesting combination. The message was clear: Brother Timothy was no country bumpkin and nobody's fool. Holliday silently reminded himself to tread carefully.

'It's complicated,' said Holliday, hesitating. The monk picked up his basket of walnuts.

'I'm a tired old man,' said Brother Timothy. 'I should not stand about too long in the hot sun. My feet swell up like little sausages. Perhaps you'd like to join me for a cup of tea? I keep a few things in the gardener's cottage.'

The monk led the way, and they followed.

The potting shed was a single, cozy room, windows on all sides, walls lined with shelves loaded down with stacks of terra-cotta flowerpots. The floor was made of fitted paving stones covered with a single braided-rope rug. Brother Timothy had made a little haven underneath one window with a small desk, a camp stove, a kettle, an old brown teapot, and several pottery mugs. There were a few small lemons in a little wooden bowl, a paring knife, and a glass jar full of sugar cubes. Above the kitchen things there was a shelf with several dusty books. Holliday read one of the titles: *Nova genera et species plantarum* by Alexander von Humboldt and Aimé Bonpland. Beside it was what appeared to be an Italian edition of George Nicholson's *Dictionary of Practical Gardening*.

There were two old chairs and a padded leather ottoman. The cell-like room smelled comfortably of pinewood and baked clay. The monk busied himself making tea for a few moments then sat down in one of the chairs, gesturing for Holliday and Peggy to seat themselves, as well. Peggy perched herself on the ottoman, and Holliday took the other chair.

'We're here about the sword,' he said slowly,

watching Brother Timothy's face for a reaction. There was none.

'Sword?' Brother Timothy replied, his expression politely curious.

'A Templar sword found by Amedeo Maiuri in the ruins of Pompeii and presented to Adolf Hitler by Il Duce, Benito Mussolini.'

Brother Timothy laughed.

'Why would a Templar sword be found in Pompeii?' the monk said. 'Vesuvius erupted in 79 A.D., long before the Crusades. And why would a renowned Italian archaeologist like Amedeo Maiuri give anything at all to Mussolini and that thug Hitler? I'm afraid someone has been telling stories to you.'

'Perhaps as you are telling stories to me?' Holliday answered. 'French historians say that the Templars were founded by Hugues de Payens, a knight of Champagne, but there is a great deal of evidence to show that Hugues de Payens was actually an Italian named Hugo de Paganis from Nocera dei Pagani in Campania, whose largest city is Naples. In a straight line the town of Nocera is about fifteen miles from Pompeii, a little farther if you travel on the coastal road, which anyone would have taken back then if they were on their way to Naples. The sword could very easily have been found in Pompeii.'

'You know something of the Templars, I see,' nodded Brother Timothy. He poured the tea. 'Lemon? Sugar?'

They took both.

Holliday continued.

'I also know that the sword found by Maiuri has an inscription on it: *Alberic in Pelerin fecit.* Made by, or for, Alberic in Castle Pelerin, the last crusader castle of the Templars in the Holy Land. St. Alberic of Cîteaux, the founder and patron saint of the Cistercian Order. *Your* order, Brother Timothy.'

'You really do seem to know a great deal, Dr. Holliday,' said Brother Timothy calmly, sipping his tea.

'I also know that this sword had a coded message embedded in it and that the key to that code lay in a particular copy of *De laudibus novae militiae*, a letter written by –'

'A letter written by St. Alberic of Cîteaux to Hugues de Payens, or Hugo de Paganis, depending on your point of view,' completed Brother Timothy. 'That particular copy having been hidden among the tens of thousands of books and papers in the Naples State Archives, which were once stored in this very place.' The elderly monk smiled pleasantly. 'As the hippies used to say back in the days of my youth, Dr. Holliday, life is a wheel and what goes around indeed does come around again.'

'You know about the sword then?' Holliday asked.

'Certainly. I have known about it for many years. Sometimes it is called the Sword of Pelerin, the One True Sword, the True Sword of Pelerin. Another myth of the Crusades.'

'No myth,' said Holliday. 'The sword exists, believe me.'

'How do you happen to know of the letter?' Peggy asked.

'Because of the warning on the cover of the holy letter written by St. Alberic: "The words within shall only be known to the holder of the True Sword of Pelerin." The cover is made of solid silver, the words chased in gold.'

'You've seen it?' Holliday asked. He felt a sudden surge of hope. If Brother Timothy had seen the copy of the letter that meant it had somehow survived the destruction of the archives.

'Yes,' replied the monk. 'It makes interesting reading. An apologia from a saint on the subject of spilling blood in the name of Christ. A philosophy espoused by less saintly men, several of your American presidents in particular.'

'You would have been too young to know about the book during the war,' said Peggy, ignoring the pointed comment and voicing Holliday's unspo-ken objection.

'I was nine, a foundling orphan. Our abbey, l'Abbazia di San Martino di Camaldoli, lies on the next hill, less than a kilometer from here. I watched the palazzo burn from the window in my room. It burned for a day and a night. It made Brother Albano, our abbot and the man who raised me, weep.'

'I'm not sure I understand,' said Holliday. 'What was the connection between your abbey and the Archives?'

'The Villa Montesano was originally the Priory of San Martino. Even after the property was sold the Abbey held stewardship of the villa's lands. It still does, which is how I come to gather walnuts here.' The monk sipped his tea, added a slice of lemon, and then went on.

'Brother Albano was more than just the abbot. He was also the sacristan, personally in charge of the scriptorium and the library for which our abbey was well-known. Mussolini despised the Roman Catholic religion from an early age. In fact, Brother Albano had taught him as a boy in the Salesian Fathers' boarding school in the town of Faenza.

'He worried that Mussolini would take his revenge on the monasteries the way Henry VIII did in England, so he hid the most precious of the monastery's volumes at the Villa Montesano just in case. Before he died Brother Albano charged me with their care, particularly the copy of *De laudibus novae militiae*.'

'How did it survive the fire?' Peggy asked. 'Why didn't Lutz Kellerman find it?'

'Do you know the meaning of the word "crypsis"?' Brother Timothy responded.

'Something to do with codes?' Holliday ventured.

'With subterfuge certainly,' answered the monk. 'Crypsis is the ability of an organism to escape detection.'

'Camouflage?' Peggy said.

'Quite so,' said Brother Timothy. 'The Dead Leaf Mantis, which looks exactly like its name. The Tawny Frogmouth owl of Australia whose feathers mimic tree bark perfectly. The Gaboon viper of Africa, colored to look like the jungle floor. These are all cryptic animals.'

He paused, plucking the lemon slice from his tea and popping it in his mouth. He chewed thoughtfully on the pulp for a moment, then put the bare rind down on the little table. He continued speaking, his voice a pleasant professorial drone.

'Brother Albano was something of an amateur

naturalist, a follower of the renowned Italian collector Francisco Minà Palumbo. Albano's great interest was the common wall lizard, a cryptic reptile, *Podarcis muralis*, a familiar creature among the rocks and stones hereabouts. The ability of the creature to disguise itself within its natural environment fascinated him.'

'I don't quite see what all this has to do with the book,' said Peggy, sounding a little frustrated.

'I do,' said Holliday, putting it all together. 'It means the book was hidden in plain sight.'

'And where would you hide a book in plain sight?' Brother Timothy asked, smiling.

'In a library,' said Peggy.

'Precisely,' said the monk, clapping his hands together happily. 'In the library of the Villa Montesano.'

'But the library must have burned along with the Archives,' said Holliday.

Brother Timothy explained.

'There had been foraging patrols in the area for some days, soldiers on motorcycles looking for food – chickens and calves and the like. The day before the Archives were burned, September twenty-eighth, one of those patrols came to the Villa.' The old man paused again and added a cube of sugar to his tea.

'They did nothing, only bullied Signora Nicolini,

the owner, and the director of the Archives who was resident at the villa, a man named Antonio Capograssi, if I remember correctly. As soon as the patrol left the premises Signora Nicolini came to the abbey to warn Brother Albano. It was everything he'd feared. He couldn't bring the precious manuscripts back to the abbey on the chance they would be found there, so he hid them again.'

'Where?' Peggy asked.

'Here,' said Brother Timothy, tapping one sandaled foot against the paving stones. 'Under the floor of the humble gardener's cottage.'

'It's not still there, is it?' Peggy asked, startled. She stared at the smooth stones beneath her feet.

'Certainly not,' laughed the old monk. 'The *De laudibus* is written on *gevil*, the processed skin of a stillborn or unborn fallow deer. It was the most common form of paper in use during the time of the Crusades. Ironically it is the same material used in the creation of Jewish holy documents like the Sefer Torah. Left beneath the floor it would have rotted away.' He smiled. 'It has been safely hidden again, however.'

'Where?' Holliday asked.

Brother Timothy sat back in his chair. Outside the cicada had stopped singing. A cloud passed overhead and for a few seconds the interior of the cottage darkened. In the distance Holliday thought he heard the faint, distant sound of summer thunder. Finally the monk spoke again.

'You have asked enough questions for the moment. Now it is my turn,' said Brother Timothy.

'What would you like to know?' Holliday asked.

'How you came to know about the Sword of Pelerin.'

'It was my uncle's. He discovered it in the Berghof at the end of the Second World War.'

'Hitler's summer house,' nodded Brother Timothy.

'That's right.'

'Who is your uncle?'

'Was,' said Holliday. 'He passed away recently. His name was Henry Granger. He was a medieval historian.'

'And my grandfather,' added Peggy.

'Henry Granger. *Watchmen of the Holy City*,' nodded Brother Timothy. 'The definitive study of the Templars in Jerusalem. A fine book. I've read it.' The old monk paused and pursed his lips. 'Where is the sword now?'

'Hidden safely,' said Holliday, 'like your copy of the Alberic letter.'

'This Nazi you mentioned, Kellerman; other than the burning of the Archives, how does he fit into this?'

'It's a long story,' said Holliday.

'I have time,' said the monk placidly.

So they told Brother Timothy everything they knew.

It took a little more than an hour. When Holliday and Peggy finished up their tale the white-haired man took off his glasses, cleaning them on the broad cuff of his habit, then set them back onto his nose again. He eyed them speculatively.

'How do I know anything of what you say is the truth?' Brother Timothy asked.

'Why would we lie?' Peggy said a little hotly. 'Besides, we have the sword.'

'Prove it,' the monk said flatly.

'Show him,' said Peggy.

Holliday stood up and undid the buckle of the Tilley Endurables money belt and stripped it off. He'd carried the belt since his first rotation in the Gulf, and it had the worn, comfortable look of a favorite piece of clothing. He turned the belt over and unzipped the twenty-inch pouch. He carefully extracted the long piece of gold wire that had been wrapped around the hilt of the crusader sword. The wire had been turned to make three loops so that it fitted into the belt. It had been carried, hidden, ever since they'd left Fredonia. He handed the wire to Brother Timothy and explained:

'If you look closely you'll see that the wire has been nicked at both regular and irregular intervals. The gold isn't solid, it's an alloy, probably electrum – gold and silver mixed. It's much more durable than solid gold, which is why the markings on the wire have survived.

'The regular nicks are all exactly the same distance apart. I'm willing to bet that they're exactly the page width of the text to your *De laudibus*. If you look closely you'll see Roman numerals scratched into the wire between the smaller nicks.

'The Roman numerals will denote page numbers, and the smaller nicks will line up with appropriate individual letters in the text. It's simple but extremely clever at the same time. The copies of the manuscript would have to have been identical for it to work. The scribe, whoever he was, must have been extremely dedicated.'

'It was a she actually,' said Brother Timothy, staring reverently down at the wire. 'Sister Diemut of Wessobrunn, a Benedictine nun. Quite famous in her time. The copies are identical, one for the abbey at Clairvaux and the other for the use of Roger de Flor and the Templars at Pelerin, the two ends of the communication route between the Holy Land and home.'

'I wonder who the knight was who actually carried the sword,' Peggy mused.

'We know that, as well,' said the elderly monk. 'His name was Sir Robert de Sales, an Englishman in the service of William de Rochefort, Vice-Master of the Temple at Jerusalem and Bishop of Acre. Robert de Sales took the overland route back to France while Roger de Flor voyaged by sea; that way they ensured the message would get to Clairvaux. Sir Robert died en route, somewhere just short of Naples.'

'And lost his sword,' said Peggy.

'As I said' – Brother Timothy smiled – 'what goes around will come around once more.'

'So we've shown you ours,' said Holliday. 'How about returning the favor?'

Brother Timothy handed Holliday the length of gold wire. The old monk gave Holliday a long searching look, then spoke.

'Do you believe in God, Doctor Holliday?' Brother Timothy asked.

'I've been trying to figure that out for most of my life,' said Holliday. 'Why do you ask?'

'Because if you believe in God you'll believe in Heaven, and if there is a Heaven, my Jesuit friends tell me there must consequently be a Hell, which is where I will damn you to if you have been lying to me.'

Holliday laughed.

'That's just about the most long-winded,

convoluted threat I've ever heard,' he said. 'Don't worry, everything we've told you is the truth, at least as far as we know it.'

'All right,' said Brother Timothy, 'I'll take you at your word.' He stood up and leaned over the table, taking one of the books down from the shelf. It was the Latin Botanical, *Nova genera et species plantarum*. He handed the leather-bound book to Holliday.

'Alexander von Humboldt, the man they named the Humboldt Current after. A little bit late, don't you think? He was born in the mid-seventeen hundreds, as I recall.'

'More crypsis. Open it,' said Brother Timothy.

Holliday opened the book. It was no nineteenth-century botanical. Instead he saw an expensively printed color photocopy of a medieval illuminated manuscript bound into the old leather cover. He read the first few lines of Latin aloud:

'In principio creavit Deus caelum et terram terra autem erat inanis et vacua et tenebrae super faciem abyssi et spiritus Dei ferebatur super aquas dixitque Deus fiat lux et facta est lux.' He paused and then easily translated the familiar verses: '"In the beginning God created the heaven and the earth. And the earth was without form, and void; and darkness was upon the face of the deep. And the Spirit of God

moved upon the face of the waters. And God said, Let there be light and there was light."' He paused again and looked up at the white-haired monk. 'It's the Vulgate Latin translation of the first lines of Genesis, taken directly from the Hebrew, not the Greek.'

'Well done,' said Brother Timothy. 'As you know most religious documents from the Middle Ages began with a prayer or a quotation from scripture. Try using the gold wire and tell me what you find.' He reached forward and opened a narrow drawer in the front of the desk, taking out a pad of paper and a pencil. Holliday pulled his chair up to the table while Peggy watched over his shoulder. Within a few moments he was able to speak the first words of a message that had gone unheard for more than eight hundred years.

'"To the reverend Father in Christ, and to all our friends in the kingdoms of France to whom this letter shall come: These are the words of the Bishop William de Rochefort, Vice-Master of the Temple. Listen and take heed."'

'It works!' said Peggy. 'Keep going, Doc!'

Dusk was beginning to fall by the time Holliday completed his translation and had written the full text of the secret message on the pad in front of him. It had clearly been intended to be read as verse:

In the black waters of the Pilgrim's Fortress
A treasured silver scroll is found,
A thirst for knowledge girded round
These holy walls without a sound.
With dead Saladin's echoing voice it calls
Us into battle once again.

'The Pilgrim's Fortress was another name for Château Pelerin,' said Brother Timothy.

'It's all very poetic, but what exactly does it mean?' Peggy asked.

'I think it means we're on our way to the Holy Land,' said Holliday. 'We're going to Israel.'

'An interesting tale,' said Raffi Wanounou, Professor of Medieval Archaeology at the Hebrew University of Jerusalem. The professor was a starkly handsome man in his late forties or early fifties with a long, square-chinned face common to many Moroccan-born Jews. His dark hair was speckled with gray and deep caliper lines extended down either side of his wide mouth. He was deeply tanned and had the slightly scorched look of someone who spends a great deal of time under the desert sun.

Peggy Blackstock and John 'Doc' Holliday were sitting in Wanounou's comfortable office at the university. They'd given the man on the other side of the desk a rough outline of their activities since leaving the United States, editing out a few dead bodies in the telling.

'Remind me again how you came to be knocking at my door in particular?' the professor asked.

'Your name came up in an e-mail from Steven Braintree at the University of Toronto to my uncle,' said Holliday.

'I know Steven quite well, of course. The Royal Ontario Museum is world-class. I only knew your uncle by reputation.'

'Professor Braintree mentioned that you knew a great deal about crusader castles,' said Peggy.

'A little.' He smiled. The smile was clearly for Peggy's benefit alone.

Holliday bristled slightly at the Israeli professor's obvious interest in Peggy. It was ridiculous; the man was almost old enough to be her father. 'Castle Pelerin in particular,' he said, a little curtly.

'Pilgrim's Fortress,' said Wanounou. 'I wrote my thesis on it. Bigger than the Krak des Chevaliers in Syria. Never breached by siege or force of arms in two hundred years. Last bastion of the Knights Templar in the Holy Land.'

'We need to go there,' said Peggy.

'Not possible I'm afraid, Miss Blackstock.'

'Peggy,' she said, giving him a smile just like the one he'd given her.

'Peggy then,' beamed the professor.

'What's the problem?' Holliday asked.

'You'd need special authorization. It's a restricted military zone. Shayetet 13 uses it as a training area.'

'Shayetet 13?' Peggy asked.

'Israel's version of Navy SEALs,' explained Holliday.

'It's the other way around, actually,' said Wanounou. 'Shayetet 13 existed long before the SEALs. They were established in 1949; the SEALs weren't organized until the early sixties, as I recall.'

'You served with them?' Holliday asked.

'Lousy swimmer.' The Professor grinned. The grin was nothing like the smile he'd offered Peggy.

'Where *did* you do your three years?' Holliday asked.

'Three years?' Peggy said, looking baffled at the rapid-fire conversation.

'Compulsory military service,' said Holliday. Now he was getting annoyed with himself. The whole thing was turning into a pissing contest all because of a smile.

'It was more like eight,' said Wanounou. '*Agaf HaModiin*. Aman.'

'Army Intelligence,' said Holliday, impressed with the man, despite himself.

The professor gave Holliday a speculative look and tilted back in his chair.

'You know a lot about the military, Mr. Holliday,' he said.

'Doctor,' answered Holliday. 'And Lieutenant Colonel; I teach Military History at West Point.'

'Then you outrank me, I guess,' said the professor, grinning again. 'I only made major.' He laughed. 'Maybe we should compare PhDs. See who got their doctorate first.'

'Sorry,' said Holliday. 'I've been a little tense since Germany.' He paused. 'If you were with Aman maybe you could pull some strings, get us into the castle.'

'I'd love an excuse to get out of the office for a while, but what pretext would I give? A couple of American tourists on a treasure hunt?' The good-looking man grimaced. 'Really, Dr. Holliday. I think not.'

'It's not a treasure hunt,' said Peggy.

'Knights Templar, a code in a crusader's sword, Cistercian monks and Nazis running around? An obscure piece of poetry instead of a treasure map? Who are you going to get for the leading role, Nicolas Cage or Harrison Ford?' He shook his head. 'Come on, guys.'

Holliday sighed.

'It's a little far-fetched, I know, but – '

'I'd have to call in a lot of favors to get us in there,' said Wanounou. 'I'm not sure I want to do that.'

Us? Holliday thought. He smiled to himself. He recognized the tone in the other man's voice; the sound of curiosity getting the jump on the cat's better instincts. The sizzle you got when you leaped from the frying pan into the fire.

'Please?' Peggy pleaded, shooting Wanounou a smile that would have lit up a dark room for at least a week. It was the straw that broke the camel's back.

'All right,' he said finally. 'I'll see what I can do.'

Two days later, under a hot summer sky, they drove out of the ancient city on the Jerusalem–Tel Aviv Highway. Highway 1, as it was officially known, was a modern thruway that arrowed northwest in a bewildering series of unsigned on- and off-ramps but that cut the driving time between the two cities to only an hour.

Wanounou drove his ancient, rust-pocked Toyota Land Cruiser like a fighter pilot, doing Immelmanns and barrel rolls through the dense traffic, all the while keeping up a running travelogue, most of it directed at Peggy, who was sitting in the cramped rear seat. Holliday had put himself in the front beside Wanounou in an attempt to cool the growing heat between Peggy and the professor, but now he was regretting his decision. After a few close calls on the highway Holliday found himself thinking about Brother Timothy's question about his belief in a higher power; whether he believed in it or not, he was praying to it. Considering his present circumstances it was a toss-up between Christ, Jehovah, and Allah to give him the best bang for his devotional buck.

Skirting Tel Aviv, the Israeli professor swept the battered old 4×4 onto the Ayalon Highway running between Tel Aviv and Haifa in the north. It was another four-lane nightmare of rushing traffic that raced up and down along the route of the ancient coastal pilgrim road that wound its way to Acre.

With the rugged slopes of Mount Carmel rising on their right and green cotton fields to their left on the plain of what had once been the land of Phoenicia, Wanounou maneuvered the clattering old vehicle on for another three quarters of an hour.

Eventually they reached Atlit Junction, another cloverleaf, and turned toward the sea. A few miles to the north the outskirts of Haifa were visible through the heat haze, climbing the slopes of Mount Carmel and spreading around the scimitar arc of Haifa Bay.

In an instant the twenty-first-century reality of congested traffic disappeared, and Holliday felt time fall away. Knights mounted on thundering coursers and even larger destriers rode along the ancient road, armor flashing in the sun. Pilgrims walked beside plodding packhorses while lords and ladies lounged in brightly painted covered wagons. Dust hung like mist in the hot, still air.

They rattled across a set of railway tracks then turned off onto a narrow, two-lane dirt road with a long, curving beach on one side and a swampy pool with a trio of pale flamingos feeding on the other.

Beyond the swampy area there was an industrial salt pool with a long elevated pipeline feeding it from beyond the sweeping bay on their left. Then the stark, bleak ruins of Castle Pelerin rose in front of them like a dark dream from the past. It made the old castle ruins on Kellerman's estate outside Friedrichshafen look puny by comparison.

Wanounou parked by the side of the road, and they climbed out into the hot, bright sun. The professor was wearing faded old fatigue pants and a T-shirt that said: ARCHAEOLOGISTS DO IT IN THE DIRT. Holliday and Peggy were both in jeans and DON'T WORRY, BE JEWISH T-shirts they'd picked up in the Muslim Quarter of Jerusalem the day before. All of them were wearing Hebrew University baseball caps against the harsh summer sun. In front of them was a rocky promontory three quarters of a mile long, forming the northern arm of a small harbor to the south. The remains of the inner keep stood like a massive square beacon against the brilliant blue background of the Mediterranean beyond.

'Holy crap,' said Peggy.

'An apt enough description,' laughed the professor. 'They dug a forty-foot-wide fosse, or moat, the entire width of the peninsula that they could flood with seawater on command. On the other side of the moat there was a colossal limestone wall sixteen feet thick, rising almost a hundred feet into the air. The whole thing was built by hand, mostly by volunteer labor from pilgrims on their way to Jerusalem, and it only took them six months.

'On the dead ground in front of the wall they built three massive towers, one at each end and one in the middle. The only way you could get beyond the towers and the wall was through a narrow entrance, angled so it was impossible to ram the gates. There were stone halls, chapels, crypts, storerooms, and everything necessary for a force of four thousand men and the workers to provide for them.

'The place was invulnerable; they had their own harbor, and in the event of a siege they could be resupplied from the sea. There was an artesian spring, a pool, and three deep wells to catch the runoff through the limestone from Mount Carmel, so water wasn't a problem either.'

'Wasn't there a fortification here before the

twelve hundreds?' Holliday asked. He vaguely remembered something about an earlier fortress. They walked toward the old moat, following a narrowing, winding path through the rough grass and sand.

'There was a small outpost called Le Destriot by the coast road, but it was long out of date even before they built Pelerin,' answered the professor. 'The Romans had a harbor here two thousand years ago, and the Phoenicians were here two thousand years before that. When the Templars were digging the foundations for Pelerin they found a treasure of Phoenician gold coins that was almost enough to finance the construction of the whole castle.'

'So we're not the first people to look for treasure here?' Peggy asked, her eyes twinkling.

Wanounou twinkled back, then turned and pointed to the craggy slopes of Mount Carmel two miles or so west across the narrow coastal plain.

'We've been excavating up there in the caves at Wadi el Mugharah since 1951,' said the professor, 'the Brits and you Yanks even before that. Where we're standing now is the biblical Plain of Sharon. We've found material dating back to the Neanderthals and even before, to the early Stone Age.

'There's been human occupation of one kind or another in this area for two million years. There's even good evidence to show that this was once the biblical Garden of Eden, at least as far as the old prophets were concerned.' He turned around, arms spread out. 'The sea, the plains, the mountains. Everything old Adam and Eve could have asked for.' Wanounou smiled. Peggy smiled back.

Holliday frowned, then sighed, wondering if it was time to have a chat with her about the potential dangers of the situation. Wiser to keep his mouth shut for the moment, he thought.

They reached a high, rusty razor wire fence that stretched across the neck of the narrow peninsula. There were faded red notices in Hebrew, Arabic, and English every ten or fifteen feet along the wire:

MORTAL DANGER – MILITARY ZONE
ANY PERSON WHO PASSES OR
DAMAGES THIS FENCE ENDANGERS
HIS LIFE

No exclamation marks, just a simple and explicit statement of fact.

'Heartwarming,' said Peggy. On the other side of the fence they could see a slight dip in the ground that marked the position of the old moat. A few yards farther in the earth thin sandy soil rose steeply, thick with coarse weeds and shrubs, all that was left of the original imposing curtain wall.

They walked on down the path for a short distance, stopping in front of a gateway set into the fence. It was secured with a heavy padlock. There was another sign on the gate. This one was even clearer:

MINEFIELD

'Are you sure we have permission for this?' Holliday asked.

'Better than that,' said Wanounou, digging into one of the pockets of his baggy fatigue pants. 'I've got a key.'

'Uh, what about the mines?' cautioned Peggy.

'There aren't any,' said the professor, smiling broadly. 'The signs are to impress the tourists and scare off any kids.'

'Said the one-legged blind guy with no fingers,' muttered Peggy.

'Your connections must be better than I thought,' said Holliday. They went through the gate, and Wanounou locked it behind them and pocketed the key again. They headed up a sandy footpath that crossed the old moat and wound its way up the hillocky remains of the old wall.

'Turns out that the navy hasn't used this place in ages,' the professor said as they trudged up the path. 'They used to train in Haifa Bay, but it got too polluted, so they moved down here. But then they cleaned up the bay, so they moved back. They might have left some equipment behind, but the property is empty. They left the fence and signs in place until they figure out who to hand it over to – the archaeologists or the tourists.'

A flight of dowdy-looking, pale brown Marbled Ducks flew overhead in ragged V formation, heading for the marshland where they'd spotted the flamingos. The air tasted of salt and the sea, and there was a light onshore breeze taking the edge off the midday heat. A hundred and fifty miles away Cyprus crouched invisibly on the blue horizon. They reached the top of the path and looked down on the ruins spread out before them.

Enough of the gigantic castle remained to make visualizing it relatively easy. From the low foundations to the seaward end of the castle was more than two football fields in length. From side to side the structure had been about half that size. There had been north and south towers on the inner wall, a higher upper ward flanked by sunken undercrofts flanking it and the massive castle keep in the center.

There had been walls on all three sides, including the side facing the sea with a seawall and a long breakwater that still remained, jutting out into the shallow, natural harbor. Lateen caravels and square-rigged cogs would have unloaded there, safely protected and out of range of any attackers from the landward side.

Ringing the keep, there had been five great halls, each one at least a hundred feet long. Now, only lines of half-buried stone and ghostly dips and patterns in the soil remained. Tufted patches of sea grass grew here and there, slabs of paving stone appearing between them, marking old walkways like long scars in the dirt.

'Needle in a haystack,' said Peggy, looking across the enormous interior of the castle's inner wards. 'That's an awful lot of ground to cover.'

Raffi Wanounou reached into his pocket again, this time taking out a folded map. It was a diagram of the castle excavations, done years ago when he'd spent three summers here when he was a graduate student. He turned it in his hands, orienting himself.

'What does your little ditty say?' he asked.

Holliday had memorized it:

In the black waters of the Pilgrim's Fortress
A treasured silver scroll is found,
A thirst for knowledge girded round
These holy walls without a sound.
With dead Saladin's echoing voice it calls
Us into battle once again.

'The "black waters" might well refer to the castle's water supply,' said the professor, looking down at the diagram and up at the huge expanse of broken ground in front of them.

'You said there was a spring and some kind of pool,' said Peggy. 'Maybe that was it.'

'I can't see them burying a treasure in an open pool,' said Wanounou. 'It's more likely near one of the wells.'

'Where were they?' Peggy asked. She came and looked over his shoulder at the diagram, her arm brushing his. 'Show me,' she said.

'They're long gone,' replied the professor. 'We never found anything remotely like a well when we were excavating.' He shrugged. 'Mind you we barely touched the surface here before the IDF kicked us out and brought in Shayetet 13.'

'Maybe I can do one better,' said Holliday, stepping between Peggy and Wanounou, glancing at the diagram in the professor's hand. 'The verse says, "A search for knowledge girded round these

holy walls . . ." That sounds like a church to me.'
He pointed down at the diagram. 'That long oval
shape with the square at one end, close to the seaward wall, what's that?'

'The undercroft – the crypt – beneath what we
think was the chapel,' said Wanounou. 'We called
it the Round Church.'

'Mimicking the Church of the Holy Sepulcher
in Jerusalem,' nodded Holliday. 'Like all Templar
churches.'

'That's right,' said the professor.

'"These holy walls,"' said Holliday. 'It's worth
a shot.'

They picked their way slowly down the
embankment and began to make their way across
the rubble-strewn expanse of the castle's middle
ward.

'From the way you speak about them I take it
you're not one to toe the party line when it comes
to the Templars,' said Wanounou.

Walking between them, Peggy laughed.

'Doc doesn't toe the party line when it comes
to much of anything.' She grinned. 'Must run in
the family.'

'You're not a believer in their Christian piety?'
the professor asked, cocking a skeptical eyebrow.

'I think some of them were religious fanatics,'
said Holliday. 'Most of them were mercenaries.

There were a lot of unemployed knights back then. A few of them might have believed in the cause, but not many.' He shook his head. 'I've been in a lot of wars in my time, Professor, and one way or another they've always been about money. The Crusades were no different.

'Castles like this one weren't built to protect pilgrims, they were built to give Europe a foothold in the Middle East. Like the Hudson's Bay Company in Canada or the U.S. Cavalry outposts in the American West. The crusaders didn't want to free Jerusalem from the infidel, they wanted to conquer it.

'The Templars called themselves the "Poor Fellow-Soldiers of Christ," emphasis on the word "poor." By the time they were disbanded in 1307 they were almost as rich as the Roman Catholic Church and richer than some countries, including France, which they virtually owned outright. The Temple fortress in Paris measured seven hundred feet on a side. That's not piety, Professor. That's greed, avarice, and power.'

'But that doesn't stop you from looking for their treasure.'

Holliday stopped walking. He turned to Wanounou.

'This isn't about treasure,' he said, a little anger creeping into his voice. 'It never has been. It's about something that concerned my uncle enough to get him to tramp halfway across Europe at the age of eighty-six when he hated leaving the study in his house. It's something that seems to concern some other people, as well; they've been looking for the answer to this riddle for a very long time. They've been willing to lie for it. Burn down buildings for it. Kill for it.'

'Then I guess we'd better find it,' said Wanounou brightly, ignoring the heat in Holliday's words. 'Right, Peggy?'

'Right,' she answered. She gripped Holliday's elbow and squeezed. 'No more lectures, Doc, okay?' She squeezed his arm again. 'Now, make nice with the professor.'

'I'm not your enemy, Colonel Holliday,' added Wanounou. 'I got us in here, didn't I?' He held out his hand. '*Shalu shalom yerushalayim*, yes?'

Holliday took the extended hand and shook it. 'Call me "Doc." '

They turned and continued on toward the ruins of the ancient castle church.

19

They reached the far end of the castle's upper ward and stopped when they came to the long oval of stones that marked the foundations of the old chapel. Wanounou consulted his diagram once again.

'One hundred and sixty feet long by forty feet wide,' he said. 'Rotundas at each end, the chancel facing north, the nave to the south. There was a cloistered walkway that connected the chapel to the main great hall over there.' He pointed toward a long, freestanding line of immense limestone blocks, even larger than the stones used to build the curtain wall. 'The builders used a lot of left-overs from the Phoenician structure that was here before them,' he explained. 'Everything done in eights and multiples of eight. Eight columns in the nave, two columns of eight in the chancel, eight arches in the cloistered walkway.'

'Why eight?' Peggy asked.

'Eight was the Templars' magic number,' said Holliday. 'If you look at a Templar cross the ends are bifurcated, making eight points.'

'What was the significance?'

'Mostly religious,' said Wanounou. 'Seven plus one equals eight, the day of the Resurrection. God created Earth in six days, rested on the seventh, and introduced man into the Garden of Eden on the eighth. Man has twenty-four ribs, divided by eight gives you three – the number of the Holy Trinity. Noah was the eighth man off the Ark. The Ark itself was three hundred cubits by fifty cubits – three plus five is eight. Lazarus was brought back to life after he'd been dead eight days. The first cubed number is eight . . . The list goes on and on.'

'Which is important to us here why?' Peggy asked, looking at the foundation work at her feet.

'Because what we're looking for will probably have something to do with the number eight or a multiple of eight,' said Holliday. He began pacing out the length of the foundation in one direction, while Wanounou went the opposite way.

'Just what are we looking for?' Peggy queried.

'"In the black waters of the Pilgrim's Fortress a treasured silver scroll is found,"' recited Holliday. '"Black waters" suggest that it was dark, maybe underground, like the undercroft, or crypt beneath the church,' he said.

'It's probably some kind of cave,' called out Wanounou. 'The land around here is all limestone.

Groundwater percolating down from the mountain creates them. The whole area under Pelerin is probably riddled with them.'

'I'm claustrophobic,' said Peggy. 'I had to do a photo shoot for National Geographic in Carlsbad, and I hated every minute. Caves are creepy.'

'We'll protect you,' laughed Wanounou.

'I may have found something,' called Holliday.

'That didn't take long,' said the professor, turning away from his own investigation of the stones. He joined Peggy, and they walked back toward Holliday's position at the far end of the chancel.

'You sound skeptical,' said Peggy.

'Archaeology's never that easy,' he answered. 'Most of us never find anything.'

'I thought the guy who found Troy was an amateur,' she answered. 'And wasn't the person who found the Dead Sea Scrolls a goat herder or something?'

'Where are you getting all this?' Wanounou asked.

'Doc and I were talking about it at lunch yesterday at a café in the souk. He said most of the great archaeological finds were accidental.'

'I don't think Doc likes me,' said the professor as they approached the spot where Holliday was standing.

Peggy laughed.

'It's not just you. Doc doesn't like *anyone* who likes me too much,' she said. 'He's very protective.'

'No kidding,' said the professor.

'Who's kidding?' Holliday asked.

Wanounou ignored the question.

'What did you find?'

'A stone,' said Holliday, pointing down into the dirt.

'Oh,' said Peggy. 'Gee, the very thing we're looking for. What's so special about this one?'

'It's octagonal,' said Wanounou, crouching down, suddenly interested. He swept off a thin layer of dirt. The full dimensions were revealed. The paving stone was about three feet across. It looked as though there had once been a design carved into it, but the pattern had long since worn away. 'Part of the church floor. In the Church of the Holy Sepulcher this would be just about where the Rock of Golgotha stands.'

'So it's an octagonal paving stone,' said Peggy. 'What's so important about that?'

Holliday knelt down beside Wanounou and started sweeping away dirt with his hands, revealing more of the stone flooring.

'Because all of the other stones are square, fanning out from this one. Whatever this was, it was the center of something.'

Wanounou stood up and brushed off his hands.

'I'm going back to the truck. We need some tools.'

'I'll go with you,' Peggy said quickly.

Holliday almost said something but then thought better of it. Instead he tried to make his expression as blank as possible.

'Don't be long,' he said.

'We won't,' answered Wanounou. The couple headed off back across the inner ward of the ruins. Holliday watched them go, 'accidentally' bumping into each other now and again as they followed the path back to the Land Cruiser. As they walked their heads were bent toward each other like old friends.

They disappeared over the rise of the inner defensive wall, and Holliday went back to sweeping away the dirt on the section of old floor. The area was butted against two sides of a jutting section of the foundation wall, indicating that it had once been a subsidiary side chapel, perhaps even the Altar of the Stabat Mater, a feature of almost every Templar church. From his long-ago life as an altar boy Holliday could still remember the Latin hymn with its rhythmic trochaic tetrameter:

Stabat mater dolorosa
iuxta Crucem lacrimosa,
dum pendebat Filius.

Cuius animam gementem,
contristatam et dolentem
pertransivit gladius.

At the Cross her station keeping,
stood the mournful Mother weeping,
close to Jesus to the last.

Through her heart, His sorrow sharing,
all His bitter anguish bearing,
now at length the sword has passed.

Pertransivit gladius. Yet another sword. The Altar
of the Stabat Mater in the Church of the Holy
Sepulcher was a carved stone niche containing a
tearful statue of the Virgin Mary with an area in
front for the lighting of candles called 'mensas.'
There almost certainly would have been a version
of the Stabat Mater at Pelerin, in which case the
octagonal stone would have stood directly in
front of it.

The brilliant sun was baking the rocks around
him as Holliday worked on. A flock of Yellow-
legged Gulls whirled and careened above him,

calling loudly to each other as they rode the roller-coaster currents of the air. A hundred yards away he could hear the dull, hammering roar of the sea battering against the low cliffs at the end of the promontory.

By the time Peggy and Wanounou returned, Holliday had roughly cleared off a twelve-by-twelve area, revealing an intricate pattern of inter-locking squares fanning out from the central octagon. Whoever had laid the floor had known something about geometry.

Peggy and the professor had brought a selection of tools from the rear compartment of the Land Cruiser including a small pick, a geologist's hammer, a spade, a toolbox full of dentist's tools and paintbrushes, three trowels, and two flash-lights. In addition to the tools he'd also brought a cooler full of Neviot bottled water, an assort-ment of sandwiches, and a thermos full of iced sweet tea.

'You've been working hard,' said Wanounou.

'Hard enough,' agreed Holliday.

Wanounou handed Peggy a waxed paper-wrapped sandwich, tossed one to Holliday, and chose one for himself. Holliday sat himself down on a foundation stone and unwrapped the sand-wich. He peeked between the slices of bread and laughed out loud.

'Where do you find a ham and cheese sandwich in Israel?'

'I have my sources.' The professor winked. They ate quickly, then the professor handed out bottles of the cold spring water.

'What's next?' Peggy asked, taking a slug of water.

'I've got an idea,' said Holliday. He stood up, holding his own bottle of water, and crossed the freshly swept area to the octagonal stone. He crouched down, then trickled water from the bottle onto the hot stone, darkening it. Wanounou came and looked over one shoulder, and Peggy looked over the other.

'I'll be damned,' murmured the Israeli archaeologist.

On the wet stone a faint faded pattern had appeared: etched in the octagon stone were two overlapping squares turned at right angles to each other, making an eight-pointed star. In the center of the star, quite distinct, were two letters: PG.

'What is it?'

'A "Lakshmi Star,"' explained Holliday. 'It's supposed to represent the eight Hindu types of wealth. Alexander the Great imported the symbol from India, and the Freemasons picked it up.'

'It's an Arabic symbol, as well,' added Wanounou. 'The mark they use at the end of each *surat,* or verse, in the Koran. There was a big controversy a few years back because the asterisk on most Western typewriters is a six-pointed star, which the Muslims identify with the Star of David, so they had to change all the keyboards to eight-pointed ones.'

'That's silly,' scoffed Peggy.

Wanounou shrugged. 'We're just as silly here – Israeli math textbooks don't use a plus sign because it's a Christian symbol, so they cut off the bottom bar, and you guys don't put a Star of David on top of the Christmas tree even though Christ was born a Jew.'

'The whole world is silly,' sighed Holliday. 'That's why we have wars.'

'What about the "PG"?' asked Peggy. 'Parental Guidance, maybe?'

'I have no idea.' Wanounou shrugged.

'I do,' said Holliday. The water was evaporating under the hot sun, and the design was fading. He poured on more water, and it reappeared.

'So give, why don't you?' Peggy said.

'*Pertransivit gladius*,' said Holliday. '"The sword is passed."'

Wanounou knelt down beside the stone with a two-inch paintbrush and a trowel. He worked his way carefully around the eight sides of the central stone, first scraping then brushing out the accumulated accretions of dirt. Whether by accident or design or simply the passage of almost a thousand years, there was no sign of grout or mortar used to bond the central stone to its neighbors. Holliday poured water along the newly cleaned joint between the stones. The water drained away.

'Interesting,' he said quietly.

'Hand me the crowbar,' said Wanounou.

Peggy put it into his hand. The archaeologist worked the chisel end of the tempered steel bar into the very narrow crack between the stones and heaved. The stone lifted an inch. Wanounou pushed the bar in a little farther and heaved again. The stone came up another few inches, and Holliday slipped an old chunk of the foundation into the space, jamming it open.

'The Musgrave Ritual,' said Peggy, watching.

'Pardon?' Wanounou said.

'It's a Sherlock Holmes story,' explained Holliday. 'A man deciphers an old family code, and he and his girlfriend find a stone like this and lever it open. The girlfriend figures out the man is going to cheat her and traps him under the stone.'

'Never trust an Englishman,' said the archaeologist. He looked at Peggy. 'You wouldn't do that to me, would you?'

She smiled. 'Not unless you tried to cheat me.'

'Let's get on with it,' said Holliday. He and Wanounou went to the far side of the stone. 'On three,' said Holliday, and counted. They heaved the stone up and back, then eased it down carefully, only dropping it the last few inches. They stood back, hands on knees, puffing from their exertions. Peggy peered into the hole the octagonal stone had covered.

'What do you see?' Holliday said.

'A staircase,' said Peggy. 'A spiral staircase made of stone.'

20

'I hate this, I hate this, I hate this,' muttered Peggy as they descended. The staircase was impossibly narrow, the stone treads dangerously smooth. The only light was the narrow puddle of illumination from Wanounou's flashlight. The air was close, heavy with the sharp scent of mold, mildew, and dissolving limestone. As they went downward step by step their shoulders brushed against the smooth rock walls.

The deeper they got the narrower the staircase seemed to get; Peggy could almost feel the enormous weight of the stone pressing in all around her. She was breathing quickly, trying to fill her lungs and failing. It felt as though she was suffocating.

'This was a really, really bad idea,' she said.

'You can always go back,' said Holliday from behind her, grinning in the near pitch dark. Wanounou led the way with the flashlight, crowbar in his other hand, while Holliday brought up the rear, carrying the geologist's hammer and the second flashlight. Peggy was sandwiched between them, which made things even more claustrophobic.

'Go back? How am I supposed to do that? There's no way to turn around, and anyway, you're blocking the way. Besides, if I was up top I'd be worrying about you guys too much.'

'So nice to feel wanted,' laughed Wanounou.

'How far have we gone?' Peggy asked, her voice urgent.

'A hundred and fifty-one steps,' said Holliday. 'I've been counting.' He did a quick calculation. 'About ten inches between the steps ... I'd say about a hundred and twenty-five feet.'

'Thirty-eight meters, if it makes you feel any better,' said Wanounou, looking back over his shoulder and grinning.

'Shut up, both of you,' she snarled in the dark. 'Or I'll scream, I really will.'

'She gets aggressive when she's scared,' commented Holliday to Wanounou.

'I picked up on that,' answered the professor.

'Shut. Up!' Peggy barked.

'Relax,' soothed Holliday. 'It can't be much farther.'

'Why do you say that?' Peggy argued. 'For all you know this is the stairway to Hell. It could go on forever.' She was almost panting now, her throat constricted, the dank cobbled walls pressing in, entombing her. In another second she really *was* going to scream.

'I can see the bottom,' called Wanounou. Suddenly he disappeared, and Peggy could hear the damp gravel crunch of his footsteps. A few seconds later she reached the bottom of the stairs and stepped out into a narrow, barrel-vaulted tunnel. It was barely wider than the stairs. The floor was covered in a thick layer of rotted, broken limestone that felt like small, damp bones beneath her feet. She shuddered. In some ways it was worse than the stairway.

Holliday stepped out behind her. Wanounou shone the flashlight ahead, illuminating the way. Silently they made their way along the tunnel, the floor gently sloping downward.

'We're going deeper,' commented Holliday.

'Thanks for mentioning it,' said Peggy acidly.

'I wonder what this place was. Some Middle Ages version of a priest hole?' Holliday asked.

'What's a priest hole?' Peggy asked. 'Or should I ask?'

'During Elizabethan times Catholic families and churches had priest holes, hiding places and tunnels they could escape to if pursuivants came after them – priest hunters,' explained Wanounou. 'Sort of like the Nazis and the Jews.'

'You history types have far too much information crammed into your heads,' said Peggy. 'Sometimes it's scary.'

The beam of the flashlight suddenly widened as they came into a large chamber hewn out of the bare rock. The ceiling overhead was at least twenty feet high, dripping with frozen limestone 'straws,' like delicate icicles. The walls were rough stone. Unlike the tunnel, the floor was set with large, quarried paving stones. There was a litter of what appeared to be broken pieces of old flowerpots that had been swept back against the walls. At the far end of the chamber was an immense doorway, the door constructed of studded iron, heavily encrusted with rust and dripping lime. An iron bar was fitted across it, held in iron brackets. Wanounou bent down and picked up a shard from the floor, examining it under the flashlight beam.

'Terra-cotta,' he said. 'From the curve I'd say a five-liter container. Wine or olive oil. Even water perhaps, although five liters is a little small; the terra-cotta kept it cool.' He ran the flashlight beam around the room. 'There's nothing else here.'

'It's chilly enough already,' said Peggy, her eyes traveling nervously around the cavernous room. She was right; it was cool, ten or fifteen degrees lower than it had been on the surface.

'This doesn't make any sense,' said Holliday.

'What doesn't?' Wanounou said, picking up another chunk of pottery.

'That staircase we came down was never used to transport jugs of wine or oil or anything else for that matter; the steps are far too narrow.'

'So?' Peggy said.

'So whatever was stored here wasn't removed up the stairs and into the chapel,' said Wanounou, nodding his agreement. 'Which means it had to have been brought in from somewhere else.'

'And that in turn means there has to be another entrance,' completed Holliday.

'Does that mean we have to go through that big door over there?' Peggy asked.

'Afraid so,' said Holliday.

'I thought you might say that,' she sighed.

They approached the door. It was enormous, at least five feet across and close to fifteen feet high. There was no sign of hinges.

'Pins in the bottom and the top,' said Holliday. 'A pivot door.'

'Let's get the bar off,' said Wanounou.

He hammered at the brackets with the curved end of the crowbar, knocking off most of the rust welding the iron bar to its supports. The rest he dug out with the chisel end. When he was done all three of them lifted the iron bar away from the door and laid it on the paving-stone floor. Their hands and clothes were stained with streaks of rust.

Wanounou hauled on the immense latch, but the door didn't budge. He fitted the chisel end of the crowbar into the narrow crack between the door and wall, then he and Holliday heaved. For a moment nothing happened, but then there was a shrieking sound and the entire door moved a few inches toward them, grinding over the stone floor.

'Anybody got any WD-40?' Peggy cracked.

Holliday and the professor rested for a second, then repeated the process. By the third time they'd opened the door a full eighteen inches – enough to squeeze by.

'Nobody's been through that door in about a thousand years,' said Holliday. 'Who goes first?'

'You do,' said Wanounou with a melodramatic sweeping gesture of his arm. 'This whole thing was your idea after all.'

'Just as long as there's no snakes,' said Peggy. 'Are there any snakes in Israel?'

'Sure,' said Wanounou. 'Cleopatra and the asp, remember?'

'Any underground?'

'Just the blind worm snake.'

'What are they like?'

'A blind snake that looks like a worm.'

'Very funny.'

'They're about ten inches long, black, and highly polished. And they're not poisonous.'

'Anything else?'

'There's a species of albino scorpion.'

'Blind snakes and albino scorpions . . . Great.'

'I'm going through,' said Holliday. 'Anybody coming along?'

Switching on the other flashlight, he turned sideways and squeezed through the opening, disappearing into the darkness beyond. Peggy went next, with Wanounou following her.

The passageway beyond the door was entirely different from the one that had led from the staircase to the storage chamber. Here the walls were raw native rock rather than dressed and quarried stone. The floor was rough, unworked limestone, and the roof, instead of being a plain barrel vault, was a soaring crevasse, its peak lost somewhere in the gloom. They were in fact now walking along an enormous crack in the earth created by some cataclysmic earthquake millennia before. When they spoke their voices echoed from the ragged stone.

'"With dead Saladin's echoing voice it calls us into battle once again,"' said Holliday, quoting from the message from the sword and swinging the flashlight around, lighting up the passage.

Shadows jumped and flared in the moving beam like flitting bats.

'Doc, you're getting spooky again,' Peggy warned.

'Sorry.'

'The passage is splitting,' called out Wanounou in the lead.

Ahead of them the passage split in two, the left fork narrower, the roof a lowered flat slab at about room height. The right fork was wider than the one they stood in, an extension of the same soaring crack in the earth. Holliday and Peggy joined the professor.

'Which way?' Holliday asked.

'It's a toss-up,' answered Wanounou. 'It's not as though they put up a sign.'

'Just like the highways,' laughed Holliday.

'I say we go right,' said Peggy firmly. 'Actually I'd like to just get the hell out of here, but that would mean going back up that stupid staircase and I don't think I could deal with that right now, so I say we go right. Maybe they'll have a Starbucks at the other end.'

Wanounou looked at Holliday. 'Well?'

Holliday shrugged. 'Suits me.'

They went to the right, where the passage was wide enough to let them walk three abreast. They walked on for another hundred yards, and then the passage suddenly opened up again, the roof soaring above their heads. The sound of falling water thundered.

'Incredible,' breathed Peggy as the light from both men's flashlights played over the way ahead. 'I've never seen anything like *that* before.'

21

In front of them lay an immense underground lake. At its far end a waterfall gushed down fifty feet before striking the main pool. Except where the waterfall struck, the water was as black as pitch.

This time it was the Israeli archaeology professor who spoke the words.

'"In the black waters of the Pilgrim's Fortress a treasured silver scroll is found,"' he whispered. 'This *has* to be it.'

'Where?' Peggy said. 'All I see is a big reservoir of water. You think an arm is going to come up out of the water like the Lady of the Lake or something?'

'Maybe,' murmured Holliday, excitement slowly coming into his voice. He pointed the beam of his flashlight into the center of the pool. A small island had formed over a million years or so, limestone in solution dripping from the roof of the cavern to fall into the water, eventually, drop by drop, eon after eon, building up and creating a small solid hillock rising into the open air.

Now the island and the long, wax-like dripping from the ceiling seemed to be reaching out to each other. In another hundred thousand years perhaps they'd even join together to form a solid column of stone.

'What?' Peggy said. 'All I see is one of those stalac-thingumajiggies. What's so special about that?'

'*Stalag*-thingumajiggy,' corrected Wanounou. '*Stalac*tites come down, *stalag*mites go up.'

'Whatever,' said Peggy, exasperated. 'It's cold, it's creepy, and there's no scroll, silver or otherwise. Can we go home now?'

'Look at the base of the stalagmite,' instructed Holliday, holding the beam of the flashlight steady.

'That's no natural formation,' said Wanounou. A right angle of stone seemed to be jutting out from the frozen ooze of dripstone, surrounding it like the corner of a cube.

'The base of a column?'

'An altar?'

'Maybe.'

'You think there might be something underneath it?' Peggy asked, suddenly understanding.

'Could be,' said Wanounou, staring out across the water.

'Well, let's go and find out,' she urged.

'How do you propose doing that?' asked the professor.

Peggy shrugged. 'Swim out with Doc's rock hammer and whack the thing until it breaks. Like opening a piñata.'

'Hardly rates as good archaeological field technique,' responded Wanounou.

'To hell with that,' said Peggy. 'Let's do it.'

'I told you, I'm not much of a swimmer,' the professor said.

'It's two hundred feet,' said Peggy. 'A hamster could swim that far.'

'I can't swim at all actually,' admitted Wanounou, coloring with embarrassment. 'I never learned.'

'Doc?'

'It was your idea,' said Holliday. 'I'm willing to come back later with a rubber raft and the right tools and do it properly.'

'And go down that stairway again?' Peggy scoffed. 'No way,' she said. She toed off her sneakers and undid her jeans.

'What are you doing?' Wanounou said, startled.

'Going for a swim,' she said, sitting down on the edge of the pool. She wriggled out of the jeans, pulled the T-shirt over her head, and put out her hand. 'The hammer,' she said to Holliday. He handed it to her, grinning, and she jammed it into the waistband of her panties. Wanounou looked at her as though she was insane.

'What?' Peggy frowned. 'Do I need a bikini wax or something?'

The professor blushed furiously.

Peggy turned around and dipped the toes of one foot into the water. She winced.

'Cold.' She shivered.

'Come on, kiddo, if you can do the creek behind Uncle Henry's in May you can do a cave in Israel during August.'

She gave him a nasty look, wrapped her arms around herself, and stepped tentatively out into the pool.

'Anything nasty likely to be in here with me?' Peggy called out, looking back at Wanounou and Holliday, her voice echoing loudly around the cathedral-sized cavern. 'The bottom feels slimy.'

'Microbial mats,' said Wanounou. 'A bit of ooze, that's all. Nothing that bites.'

'No blind worm snakes?'

'No blind worm snakes.'

She was up to her waist now. She took a breath, held it, then ducked herself completely under the surface. She came up sputtering.

'Freezing!' she yelped. 'And salty.'

She arched forward gracefully, slipping into the water fully, stroking across the surface of the pool with barely a ripple, doing a perfect, powerful Australian crawl.

'Astounding,' said Wanounou, clearly in awe. 'Beautiful.'

'She was always the porpoise in the family,' said Holliday proudly, touched by the Israeli's appreciation of her. 'As far as I know this is a first for her.'

It took Peggy less than a minute to swim to the little stone island. Reaching it, she pulled herself out of the water, slicked the hair off her face in a quick gesture, then pulled the geologist's hammer from the waistband of her panties. She turned back to the men waiting on the far shore.

'Anywhere in particular?' she called out, raising her voice over the steady noise from the waterfall.

'They're a lot more fragile than they look,' Wanounou called back. 'Just about anywhere should do it.'

Peggy turned back to the stone and raised the hammer.

'There goes a thousand years of work by Mother Nature,' muttered the professor under his breath.

Peggy brought the hammer down hard, the sound ringing like a church bell. Nothing seemed to happen. She raised the hammer and brought it down a second time.

'It's cracking!' she called out, excited. She began pounding at the rocky extrusion, finally shattering it. 'It's some kind of statue, I think!' She pounded harder. On the shore Wanounou winced with every blow.

'A statue,' he whispered. 'And she's destroying it.'

Peggy kept on hammering. Suddenly she stopped.

'What is it?' Holliday called out.

Peggy started hammering again, more carefully and with less force.

'There's something inside!' Peggy boomed.

'What is it?' Holliday called again. Peggy turned, put the hammer back into the waistband of her panties. She had something else tucked into the crook of her arm.

'What is it?' Wanounou asked Holliday.

'I can't see. Some sort of jar, I think.'

Peggy slipped into the water again and began sidestroking back to shore. In another minute she was back again and climbing out of the water. Shivering and covered in goose bumps, she handed the object in her hand to Holliday. It appeared to be a plain alabaster jar about ten inches long, three in diameter, and sealed with some black, tarry substance at the upper end.

'I think the statue was of the Virgin Mary,' said

Peggy, shivering uncontrollably, her teeth chattering as she pulled her T-shirt over her head. 'Made of clay. There were praying hands, I'm pretty sure.' She sat down on the stone and began tugging on her jeans again. 'That was inside. Is it the scroll, do you think?'

'Someone went to a great deal of trouble to keep it hidden, that's for sure,' said Holliday.

'Then let's get it open,' said Peggy.

'Not here,' said Wanounou firmly. 'We don't have the right tools.'

'Tools?' Peggy said. 'Who needs tools? We've got a hammer.'

'Sorry, Peg. Raffi's right,' said Holliday. 'We have no idea what's in that jar or what condition it's in. We'll have to open it in a controlled environment.'

'Specifically my lab at the university,' said Wanounou.

'If you say so.' Peggy shrugged. 'So *now* can we get out of here?'

In the distance, muffled but distinct, they heard the undeniable sound of a human sneeze.

They froze.

'Oh, crap,' whispered Peggy.

'Somebody's down here with us,' said Holliday.

'Who?' Wanounou asked nervously.

'Nobody knows we're here,' said Peggy.

'Kellerman's people; they must have followed us,' grunted Holliday.

There was the sound of a second sneeze. Closer now. Then a rusty grating sound. Someone hauling away on the big iron door.

'*Benzona*,' muttered Wanounou in Hebrew.

'What do we do now?' Peggy said.

'Scram,' said Holliday.

'Which way?' Wanounou asked. 'We can't go back the way we came. We'll run right into them.'

'The other tunnel?' Peggy said.

'What if it's a dead end?' Holliday said. 'We'd be trapped with our backs against a stone wall.'

'We're trapped now,' said Peggy. She hefted the rock hammer. 'Maybe we should stay and fight.'

'With a hammer?' Holliday said. 'The last time we ran into these people they were carrying machine pistols.' He shook his head. 'He will win who knows when to fight and when not to fight.'

'Sun Tzu?' Wanounou asked.

Holliday nodded.

'Nice philosophy, guys, but what are we supposed to *do*?'

Wanounou looked around, then turned to Peggy.

'You said the water tasted salty?'

'That's right.'

'Look at the edge of the pool – those dark stains on the limestone walls.'

'High tide,' said Holliday, brightening suddenly. 'This is a tidal pool.'

'Which means it must have an outflow somewhere; the runoff from that waterfall has to empty somehow,' nodded Wanounou.

'Look,' said Peggy, pointing.

They turned. Behind them, at the mouth of the passageway leading to the pool, they could see the faint, wandering beams of multiple flashlights playing over the rock walls.

'Come on,' whispered Holliday urgently.

They made their way around the narrow shelf between the edge of the water and the wall of the cavern, looking for the pool's outlet. A third of the way around they found it: a narrow tunnel in the stone only a few feet wide, barely visible in the shadows of the jutting, smooth rock walls. The tide was clearly low, and the flow seemed to be only about knee-high, if the high-water mark on the wall of the cavern was any indication.

'Quick!' Holliday urged, looking over his shoulder. The flashlight beams behind them were getting brighter as their pursuers approached. They had to get into the relative safety of the outlet tunnel before Kellerman's men reached the cave.

'What if it gets deeper?' Wanounou asked nervously. 'I told you, I can't swim.'

'I'll protect you.' Peggy grinned. She put her arm around the professor's waist, and they stepped into the water with Holliday right behind, holding the alabaster jar.

The swift undertow took all three of them by surprise, sweeping them off their feet and tumbling them into the lake's narrow outlet. Wanounou yelled, but the sound was swallowed up as he drank in a mouthful of the freezing water and gagged. He began flapping his arms and struggling in the water, but Peggy managed to get his head above the surface, her arm now crooked, elbow under his chin, as they hurtled along the underground river.

'You're okay! You're okay!'

Peggy turned her head, looking for Doc in the almost absolute darkness, then spotted the sweeping beam of his flashlight a few yards behind, swinging wildly back and forth as the speeding current dragged him along.

Suddenly Peggy felt something hard slam against her back and realized that it was the stone bottom of the stream. It was getting shallower, not deeper. She began to call out a warning to Holliday, but before she could speak the world dropped out from beneath her, and then she and

Wanounou were sliding down a long curving tube, the rock slippery with the same sort of microbial muck she'd felt under her feet when she swam out to the island in the pool.

She and Wanounou clutched each other desperately as the tube descended, slamming them back and forth with every twist and turn, the rush of water from the pool following the course it had carved through the rock for a million years. Then, abruptly, there was daylight, and just as abruptly they were thrown out into the air as the tube emptied into another cave, this one with an entrance open to the sea.

They dropped six or seven feet, straight down into the ocean, and once more Wanounou was struggling as he breathed in water, choking and flailing. Again Peggy dragged him to the surface as she oriented herself, then pointed him toward a narrow shelf of beach a few yards away. He slapped the water with both hands, doing a frenzied version of the dog paddle.

After three steps she felt the bottom beneath her feet. Wanounou reached safety first and slumped down onto the sand. There was a loud splash behind her, and Peggy turned as Doc came flying out of the water's yawning exit point on the sidewall of the cave and plummeted into the water. A few seconds later he surfaced, the alabaster jar still clutched under one arm. Peggy gave him a hand, and they staggered to the shore and dropped down on the little beach.

Finally they had a moment to get their bearings.

'I lost the hammer,' said Peggy, pushing hair out of her eyes and getting to her feet. 'Where the hell are we?' Beside her, Wanounou, gasping and retching, was still coughing out the last of the water from his lungs.

Holliday looked around the chamber. It was a typical sea cave, narrow and relatively shallow, perhaps fifty feet across and a hundred feet deep, the far end sloping up into a sandy beach with darker limestone chert pebbles strewn around. The walls arched steeply up to a rotted stone ceiling, and there was sea salt encrusted here and there, left by the rising and falling tides. At the sea end of the cave the Mediterranean glowed like sapphire in the early-afternoon sun.

There was evidence of recent occupation everywhere: rusting fifty-gallon drums lined up at the far end of the cave beyond the high-tide line, a coil of rope, several broken crates, and something that looked like a portable air compressor of some kind.

Tethered to a roughly hewn pier carved out of

the ancient rock was what appeared to be a perfectly seaworthy RIB – a rigid-inflatable boat, military grade, painted in shades of dull gray and brown, with a shield and bat wing emblem on the prow. It was about fourteen feet long with a center-mounted console and some kind of inboard drive.

'Is that our ride?' Peggy asked.

'It is if I can get it started,' answered Holliday. He handed Peggy the alabaster vase, then crossed the little strip of beach and climbed up onto the stone pier. He walked along it to the point where the boat was tethered. The boat was neatly attached to a very old-looking iron ring with a round turn and two half hitches, a sailor's knot that even a hurricane couldn't undo.

Holliday dropped down into the boat and made his way to the console. It looked simple enough: five gauges, all in Hebrew, a key-slot ignition, a starter button, a throttle lever, and a padded plastic wheel for steering.

There was a small panel underneath the wheel. Holliday reached down, opened it, and pulled out a handful of wires. There was a green one, a yellow, and a red. Presumably the red was the hot wire, and the green was the crank.

He stripped off the insulation on both and touched them to each other. All the gauges lit up.

Leaving the two wires connected, he hit the starter button, and the engine fired instantly.

'Your chariot awaits,' said Holliday.

Peggy untied the boat, and she and Wanounou climbed down into it. Holliday eased them away from the pier, then spun the wheel, turning the small boat in a tight circle until the bow was facing toward the cave exit and the open sea.

'Which one of these gauges is fuel?' Holliday asked.

'That one,' answered Wanounou, pointing. 'According to it we've got half a tank.'

'How far is Haifa?' Holliday asked.

'Bat Galim is about seven miles or so. The harbor is a little farther around the headland,' said Wanounou.

'Then let's get the hell out of Dodge,' said Holliday, and he pulled back on the throttle.

22

The inflatable made the short trip up the coast in a little less than half an hour, with Wanounou turning several shades of green in the process. Not only wasn't he a swimmer, he wasn't much of a sailor either.

Rather than get into a tangle of bureaucracy by trying to return the boat to its rightful owners Holliday simply drove it up onto the beach in front of the Méridien Hotel and left it there.

Getting back to Jerusalem with the alabaster vase turned out to be just as simple. At the hotel they bartered with a taxi driver named Bashir for a two hundred shekel ride back to the Land Cruiser, which they found exactly where they'd left it, apparently unharmed and untouched. There was no sign of any other vehicle except for a fresh set of tread marks in the soft dirt by the side of the road. A good-sized truck or SUV, from the width of the tires.

As far as Holliday could tell no one followed them on their return to Jerusalem. After a completely uneventful journey on the busy highway they arrived back at the university shortly after five o'clock that afternoon. They went to Wanounou's lab in the basement of the Archaeology Building.

The lab was a long, narrow, windowless room approximately twenty feet wide and the length of an Olympic swimming pool. The length of one entire wall was taken up with floor-to-ceiling metal shelving units, and the opposite wall was a collection of benches, computer work stations, and equipment pods that ranged from spectroscopes and comparison microscopes to laser saws, portable X-ray machines and megasonic cleaning tanks.

The center of the room, from one end to the other, was taken up by a long row of light-box tables for sorting, examining, and preliminary sorting of artifacts. On the tables were trays of tools, solvents, acids, and adhesives to aid in conservation, ongoing maintenance, and reconstruction of individual finds.

It was midsummer, and the laboratory was empty except for Peggy, Holliday, and the professor; the rest of the faculty and most of the grad students were either in the field or on holiday.

Wanounou took the vase to one of the light-box tables and switched it on. The table glowed bright white. He sat down on a stool, with Peggy and Holliday on either side. He took a pair of disposable gloves out of a pop-up box, then selected a long-bladed X-Acto knife from one of the trays. He weighed the jar on a small digital scale and noted the weight in a notebook he'd taken from a drawer in the table. That done, he pulled over an illuminated fluorescent magnifier and examined the jar more closely.

'Sealed with some sort of mastic,' said Wanounou.

'Mastic?' Peggy asked.

'A resin gum. They used it for medicinal purposes in the Middle Ages, but they also used it as a sealant, like a gummy varnish. It dries that yellowy color and gets very brittle.'

'Isn't there some kind of solvent?' Holliday said, eyeing the X-Acto knife.

'Sure, there's even some pretty inert ones, but it's safer to chip it off; less likely to damage whatever's inside.'

Using the scalpel-bladed knife, Wanounou scored the surface of the sealant covering the ceramic stopper of the jar, working the gouge deeper and deeper until after about ten minutes' patient work the knife slipped into the crack between the stopper and the vase itself.

As Peggy and Holliday watched, Wanounou put the knife down, chose a pair of long-nosed, locking surgical forceps, and gently lifted the lid off the vase. He set the lid aside and tilted the vase so the light from the magnifying lamp shone into it.

'Anything inside?' Peggy asked.

'Something.'

'What?'

'Hold on.'

The professor picked up the forceps again and eased them down into the neck of the vase. Concentrating hard, he worked the forceps around for a moment, then withdrew them.

'Wrong tool,' he said. He rummaged around in the tray and found what he was looking for. He held it up.

'Looks like something I saw at my gynecologist's,' said Peggy uncomfortably. They looked like the surgical version of cooking tongs with blades that locked like vise grips.

'Close,' answered Wanounou. He teased the device down into the vase. 'They're obstetrical forceps for delivering babies.' He used his free hand to lock the smooth steel blades of the forceps in place and then gestured to Holliday. 'Hold the vase steady.'

Holliday did as he was told, leaning forward and gripping the vase with both hands. With slow, agonizing care Wanounou slipped the forceps out of the vase, their captured prey in tow.

'It's a boy,' said Peggy, staring. 'Either that or a piece of the muffler from my old Ford Escort.'

'It's a scroll,' said Wanounou, excitement in his voice.

'I don't want to say what it looks like,' said Holliday.

'What he means,' said Peggy drily, 'is that it looks like a big dookie.'

She was right. The object caught in the locked rounded blades of the forceps was ten inches long, roughly circular, lumpy, dark in color, and with a crusty surface.

'Corrosion,' explained Wanounou. 'Silver tarnish taken to its logical conclusion.'

'How do you get it off?' Peggy asked.

'Carefully,' said the professor. 'First an electrolytic bath, then run some current through it, and after that give it a few minutes in the megasonic cleaner to shake off anything left.'

'After that?' Peggy asked. 'Will you be able to unroll it?'

'Doubtful,' said Wanounou. 'It would probably crumble.' He shook his head. 'After it's been cleaned I'll put the scroll into the laser saw and cut it into strips. If there's corrosion within the scroll I'll have to put each strip into the electrolytic bath again. Then I'll X-ray the strips, photograph them, put them between sheets of inert

plastic, and then maybe you can read what's on it
– if anything.'

'So what's the next step?' Holliday said.

'Go back to your hotel. Have dinner in the old
city. Go to a place called Amigo Emil. It's a little
hole-in-the-wall place in the El Khanka Street
Bazaar. Tell Emil I sent you. Call me in the morning, and I might have something for you to see.
I'll probably be at this all night.'

'We could hang around,' said Peggy.

'No, we couldn't,' said Holliday firmly. 'Leave
the man alone to do his job.'

'Sure you don't want us to stay?' Peggy said.

'Go, let me work,' said Wanounou. 'You'd be
bored stiff in half an hour if you stuck around.'
He grinned. 'Buy a book about the Copper Scroll
at the university book store on your way out.
There's lots of them. Educate yourself.'

'All right,' she said.

'Come on,' said Holliday, heading for the door.
Peggy followed, but not before she leaned over
and gave the startled professor a quick peck on
the cheek.

The Old City of Jerusalem is an ancient walled
district occupying an area of slightly less than
half a square mile in the southwestern corner of
the modern city. Since the mid-1800s it has been

divided into four distinct zones: the Christian Quarter in the northwest, the Muslim Quarter in the northeast, the Jewish Quarter in the southeast, and the Armenian Quarter, the smallest of the four areas occupying a sliver of territory in the southwest corner.

During the British Mandate period of the 1920s a man with Walt Disney-like foresight named Sir Ronald Storrs, the newly installed governor of the city, decreed that all construction within the city, new and old, would use locally quarried 'Mezzah,' or Jerusalem stone. Not only did it provide needed jobs for an almost bankrupt city, it also gave the city a uniform look and prevented the Old City from being radically altered over the years. Conservationists, town planners, and tour guides still praise his name.

The walled area of the Old City looks like a complex web of winding streets that has been grasped in a pair of giant hands and squeezed down to Lilliputian dimensions. There are less than a score of streets wide enough to support traffic, and many of the alleyways in the old city are no wider than an average person's outstretched arms.

Amigo Emil's was just as Wanounou had described it, a hole-in-the-wall on a narrow street just inside the Damascus Gate in the Christian Quarter, the restaurant marked only with a rudimentary oval sign over the door painted with a cup, knife and fork, and something that looked like a steaming bowl of soup.

The dining area inside looked as though it had been carved out of native stone. The tables were blond wood inset with blue patterned ceramic tiles, the seats were straight-backed wooden chairs with comfortable cushions, and the food was wonderful. Peggy had once done a month-long shoot in war-ravaged Beirut so she worked the menu, ordering up a meze of Arabic dishes in square, white ceramic bowls and a pile of freshly baked pita bread.

They ate their way through an array of tapas-like portions of hummus; baba ghanoush; spicy kibbeh, a meat dish; *carabage halab*, an Arab pastry; tahini; and *muhammara*, a hot pepper dip. All of this was washed down with icy bottles of Maccabee pilsner.

The meal finished, Emil, the owner, took them down a few steps into the tiny establishment's back room, where they rested on enormous lounging pillows and had coffee and several slices of tooth-numbingly sweet baklava.

'Trapped in a crusader castle one minute, defying dental hygiene the next,' said Peggy happily, licking honey syrup off her fingers. 'This is the life for me.'

'Let's not forget a body count that's up to five

now,' said Holliday. He sipped his coffee. 'This isn't a game of Where in the World Is Carmen Electra or whatever her name was.'

'Sandiego,' said Peggy. 'Cool your jets, Doc. I was just trying to lighten things up.'

'Sorry,' answered Holliday. 'But I've been doing a lot of thinking in the last little while, and things aren't adding up.'

'Like what?'

'Lots. Like Broadbent's father finding the sword with Uncle Henry, for instance. We know that was a lie. Carr-Harris never mentioned his name, so how did Broadbent junior even know about the sword?'

'What else?'

'How did Kellerman's men know we were going to England? They knew we were in Friedrichshafen from the minute we got off the ferry. That monk . . .'

'Brother Timothy?' Peggy asked.

'Right. How did Brother Timothy know we were coming to the Villa Montesano exactly when we did? It was almost as though he expected us.' He paused. 'And then there's the good professor to consider,' he said slowly.

'Raffi?' Peggy frowned. 'What about him?'

'He's almost too good to be true.'

'The guy in Toronto, Braintree, was the one

who suggested him,' argued Peggy. 'Are you saying he's involved in some kind of worldwide conspiracy, too?'

'I don't know, Peg. I told you, it's just that none of it makes any sense.'

'I think you're just being paranoid.'

'Carr-Harris is dead. One of the guys shooting at him is dead. Two of Kellerman's guards are dead. The old man, Drabeck, is dead. That's not paranoia, that's fact.'

'None of which has anything to do with Raffi.'

'He's too convenient,' grumbled Holliday.

'What exactly is that supposed to mean?' Peggy said.

'The code on the gold wire takes us to Castle Pelerin. The Castle is in a military zone. Lo and behold, Raffi Wanounou has a pal who gets him clearance. We get trapped with someone on our tail, and there just happens to be a boat waiting to spirit us away. I don't believe a word of it.'

'The man Raffi phoned at the Méridien to tell him where the boat was explained that,' said Peggy. 'They were going to use it for some special exercise next weekend or something.'

'Or something, sure,' scoffed Holliday.

'You're just worried that he likes me too much and that the feeling is mutual,' replied Peggy.

'That, too,' grunted Holliday.

'You're being an old fogey,' laughed Peggy. 'Have another piece of baklava.'

Emil materialized at the top of the stairs with the kind of fixed smile on his face that suggested he wanted to close up for the evening. Holliday looked at his watch. It was past eleven.

'Time to get back to the hotel,' he said. They were staying at the American Colony Hotel, a Jerusalem landmark just a ten-minute walk from the Damascus Gate. They paid the bill, thanked Emil for a wonderful meal, and stepped out of the restaurant onto the narrow street known as Souk El-Khanka. It was getting cool, and Peggy shivered.

Even though it was late, the quarter was still busy, and the little street was crowded with tourists and deliverymen balancing huge trays of fruit and bread on their heads. The air smelled of hot stone and spices, and a dozen kinds of music could be heard over the chatter of voices speaking half a dozen languages.

Take away the rock and roll and add a few donkeys and it could have been two thousand years in the past. Halfway back to the Damascus Gate Holliday could feel the hairs on the back of his neck rising. He tensed, then gripped Peggy's elbow.

'What's the matter?'

'We're being followed.'

23

'You're sure?' Peggy said.

'Certain,' answered Holliday. 'He was outside the restaurant, smoking a cigarette. Waiting. Dark hair, jeans, sneakers, and one of those zip-up hoodie things, dark blue.'

'He could be a student.'

'He looks like a cop. Moves like one, too.'

'Why would cops be following us?'

'I have no idea, but I'm going to find out.'

They reached the corner of Souk El-Khanka and turned right, heading south down Bab Khan El-Zeit, a busy market street, well-lit and with lots of stalls and shops still open.

'This isn't the way back to the hotel,' said Peggy. 'We should have turned the other way, back toward Damascus Gate.'

'I know that,' said Holliday.

'So what are we doing?'

'Finding out what's going on, once and for all.'

Holliday turned again onto a narrow side street called El-Khayat that ran behind. It was darker here, lit only at the entry to the alley. They went down a short flight of old stone stairs and kept on walking. A few seconds later, the man in the hoodie appeared and turned down the alley, as well.

'Is he still behind us?' Peggy asked nervously.

'Yes,' said Holliday. 'That proves it; he's on our tail.'

'Now what?'

'I'm not sure.'

'Maybe we should just go back to the hotel,' said Peggy, 'ask Raffi about it tomorrow.'

'You ask him,' said Holliday. 'I want answers now.'

'You're sure he's a cop?'

'I'm not sure of anything. He could be just a mugger, but I don't think so.'

'A mugger in Jerusalem?'

'They have suicide bombers, why not muggers?'

'It's creepy, like pickpockets in Bethlehem. It's just not right.'

They reached the end of the street and turned south again, this time onto a slightly wider street called Christian Quarter Road, once more filled with strolling tourists and lined with shops and restaurants. A lot of the folding wooden shutters were closed, and half of the sky was blotted out by wooden, shelf-like awnings that jutted out over the paving stones. Every few yards the dark, shadowy entrance to a narrow laneway loomed.

As they reached the corner of Christian Quarter Road and David Street Holliday saw another figure smoking a cigarette and leaning against a wall. This one was wearing an old Rolling Stones *Tattoo You* tour T-shirt from 1981. The T-shirt was so old the lolling tongue had faded to light pink.

Holliday stopped in front of some kind of pottery store and watched an enormously fat woman in a straw hat and sweatpants with JUICY in big letters across her straining buttocks bargain for a pot in booming New Jersey-accented English. Maybe the Muslims were right, thought Holliday, trying not to stare: some women's improperly covered bodies *were* an offense to God.

Out of the corner of his eye he watched Tattoo You in conversation with the man in the dark blue hoodie. Blue Hoodie nodded and then walked away, heading back down Christian Quarter Road.

'We've been handed off,' said Holliday.

'What do you mean?'

'Blue Hoodie just passed us on like a relay runner. The guy on our tail now is wearing a Rolling Stones T-shirt.'

'Is that important?'

'It means they're organized,' answered Holliday.

It also meant they had enough resources to scatter men around the Old City and that they had some way to communicate, probably earpiece radios. Cops or better; he doubted that Kellerman's people could put together something that sophisticated that quickly, especially in Israel.

They moved away from the pottery store and turned left. Ahead of them, in the distance and glowing splendidly in a bath of brilliant light, was the Dome of the Rock, the mosque occupying the historic site of King Solomon's Temple, the near-mythic source of the Templar Knights' original wealth.

The actual dome was covered in a hundred and seventy-six tons of gold donated by King Hussein of Jordan shortly before he died. They crossed El-Lahamin Street and walked to Bab-Alsilsileh, the Dome of the Rock like a fabulous beacon ahead of them rising from the rabbit warren of limestone buildings surrounding it. There were even more tourists here, heading for the Dome of the Rock or to the Wailing Wall, built by Herod to enclose and support the original Temple Mount.

Even from blocks away Holliday could see the blaze of strobing flashes from people taking pictures of the famous holy place, one more treasured trophy shot so that JUICY from New Jersey

288

could prove to her Bergen County buddies that she'd been there and they hadn't.

Among the tourists Holliday could spot at least half a dozen Catholic priests, a black-robed Greek Orthodox priest, a flock of Mother Teresa nuns in their distinctive tea-towel blue and white striped habits, and several big-hatted, long-bearded rabbis.

Instead of following them, Holliday and Peggy ducked down a narrow winding alley that led them south again. Behind them, Tattoo You followed at a discreet distance. The T-shirt was at least one size too big, and the man tailing them wore it loose, not tucked in, probably to hide a weapon on his belt. The man was no more than thirty, with muscular biceps and an athletic look; even without a gun he'd be more than a match for Holliday. No confrontations here, that was for sure.

The alley was leading them to the west, into the Armenian Quarter. Like all the street signs in Old Jerusalem there were three languages: Hebrew, Arabic, and English. The signs were bolted or inset into the walls at every street corner. The directions in the ancient city were easier to follow than the superhighways.

Holliday still wasn't quite sure what he wanted to do, but he knew he didn't want to just scurry back to the hotel and play possum. It wasn't in his nature to run from a fight, but by the same token he knew better than to take on insurmountable odds. The question still remained, however: what would interest Israeli cops, local or otherwise, in their activities?

They turned down yet another narrow street, this one called Tiferet Yisrael. Once again it took them farther west, with the Dome of the Rock at their backs now. The streets were empty of tourists, and the only footsteps other than their own were the ones of the man behind them.

'Let's get him off our tail,' said Holliday, finally exasperated and just a little tired of the prolonged game of cat and mouse. They slipped off Tiferet Yisrael down a stony little crack between two rows of anonymous buildings. The pathway was too narrow even to have a name.

They reached the end of the shortcut and turned back the way they'd come, following a street broken into long, wide steps leading north. The sign on the wall said they were on Hakraim Gilaad. The street eventually took them back to Tiferet Yisrael, where they paused. There was no sign of Tattoo You.

'Did we lose him?' Peggy asked.

'Looks like it,' said Holliday, looking around.

The little street was empty, all the shutters drawn against the evening chill.

'So what was that all about anyway?' Peggy asked. 'If you saw them like that they couldn't have been very good at their jobs.'

'Intimidation, I think,' said Holliday. 'Just letting us know we were being watched.'

'Do you think there's any connection to whoever was down in those tunnels today?'

'I don't know. Maybe we should ask your friend Raffi tomorrow, like you said.'

'Let's not start that again,' said Peggy.

They turned and headed back along the length of Tiferet Yisrael, heading to El-Lahamin Street and the way back to the Damascus Gate. A man dressed entirely in black came out of a doorway and turned toward them, walking casually. Holliday noticed a flash of white at his collar. A Catholic priest. Red-haired, red-cheeked, and wearing half-glasses. A man in his fifties. He wore a baggy black suit jacket over a regulation bibbed black shirt.

The priest nodded to Holliday and Peggy as they passed. Holliday nodded back. In the one brief glance Holliday noticed something in the priest's eyes. Something hard. He shook off a vague feeling of unease and walked on. From behind them he heard a short, metallic sound and turned. The noise had been familiar: the slide of an automatic pistol snapping into place.

The priest stood less than ten feet away, his baggy jacket swept back, revealing a sling holster. In his hand he held a folding stock Czech Skorpion machine pistol, the short barrel fitted with a fat, black sausage suppressor. There was no time to react; the man lifted the gun to chest level, his finger already squeezing the trigger. There was no way out; they were dead where they stood.

There was a sound like a huge hand slapping a door. For a split second Holliday thought he saw the priest's jacket riffle, suddenly fanned by a rush of air. Then the red-haired man crumpled to the ground, falling forward on his face, the machine pistol dropping out of his extended hand and clattering onto the cobbled street.

From the dark entrance to the alley they'd just come out of, Tattoo You appeared, a black polymer Jericho automatic pistol in his hands, the one they called a 'Baby Eagle' back in the United States. He looked at Holliday and Peggy briefly, then holstered his weapon underneath his shirt again.

'Get out of here, quickly,' said Tattoo You. He turned and disappeared into the darkness of the alley.

Holliday stepped forward a few paces and knelt

down beside the corpse of the priest. Blood was oozing beneath the left arm. Tattoo You had shot him through and through, perfect center of mass, the bullet blowing out the heart and lungs together.

He felt around in the inside pocket of the dead man's jacket and found a wallet and a passport. The passport had a red cover with the miter and crossed key insignia of the Holy See stamped in gold. He flipped open the Vatican passport and checked the I.D. page.

The dead man's name was Brendan Jameson, born October 22, 1951 in Mount Kisco, New York, presently a resident in Rome, Italy. His occupation was listed simply as 'priest.' A priest with the Czech version of an Uzi? He slipped the passport back into the man's inside pocket and checked the wallet. The I.D. in the wallet matched the passport. He replaced the wallet and climbed to his feet. In the distance Holliday could hear the approaching warble of sirens.

'Let's get out of here,' he said.

'Shouldn't we call the cops or something?' Peggy said.

'They're on the way. Someone must have heard the shot.'

'Shouldn't we stay and explain?'

'Explain what? Why we're standing here with a

dead priest? I can't explain it to myself let alone the cops. I've killed people in England and Germany. In most countries they call that murder. And don't give me the innocent until proven guilty stuff; justice only works on *Law and Order.*' He took Peggy by the arm, turning her away from the priest's dead body. 'Come on.'

Twenty minutes later, the Old City behind them, Holliday and Peggy reached the American Colony Hotel on the Nablus Road and stepped into the small, multi-arched lobby. A stout man with a horseshoe of curly dark hair and dressed in a wrinkled gray suit stood up from one of the old red brocade couches and approached them. As he walked Holliday could see that he was wearing a shoulder holster. He tensed. The fat man smiled pleasantly, extending his hand.

'Colonel Holliday? Miss Blackstock, yes?'

'Who wants to know?' Holliday asked.

The smile on the fat man's face faltered just a little.

'I am Prakad . . . Chief Inspector Isidor Landsman of the Israeli Police Department.'

'Yes?' Holliday said.

'You are Colonel Holliday?'

'Yes.'

'There has been an accident. Your friend Dr. Wanounou of the university.'

'Accident?' Holliday asked.

'What happened?' Peggy asked. 'Is he hurt?'

'Dr. Wanounou was very badly beaten. He is at the University Medical Center. I can take you to him if you wish.'

24

They didn't actually get to see the professor until early the following morning. According to Wanounou's doctor at the Hadassah University Medical Center, a middle-aged man named Menzer, the archaeologist had suffered a fractured skull, a broken nose, a broken arm, several broken ribs, and assorted cuts, bruises, and contusions. If the fracture had been any worse he would have died.

'In other words, they kicked the crap out of him,' said Menzer, eyeing them a little skeptically, wondering if they knew why this had happened to an innocent archaeology professor working late in his laboratory.

Isidor Landsman had looked at them the same way. On the drive up Cheil Handasa to Mount Scopus Hospital on the university campus, the police detective had asked Holliday and Peggy why, according to the security log in the Archaeology building, they had been the only names listed along with Wanounou's. What was their relationship? Why were they with the professor in his lab? Where had they been before arriving at the university? Where did they go after they supposedly left the professor alive and well? And over and over again: did they know of anyone or any reason why professor Wanounou would wind up being beaten within an inch of his life and left to die alone on his laboratory floor?

Holliday and Peggy stuck to the same basic story: They'd come to Israel on the advice of Professor Steven Braintree of the Centre for Medieval Studies at the University of Toronto. They wanted to consult with Wanounou regarding the provenance of an artifact that had been part of Henry Granger's estate. The fact that Holliday was a decorated active soldier and a teacher at West Point seemed to mollify the chubby cop, but it didn't stop him from continuing to ask questions. In the end he'd left them with the classic warning: don't leave town.

At seven thirty in the morning they were finally allowed into Wanounou's room. It looked like every other hospital room that Holliday had ever seen. The floors were dark vinyl tile, the walls were cream-colored, and the door was big enough to maneuver a gurney through.

There was an ominous blue panic button on the wall with white lettering that read simply CODE. There were two beds. The one nearest the door was empty but obviously in use. Wanounou was in the bed by the window, up five floors with a view of bright blue sky. The room smelled like rubbing alcohol and floor wax. People moved quietly up and down the halls carrying bouquets of flowers and peeping in doorways.

The professor looked like hell. Both eyes were black and swollen three-quarters shut. His lips were swollen and the color of eggplant. He had a plaster skullcap and a plaster bandage on his nose. He had a cast on his left arm and wires and tubes everywhere.

Machinery clicked and hummed all around the room. Things dripped into him, and things dripped out. The nurse, a skinny thin-faced man named Joseph with some kind of Slavic accent and a thick scar on his chin, told them they had exactly half an hour to visit. He looked like he meant it.

Wanounou was conscious and a little groggy from assorted medications he'd been given. He gave them a puffy-lipped smile as they stepped up to the bed. Two of his front teeth were broken, their ends jagged. He lisped a little when he talked.

'I'd kiss you, but it might be too painful,' said Peggy, pulling up one of the visitor's chairs and sitting down. She extended her hand and let it rest on the professor's sheet-covered leg. Wanounou's smile broadened. It looked as though his lips were going to split open. Holliday winced.

'Feeling better now,' said the professor. 'A bit hungry though.'

'That's a good sign,' said Peggy.

'What happened?' Holliday asked.

'I was working on the scroll. It was about ten thirty or so. Three guys came into the lab. One of them had an attaché case. He took the sections of the scroll, and the other two started beating me. One of them had a piece of pipe with duct tape wrapped around it. The other one just used his fists.'

Peggy winced.

'What did they look like?' Holliday asked.

'Ordinary, but like they went to the gym a lot.'

'Military?'

'Maybe. They didn't have particularly short hair, except the one with the attaché case. He was bald.'

'Tattoos?' Holliday was thinking about the sword and ribbon symbol he'd seen on the killer's wrist at Carr-Harris's summer house.

'Not that I saw.'

'Accents?'

'They didn't talk much.'

'Anything?'

Wanounou thought for a moment. The machinery ticked, dripped, and wheezed.

'The one with the attaché case.'

'What about him?'

'He was a Christian.'

'How do you know?'

'He had a little crucifix on a chain around his neck. Gold.'

That really didn't mean much these days.

'Anything else?'

Wanounou thought again.

'One thing. Silly.'

'What?'

'One of the guys kicking me. Before I passed out.'

'What?'

'His boots. Motorcycle boots, you know? The ones with a buckle.'

'Okay.'

'They were Rogani Bruno e Franco. I know the brand. Pricey. I've always wanted a pair. They make beautiful street shoes, too.'

'So?'

'They're Italian. The only place you can get them is a town called Macerata, near the Adriatic Coast.'

'Now why would you know a thing like that?' Peggy asked.

'Fanum Voltumnae,' said Wanounou as though it would mean something to them.

'"*Fanum*" means "temple" or "shrine," doesn't it?' Holliday said, his mind skipping back to Mary-Lou Gemmill's senior Latin class and her threats to deny prom tickets to anyone who couldn't decline neuter i-stem nouns by the end of class.

'That's right,' said Wanounou. 'There's a big archaeological site there. Etruscan. It's not far from Orvieto, a big gathering center for crusaders shipping out to Jerusalem. I've visited the site a number of times.'

'How far along were you with the scroll before they got to you? Did you manage to read it?'

'I didn't even get to clean the pieces.'

'How many slices?'

'Nine.'

'How long do you think the whole scroll was?'

'Thirty centimeters. I measured the pieces.'

'About twelve inches.'

'More or less.'

'And he took them all?'

'I guess so. My concentration was elsewhere,' answered Wanounou.

Peggy gave Holliday a sharp look.

'Would you like some water?' she said.

Wanounou nodded.

There was a carafe and a plastic cup with a flex straw in it on a rolling side table beside the bed. Peggy poured some water into the cup then held the flex straw to the professor's lips. He drank and then his head dropped back against the crisp linen of the pillow as though even sipping a little bit of water had exhausted him.

Holliday sighed. Maybe losing the scroll and whatever secret it possessed was an omen. The priest in the Old City alley brought the body count to an even half dozen. And those were the people he knew about. How many other people had died because of the sword and its hidden message? With the scroll gone there was no way to go on. They'd reached the end of the line. It was time to go home.

'Well, that's it, I guess,' he said. 'We've got nowhere else to go with this. We'd better pack up and go.'

'You're going to leave it like this?' Wanounou said. 'After everything you and Peggy have been through? After everything *I've* been through on your behalf?'

'You'd make a great Jewish mother,' said Holliday, smiling weakly.

'I *have* a Jewish mother; it rubs off,' said Wanounou, trying to smile back. It obviously hurt. He grimaced instead.

'Without knowing what's on that scroll I'm stumped.' Holliday shrugged. 'Unless a really suspicious customs guy at the airport finds your Italian thieves the scroll is gone forever.'

'The scroll may be gone,' said Wanounou, 'but we might still have the message.'

'Explain.'

'X-ray fluorescence. Know anything about it?'

'Something to do with X-rays?' Peggy ventured.

'Fluorescent X-rays,' said Holliday.

'Never mind,' said Wanounou. 'It's a relatively new process they use for all sorts of analysis, including archaeological artifacts. They used it recently to uncover a hidden text under a painted over section of the Archimedes Palimpsest, a copy of some of Archimedes's theories from about 300 B.C.'

'And?'

'The silver the scroll is made of is brittle and thin, extremely fragile. It occurred to me that even the cleaning process might harm whatever images or script was on the silver.' He paused, his voice croaking. Peggy gave him another sip of water. He went on. 'So before I put them into the electrolyte bath I took them upstairs to the imaging department and ran the individual slices through the big Philips machine they have up there. I fed the imaging data back down to my computer in the lab. I was just about to check it when the goons came in.'

'So the data is still in your computer?'

'It should be,' said the professor.

Using Wanounou's key and with the password to his computer written on a slip of paper, Peggy and Holliday let themselves in to the professor's laboratory later that morning. Except for a dark stain on the floor there was no evidence that anything untoward had happened. There was nothing broken and nothing that looked out of place.

The vase that had originally contained the silver scroll had been placed on a photographic copy stand waiting to be documented. There was a scattering of rust-colored crumbs on a white plastic tray that had held the laser-sawn strips of the scroll, but the scroll itself was gone.

Peggy sat down at the computer terminal, booted it up, and entered Wanounou's password. She entered the name he'd given to the data from the X-ray fluorescence scanner upstairs and then opened it. A screen full of brightly colored, slightly fuzzy images appeared.

'According to your friend Raffi the X-rays react to particles in the iron gall ink they used back in the Middle Ages,' said Holliday, peering over her shoulder.

'Why would they use ink on silver?' Peggy asked.

'As a guide for the engraving tool they used to scratch into the metal,' explained Holliday.

Peggy looked at the screen.

'It's fuzzy,' she said. 'Some of the words and letters are missing. And it's in Latin.' She looked around at Holliday. 'Can you read it?'

Holliday bent closer.

'"*Innocent III, Episcopus, Servus Servorum Dei. Sancti Apostoli Petrus et Paulus: de . . . potestate et auctoritate confidimus ipsi intercedant pro . . . ad Dominum. Precibus et meritis . . . Mariae semper Virgi . . . beati Michaelis Archangeli, beati Ioannis Bapti . . . et sanctorum Apostolorum Petri et Pauli et Sanctorum misereatur vestri omnipotens Deus; et dimissis omni . . . peccatis vestris, perducat vos Iesus Christus ad vitam aeternam.*"'

'Easy for you to say,' snorted Peggy. 'What does it mean?'

'It's an apostolic blessing from Pope Innocent the Third,' replied Holliday. 'I think it's called the *Urbi et orbi* – blessings to the city and to the world. "May the Holy Apostles Peter and Paul in whose power and authority we have" – uh, "confidence" would be the best translation, I guess – "intercede on our behalf to the Lord . . ." Et cetera, et cetera. Innocent was Pope during the Crusades. He was the one who eventually ordered the Templars to be arrested and killed.'

'That's it?' Peggy said. 'A blessing?'

'There's more,' said Holliday, scanning the text. 'Is there any way you can print this out?'

'Probably,' answered Peggy. She fumbled around with the keyboard and the mouse, then finally found the right command. Somewhere nearby a photo printer began to hum and whirr.

'Yada, yada, yada . . . "May Jesus Christ lead you into everlasting life . . ." Yada, yada . . . "Descend on you and remain with you always . . ." Here we go. "I hereby give you, Rutger von Blum, also known as Roger de Flor, Admiral of Naples and the Holy Order of the Temple, full license and authority to remove these treasures to a place of safety across the sea and out of the hands of the infidel Saladin . . .'"

'Does it say where this place of safety is?' Peggy asked.

'Not really. All it says is . . . *"fanum cavernam petrosus quies."*'

'Which means?'

'Roughly translated: "a rocky, holy cave-place of peace and quiet." Something like that.'

'We need to talk to Raffi again.'

*

When they returned to the hospital on the far side of the campus, Raffi was sitting up in his bed and half of the tubes and wires were gone. He was eating green Jell-O, sucking it carefully through his bruised and battered lips. They showed him the photo prints of the scroll sections, holding each one of them up in front of his swollen eyes. Holliday gave him the rough Latin translations.

'It's a papal bull. A proclamation. A license, like letters patent they used to give to privateers and pirates.'

'I could never figure out why they called it a bull,' said Peggy. 'What do bulls have to do with it?'

'A *bulla* is the lead seal they used to attach to the end of them,' explained Raffi.

'What about this "rocky holy cave-place of peace and quiet"?' Holliday asked. 'Ring any bells?'

'Not a one,' said Wanounou. 'But I know who you could ask.'

'Who?'

'A friend of mine, Maurice Bernheim. He's a curator at the Musée National de la Marine in Paris. He wrote a book on the history of Mediterranean shipping. If anyone is going to know about this Roger de Flor, it'll be Maurice.'

25

The Musée National de la Marine is located in one wing of the 1930s Palais de Chaillot and looks out across the Champ de Mars. When you see a photograph of Hitler with the Eiffel Tower in the background during his whirlwind visit to Paris after the city fell, the Führer is standing on the terrace of the Marine Museum.

Maurice Bernheim was in his early forties, bluff and hearty and full of laughter. When he saw Holliday his first comment was about how easily a man with a patch on his eye could be a pirate. Bernheim was comfortably chubby, brown-haired, wore a lovely Pierre Cardin suit and expensive-looking shoes, and smoked a particularly foul-smelling brand of cigarettes known as Boyards. Holliday hadn't known you could still get them, and the only reason he remembered them at all, other than once choking on one, was because, oddly, they were the only brand of cigarette anyone smoked in the movie *Blade Runner*. They smelled like old sneakers that had somehow caught fire.

Bernheim's office was a lavish room with the same view that Hitler had gotten, French doors leading out to the same terrace, paintings of ships where there were no bookcases, and ships in bottles on the few shelves that had no books. The furniture was expensive, leather and comfortable. Bernheim's desk was huge, carved, and very old. The carpets on the floor were Isfahan Persian and beautiful. Either Bernheim was independently wealthy or he had a lot of juice in his job.

'Ah, yes,' said Bernheim, leaning back in his chair. Smoke writhed up from the corn-paper cigarette in the big, cut-glass ashtray, already overflowing with butts from previous brushfires. 'The infamous Roger de Flor. I know him well.'

'Why infamous?' Holliday asked.

'He was something of a bad boy, you know. An adventurer and a mercenary. Sometimes he would rise up against his employers and take them over. He was like his Templar friends – far too successful. A great sailor by all accounts.'

'Why did the scroll we found refer to him as Rutger von Blum?' Peggy asked.

'That was his name,' said Bernheim with a very Gallic shrug. He picked up his cigarette, and it found its way to the corner of his mouth. He sucked, then puffed, excreting a cloud of smoke up toward his high ceiling. 'He was born in Italy where his father was royal falconer in Brindisi. Blum means flower in German. De Flor was nothing more than political expediency . . . When in Rome and all that, yes?'

'How did he connect with the Templars?' Holliday asked.

'He was a second son, which in those days meant his father didn't know what to do with him. It was either the priesthood or the sea. When the young Roger came of age he was indentured to a Templar galley of which he later became captain. Like that.' He took a puff of his Boyard. 'He eventually built up a fleet of warships and cargo ships for hire. His flagship was the *Wanderfalke* – the *Peregrine Falcon*, a caravel. Two hundred tons; quite large for the time.'

'I read you the translation of the Latin over the telephone,' said Holliday. 'Did it mean anything to you?'

Bernheim smiled broadly and took another drag on his cigarette.

'Not at first. My Latin is sparse to say the least; it was never my subject even years ago. I think perhaps your translation was a little . . . rough, as well.'

'I'll grant you that.' Holliday nodded.

'So,' continued Bernheim, 'it did not *sonner les cloches*, yes? Ring the bells?' He shrugged again.

'So I thought, I smoked a few cigarettes and thought some more. *Fanum cavernam petrosus quies.* So I did what my old teacher Monsieur Forain instructed. I, how do you say it, *decomposer la phrase?*'

'Parse,' said Holliday.

'Yes, parse,' nodded Bernheim. 'I parsed the phrase. *Fanum.* Shrine. Holy Place. *Cavernam.* Cave. Hollow place. *Petrosus.* Rock. Stone. *Quies.* Resting place.'

'Bells rang?' Peggy asked.

'Indeed, yes, they rang loudly because I also remember Monsieur Forain telling us that Latin is often a matter of the turn of phrase. What are the phrases that we have here?'

'*Fanum cavernam* and *petrosus quies,*' responded Holliday.

'Quite so, *les phrases descriptives*, the descriptive phrases "holy cave" and "rock of quiet." Then I see it. A pun, or perhaps even a code. *Quies*, a place of safety. A harbor perhaps. The Harbor of the Rock, yes?'

'Is there such a place?' Peggy asked.

'Certainly,' nodded Bernheim, triumphantly crushing out the fuming end of his cigarette. 'Roger de Flor's home port: La Rochelle, the harbor of the rock.'

'And the holy cave?' Holliday said.

'Saint-Émilion,' said Bernheim.

'I thought that was a wine,' said Peggy.

'Also a town not far from La Rochelle. Also a monolithic church carved out of the limestone where the hermit St. Émilion had his home. In a cave beneath the church. The Harbor of the Rock. The Holy Cave, *n'est-ce pas?*'

'It could be,' nodded Holliday.

'I am sure of it,' said Bernheim. 'Go to see this person in La Rochelle.' He sat forward and scribbled something on a notepad. He tore it off the pad and handed it to Holliday. A name and address: Dr. Valerie Duroc, Université de La Rochelle, 23 avenue Albert Einstein, La Rochelle, France. 'She will be your guide.'

They left the museum and crossed the Seine on the Pont d'Iéna by the tour boat landing stage. They turned and walked along the quayside, enjoying being in Paris once again. Peggy had been there on assignment several times, and when Holliday had done a brief stint at NATO headquarters in Belgium, Paris had been his favorite go-to place for R&R.

Paris. Arrogant, self-involved, pompous to the point of buffoonery, and populated by roughly six million elitist snobs forever looking down their noses at everyone else in the world, including the rest of their fellow Frenchmen, Paris was without a doubt still the most beautiful city in the world and one of the most fascinating. You could hate Paris for all its shortcomings, but at the same time you could have a wonderful time meeting the challenges the old bitch has got waiting for you around every corner.

They eventually reached the Quai d'Orsay and turned down the boulevard Saint-Germain, heading toward their hotel. Saint-Germain was in full summertime riot gear, selling everything from Armani suits to ten-thousand-dollar cufflinks and solving the problems of the world over coffee and a *sandwich jambon* in any number of cafés that ran the length of the long, tree-lined *grand boulevard*.

Half the store windows announced a *grande vente* to lure in the tourists, and the other half had signs in their windows warning of the dreaded *fermeture annuelle*, the city's classic July–August vacation when all Parisians make their once-yearly trek to the country or the seaside and pretend to enjoy it.

As Holliday and Peggy made their way down the street to their pension-hotel on the rue Latran they heard a dozen different languages being spoken and saw tour buses rolling by from at least that many countries. It was hardly the Left Bank of Hemingway's time, but it was still a great show, complete with striped jerseys, berets, old Citroëns, and *les flics*, the smiling pillbox-hatted policemen twirling their nightsticks and caressing the nasty little automatic pistols holstered on their hips. Here and there Bosnian beggars lurked, often with landmine-blasted arms and legs, rattling paper cups in hand.

They bought mustard slathered sausage rolls from a street vendor and continued down to the hotel, a six-story run-of-the-mill pension with no particular amenities other than the fact that, for a city like Paris, it was relatively cheap. Holliday and Peggy trudged up the narrow stairs to the second floor, said their good-byes in the hallway and retreated to their separate rooms. Neither one of them had slept since Jerusalem.

The room was classic third-rate Paris. The bed was cast iron with a mattress so soft it almost hit the floor. The chest of drawers had survived two World Wars and had the scars to prove it, and the bidet was ridiculously crammed between the bathroom door and the window, which overlooked a back alley. The view was just as classic: chimneypots on rooftops that drifted down to the Seine and a corner of Notre Dame if you hung out over the fire escape like an acrobat.

Holliday stared. The room had been completely trashed. The mattress looked as though someone had gone at it with a butcher knife; there were feathers and shreds of ticking everywhere. The drawers in the bureau hung open like lolling tongues, and clothes were scattered all around the room. His overnight bag had been torn to ribbons and the lining hacked out.

He paused. A sound? His heart hammered in his chest; the smart thing would be to turn around and run. Instead he went across to the closed door of the bathroom, wincing as a floorboard creaked under his foot like a rifle shot. He paused again at the door and listened.

Breathing, or the sound of a breeze blowing down the alley outside? Water dripped in the bidet. Holliday thought about the knife that had torn up the room. He stripped off his jacket and wrapped it around his arm. He pushed open the door. The bathroom was empty.

He turned back into the room, but something was nagging him. The shower curtain had been drawn around the bathtub. He was sure it hadn't been like that when he left the room. He whirled. A knife razored past his shoulder, and he had an image of a slim, lean-faced man in a white shirt with the tails out. His head smashed against the doorframe, and he reeled back as the man lunged toward him.

Holliday scuttled backward through the open

doorway. His assailant tried to bring the knife up under his ribs, but he managed to twist away, the long stiletto blade slicing through his shirt and grazing his skin. Holliday managed to launch a sharp kick to the man's groin.

The intruder screeched and dropped one hand between his legs. Holliday staggered back, tripping over the slashed remains of the mattress. Suddenly the man was on top of him, straddling his chest, his free hand coming up underneath Holliday's jaw, pushing his head back, leaving the throat open to attack.

Holliday bucked frantically as the knife arced down toward him. He tipped the other man off his chest and slammed him into the iron bed, his knife hand snagging on the metal springs. Holliday ground his knee into the other man's cheek, putting his weight into it.

There was a wet cracking sound, and the man with the knife let out a muffled, choking scream. Holliday reached up and grabbed the man's arm, pulling the wrist back over the edge of the iron bed, almost bending it back double on itself. The man let out a desperate groan, and the knife dropped out of his hand, clattering onto the floor.

Somehow the man twisted out of Holliday's grip and staggered to his feet. He was a lot larger than Holliday had originally estimated, and there was a frighteningly feral look about him. He was an attack dog, and even with a broken cheekbone and a nose gushing blood he looked as though he was in his element; this kind of thing was his business.

A quick glance told Holliday that the knife was now behind him; to make a play for it would mean turning his back on the man in front. He also noticed that the man's hands had a hard line of callus on the outer edge of the palm. He knew what that meant; Turner, one of the martial arts instructors at the Academy, had hands like that. The kind of hands that could slice through a three-inch board or a concrete block. Or crush an esophagus. This guy didn't need a knife at all.

Things suddenly got even worse. The man smiled through the mask of blood covering the lower half of his face, the teeth like dirty little yellow pearls.

'*Connard,*' he murmured.

His right hand swept back under his shirt and came out with a stubby little Beretta Tomcat, a mini-pistol from the late seventies. It sounded like a rat sneezing and was only .32 caliber, but a .32-caliber hole in your forehead was a hole nonetheless. He stepped forward, still smiling, bringing the gun up, his finger tightening on the trigger.

From the right side Peggy swept in under Holliday's arm, the long-bladed stiletto underhanded in her fist. She drove it like an uppercut up under his chin, the stainless steel spike cutting through throat, tongue, and soft palette, eventually lodging deep in the man's midbrain.

Peggy let go of the blade. The man collapsed like a venetian blind. He fell forward, his cheek resting on Holliday's shoe. Peggy was shaking, her eyes like saucers.

'Is he dead?' she whispered.

'You're kidding,' answered Holliday. 'He couldn't get any deader.' He shifted his foot. The man's head thumped lightly against the floor. He was barely bleeding at all.

'Oh, God,' groaned Peggy. 'I killed him.'

'About a millisecond before he was going to kill me,' said Holliday. He put his arm around her, squeezing hard. 'You saved my life, kiddo.'

'Don't mention it.'

They both stared down at the body.

Holliday crouched down and turned the man over on his back. He checked the man's wrist. There was a tattoo: the same sword and ribbon insignia he'd seen on the man in England.

'One of Kellerman's people,' said Holliday. He checked the man's wallet. His *carte d'identité* said his name was Louis Renault, a citizen of Morocco, born in Casablanca. There was also a small leather folder that identified him as a captain in the elite *Groupe d'Intervention de la Gendarmerie Nationale.* 'He's a cop,' said Holliday. 'Antiterrorist squad. We just stepped in it big time, I'm afraid.'

26

'How can he be a cop?' Peggy said, her eyes still glued to the body on the floor. The room was starting to smell like a slaughterhouse. It was high summer. The flies would be next. 'You said he was Kellerman's. He was trying to kill you.'

'He's still a cop.'

'So what do we do?'

'Get out of here as quickly as we can. The desk clerk downstairs has our passport numbers. They know whose room this is.'

'The old guy sits down there like a vulture. He sees everyone going in and out.'

'He probably saw our cop come in. Kept his mouth shut about him being in the room. Took a bribe. We can't let him see us leave.'

'How do we manage that?'

'Go back to your room. Get your things. I've got an idea. Meet me back here.'

Peggy left. Holliday took the man's gun, his wallet, and his identity card. With nothing on him it might slow down the identification process and buy a little more time. Peggy returned with her bag over her shoulder. Holliday led the way out of the room and back down the stairs.

Instead of going through the lobby he stopped on the second floor and turned in the other direction. There was a window at the far end of the hall that looked out onto the alley. Ten feet below the window there was a small lean-to shed for keeping the wheeled plastic garbage bins used by the hotel. Holliday boosted Peggy up onto the windowsill. She turned and dropped onto the little shed, then down to the ground. A few seconds later Holliday joined her.

'Now what?'

'We get away from here.'

They tidied their clothes, then walked down the little alley and out onto the rue Latran. Nobody paid them the slightest attention; it was as though nothing had happened, which of course it hadn't at least as far as the people on the street were concerned.

Peggy and Holliday walked down to the rue Saint-Jacques, then turned right and headed for the Seine and the Petit Pont. They walked past rue de la Huchette and reached the bridge. On the other side was the immense block of the Prefecture of Police and across from it the familiar shape of Notre Dame Cathedral.

Halfway across the bridge Holliday stopped and looked upriver. There were bookstalls set up against the stone embankment to his left. Down below on the quai by the river half a dozen homeless people huddled. A glass-topped tour boat slid under the bridge and headed west. A few fluffy clouds rolled peacefully through a mid-afternoon summer sky. Without a dead body decomposing in his hotel room, it would have been a perfect day to be in Paris.

'Somebody's on our tail,' said Holliday.

'Who?' Peggy asked, gripping her shoulder bag and trying not to look nervous.

'We're being double-teamed. They're almost certainly with Renault,' answered Holliday. 'There's a guy back there in a leather bomber jacket even though it's about ninety degrees out, and there's another one who's supposed to be a tourist, but he just doesn't look right.'

'Most tourists don't look right,' said Peggy. 'I've taken a million pictures that prove it.'

'Tourists in Hawaiian shirts and fatigue hats with cameras around their necks don't usually travel alone. They come in groups, pairs at least. And he's too young for the whole Ugly American outfit.'

'More cops?'

'Cop or not, Monsieur Renault back there was

working for Kellerman. We have to assume these two mooks are his men, too.'

'How do we get rid of them?'

'You know Paris better than I do. East and west, where will the subway get you?'

'The RER, the regional express, can get you out to Poissy and Cergy le Haut in the west, Chessy in the east – that's Disneyland.'

'And the regular Metro?'

'La Défense in the west, Porte de Vincennes and the Paris Zoo in the east.'

'Where's the closest Metro interchange, where the most lines cross?'

'Châtelet, just across from here. A few blocks away. All the main lines cross there, including the RER.'

'Then that's where we'll lose them,' said Holliday.

The Châtelet Metro station was built in 1900, and over the next century it expanded and grew up, down, and sideways, connecting the four main lines of the original Metro plus the high-speed lines of the RER located below the main lines.

The station has eleven access points, stairs, elevators, escalators, and even two moving side-walks called *'tapis roulants'* or rolling carpets. You can go north, south, east, or west, get to the air-port and any one of four major train stations, including the TGVs into Europe and under the English Channel to England, buy everything from condoms to croissants, have a glass of wine, eat *pommes frites*, or buy any one of a dozen newspapers.

At any one time during an average day in the summer there are between five and eight thousand people moving through the intricate web of platforms, corridors, and gateways into the station. Trains pull in, trains pull out, horns sound, recorded voices make announcements, beggars beg, and licensed chamber musicians play Johann Pachelbel's entire Canon. Rock ensembles do all seventy-four minutes of *Tommy*, the rock opera by The Who.

With Peggy in the lead they slipped into the Metro at one of the three entrances on avenue Victoria, bought a *carnet* of tickets next to one of the turnstiles, and started up and down a dizzying array of walkways and corridors, trying to leave their surveillance behind.

They faked taking a ride on one of the westbound trains, but got off at the last second, doubled back, and finally climbed onto a train heading for Château de Vincennes just as the doors were hissing closed. The horn gave its warbling warning, and they moved off. At the far end of the car a young woman with a clarinet started doing an excellent rendition of Benny Goodman's 'One O'Clock Jump.'

'Did they get on?' Peggy asked.

'American Tourist did, I think; three or four cars back. We ditched Bomber Jacket.'

'Presumably they'll have cell phones. They'll be in contact.'

'Where's the best place to get off?' Holliday asked.

'To leave American Tourist behind?' Peggy shrugged. 'Nation. It's the next big multiple-line station, just this side of the Périphérique, the ring road we took in from the airport, like the Beltway in D.C.'

'And after that?'

'Saint-Mandé, on the other side of the ring road.'

'What's there?'

'Old apartment buildings. Upper middle class, doctors, lawyers. There's some kind of farmers' market there; I don't know what days.'

'Taxis?'

'There should be a taxi stand right outside the Metro.'

Holliday looked up at the Metro diagram above the doors a few feet away. There were seven stations between Châtelet and Saint-Mandé.

'How long to Nation?' he asked.

'Ten minutes.'

'Saint-Mandé?'

'Three minutes more. What are you thinking?'

'Get off at Nation. Make him believe it. Then get back on again. If we shake him, great. If we don't, we get a taxi at the Saint-Mandé stop and see if we can lose him that way.'

'Okay,' she nodded.

Holliday looked at his watch. Three in the afternoon. The train was half-filled with tired looking civil service types. Men in jackets and ties, women in dresses and high heels. These people were going home.

A baguette was sticking out of a woman's shopping bag, and Holliday realized that the only thing he'd eaten since getting off the plane had been a single slightly greasy sausage roll. Neither he nor Peggy had slept since leaving Jerusalem. If they didn't find somewhere to go to ground soon they were both going to collapse.

The train pulled into Nation with a roar and shuddered to a screeching stop. The doors sucked open, and they stepped out onto the platform. The train was emptying almost completely. Three cars up they saw American Tourist, and they suddenly had a bit of luck. Somebody made a grab for the Nikon prop around the fake tourist's neck and in the process dragged American

Tourist off balance. They fell together in a tangle just as the warning horn sounded. Peggy and Holliday stepped back into the train. The doors shut, and they moved off, leaving American Tourist behind.

At Saint-Mandé they climbed up into daylight again. The farmers' market, a double row of tent-like booths set up in a parking area, was winding up. The air smelled like fresh cabbage and chicken blood. Across from the Metro exit and the farmers' market there was an intersection of two main streets with a florist on one side and a café with an awning and a red, glowing neon sign: LA TOURELLE.

They crossed to the café, picked a table where they could keep an eye on the Metro exit and sat down. A waiter came and sneered silently. They both ordered Kronenbourgs and a *sandwich jambon* with fries. The sneering waiter disappeared.

'We can't stay exposed like this for too long. We have to get off the street.'

'Another hotel?'

'If Captain Renault was really with the *Groupe d'Intervention de la Gendarmerie Nationale* he'll have the hotels covered. Every registered guest is on a police report somewhere. They've gotten even tighter since 9/11. They'll find us within hours.'

'So what do we do?' Peggy asked.

The beer and sandwiches arrived. The sneering waiter served them and then disappeared again.

'I'll think of something,' said Holliday. They began to eat.

Holliday was always fascinated by the way the French took their food so seriously. Here he was in the Parisian equivalent of a New York diner, and the food was worthy of a four-star bistro in the Village. The crusty bread was unbelievably fresh, the butter was sweet, the ham was lean, thinly sliced, and smoked to perfection, and the fries were hand-sliced and golden brown. No wonder the waiter sneered; he had a right to. He was serving the perfect sandwich to people who were used to something vaguely pinkish being slipped between two slices of Wonder Bread and sprinkled with shredded green cellulose that said it was lettuce.

Holliday looked down the long, tree-lined street on his left. According to the plaque high on the wall of the florist's across from the café it was avenue Foch. Probably named by some developer a hundred years ago hoping to confuse it with the much more prestigious avenue Foch that led away from the Arc de Triomphe on the other side of town.

This avenue Foch looked like a good, solid

middle-class place to live: trees neatly trimmed and unbroken lines of faintly Edwardian-looking apartment buildings butt-ended together to form a solid block, protected by well maintained wrought iron fences. Here and there along the row of buildings Holliday could see the gleaming brass plaques beside some of the doors discreetly advertising doctors, dentists, and maybe even a few lawyers.

Five doors down on the other side of the street a domestic drama was unfolding that caught Holliday's attention for a moment. A man in his thirties was loading up a pale blue Peugeot Partner, a compact minivan that looked vaguely cartoonish. The trunk was filled to overflowing, and he was working on the roof rack, building a precarious pile of cardboard boxes and suitcases.

The man was dressed in gray flannels and a white shirt, but the shirt had the sleeves rolled up and he wasn't wearing a tie. The shoes on his feet were open-toed sandals; a man preparing to go on vacation. The front door of the building opened and a pretty dark-haired woman appeared with three small children in tow, all girls. Two of the girls had suitcases while the youngest one had a pink overnight case wedged into a doll's baby carriage.

There was a brief argument about the baby

carriage, and the youngest girl began to cry. A moment later the second youngest started crying, too, while the oldest, a girl of about twelve or so, simply looked bored. Eventually the man in the gray flannels realized he was outnumbered four to one, and he capitulated, putting the baby carriage on the roof rack. The youngest girl, still crying, then took it upon herself to prolong the melodrama and bolted for the door of the apartment building, wailing in full voice. A drill sergeant's bark from the mother stopped her dead in her tracks.

'*Marie-Claire Allard! Viens ici im-med-i-ate-ment!*'

The little girl stood her ground for a moment. Her mother stamped her foot once. Marie-Claire realized that further resistance was useless. Head bowed, the little girl trudged down the sidewalk and climbed into the minivan, followed by her two sisters. The mother got into the passenger seat, the man got behind the wheel. The Peugeot pulled away from the curb, heading east, out of the city.

'Parenthood,' said Peggy, who'd been watching, as well. She popped the last *pomme frite* on her plate into her mouth. 'No ketchup,' she said mournfully. 'Typical.'

'You done?' Holliday asked.

'Yup,' said Peggy. 'You figured anything out yet?'

'Absolutely,' nodded Holliday. 'Little Marie-Claire Allard just gave me an idea.'

They paid the bill, then crossed avenue Foch and went down the street to number ten. They went through the main door and stepped into a marble-tiled foyer. There was a brass plate array of apartments and buzzers. They scanned the names, but there was no Allard listed.

Holliday heard a faint creaking sound. A breeze was gently moving another door at the end of the hallway. The door was inset with a panel of frosted glass. Behind it Holliday saw a square of what appeared to be natural light. A courtyard? They went down the hallway, and Holliday pushed open the door.

They stepped out onto a flagstone path in a vest-pocket garden that led to the front door of a two-story stone house with a red-tiled roof. Once upon a time the house had probably been the original number ten avenue Foch, but over the years it had become enclosed by a looming can-yon of apartments.

They went down the walk to the front door. The door was dark oak, deeply carved with deco-rative squares. The keyhole was ancient, big enough to stick an index finger into. Holliday could have picked the lock with a bent nail. He reached up to the lintel above the door and felt along it. He pulled down a huge iron key and slipped it into the lock. He turned the key and the door opened. They stepped inside.

The house was a far cry from the hotel on rue Latran. To the left was a large, paneled library with a fireplace, a giant antique globe on casters, and an enormous plasma TV nestled in a wall of books. There was a leather couch, a couple of comfortable-looking leather chairs, and a heavy oak desk that matched the front door.

A row of shuttered windows looked out onto the little garden and an old stone wall. The late-afternoon sun trickled in through the shutter slats, throwing bars of pewter light onto the dark green Persian carpet. A quick shuffle through the papers on the desk told Holliday that M. Pierre Allard was a professor of philosophy at the University of Vincennes, and Madame Allard was actually Dr. Allard, an orthodontist.

To the right of the front door there was a good-sized dining room with a state-of-the-art kitchen in the rear of the house. Upstairs there were four bedrooms, three small ones for the girls, a larger one for M. and Dr. Allard. Holliday and Peggy didn't even say good night to each other. Holliday took the bedroom with the Barbie dolls, and Peggy took the one with the posters of Coldplay on the walls. They were both asleep in minutes.

27

They woke up the next morning refreshed but a little disoriented. Holliday opened his eyes to a shelf full of Barbies staring down at him in busty, well-coiffed splendor, and Peggy found herself squeezing into her jeans under the baleful James Dean gaze of Gwyneth Paltrow's husband, Chris Martin. Once dressed, they met up in the library. Holliday was watching the big plasma TV and drinking coffee.

'There's coffee in the squeeze pot on the counter, but there's no milk,' he said. 'Madame Allard cleaned out the fridge before they headed out.'

'Are we on the news?' Peggy asked.

'Nothing on TF1 or Canal Plus. Nothing on Sky News or CNN.'

'Maybe they haven't found the body.'

'Maybe,' said Holliday. 'Or maybe the *Sûreté* just put a clamp on the networks.'

Peggy fetched herself a cup of coffee, then came back into the library and sat down in one of the big leather chairs, her eyes on the television.

There was an ad for the French-translated version of *The Lost* playing.

'Maybe we should have hightailed it out of the city yesterday,' said Peggy. 'Maybe we're trapped. Eventually the Allards are going to come back from their holiday.' Peggy's expression soured. 'I feel a little bit like Goldilocks here.'

'There won't be any baby bears coming back to taste their porridge for a while,' said Holliday. 'They had enough stuff packed into that minivan to last them for a year.' He smiled. 'Not to mention the fact that there's no porridge in the house; the French don't seem to like canned goods or frozen pizza.'

'I could use another one of those *sandwichs jambon*,' said Peggy. 'I'm famished.'

They locked up the house and went back to La Tourelle. It was nine o'clock, and the streets were jammed with traffic. They sat down at the same table they'd had the day before, and the same sneering waiter appeared with menus. Peggy chose an herb omelet, and Holliday settled on ham and eggs. They both had more coffee. Once again the food was wonderful and the service surly.

'We've got to get to La Rochelle,' said Holliday. 'But if the police are onto us they'll have the airport under surveillance and the train stations.'

'We could rent a car,' suggested Peggy.

'If they know who we are then they'll be monitoring car rental agencies, as well.'

'There has to be some way,' said Peggy. 'We can't stay in the Allards' place forever.'

They ate their breakfasts and sipped their coffee. The waiter didn't seem disposed to provide refills. Peggy looked down avenue Foch at the parked cars and the slowly moving traffic.

'Did you notice Madame Allard's business address by any chance?' Peggy said thoughtfully.

'Avenue Victor Hugo. A low number, I think. Six maybe.'

'That's only a block from the Arc de Triomphe,' said Peggy.

'So?'

'Think about it,' said Peggy. 'The Allards have a minivan. Why?'

'Because they've got three kids and a place in the country.'

'Almost guaranteed wherever those kids go to school is nearby. The University of Vincennes is only three or four miles away in Saint-Denis. They probably have a day-care center there for the faculty.'

'I repeat . . . so?'

'It means Monsieur Allard, the young professor, is probably the one who takes them to school.

In the minivan. And I don't see Dr. Allard, the woman who can afford to have her dental practice next door to the Champs-Élysées, taking the Metro to work with the rest of the sweaty petite bourgeoisie.'

'You think they have another car?'

'Almost certainly,' said Peggy. 'Her car.'

Holliday looked down the street. There were cars parked on both sides, and there were half a dozen side streets nearby.

'How are we supposed to find it? There are hundreds of cars in the neighborhood.'

'You don't watch enough television, Doc. I told you before – welcome to the digital age.'

They finished up their breakfasts and went back to the stone house hidden in the courtyard. Peggy found the keys exactly where you'd expect: in a little candy dish on a table beside the door. The keys had an electronic door opener on a Mercedes key ring. Ten minutes later, beeping the door opener every few feet, they found the lady dentist's car around the corner on rue Cart.

'Now ain't that something?' said Peggy, staring.

Parked at the curb, deep green and gleaming, was a brand-new Mercedes S Class sedan, eighty thousand dollars on four very expensive wheels. Less than an hour later, stocked up with a polystyrene cooler full of food and drink for the five-hour drive to La Rochelle, they headed out of the city, traveling southwest toward the Bay of Biscay.

They drove to Versailles, then continued south to Chartres and then Tours, navigating the length of the Loire Valley. They stopped just outside Tours for a picnic lunch by the gently flowing River Cher and then drove to Poitiers and finally to La Rochelle, arriving in the port city at three thirty in the afternoon.

The city of La Rochelle was established as a small fishing village in the year A.D. 1000, but the University of La Rochelle was so new it squeaked. Opened in 1993, the campus was ultramodern, and so were the students. The biggest faculty was Mass Communications, and the university was a correspondence school with half a dozen institutions, including SUNY in the United States. The university was located in the southern part of the city, close to the water and within a stone's throw of Minimes, once a fishing port in its own right and now an immense marina.

Dr. Valerie Duroc's office was in the Humanities building at the university, on the top floor. The room was austere to the extreme. Metal desk, metal bookcases, metal filing cabinets, and a framed photograph of an anonymous beach with palm trees at sunset that could have been the Seychelles or San Diego.

Duroc was a woman in her sixties who looked like a slightly less emaciated version of Lauren Bacall with a voice to match: throaty smoke over buckwheat honey. She had huge Bette Davis eyes, sculpted cheekbones and gray hair cut in a shaggy pageboy that looked as though she might have done it herself but which probably cost a fortune. She was wearing a wine red silk blouse, a pleated skirt, and Arche sling-back flats. She smoked unfiltered Gitanes Brunes; not quite as foul as Bernheim's Boyards, but close.

They introduced themselves and dropped Maurice Bernheim's name and then repeated their story, leaving out the mounting number of bodies, dead policemen in Paris pensions, Axel Kellerman and his father, the appropriation of the Allards' house in Paris, and the theft of their expensive Mercedes. Edited down that way the story had at least some semblance of normalcy.

Duroc lit a cigarette with a slim little gold lighter then clicked it closed. She put the lighter down on the blue and white package of Gitanes and let two wandering plumes of smoke escape slowly from the flared nostrils of her patrician nose.

'I'm afraid the Internet has given currency to rather shoddy mythologies about men like Roger de Flor,' she began. 'One can play Google like a piano keyboard and construct entire symphonies of misinformed conspiracy.' Her voice had the mid-Atlantic toneless accent of someone who has spoken English as a second language for a very long time. Holliday was willing to bet that she'd taught at an American university once upon a time.

'The truth of the matter is that Roger de Flor was nothing more than a German wine merchant. He was no Templar knight, he was no hero, and he was no warrior for God who fetched the Holy Grail from out of Jerusalem. He was a business-man, plain and simple.'

'But he did exist?'

'Certainly,' said Duroc. 'That much is borne out by the records of the Port de La Rochelle. The archives of my own family bear that out, as well.'

'Your own family?' Peggy asked, intrigued.

'The *famille Duroc* has lived in La Rochelle since the twelfth century,' she said, a hint of pride creeping into her voice. 'We are one of the oldest families in Aquitaine.' She blew out more smoke as punctuation.

Listening to her and looking at her aristocratic face Holliday could see some of the reasons for the French Revolution and the rise of a little Cor-sican nobody like Napoléon Bonaparte. There was a studied arrogance to the woman that went back for hundreds of years.

'Originally the name was de la Rochelle, but as the centuries passed it was shortened to Duroc,' the professor continued.

Holliday couldn't resist.

'They were wine merchants like de Flor?'

'They were hereditary Dukes of Aquitaine,' said Valerie Duroc a little stiffly. 'My ancestors include Edward Iron Arm and Richard the Lion-heart.'

'Crusaders presumably.'

'Indeed. One of my ancestors was William the Pious.'

'Did they lease ships from de Flor's merchant fleet?'

'Of course. By that time de Flor was the largest shipper of wine in France. He even had royal warrants to bring wine to England.'

'So there is a connection between the two families then.'

'In a business sense. I doubt if you could transport anything during those times without some connection to Roger de Flor.'

Duroc glanced at her watch.

'It's almost four o'clock,' she said, smiling. 'Coffee break time. Would you and Miss Black-stock care to join me?'

They walked across the virtually deserted campus and through the new developments around Le Lac de la Sole to a restaurant-bar overlooking the Minimes marina called Les Soeurs Dogan. They found a table on the patio and sat down. Duroc lit another cigarette. She ordered a licorice-flavored pastis. Not a coffee break at all. Holliday and Peggy ordered beer.

They sat in the bright afternoon sun and looked out over the forest of masts in the marina to the ancient stone breakwaters of the *vieux port* and beyond to the Bay of Biscay and the open sea. Gulls whirled and screeched. A breeze made the taut lines on the sailboats hum, and under it all was the steady heartbeat of the breaking sea.

It wasn't hard to imagine this place a thousand years ago, the sailboats gone, the port filled with lateen caravels, multi-oared galleys and tough, stumpy looking little cogs making ready for sea. Some ships bound for England, some to Lisbon, and some to Gibraltar and finally the Holy Land. The man who owned such a fleet would have had a great deal of power. A Duke of Aquitaine who was also a Templar in partnership with such a man would have represented a serious threat to the Catholic Church. Things were beginning to come together.

'What happened to de Flor?'

'He was assassinated in Turkey in 1305,' said Duroc, sipping her milky, banana-colored drink.

'On whose order?'

'Some say Michael IX Palaiologos, the young emperor of Anatolia. Others credit Pope Clement V.'

Clement was Bishop of Poitiers, which included La Rochelle, and the man who ordered the arrest and execution of the Templars two years later in 1307 – a new broom sweeping clean, and also managing to absolve the almost bankrupt Philip IV, king of France, from his enormous debt to the Templar banks. A circle closed.

'It sounds like this Pope Clement really didn't like de Flor,' commented Peggy.

'By then the Templars had too much power and too much wealth for their own good,' replied Valerie Duroc. 'It was the Holy Office of the Inquisition that saw fit to disband them.'

'As in the Spanish Inquisition?' Peggy asked. 'Burning people at the stake, that kind of thing?'

'Only in part,' answered Duroc. 'The Inquisition was much more than that. In effect it was the CIA of the Catholic Church, seeking out not just heretics among the general public but dissenters within the Church itself.' She shook her head. 'If there is one thing the Catholic Church abhors it is change.'

'CIA?' Holliday said. 'Isn't that a bit extreme?'

'Not at all,' said Duroc. 'The Dominicans, the so-called Hounds of God, actually sent spies to infiltrate other orders. Groups of papal assassins have been known since the time of the Borgias; during the Renaissance religious murder became a fine art. In more modern times there was the institution known as *Sodalitium Pianum*, the Fellowship of Pius, an organization within the Vatican that sought out officials within the Church teaching the so-called condemned doctrines.

'In France the group was obscurely called *La Sapinière*, the Tree Farm – much like the CIA's training school in Maryland called "The Farm." It was such an organization that masterminded the flight of SS officers through the ratlines of Rome and funneled black operation funds out of the Vatican Bank during the 1970s.' Duroc paused. 'Oh, no, Monsieur Holliday, the intelligence networks of the Holy See are very much alive.'

Which explained the murderous priest in Jerusalem, but not why he was there in the first place. What possible secret could the Templar sword contain that would interest the Vatican a thousand years later? Axel Kellerman might be searching for war booty and his father's legacy, but the Roman Catholic Church had more money than it knew what to do with.

Not money – power.

'What about Professor Bernheim's idea about Saint-Émilion and the cave?' Peggy asked. 'Is it worth a look?'

'Rubbish,' said Valerie Duroc, stubbing out her cigarette. 'Saint-Émilion is almost two hundred kilometers from here – a hundred and twenty-five miles. During the Middle Ages that would represent at least a week's travel. The caves of the hermit St. Émilion have been receiving pilgrims since the eighth century, and the underground galleries have been used to store wine for at least as long. It's hard to imagine a worse place to hide a treasure.' She laughed.

'Maurice has a fanciful imagination; he would have made a wonderful lawyer but a very bad scientist. He tends to bend facts to his hypothesis rather than the other way around.' She shook her head again. 'No, Monsieur Holliday, I am afraid your search for the mythical treasure of Roger de Flor ends here in La Rochelle.'

Holliday looked out over the marina and sipped his beer. Valerie Duroc lit another cigarette and leaned back in her chair. Peggy looked depressed. A huge yacht lumbered past them, big diesels throbbing. Two unbelievably beautiful women lounged on the afterdeck in their bikinis. The name on the ship's transom was picked out in black and gold:

LA ROCHA
PONTA DELGADA

'La Rocha,' he murmured to himself.

'Pardon?' Duroc said.

'The name La Rocha.'

'Portuguese,' replied the French professor. 'The same as mine actually. It means "The Rock."'

'Where's Ponta Delgada?' Holliday asked, watching as the yacht motored out through the breakwater entrance.

'The island of São Miguel in the Azores,' said Duroc. 'It's the main way station for sailboats crossing the Atlantic.'

'Didn't the Templars settle in the Azores after they were disbanded?' Holliday asked, vaguely recalling something about it from his reading on the subject.

'They exiled themselves to Portugal and called themselves the Knights of Christ. The ships Columbus used to cross the Atlantic carried the Catalan Cross on their sails.'

'Could de Flor have reached the Azores with his fleet, or at least a single ship?'

'Certainly,' said Duroc. 'With ease.'

28

They drove the big Mercedes south, following the long azure curve of the Bay of Biscay. They flinched a little every time they saw one of the Gendarmerie Nationale's blue Subaru chase cars speeding by but traveled without incident into the Basque Country and the rugged coastal mountains of the Pyrénées Atlantiques, crossing the border at Hendaye with barely a ripple. The only visible sign that they had left one country for another was the change in highway signs from blue to black on white.

Gone were the days of barbed wire and Franco's bully boys armed with machine guns poking through your luggage; now there were only blue and gold Eurostar welcome signs and the occasional multilingual tourist information kiosk.

They drove through the wine country of Navarre and west across the plains of old Castile and finally to Salamanca and the old battlefields Holliday had only read about in Bernard Cornwell's almost addictive Sharpe novels. They crossed the border into Portugal with even less fanfare than there had been crossing into Spain and continued south through the old capital of Coimbra then took the toll route down to Lisbon. The entire trip took two full days, and during that time there wasn't the slightest indication that they were being pursued by the police or anyone else.

In Lisbon they booked a flight to the Azores on SATA and flew out of Portela Airport the following day. Holliday had picked up a Bradt guide to the Azores at their hotel the previous afternoon and had been reading it ever since.

'Of course this whole thing could be a wild-goose chase you know,' said Peggy. The Airbus A310 had reached cruising altitude, and they were heading out over the Atlantic, the European Continent falling away behind them. 'Grandpa could have been chasing fireflies.' She shrugged her shoulders. 'Maybe the Duroc woman is right; the search ended in La Rochelle.'

'I don't think Henry Granger ever chased a firefly in his life,' answered Holliday. 'It simply wasn't in his nature. He was a historian; he gathered facts, checked sources, did his research, developed hypotheses, and constructed theories.'

'In other words he did it by the book.'

'That's right,' nodded Holliday.

'But it doesn't make sense,' argued Peggy. 'He had the sword for decades, and he kept it hidden.

Then all of a sudden he gets in touch with Carr-Harris and goes running off to England.'

'And then Germany,' added Holliday.

'Assume that means Kellerman,' said Peggy. 'So what got him going after all those years?'

'Maybe it wasn't his interest,' said Holliday. 'Maybe it was someone else's interest in him.'

'Like Broadbent?'

'The lawyer?' Holliday said. He shrugged. 'I think Broadbent's a latecomer, nothing more than a hired gun. I think Kellerman's people used him. That story about his father and the sword was completely bogus. He was fishing for information.'

'So you think Kellerman is behind this?' Peggy asked.

'It's either him or this *Sodalitium Pianum* or whatever Duroc called her Vatican assassins.'

'You believe her?' Peggy said a little skeptically. 'We're getting into grassy-knoll-people-going-around-with-aluminum-foil-on-their-heads-to-keep-out-the-cosmic-rays territory here, don't you think?'

The stewardess came around with a cart loaded down with cheese sandwiches wrapped up in plastic and cans of Fanta Orange. They took one of each. The cheese tasted like something you'd use for an insole. They were a long way from La Tourelle, the little café in Paris.

'Did you know that Fanta was invented in Nazi Germany by a chemist from Atlanta to replace Coca-Cola?' Holliday said. 'They made it from saccharin, scrapings from apple cider presses, and cheese curds.'

'And that is relevant how?' Peggy asked, frowning at the familiar can in her hand.

'It just shows how truth really can be stranger than fiction,' he explained. 'The Borgias did exist, and some of them really were assassins just like she said.'

'But really, secret societies, Doc? Come on.'

'Why not?' Holliday said. 'A secret society is really nothing more than a network, like the Mafia is a network, or the Bush family and Skull and Bones at Yale. Put it in the right context, and you've got something that Oprah would approve of.'

'Dead priests in the streets of Jerusalem would never wind up being on her approved list of things to see on your next summer vacation,' said Peggy with a snort.

'The point is, things like Duroc's *Sodalitium Pianum* or *La Sapinière* really exist. That priest was sent to kill us, there's no disputing that. He was an assassin. Even the Portuguese have secret societies – the *Carbonária* was a military group of Freemasons who were responsible for killing King Carlos I back in the early nineteen hundreds.'

'Another history lesson, Doc?' Peggy warned.

'Sorry.' He took a sip of the Fanta, thought about cheese curds and Nazis and put the can down on his seat table.

'The Azores is a long way to go on the basis of a name you saw on the back of a boat,' said Peggy, staring out the window at a fleet of fluffy white clouds sailing by, all sails set.

'It's more than that,' responded Holliday. 'I'm doing this the way Uncle Henry would. Make the hypothesis fit the facts, not the other way around. When you get enough facts together to make an overwhelming case then you go from hypothesis to theory, and the only way to prove the theory is by –'

'Finding the treasure that Roger de Flor took away from Castle Pelerin,' completed Peggy.

'Which is why we're going to the Azores,' said Holliday.

'You have enough facts to prove the hypothesis?' Peggy asked.

'A lot of suppositions at least.'

'So suppose away.' Peggy grinned.

'Suppose you're a pirate. Where do you bury your treasure?'

'A desert island.'

'Not a hermit's cave in France or a busy port like La Rochelle.'

'Why not leave it at Castle Pelerin?' Peggy argued.

'Because like Jerusalem itself, you have no idea of how long it's going to be before the place is overrun by the godless infidels. Pirates bury treasure to keep it away from prying eyes and sticky fingers.'

'But maybe it's all smoke and mirrors,' argued Peggy. 'Like I said before, what if the whole idea of a Templar treasure is a myth?'

'They dug up the Temple Mount for nine years; they were looking for something. The stories say it was the Ark of the Covenant, but who knows?'

'People dig for treasure all the time,' said Peggy. 'I used to do it in Grandpa's backyard, looking for artifacts from the Cattaraugus Indians. I never found so much as an arrowhead.'

'Templar *treasure* is one thing. Templar *wealth* is another. They were unbelievably rich; that's established fact. It's also fact that they liquidated their assets shortly before they were disbanded. Those assets went somewhere. The money is out there.'

'And you think it's in the Azores?'

'It fits. For one thing, they're the nearest thing to desert islands close enough to La Rochelle to be useful. The Catalan Atlas shows a few of the islands in 1375, but colonization didn't really begin for another hundred years or so. According to the guide I just read, Corvo, the smallest of the islands, wasn't discovered until the middle of the fifteenth century. Even now only about three hundred people live there.'

'Okay,' nodded Peggy. 'I'll give you the desert island.'

'What?' Holliday laughed. 'Now we're doing *Deal or No Deal*?'

'Something like that,' said Peggy. 'I need more proof.'

'Kellerman,' responded Holliday.

'What's Kellerman's connection with the Azores?'

'A ship called the MS *Schwabenland*. It operated under Himmler's orders for the *Ahnenerbe*, looking for evidence of their so-called Aryan ancestors in South America and Antarctica in particular. The ship operated out of the Azores before the war and even during, even though Portugal was supposedly neutral. Maybe one of the people on the *Schwabenland* got a whiff of a Templar treasure somewhere on the Azores, and the mythology grew from there.'

'Thin, but barely possible, I suppose,' she said. 'What about Duroc's Vatican assassins?'

'Settling old scores?'

'Really thin,' said Peggy. 'Can't you do any better than that?'

'At a guess I'd say it probably had something to do with keeping secrets. The Vatican has been getting a lot of bad press recently, and with a German Pope on the papal throne they'd be particularly vulnerable to bringing up old ghosts connected with Nazi Germany.'

'So that's it?'

'Pretty much, except for the most important thing.'

'Which is?'

'Uncle Henry again.'

'What about him?'

'He never started anything without finishing it, not in his whole life,' said Holliday emphatically. 'Everything we've done so far has been at his direction. He didn't put that sword where he knew we'd find it for no reason. He *wanted* us to do this. He planned on it. He knew we'd follow in his footsteps no matter where the trail led.' Holliday held up his hand and counted off the fingers one by one: 'England, Germany, Italy, Jerusalem, France, and now the Azores. It's the last link in the chain.'

'I still don't get why he waited more than half a century to start this wild-goose chase,' said Peggy. 'If he'd known all this for all that time you'd think he would have found the treasure a long time ago.'

'I know,' said Holliday. 'I can't figure that out either.'

Two hours later the big, wide-body jet landed at Ponta Delgada Airport on the island of São Miguel. It was small, fewer than fifty thousand people, a city of churches and fine seventeenth- and eighteenth-century buildings reflecting the island chain's rich past as the staging base for virtually anyone hoping to reach the riches of the New World. For the most part it was now a city of tourists.

They booked in to the Hotel do Colégio in the town center, ate a tasty bouillabaisse of various unidentified bits of seafood to counteract the cheese sandwich and the Fanta, and then went to bed, reconvening at the breakfast buffet the following morning. Once again the weather outside was perfect: clear skies, bright sunshine, and a cool onshore breeze coming in off the bay.

'So what's the plan?' Peggy asked, starting on her second cinnamon roll. 'Get some spades and start digging up the beach?'

'Caves,' said Holliday. He sipped his *chávena quente* – black coffee, very strong. 'It's the only thing that makes sense.'

'Are there any caves in the Azores?'

'Lots of them,' said Holliday. 'The islands are all volcanic; there are lava tubes everywhere.'

'So how do we figure out where to look?'

'Logic,' Holliday answered. 'Most of the caves here are famous; they even had a convention of cave explorers here once or so the guidebook says.'

'Ergo?'

'Ergo we find the caves that no one's ever explored before, which means going to Corvo, the smallest of the islands and the most remote.' Holliday smiled. 'Not to mention the fact that Corvo is also known as *"Pequeno Rocha,"* the "Little Rock." '

'So how do we get to this little rock of yours?'

'There's a plane you can take, but I'd rather see it from the sea the way Roger de Flor must have. We need a boat.'

29

The Azores are a volcanic archipelago of nine major islands in the North Atlantic a thousand miles from Lisbon and twelve hundred miles from St. John's, Newfoundland. During the age of New World exploration between the fifteenth and seventeenth centuries, the string of islands provided a perfect way station for ships heading west or returning to Europe on the easterly trade winds. There are three major population centers on the islands: Ponta Delgada on the island of São Miguel, Angra do Heroísmo on the island of Terceira, and Horta on the island of Faial. There has been volcanic activity in the Azores as recently as a hundred years ago.

The westernmost island in the group is Corvo, barely six and a half square miles in size. There is one small village on the island, Vila Nova do Campo, with a population of approximately three hundred people. Corvo, the Little Rock, is essentially nothing more than a collapsed volcanic cone or 'caldera.' The island's only occupation is farming. Half of the time the island is shrouded in fog, the caldera hidden by low-lying clouds. The northernmost end of the island, hammered by an unrelenting Atlantic, is a ring of surf-shattered cliffs rising up the steep slopes of the old volcano.

There is one guesthouse with seven rooms, one restaurant, one bar, and an open-air barbecue which shares a small walled-in pasture with a motley, ill-tempered herd of goats. Corvo is fifteen nautical miles from Flores, its immediate neighbor, and a hundred and thirty-five miles from Horta, the nearest town of any size.

On the afternoon of their first full day in the Azores Holliday and Peggy took the short-hop commuter flight from Ponta Delgada to Faial and went searching for a boat to take them to Corvo the following morning.

Horta turned out to be a hilly little town of fifteen thousand built around two small bays that make up the port and divided by yet another volcanic crater. There is a sports bar, some appropriately charming restaurants and craft shops, and the occasional second-level cruise ship snuggled up to the fairly modern concrete pier and breakwater.

The most notable visitor to Horta was Mark Twain, who stayed there briefly in the early stages of his long journey to Jerusalem in 1867. Setting foot in the town he was immediately assaulted by a throng of barefoot beggar children who haunted his every step for the next two days. He never came back.

The boat, when they found it, was an old Chris-Craft 38' Commander from the sixties, and looked eerily like the raggedy vessel piloted by Humphrey Bogart in the movie version of Ernest Hemingway's *To Have and Have Not*. It smelled of fish and beer, needed a paint job and was named the *San Pedro*.

Her owner and captain was a man named Manuel Rivero Tavares. Tavares smelled like the boat and looked like a bowling ball with a two-day growth of stubble, but by all reports he was the best and most knowledgeable charter-boat captain in Horta.

'Why you want to go to Corvo?' Tavares asked. 'No food there, no hootchie-hootchie nightclub with Michael Jackson. No nothing. Not even no fish.' According to the men drinking in Peter's Sports Bar in town, Capitano Tavares was the finest white marlin fisherman in all of the Azores.

'We don't want food or hootchie-hootchie nightclubs, and we don't want Michael Jackson,' said Holliday. 'We want to see it from the ocean the way the old explorers did.'

'Old explorers are dead,' replied Capitano Tavares. 'All of them.'

'I know that,' said Holliday. 'How much to take us to Corvo?'

'If you are not liking hootchie-hootchie and not liking fishing what will we talk about? A long way to Corvo. One hundred thirty-five nautical miles. Seven, eight hours to get there, seven, eight hours to get back. Long time.' The captain didn't look happy.

'We don't have to talk about anything,' sighed Holliday. 'How much?'

'Manuel Tavares likes to talk,' said the captain, frowning.

'How much?'

'A thousand euro.'

'Five hundred.'

'Seven hundred and fifty.'

'Seven hundred.'

'You will pay the gasoline?'

'Yes.'

'Beer?'

'Yes.'

'Seven hundred twenty-five. I cook you an' your little sister-girlie nice fish stew.'

'Deal.'

Two hours later, stocked with food and a case of the captain's favorite Sagres Branca beer, they motored slowly out of the port, turning around the long breakwater then swinging sharply around the remains of the old volcano before heading west along the rugged coastline of the island, bearing a little north into the open sea, heading toward Corvo.

Peggy had taken Holliday's Bradt guide and was sunning herself on the forward deck while Holliday sat beside Capitano Tavares in the companion chair on the flybridge high above the main deck of the boat. The *San Pedro* was doing a steady eighteen knots, muscling easily through the gentle swell. The sea was dark blue, almost a steely black. A few petrels whirled and dipped in their wake, but except for the birds they were alone on the ocean.

Far ahead on the distant horizon Holliday could see a broadening line of dark clouds gathering. They were heading into a storm. It occurred to him that the weather had been absolutely perfect ever since he'd left West Point. The closest thing to a problem had been the fog approaching Friedrichshafen. From the looks of the sky ahead, that was about to change.

'Storm coming,' commented Holliday.

Tavares took the bottle of beer out of its polystyrene holder in front of him and sucked on the neck for a few seconds. He gave a little belch and put the bottle back in its holder.

'Long time yet,' he said. 'Manuel Tavares knows

these things.' He turned and smiled. He poked himself in the eye. 'Captain Jack Sparrow has no need to worry, yes?' He laughed at his own joke. 'That Johnny Depp, he's a funny guy, no?' He laughed again. 'What kind of name is that – Depp? Something you put in the hair to make it shiny, yes? Depp! Ha!'

'You know Corvo?' Holliday asked.

'Do I know Corvo! Of course! I was born there! Corvo is one cattle, a big fat brown one with udders like Scotland bag flutes. Lying down in the grass. Looking out at the ocean, chewing grass. Waiting for the milk. That is Corvo. Maybe one goat, as well.'

'Are there any stories of treasure?' Holliday asked.

'Sure! Sure!' nodded Tavares. 'Moby Dick!'

'The whale?'

'Yes, of course. It was written in the book about Corvo. The courage of her men. "Call me Ishmael," yes? There was a statue. A man with a finger pointing west to Boston, the Holy Virgin. A whaler. Who knows? A statue and a pot of gold coins. Very old. Phoenicia, yes? You know it?'

'You're kidding, right?' Holliday said.

Phoenicia was the ancient name for Canaan. Phoenician coins had been found in the old foundations of Castle Pelerin. It was too much of a coincidence. Myths turned to reality, legend to fact, like Schliemann discovering Troy.

'No! No! True, swear to God! Coins. Found in fifteenth century by a priest named Gao, I think. Ponta do Marco, the very edge of the world! I will take you there!'

Bless you, Uncle Henry, Holliday thought. Somehow he'd managed to make the right choice; the odyssey continued.

The weather worsened with each passing hour. The dark smudge of clouds staining the western horizon became a black, roiled wall of thunderclouds, their flattened undersides stretched out like hammered anvils blocking out the sun and the blue sky. Peggy came in from her sunbathing, then Holliday and finally the captain climbed down from the flybridge. All three of them huddled in the protection of the lower helm overhang as the blustering wind blew up the waves into a frothing mass of spume-tossed peaks and valleys. The *San Pedro* continued to hammer forward, the old fiberglass hull crashing through the heaving swell, forcing itself along the line Manuel Rivero Tavares had decreed.

It began to rain. The drops fell in sheets as one gale after another roared over them. Peggy finally disappeared into the forward cabin while Holliday remained with Tavares at the helm.

'How long will it last?' Holliday yelled into the Portuguese captain's ear.

'At least through the night, perhaps longer,' he answered. 'There is no point in making for Corvo; the harbor at Flores is a better choice.'

'You're the captain,' said Holliday. 'Whatever you say.'

Tavares nodded and spun the wheel. They turned a little further west, away from their goal. An hour later Flores came in sight, and an hour after that the *San Pedro* reached the tiny harbor of Santa Cruz das Flores, a single concrete pier in the lee of a tiny village huddled at the base of a battery of rugged hills.

The buildings of the village were rough lava stone mortared together and topped with the standard Portuguese style terra-cotta tiles. They found a restaurant in the town square and had a meal of octopus stewed in wine, rabbit stew, and fresh-baked bread and creamery butter.

After the meal Tavares disappeared for a few minutes, returning with an elderly man in tow whom he introduced as Dr. Emilio Silva. Dr. Silva wore enormous rubber boots, a completely transparent raincoat, and what appeared to be a very old-fashioned military uniform underneath.

He smoked a long, fuming clay pipe and appeared to be heading toward a hundred years of age, his face a wrinkled map of a long, arduous life. His eyes were clear, however, and when he spoke his voice, though as wispy and cracked as his face, was firm and coherent. According to Tavares the doctor had lived in the islands all of his life, and anyone or anything he didn't know wasn't worth knowing.

He told the story of the statue and the coins, again with Tavares as his translator. The man's name was Damien de Goes, not Gao as Tavares had thought, and the statue had been of a bare-headed 'Moorish' man – presumably black or at least swarthy – wearing a cape and seated on a horse, his right arm raised and pointing to the west. At his feet there had been a cauldron or kettle containing a hoard of treasure including five bronze and two gold coins from Cyrene in North Africa and from the Phoenician colony of Carthage, now modern Tunisia. Remarkably detailed for a myth or an old wives' tale.

As the old man recounted the story, Holliday remembered an old map he'd once seen in a museum drawn by the Pizzigano brothers, a team of cartographers working in the early 1300s – long before the Azores had actually been discovered and almost two hundred years before Columbus.

The Pizzigano brothers, illustrating an ancient

Phoenician myth, showed a man on horseback at the edge of their map, just about where the Azores would be located. The man was pointing westward, and a medallion at his feet warned that anyone venturing further would be swallowed up in 'The Sea of Fog and Darkness' – not a bad description of the North Atlantic when it was in bad humor.

Interestingly the same 'sea of fog and darkness' term had once been used by a Moorish Muslim cartographer in Spain named Khashkhash ibn Saeed ibn Aswad to describe a voyage made in the ninth century – a full five hundred years before Columbus. Even the name of the place where the statue had been found on the island of Corvo rang true: Ponta do Marco – the boundary marker – go no further. X marks the spot.

'He says,' said Tavares, continuing to translate, 'that there is a man on Corvo who we should see if we have any more questions.' He turned to the old man again. *'Como o senhor te chama?'* What is his name?

'Rodrigues,' said the old man clearly, his yellow teeth clamped around the stem of the long clay pipe. *'Helder Rodrigues. Clerigo.'*

'A priest,' said Tavares. 'He says the man you should see is a priest.'

30

Capitano Tavares ferried them across to Corvo
the following morning. The day was moody, the
skies full of broken clouds that scudded low on
the horizon over a choppy, restless sea. The *San
Pedro* slapped the small waves sullenly, the movement jarring. Corvo was visible from the time
they rounded the breakwater at Santa Cruz das
Flores. It stood like a massive cupcake, one side
slumped in the pan, a single volcanic cone worn
by a million years of winds and storms, shoulder-
ing its way through the eons, the fire that had created it long since cooled, the steep slopes covered
with a thick carpet of greenery, its giant cliffs like
the massive bow of an ancient ship.

Barely fifteen miles separated Flores from its
smaller sister; the voyage in the *San Pedro* lasted
barely forty minutes. The town of Corvo clung to
the sloped, southernmost portion of the island, a
scattering of red-tile-roofed houses wedged in
around a straight concrete pier with no breakwater.

Instead of docking, Tavares guided the old

Chris-Craft north, following the steep coastline away from the town.

'Where are we going?' Peggy asked as the town receded in their wake.

'Around the island. A few minutes only. I show you Ponta do Marco. End of the world.'

They continued northward, the coast steepening to dark, plunging cliffs of volcanic basalt, the sea breaking in huge shuddering waves at the bottom. There was no middle ground, not even a rocky beach. There was the sea, and then there was the land, an irresistible force meeting an immovable object, one trying to wear down the other in a never-ending battle that had already lasted millions of years.

Holliday thought about the sword and the man who might have carried it. Was this his destination? Was this lonely island in the middle of an even lonelier sea the final resting place of the great treasure that had been hidden since the time of Christ beneath the Temple of Solomon in the holy city of Jerusalem? Or had it all been nothing more than a story, a fancy like King Arthur and his sword, Excalibur?

Standing there, feet braced against the rocking of the boat, it occurred to Holliday that perhaps it didn't matter. The sword, the story behind it, and the long journey were enough to have changed and molded events and men's lives across two thousand years, and a story told that long and with that effect had to have some meaning behind it. Arthur and Excalibur may well have been nothing but childish myth, but it was a myth that had moved millions and changed lives.

'You've got that thousand-mile-stare expression on your face, Doc,' said Peggy, standing at his side. She smiled fondly at him. 'Looking into history again?'

'Something like that,' he nodded.

Tavares spun the wheel, and the *San Pedro* heeled over slightly as they turned around a rocky headland. He pointed.

'There!' he said. 'Ponta do Marco. The end of the world!'

They were at the northernmost tip of the island. The caldera of the old volcano rose like a jagged green wall, slightly terraced into narrow overlapping ledges that ran directly down into the crashing sea. The heights of the caldera were shrouded in gray rags of cloud and mist.

Standing in front of this looming wall were three black slabs of rock, each one lower than the first, their spires sharp and splintered like giant flakes of obsidian. The three formations each stood separate from the others, the caldera cliff rising like spidery stone fingers clawing up from the sea. The base of the spires was hidden in deep shadow and skirts of rising foam, but for a second Holliday thought he saw a darker patch that might have been the narrow entrance to a cavern.

'The statue stood at the top of the black pillar!' Tavares yelled, pointing upward. Holliday stared.

The foot of the three bony fingers was a froth of crashing surf that threw up enormous curtains of foaming spray, the sound like echoing thunderclaps. Tavares was right; it did look just like the end of the world. Beyond it there was nothing but empty sea. The captain threw the throttles into neutral.

The engines surged and whined and the *San Pedro* bobbed unhappily on the rolling chop racing under her hull to throw itself onto the great black rocks directly in front of them a few hundred yards away. Peggy was starting to look a little green.

'I thought I saw the mouth of a cave!' Holliday yelled, raising his voice over the booming surf.

'Perhaps!' Tavares shrugged. 'No one has ever landed here! There is no beach, only the cliffs!' He shook his head. 'A dangerous place. The home of the great beast god, Adamastor!'

Holliday hadn't heard that name in years. Once, when he was no more than a child, Uncle Henry had told him a bedtime story from memory that had scared him out of his wits. He could still hear his uncle's rich voice, rolling out of the darkness of his bedroom like the surf upon this broken shore:

> *Even as I spoke, an immense shape*
> *Materialized in the night air,*
> *Grotesque and of enormous stature*
> *With heavy jowls, and an unkempt beard,*
> *Scowling from shrunken, hollow eyes,*
> *Its complexion earthy and pale,*
> *Its hair grizzled and matted with clay,*
> *Its mouth coal black, teeth yellow with decay –*
> > *Adamastor!*

It was the kind of thing that would have given Edgar Allan Poe food for thought. Much later Holliday had learned that Henry's tale was from the epic Portuguese poem *The Lusiads*, which contained the famous threat: 'Defy me not for I am that vast, secret promontory you Portuguese call the Cape of Storms . . .'

He stared at the black spires and the foaming surf, trying to see in his mind's eye a Templar ship and its precious cargo. Had it somehow managed to find a safe landfall here? If that were true it wasn't hard to imagine that no other ship had followed for the last eight hundred years. The sword's secret would have been safe in the protection of these bleak, stone monsters and the pounding sea.

'*Bastante,*' said Tavares. Enough. He engaged the big twin diesels and pushed the throttles forward, spinning the wheel and turning away from the rocky headland. A few minutes later and they rounded the island onto the lee side. Almost instantly the sea calmed, and the wind died as they chugged their way along the opposite coastline. The cliffs here were less precipitous, the slopes of the caldera thick with clover.

The further south they went the easier the slopes became, and eventually Holliday could see Tavares's fat brown cows in the little fields, legs tucked beneath them, staring blankly out to the ragged, uneasy sea. Less than half an hour later they rounded the south cape and came in sight of the little village once again. More storm clouds were gathering as Tavares guided the *San Pedro* toward the wharf.

'I radioed ahead last night,' said the heavyset captain. 'My cousin Sebastian will rent you his motorcycle. Only twenty euro plus gas. He is waiting on the dock. He will give you directions to find this priest, Rodrigues.'

'You'll wait for us?'

'I'll be here until an hour before sunset. Then I

go back to Flores for the night. I do not like the look of this weather.'

'All right,' agreed Holliday.

Sebastian Brigada, Tavares's cousin, was a man in his thirties, tall, dark-haired with a big caterpillar mustache and caterpillar eyebrows. He smoked a pipe, wore an old tweed cap and giant rubber boots. As promised he was waiting for them on the dock with his motorcycle, a rickety old Casal with a square gas tank, almost no instruments, and a homemade bullet-nose sidecar fitted with its own windscreen and two skinny bicycle tires on a fragile-looking axle.

'No way,' said Peggy, looking at the sidecar. 'You expect me to ride in *that*?'

'Not much choice.' Holliday shrugged. 'It's the only game in town.' He dug into his wallet and handed Sebastian Brigada a twenty-euro note. Brigada nodded his thanks and handed over the bike. As it turned out the directions to Rodrigues's house were simple enough since there was only one road and one turnoff. You either followed the branch that led to the rim of the old crater or the branch that took you down to the crater floor. Rodrigues lived in a cottage at the end of the branch leading to the crater floor.

Holliday thanked Tavares's cousin once again and climbed onto the bike. Peggy eased herself into the sidecar and sat down. Brigada showed Holliday how to switch on the engine, and a few moments later they were chattering off down the island's single paved road, tiny pocket-handkerchief fields on either side, divided at irregular intervals by dry stone walls that looked as old as time. Ahead of them the sweeping slope of the volcano rose up into the sullen mist. A few big shearwater gulls rode the air currents like shifting ghosts, and a few of Tavares's fat brown cows lounged in the heather, but except for that the landscape was silent and empty. There seemed to be no people and no houses anywhere, and there was no traffic on the unmarked one-lane road at all.

'Pretty spooky,' commented Peggy over the clattering of the old motorcycle. 'Hound of the Baskervilles time.'

She was right, thought Holliday: the whole island had the sinister, primordial tension of a place like Dartmoor. Man had no business in a place like this; it was a land of bad dreams and banshees. He shivered. An old wives' tale – somebody walking over his grave.

They followed the road upward for another mile. Finally they reached a crossroads, one section of the road rising away into the fog on their right, the other fork dropping away on their left.

Holliday braked, and they came to a stop. There was a plain sign pointing down the lower road that said simply CALDEIRÃO – the crater.

'Why would a priest live out here in the middle of nowhere?' Peggy asked from the sidecar.

'Only one way to find out,' answered Holliday. He put the bike in gear, eased off on the brake and opened the throttle. They turned down the road leading to the crater. Five minutes later Holliday slowed and stopped again as they climbed a final hill. There, below them, almost a thousand feet deep, lay the bottom of the crater, a gigantic punchbowl amphitheatre at least two miles across, the walls rising, green and steeply sloping, on three sides. At the very bottom of the crater were two small lakes, and between them on a connecting strip of pasture they could see a small cottage surrounded by a stone wall. The priest's house.

Suddenly, out of the rags and tatters of fog and cloud there was an alien sound: the steady drumming beat of an aircraft engine. A few seconds later Holliday and Peggy spotted the source of the noise – a big Cessna Caravan flying low over the caldera, looping south almost directly overhead.

The colors of the aircraft's livery were green and red, not the simple blue on white of SATA airline; not a scheduled flight – a charter. Holliday looked up uneasily as the airplane droned off into the distance. He tried to shake off the feeling of apprehension; the flight was probably just a group of tourists on a day-tripper outing to the little island. He dropped the motorcycle into gear with a bone-jarring clank, and they headed down into the crater, engine coughing and rattling as they went.

The cottage was small and typically Portuguese: whitewashed lava stone and mortar, gently sloping roof of terra-cotta tiles, shuttered windows bracketing a sun-worn door of bleached planking. A man stood in the doorway, watching them approach, one hand up, shading his eyes.

He was very tall, at least six five and slightly stooped. His shoulders were as broad as a stevedore's, and he was barrel-chested with heavy arms and massive, stoneworker's hands. His face was square, the eyes deep-set with dark rings around them. He was clean-shaven, the dark stubble flecked with gray. His hair was thick and white as snow. The man was wearing faded twill trousers and a rough cotton shirt, faded and thin. He wore sandals on his feet. At a guess he was in his early sixties and clearly very fit.

Holliday braked, and the old motorcycle ground to a halt on the dark gravel path in front of the cottage. He climbed out of the saddle, and

Peggy levered herself out of the sidecar. The tall man in the doorway smiled and stepped forward, his hand extended. He spoke.

'Doctor Holliday, Miss Blackstock. I've been expecting you. Welcome to my home. My name is Helder Rodrigues.'

'You know who we are?' Peggy asked, surprised.

'Of course,' said the tall, stooped man. 'Very little goes on in Corvo that I am not privy to.'

'You said you were expecting us,' said Holliday.

'Yes, for some time now,' nodded Rodrigues. When he spoke it was without accent, the voice cultured and educated. The white-haired man might live in a cottage in the middle of nowhere, but it was clear that in his time he had traveled the world.

He stepped aside and gestured.

'Please, come in,' he said. 'I was just making coffee for us.'

They stepped inside. The interior of the cottage was plainly furnished. An open fireplace stood at one end of the single room, and an old-fashioned trundle bed was fitted into the wall opposite. A very old-looking double-barreled shotgun hung on pegs above the fireplace. In front of the hearth was a large, oval braided rug, the once-bright twisted rags faded to soft pastels. There was a plain wooden table in the middle of the room with four chairs around it. Kitchen things were arranged on a counter under one window and a small desk and a shelf of books beneath the other.

There were a few electrical fixtures, but most of the lights seemed to be glass-chimneyed, oil-fed hurricane lanterns. Holliday hadn't seen any electrical wires on the road so the cottage had to be powered with a generator. There was no television and no obvious telephone anywhere. A very old-looking dark brown Bakelite radio sat on the windowsill.

Rodrigues indicated that they should sit down, and then busied himself finding cups and pouring coffee from the old enameled pot hanging over the coals in the open fireplace.

'Expecting us for some time?' Holliday said. 'How's that, Father Rodrigues?'

'Not Father, Doctor Holliday, not for many years. Just call me Helder.'

'Why a Dutch name like Helder?' Peggy asked.

The big man shrugged.

'The Dutch and the Portuguese were both great seafaring nations in times gone by. A Dutch ship in a Portuguese port, a Portuguese ship in a Dutch port. Who knows how the world entangles itself?' He laughed. 'Den Helder is a small village in North Holland, that I know. I believe the name comes from the word *"Helledore,"* which means "the Gates of Hell."'

'Interesting,' said Holliday. 'But it still doesn't answer the question of why you've been expecting us for some time. I didn't even know where Corvo was until a few days ago.'

'You don't need to know where you're going to get there,' said Rodrigues obscurely with a soft smile. 'I knew you would get here eventually because I knew the kind of man you were.'

'And how did you know that?' Holliday asked.

'Because I knew what kind of man your uncle was.'

'You knew Grandpa?' Peggy asked.

'I knew him quite well,' said Rodrigues. 'I read him while I was at Cambridge studying Classical Archaeology. I met him later in Madrid, which is where we became friends. We ran into each other regularly over the years. Cairo, Athens, Berlin, even Washington.'

Washington, thought Holliday. So the priest had also been a spy, but for who?

'But why did you expect us in particular?' he asked.

'Because I heard that Henry had died,' answered Rodrigues. 'I knew that you would come eventually.'

'How does that follow?' Peggy asked.

'I knew the sword would bring you,' said Rodrigues simply. He sipped his coffee, looking at them over the rim of his cup, dark eyes twinkling.

'You knew about the sword?' Holliday said, stunned.

'Four of them actually,' offered Rodrigues. '*Aos*, *Hesperios*, *Boreas*, and *Anatos*. The so-called *Xiphêphoros Peritios Anemos*.'

'East, West, North, and South, the Swords of the Four Winds in ancient Greek,' translated Holliday.

'Quite so,' said Rodrigues. 'The benefits of a classical education, I see,' he smiled. 'The Swords of the Four Winds. The sword your uncle had was named *Hesperios*, the Sword of the West. It was carried by a man named the Chevalier Guillaume de Gisors, not to be confused with the man of the same name who is sometimes reputedly referred to as a Prior of Sion. This Gisors was a simple knight in the service of Henry II of Jerusalem. The city of course had fallen long before, but by then Saladin's treasure had been removed, first to Castle Pelerin and then to Cyprus.'

'Saladin's treasure?' Holliday asked. 'Richard the Lionheart's Saladin?'

'His full name was Salah al-Din Yusuf ibn Ayyub, a warrior born in what is now known as Iraq. Tikrit to be precise.'

'But how is it *his* treasure?' Holliday said. 'Didn't the Knights Templar excavate the treasure from the Temple of Solomon?'

'The Templars never excavated anything from Jerusalem,' said Rodrigues. 'Saladin was no fool. He knew that he couldn't hold on to Jerusalem forever. Eventually it would fall again, and given the emotions involved it would probably be pillaged and sacked by whoever held it next.

'Saladin knew bloodshed was almost inevitable, but he knew that the treasure had to be saved above all else. At that point the Knights Templar were the greatest united force Saladin had to negotiate with; on the promise that they would neither reveal the origins of the treasure nor disperse it he secretly let the Templars remove it from the city. Had the negotiations ever come to light it is probable that both Saladin and the Templar leaders would have been executed for treason.'

'This makes no sense at all,' said Holliday. 'You're saying that Saladin, the crusaders' nemesis, the arch-enemy of Christianity, gave away the treasure to the Templar Knights?'

'He *saved* the treasure,' said Rodrigues. 'Had he not, it would almost certainly have been destroyed. It was the act of a noble and honorable man.' Rodrigues smiled sadly. 'Unfortunately it was not an act that ingratiated him to Pope Clement or to Philip of France, both of whom wanted the treasure for themselves.'

'There's no documentation of this in the historical record,' said Holliday. 'Nothing at all.'

'The historical record, as you well know, Doctor, is written much later than the history itself. All history is hindsight. It is well-known that the Templars did business with their enemies; trading with the enemy is a fact of life, even now. Standard Oil filled the tanks of submarines sinking British ships during World War Two. IBM facilitated the record keeping of Adolf Eichmann at Dachau and Auschwitz-Birkenau. American-owned hotels line the beaches of Veradero in Cuba. It was the same during the Crusades. After all, Richard the Lionheart used a sword forged in Damascus.'

'So what happened to the four swords?' Peggy asked.

'The four swords, each with the same message to the Templar hierarchy at Clairvaux, were sent off with four separate messengers, each blade backing up the others in case one or more was lost. None ever reached their destination. Roger de Flor sailed off with Saladin's treasure and vanished into history, its location a secret.'

'First to La Rochelle, and then here,' said Holliday.

'So some people say,' murmured Rodrigues.

'How does Uncle Henry figure into all of this?'

'There had always been rumors that *Boreas*, the Sword of the North, had reached Scotland with some of Roger de Flor's ships. Sir Henry St. Clair was thought to be the *Boreas* messenger, which is probably how the rumors started. Your uncle became interested in the sword mythology during his time at Oxford, which is of course where our paths begin to cross. It was Henry who discovered the connection to Mussolini and the *Hesperios* sword, which he eventually traced to Berchtesgaden and Hitler's lair.'

'The existence of which he kept a secret for the rest of his life,' said Holliday flatly, still finding it difficult to believe that he was having this conversation in the belly of an extinct volcano in the middle of the Atlantic Ocean.

'Of course he kept it a secret,' said Rodrigues. 'To reveal it would have had disastrous consequences. It was the end of the war; the Middle East was in ferment; Israel was barely a dream, and a fragile one at that. The Catholic Church wasn't in much better shape. Over the years the situation has gone from bad to worse.'

'How does *La Sapinière* fit into all of this, the *Sodalitium Pianum* or whatever it was called?'

'Why do you ask?'

'Because one of their people tried to kill us in Jerusalem,' said Holliday. 'A priest, like you.'

'I told you,' said Rodrigues, 'I am no longer a priest.'

'That doesn't matter. What interest does the Vatican have in all of this?'

'The same as it did eight hundred years ago,' answered Rodrigues. 'Power. Or the lack of it. The Saladin treasure would make the Roman Catholic Church an irrelevancy in one blow if it was revealed. The political machinery that has evolved in the Holy See over a thousand years would come down like Humpty Dumpty off his wall. There would be no way to put it back together again.'

'I don't get it,' said Peggy. 'The Vatican has more money than it knows what to do with. You're trying to tell me they'd hire killers just to get more?'

'You'd be surprised at what the Church is capable of,' said Rodrigues. 'But this is not about money. It never was.'

'What else is treasure about?' Peggy said.

'When is a treasure not a treasure?' Rodrigues responded.

'What's *that* supposed to mean?' Peggy asked, exasperated by the tall man's roundabout answers.

'I think I see,' said Holliday slowly.

'Well, I sure don't,' said Peggy.

There was a sound from the road outside the cottage: tires on gravel, and more than one vehicle from the sounds of it. Doors slammed, and they heard the low sound of voices speaking quietly.

Rodrigues stood and went to the window. He looked for a few seconds, then turned away and went to the fireplace. He took down the shotgun, carried it to the desk, and rummaged in one of the desk drawers. He took out a handful of shells, broke the barrels of the shotgun, and loaded it. He snapped the barrels closed and turned to Holliday and Peggy.

'We have visitors,' Rodrigues said. 'Unwelcome ones by my estimation.'

32

Through the window, Holliday saw two cars, an old Citroën 2CV and an even older Mercedes sedan, standing on the gravel in front of the cottage. There were six men, all big, blond, and hard-faced. One of them stood at the trunk of the Mercedes handing out weapons to the others. Shotguns and small, brutal-looking machine pistols, Uzis and MAC-10s. Holliday caught the flash of a tattoo on the wrist of one of the men.

'Kellerman's people,' said Holliday.

'*Ordo Novi Templi,*' nodded Rodrigues. 'The Order of the New Templars.'

'You know about Kellerman?' Peggy asked, startled.

'There have been White Templars and Black since the beginning,' answered the ex-priest. '*Ordo Novi Templi* is simply one of the Black Templars' more recent incarnations.' The tall man shook his head. 'There is no time to explain further. We must leave this place immediately.'

'And how are we supposed to do that?' Holliday

asked. 'Those men outside aren't about to give us a free pass.'

'*Vis consili expers mole ruit sua,*' said Rodrigues, stuffing the pockets of his trousers with more shotgun shells.

'Horace,' answered Holliday. '"Discretion is the better part of valor." You don't happen to have another weapon by any chance, do you?'

Rodrigues reached under the desk. There was a faint tearing sound: Velcro. He handed Holliday a well-oiled Czech CZ 75 automatic pistol in a belt-clip holster.

'It's loaded with Smith and Wesson .40-caliber copkillers – Teflon coated.'

'Strange priest,' said Holliday, stuffing the holster into the waistband of his jeans.

'Strange times,' responded Rodrigues. 'Follow me.'

Rodrigues stepped quickly to the center of the room and threw back the braided rug. Beneath it was the obvious square and iron ring of a trap-door set into the floor.

Peggy groaned. 'Not this again!'

Rodrigues grabbed the ring and pulled up the trapdoor. Beneath it was a narrow set of stone steps leading downward. The ex-priest motioned them toward the opening.

'Go down. I'll come after you.'

'It's dark,' objected Peggy.

'The fifth step down on the right,' instructed Rodrigues. 'There's a switch on the wall.'

'Go,' said Holliday to Peggy.

She eased herself onto the stairs and went downward, feeling her way with one hand against the stone. A few seconds later there was a wash of light, and Holliday heard the distant grumbling of a generator coming from far below.

'Your turn,' said Rodrigues.

'They're going to follow us, you know,' cautioned Holliday.

'I think I can cool their ardor somewhat.' The ex-priest smiled. 'Go.'

Holliday went down the steps, following Peggy. He could see her below him on the stairs carved into the ancient, porous, pumice-like stone at a steep angle. A thick old-fashioned strip of flat cable was threaded through rusty old staples in the roof of the stairway, and bare bulbs hung every ten feet or so, the light pulsing with each cycle of the generator.

The stairway turned sharply at almost right angles and suddenly ended in a low, wide tunnel that looked man-made but wasn't. Peggy was waiting for him. The tunnel went left and right; the left-hand path was dark while the right-hand path was lit by the same bulbs as the stairway.

Holliday stretched out his hand and ran his fingers along the rows of parallel ridges in the frozen stone.

'A lava tube,' he said. Once upon a time molten stone had flowed in a white-hot liquid river down this subterranean path, eventually ending in the sea. Ahead of them Holliday could hear the echoing, out-of-place sound of the generator powering the lights in the ceiling overhead.

'What do we do now?' Peggy asked, staring down the tunnel.

'Wait for Rodrigues,' answered Holliday. He drew the pistol, racked the slide, and waited at the foot of the steps. The ex-priest appeared a few moments later, his expression tense.

'I've been expecting something like this for many years,' said Rodrigues as he stepped into the tunnel, the shotgun cradled in his arms. 'Secrets never remain secrets forever. As Shakespeare said – "the truth will out." '

From above them there was the sudden sound of an explosion. Rodrigues smiled grimly.

'That should even the odds a little,' he said. 'This way.' He headed off down the tunnel. The lava tube went noticeably downward for two or three hundred yards, meandering around extruded rock formations as it found its petrified path, narrowing until it was barely wide enough to navigate.

Finally it was no more than a crack in the seamed, black stone.

Peggy felt her chest constricting. Without the naked lightbulbs in the roof of the now two-foot-wide passageway, she knew she'd be having a severe case of the screaming meemies. Tight spots and stalled elevators had never been her favorites. The fact that there was probably a squad of armed goons behind them wasn't making her feel any better.

'Getting a little claustrophobic here,' she muttered warningly to Holliday, who had taken up a position right behind her.

They were shuffling sideways now, faces inches from the rock walls.

'It'll be over in a few seconds,' soothed Rodrigues ahead of her in the impossibly narrow corridor.

Peggy wasn't quite sure she liked his choice of words.

Suddenly Rodrigues vanished. She heard his voice.

'Mind the step,' he said. Peggy squeezed out through the crack and stopped dead in her tracks. She felt Holliday slip out behind her onto the small stone platform.

'Holy crap,' she whispered.

'My God,' breathed Holliday, stunned by the vision that rose before him.

The scale was almost beyond belief.

They stood at the foot of a cavern almost as large as the main concourse of Grand Central Terminal in New York City. It was as wide as a football field and twice as long. The ceiling, towering more than a hundred feet overhead, seemed to pulse with life. Color, form, and texture danced up from the mists of time long past as giraffes and wildebeests wandered across endless plains; ibex, scores of them, raced in bent-legged flight, horns swept back as black stick figures pursued them over the great veldts.

Bears, not seen in the Azores since the dawn of the last ice age, roamed through ancient forests. Life-sized Phoenician triremes, sails bent above twin hulls, drove across restless seas through the Pillars of Hercules and beyond into the great unknown sea. Crusader ships followed them, white Templar crosses proud on red sails. Soldiers in armor and chain mail, thousands of them, marched forever out through Jerusalem's gates. Red, green, black, yellow, and ochre, blues azure and aquamarine, blacks and browns and silver, flowing muscle, finely wrought bone, men, animals, creatures that were both and neither, hundreds of them, herds of them, armies and oceans of them, all danced, sailed, rode, and ran across time and the arching ceiling overhead in a strange fantastic vision on the stone.

It was the most awe-inspiring work of art either Holliday or Peggy had ever seen, the great ceiling of the Sistine Chapel paling in comparison. Even illuminated by the electric bulbs set along the walls, Holliday knew that he was only seeing half of what was there, the rest lost in permanent shadow. Heaven only knew how the artists had created such an enormous spectacle; it defied the imagination. It was magnificent.

Steps had been cut into the stone down into the great bowl of the chamber floor, and terraces of frozen lava rode up against the curving walls in lapping waves. Here and there around the base of the cavern Holliday could see the shadows that marked other lava tubes running through the caldera's foundation.

On one of the shelf-like terraces closest to them there were a number of iron chests that looked hundreds of years old, and stacked beside them, almost incredibly, were piles of what could only be iron spears, their flanged points still visible. In the middle of all this was a long, zinc-topped table and an assortment of power tools. It was like a rough version of Raffi Wanounou's lab in Jerusalem.

Sitting under a magnifying lamp on a pair of

padded pedestals in the middle of the table was a sword, the perfect mate to the one Holliday had discovered in Henry's secret drawer. On a second table, set at right angles to the first, was another table, this one holding a large, plain terra-cotta amphora, a delicately shaped clay container about five feet long and used until the late Middle Ages for transporting wine.

On the far left in the darkest corner of the cathedral-like cavern was something that looked like the blackened skeleton of some enormous sea monster, claw upheld, dark spine broken, and huge bony rib cage revealed. It lay partially on its side along a sloping ledge of flowstone that oozed into the shadows. It took Holliday a second, but he managed to decipher the image: it was a ship-wreck, perhaps a hundred feet long and thirty wide, the planking long since rotted away, leaving only the stark outline of the hull.

Rodrigues gestured toward the wreck. 'All that is left of the *Wanderfalke*, the *Peregrine Falcon*, Roger de Flor's flagship, loaded with the great treasure from the Temple of Solomon, Saladin's gift to the Templar Order and to the world, brought here by a Castilian knight named Fernan Ruiz de Castro. The sword on the table belonged to him. It is *Aos*, the Sword of the East.'

'De Flor knew about this place?' Holliday

asked. He stepped over to the table and bent down, examining the ancient weapon.

'By my estimation this cavern has known human occupation for at least ten thousand years,' said Rodrigues. 'There are paintings in the back of the chamber clearly showing the European cave lion, which lived during the Upper Pleistocene Era, probably contemporary with the last ice age. The illustrations of some of the Phoenician ships predate Christ by at least a thousand years. The Phoenicians certainly knew of this place, perhaps the Vikings, as well. One of de Flor's captains discovered the island when his ship was blown off course. The sea entrance to the cave was much larger then, and there was a much easier landfall. From the evidence I have seen there was some sort of seismic activity in the 1600s, and a large section of the entrance collapsed, making it almost invisible. There could have been no better place to hide the treasure.'

'You keep on talking about treasure,' said Peggy. 'But I don't see any.'

Rodrigues went to the second table and put his hand on the terra-cotta wine jar under examination. It was sealed around its upper end with some dark, resinous substance.

'This is the treasure,' said the ex-priest softly.

'Wine?' Peggy laughed. 'We've traveled halfway

round the world and back, putting our lives in jeopardy for a big bottle of wine?'

'No,' said Rodrigues gently. 'You've traveled halfway around the world and back putting your lives in jeopardy for this.'

He picked up a small, rubber mallet from the worktable and brought it down hard on the side of the amphora. The jar shattered, pieces of brittle clay dropping to the zinc surface of the table. Half a dozen gleaming cylinders of pure, butter-colored gold tumbled out, each one about ten inches long and three inches in diameter. The cylinders, like the wine jar, were sealed with resin at one end. Rodrigues picked up one of the tubular objects.

'A scroll from the ancient royal library at Alexandria, saved by the military commander Amr ibn al-As, not destroyed by him during his conquest of Egypt in the sixth century – a story, by the way, that Saladin was quick to quash, since Amr ibn al-As was a contemporary of Muhammad and many of the works in Alexandria were in contravention of the Koran and thus should have been destroyed under strict Muslim law.'

Rodrigues shrugged, shifting the gold cylinder into his other hand. 'Perhaps an unknown work by Homer? One of the Greek tragedies by Euripides? Mathematics from Archimedes? A map to the secret location of Imhotep's fabulous tomb? The way to King Solomon's Mines? A treatise on medicine by the first true doctor, Aesculapius?' He paused. 'The Holy Church's greatest fear is in this place – I have seen the evidence myself – the Lost Gospels of the Apostles from their own mouths, in Aramaic, not handed down through centuries of translations each with their own interpretation. Somewhere hidden there might well be the most sacred and dangerous of them all – the Gospel of Christ himself.' He shook his head. 'No wonder the Vatican and the *Sodalitium Pianum* would have you dead, and me, as well. News of this place would shake St. Peter's Basilica to its very foundation.' The ex-priest lifted his broad shoulders once again.

'Who knows what else lies here? I have been working at this for more than fifty years and have only barely scratched the surface; others were here before me, as well.

'It is not just the Library of Alexandria that was hidden in Jerusalem. Hadrian's library is here, as well, the Library of Pergamon in Athens, the texts from the Villa of the Papyri in Herculaneum, long thought to have been destroyed in the eruption of Vesuvius, all of them are here and more. It is the wisdom of the world, nothing less, wrapped in skins of gold, all of it.'

'There are more scrolls then?' Holliday asked, excited. 'More amphorae?'

'Thousands,' answered Rodrigues. 'Enough to fill the hold of the *Wanderfalke* and its sister ship *Tempel Rose*, the *Temple Rose*. Ten thousand, perhaps more; I've never bothered to count. De Flor was a well-known trader in wine out of La Rochelle and the Levant; what better and safer way to move such a treasure about than hidden in clay casks? Even in crusader times they knew that gold was inert and would be the safest form of transport; that is why they had a smelter at Castle Pelerin. The scrolls have remained intact for the better part of a millennium. The ones still to be examined wait in the lava tunnels that you see around the cave. The rest are in the good hands of friends of the Order.'

'Order?' Holliday said. 'You mean the Templars?'

'Of course,' said Rodrigues. 'As I said to you, there have been White Templars and Black since the beginning. We couldn't let all this great knowledge fall into the wrong hands. That's why your uncle joined us.'

'Grandpa was a Templar?' Peggy asked. 'He knew about all this?'

'Yes,' nodded Rodrigues. 'That is why he hid the sword.' The ex-priest turned to Holliday. 'To protect and pass the secret on to you if you proved yourself worthy of the task.' He turned back to Peggy. 'And you, as well.'

Suddenly the dim lights in the huge cavern flickered. Almost instinctively Holliday's hand reached out and swept up the old sword from its pedestal mounts. With his other hand he wrenched the Czech automatic from its holster and thumbed off the safety. Then the lights flickered again and finally went out. Utter darkness fell.

33

The lights came on again almost immediately.

'What the hell?' Peggy said.

'A crude approximation of an alarm,' said Rodrigues, hefting the shotgun. 'Apparently my fireworks didn't disable all our visitors. They're almost here. We have to leave. Now.'

'We could stay and fight,' said Peggy.

'No. He's right. They've got automatic weapons; we've got a shotgun and a pistol. Time to bug out.'

'This way,' said Rodrigues. He bent down and picked up a battery-powered lantern from beneath the table with the shattered wine jar and headed across the cavern toward one of the lava-tube entrances. As they climbed the ascending layers of petrified lava Holliday saw a flicker of movement out of the corner of his eye and turned.

'Go!' he commanded. On the far side of the cavern one of Kellerman's men appeared, a squat weapon in his hands and a set of American Technologies lightweight night-vision goggles balanced on his forehead. Holliday saw a red beam flash across the cavern from the man's weapon: a fire-and-forget laser scope. He didn't wait to see the man's elected target, or take the time to aim his own weapon; at this range it would be futile. He simply aimed high and squeezed the trigger of the Czech pistol, spraying the entire clip of twelve rounds in the enemy's general direction. Delay was the objective now, not accuracy. The inside of the cavern rang with shattering echoes as he emptied the gun. The man got off one shot and ducked away. Behind Holliday there was a grunt of pain and surprise. He turned. Rodrigues had been hit, blood blossoming on his shirt, low on his right side. Hopefully no more than a flesh wound. He sagged against the smooth wall of the cave by the entrance to a lava tube. Peggy took the big flashlight and the shotgun from his hands, supporting him under one arm.

'Into the tunnel, as fast as you can,' the ex-priest moaned.

Holliday tossed away the empty gun, transferred the sword into his right hand, and ran up the last few levels to take Rodrigues by the other arm. Together he and Peggy helped him into the relative safety of the lava tube. Behind them there was the sound of ringing automatic fire. More than one weapon. Kellerman's people had arrived in force.

'Twenty paces into the tunnel. The generator,' grunted Rodrigues. 'Be careful,' he warned.

Holliday and Peggy eased the wounded man forward, the tunnel barely wide enough to allow them passage, the ceiling low above their heads. Ahead of them they could hear the roar of the diesel generator, the fumes souring the air slightly. Holliday could also feel a slight movement of the air across his face. Fresh air.

At twenty paces there was a widening of the tunnel, man-made, and a deep, square-cut little chamber on the left. Inside the tiny room there was a bright yellow six-thousand-watt Yamaha diesel generator chugging quietly and a hundred gallon tank of kerosene. A length of PVC tubing led up into a narrow crack in the ceiling, carrying most of the fumes away.

'The switch,' managed Rodrigues.

Holliday found the switch on the side of the generator and threw it. The sound of the generator stopped in mid-cycle, and the lights went off. It might slow their pursuers for a moment, but with the active infrared goggles it wouldn't stop them. Peggy switched on the battery-powered lamp. A cone of light bloomed, showing the way ahead.

'Another ten paces,' muttered the ex-priest. He coughed and dark, coffee-ground blood poured over his lips and down his chin. Not a flesh wound then, noted Holliday. The man was bleeding internally. He needed medical attention, and quickly.

'What about ten paces?' Holliday asked urgently, helping Rodrigues down the tunnel. Their pursuers couldn't be much more than a minute or two behind them.

'Trip wire. Fishing line,' the ex-priest managed, coughing again and doubling over.

They stepped forward carefully, Peggy shining the light ahead, keeping the beam down, illuminating the base of the tunnel. Holliday, supporting Rodrigues, now came up behind her.

Fifty feet farther on the light caught a length of taut, black fishing line stretched across the tunnel, calf-high, invisible unless you were looking for it.

'Where is it?' Holliday asked.

'Up,' muttered Rodrigues.

Peggy swept the light up toward the ceiling. The trip wire led upward, threaded through blackened eyebolts, to a small hole in the roof about eight inches across. In the hole were two round, olive-green metal objects, each about four inches in diameter. Holliday recognized them instantly: OZM-72 antipersonnel mines, the Russian version of the American M16 'Bouncing Betty' he'd used in Vietnam and the Yugoslavian PROM-1's he'd seen during the Bosnian War. Triggered on the ground, the device would bound into the air to waist height before exploding. In the case of these two mines they would fire downward into the lava tube. Each of the OZM's carried a charge of slightly more than a pound of cast high explosive. The slaughter in the lava tube would be horrifying. On ignition anything for a hundred feet in either direction would be shredded into hamburger.

'Help him over the trip wire,' said Holliday.

Together he and Peggy managed to get the failing ex-priest over the deadly thread. They headed on, hurrying now more than ever, trying to put distance between themselves and the hideous booby trap behind them. A dozen yards along the tube, the passage suddenly veered sharply to the right and began heading upward at a steep angle. Holliday could feel a rush of cool air on his face now, and in the distance he thought he heard the sound of thunder. Somewhere above them yesterday's storm was returning.

Around them the lava tube was changing; as they neared the surface the walls of the tunnel began to close in. The smooth floor felt slick with mud, and the walls were coated with heavy bacterial slime. It was getting harder and harder to get

Rodrigues to keep walking, his coughing increasing with each step, his legs dragging, and his body beginning to shake uncontrollably as he went into shock. Holliday knew the signs. He wasn't going to last much longer.

'Pocket,' moaned the dying man. 'Book. Take it.'

'Later,' soothed Holliday. 'There'll be time for that later.'

'*Now!*' Rodrigues demanded with authority.

Still moving forward Holliday fumbled in Rodrigues's back pockets and found a small leather-bound notebook at least half an inch thick. It looked very old. Holliday stuffed it into the pocket of his jacket and carried on. The ground began to rise even more steeply, and their knees bent with exertion. Rodrigues was almost deadweight now. Ahead Holliday thought he saw a crack of light.

Without warning all three of them were picked up and thrown to the ground by a massive concussion. A split second later there was a rolling, earsplitting explosion and a second concussive blast as a gusting roar of heat enveloped them and passed on.

Holliday got to his feet, still hanging on to the sword. The glass in the battery-powered lamp was broken, but enough light was coming down from above to light their way. Peggy abandoned the lamp, and clutching the shotgun, she and Holliday managed to get Rodrigues up. They stumbled forward toward the light. Holliday felt a few splashes of rain on his face, and above them thunder roared. A moment later they reached the ragged end of the lava tube exit and stepped out onto the rugged surface of the ancient crater and into the teeth of a biting wind and a growing storm. A bolt of spiked lightning flashed across the gray-black clouds roiling overhead.

'The badger comes out of his lair,' said a voice. 'A little the worse for wear, it would seem.'

Axel Kellerman. He was dressed like the quintessential British country squire in a tweed suit with a waistcoat, walking boots, and a rabbit-skin trilby hat. He sat perched on a flat ledge of broken stone a few feet from the entrance to the lava tunnel. In the distance, almost half a mile away between the two volcanic lakes, Holliday could see Rodrigues's isolated cottage. More rain began to spatter down. Above them the storm was breaking, the winds pulling at their clothes. Thunder rolled.

Seeing Kellerman standing there dressed like that and in those circumstances, Holliday suddenly realized just how insane the SS officer's son really was, living out some Goethe-like *Sturm und Drang* aristocratic fantasy. Kellerman wasn't alone; one of his blond thugs stood close to him, machine pistol held to the neck of Manuel Rivero Tavares, the captain of the *San Pedro*.

Between Peggy and Holliday, Rodrigues sagged to the ground.

'Put the shotgun down, Miss Blackstock,' said Kellerman, smiling. 'You can keep the sword for now, Dr. Holliday. It suits you.'

Peggy carefully did as she was told.

Holliday kept his eyes firmly on Kellerman.

'I'm very sorry, *Doutor*,' said Tavares, his eyes pleading. 'I could not help it.'

'A few simple threats,' said Kellerman. 'Apparently the good captain has grandchildren. Little girls.'

He looked past them down the ragged hole in the ground.

'I gather from the noise a few moments ago that some of my employees fell afoul of some sort of IED.' Kellerman grimaced. 'That's more lives you owe me, Dr. Holliday, although they served their purpose. Now at least I know where my legacy is hidden. It only remains for me to retrieve it.'

'The legacy isn't yours any more than it was your father's,' said Holliday. He gripped the hilt of the sword tightly in his hand. 'It doesn't belong to any one man.'

'It belongs to anyone who takes it,' spat Kellerman, getting to his feet and stepping closer. 'The world has always been that way. Victory to the strong.' He sneered down at the curled still figure of Rodrigues. 'Defeat to the weak.'

'We've all heard that filth before,' said Holliday. '"*Arbeit macht frei,*" "*Kraft durch Freude,*" "*Drang nach Osten,*" and in the end none of it came to pass.' He shook his head. 'You're nothing more than a dirty joke gone wrong, Kellerman, just like your father before you.'

Light flashed in the New World Nazi's eyes. He surged forward, fumbling beneath his tightly buttoned jacket, spittle forming at the corners of his mouth. There was a blinding flash of lightning and an enormous thunderclap. The heavens opened.

It happened in the blink of an eye.

'*Vai-te foder!*' Tavares said furiously. He brought his foot down hard on the blond thug's instep and threw himself wildly to one side. Reacting instantly, Peggy dropped to the ground, swept up the shotgun, and pulled both triggers. The heavy gun jumped in her hands, the butt thumping back into her shoulder. The thug made a grunting sound and sat down on the ground abruptly, staring down at the plate-sized bleeding hole in his belly as the torrential rainfall began.

Kellerman had his weapon out, a flat little Walther PPK. He kept coming, lifting the pistol in his hand.

Holliday didn't even think twice. The sword came up, and he took one step forward, setting his leg with the knee slightly bent and his elbow locked. Unable to stop his forward momentum Kellerman ran onto the blade, unblooded for more than seven hundred years. It sliced through the thick tweed of his waistcoat, his shirt and the flesh just beneath the xiphoid process of his diaphragm. Still going forward, the broad wedge of Damascus steel thrust through both the right ventricle and left atrium of his heart before it finally ground against his spine. The furious light went out in the madman's eyes, and Kellerman died, skewered.

Holliday stepped back, pulling the sword out of the man's body with a light twisting movement to break the inevitable suction. There was a ghastly sucking sound as the blade slid out of Kellerman's chest. The dead man slithered to the ground. Holliday dropped the sword and turned, trying to wipe the rain out of his eyes.

Peggy was on her knees, one hand cradling her bruised shoulder, staring at the corpse of the blond thug, the blood from his wound diluted by the rain into a spreading pink puddle on the rocky ground.

'Are you all right?' Holliday asked, bending over her.

'Just fine,' she said quietly, staring vacantly at the man she'd just blown out of his socks. 'Peachy.'

Tavares sat on the ground, cradling Rodrigues's head in his lap, the steady rain soaking them both. Holliday knelt beside them.

'He is my friend,' whispered Tavares, weeping, the words catching wetly in his throat. He stroked Rodrigues's forehead soothingly. 'My dear, dear friend for all these years. I cannot let him die.'

Rodrigues opened his eyes, blinking them hard against the rain.

'We all die, Emmanuel,' murmured the ex-priest.

He made a small sighing noise, managing to lift his hand and grip Tavares's broad, hairy wrist. He turned his head slightly so that he could see Holliday above him.

'Keep Manuel close. He is brother to my soul and knows about everything. He has been my eyes and ears in the world of men for a long time.'

'I will,' promised Holliday, feeling his own eyes dampen, trying to tell himself it was the rain.

'Kellerman is dead?'

'Very,' nodded Holliday.

'Good enough,' murmured Rodrigues. 'Good enough.' He sighed again. 'Then the torch is passed. *Iacta alea est. Vale, amici.*' The ex-priest lifted his head from Tavares's lap. His eyes stared up at the dark sky, seeing nothing now. 'Too many secrets,' he whispered. 'Too many secrets.' He made one last, small sound, closed his eyes, and died.

The rain crashed down in long, weeping curtains all around them in the bowl of the island crater.

Peggy rose, turned away from the two dead men, and put her hand on Holliday's shoulder.

'We never really knew him,' she said sadly, looking down at Rodrigues.

'And now we never will.'

'What was that he said at the end?'

'*Iacta alea est.* It's what Julius Caesar said when he crossed the Rubicon and entered Roman territory, defying the Senate and starting civil war.'

'What does it mean?'

'"The die is cast." There's no way to turn back from destiny now. He meant for you and for me.'

'And the last *"Vale, amici"*?'

'"Farewell, friends,"' said Holliday softly.

Two hours later they sat in the snug cabin of the *San Pedro*, wrapped in blankets, a kettle whistling on the small gas stove. Peggy got up from the little table and began making tea. With Holliday and

Peggy in the *San Pedro* bobbing gently at anchor in the tiny harbor, Tavares was dealing with the embarrassment of dead bodies back at Rodrigues's little cottage. The rain still thundered down, hammering on the cabin roof of the old Chris-Craft, and, according to Tavares at least, making his job much easier. They would stay aboard the *San Pedro* tonight, and tomorrow the rotund captain would take them across the narrow strait to Flores and a flight back to civilization.

Holliday sat at the table, leafing through the fat little notebook Rodrigues had insisted he take from his pocket. *Aos*, Sword of the East, cleaned and dried, lay on a folded towel in front of him. Peggy put two mugs of hot sweet tea on the table and slid down the upholstered bench beside Holliday. Rain streaked against the cabin window behind her, and she snuggled down into the blanket, pulling it around her more tightly. She shivered and took a sip of the tea.

'What's in the book?'

'Names and addresses,' said Holliday. 'Hundreds of them. People all over the world. Something called the Phoenix Foundation and some sort of special prefix number I've never seen before. Figures and letter codes that look like they might be bank accounts.'

'Is Raffi in the book?'

'No.' He smiled. 'I haven't seen it so far.'

'But you checked, didn't you, Doc?'

'Of course.' He grinned.

'Still suspicious?' Peggy asked.

'Always,' said Holliday.

'I'm going to see him when we get out of here,' she said, a little defensively. 'See how he's doing in the hospital. See if he could use some help.'

'Bring him a box of candies?'

'Maybe even flowers.' She smiled. 'Guys never get flowers.'

'Give him my best,' said Holliday. 'I mean that.'

'Thanks, I'll tell him.'

There was a long pause. They sipped their tea and listened to the raindrops rattling on the cabin roof, both wondering how they'd come from here to there and back again, wondering what was coming next. Finally, Peggy spoke.

'It's not over yet, is it, Doc?'

Holliday glanced at the gleaming sword on the table, bright steel forged an eon ago in the desert sun of Damascus, reaching across time to slay its enemy.

'No,' he answered, flipping the pages of the little book. 'I don't think it's over, not for us, not by a long shot.'

*

It was late September now. There was a chill in the air, and Holliday had laid kindling in the little tiled hearth of the fireplace in his living room. It was blazing well, the flames making flickering shadows dance across the book-lined walls. Time to add a log or two and then relax after a long day of teaching.

The reinforced FedEx box from José de Braga's shop in Quebec City was leaning up against the armchair by the fire. A glass of Ardbeg Lord of the Isles single malt stood waiting for him on the side table. But he wasn't ready for either the box or the drink just yet.

Holliday went to the window at the front of the room and stared out into the gathering night. Through the trees and down the hill he could see the modern brick bulk of Eisenhower Hall. Beyond it the Hudson River wound its dark way toward Manhattan and the sea.

A thousand miles or so farther were the Azores, where Rodrigues and Kellerman had both died and where his life and Peggy's had changed forever. After Peggy had gone back to Jerusalem to be with Raffi, Holliday had returned here to West Point.

Everything seemed as it should be. A thousand fresh-faced and earnest plebes, triumphant survivors of Beast Barracks, back from six weeks of basic-training hell and willing to learn – even if it was just history. A thousand ring-thumpers who were sure they knew everything, but who really didn't know anything at all about what waited for them in the real world. And him, Lieutenant Colonel John 'Doc' Holliday, who was starting to think that he'd fought one too many battles and seen one too many good people die for no good reason. *Gung ho!* and *Huah!* were Hollywood, but it would take these kids a long time to learn that. Too long for some of them, and some wouldn't have time to learn at all.

He let out a long breath and turned away from the window. He went back to the armchair and tore open the heavy box. He drew out the restored weapon from the famous swordsmith's shop and examined it in the glimmering light of the fire.

De Braga had done a wonderful job; the gold wire with its coded message had been perfectly rewound over the tang, and the silky, iridescent sheen of the yard-long Damascus blade had been polished to an almost magical brilliance. Somewhere, four thousand miles and almost a thousand years away, a dead knight smiled in his grave. *Hesperios*, the Sword of the West.

Holding it carefully in both hands Holliday took the sword to the fireplace and eased it onto the slotted wooden pegs that awaited it above the mantel. He stood back. It looked as though it belonged. But for how long?

'Sword of the Templars,' said Holliday to the empty room. What had Rodrigues said? 'Too many secrets'? He'd told Peggy that he didn't think the story had ended for them, and now he was even surer of it. Something was coming, something dark and forbidding. He stared up at the gleaming sword, its purity and perfection suddenly nothing more than a shallow arc of malevolent steel.

'Now what?' he asked.

Author's Note

The research contained in *The Sword of the Templars* is accurate. Saladin really did offer Richard the Lionheart terms on the fall of Jerusalem that were refused, resulting in great slaughter.

A hoard of Phoenician coins really was discovered during the building of Castle Pelerin (Pilgrim Castle) by the Templars in A.D. 1213. Exactly the same type of coins were discovered on the remote island of Corvo in the Portuguese Azores in the mid-1800s, more than six hundred years later.

Roger de Flor, also known as Rutger von Blum, commanded the Templar fleet out of La Rochelle, France, and both his ships, *The Peregrine Falcon* and *The Temple Rose*, existed.

Both the *Ordo Novi Templi*, the Order of the New Templars, and *Sodalitium Pianum*, the Vatican intelligence network, existed exactly as they are described.

And last but definitely not least, an SS officer named Kellerman really did sign off on the destruction by fire of the Naples State Archives being stored at the Villa Montesano near San

Paolo Bel Sito, about thirty kilometers from Naples, on September 30, 1943. The ruins of the villa still exist not far from the local monastery. Go and see for yourself if you don't believe me.

– Paul Christopher

Read on for the first
chapter from Paul
Christopher's new thriller

The Templar Cross

Available from Penguin
in July 2011.

I

The United States Military Academy at West Point was deserted. There were no platoons practicing close order drill on the Plain, marching under the tarnished eternal eye of a bronze George Washington on horseback. There was no echoing sound of polished combat boots on asphalt in the Central Area as cadets did punishment duty. No barking orders echoing from stone walls. No drill sergeants calling cadence.

Graduation was over. Firsties transformed into newly minted soldiers were gone to their posts – plebes, cows and yuks all gone on summer training tours of one kind or another. No bands played, and the trees whispering secrets in the early-summer breeze was the only sound. The complex of old gray buildings was fading to a warm golden hue in the waning light of the sun. It was the last Sunday in June. Tomorrow was 'R' Day.

Lieutenant Colonel John 'Doc' Holliday walked across the broad, empty expanse of the Plain in his dress whites, feeling just a little bit tipsy. He was returning home from his farewell dinner at the West Point Club on the far side of the campus and he was relieved that there was no one around to see him in his present condition. Drunk history professors in tailcoats reeling around on the grounds of the nation's premier military school didn't go down well with civilian cadet moms and dads; definitely not good public relations.

Holliday stared blearily into the gathering darkness, the scarred eye socket under his black patch giving him phantom pain probably caused by one too many single malts. The gloomy breadth of the Plain was as empty as the rest of the Point. Tomorrow the fathers, mothers, brothers, sisters and friends of twelve hundred new cadet recruits would swarm over the big, neatly clipped field like ants with video cameras recording the doomed twelve hundred's last hours of freedom before they were swallowed up by the U.S. Military machine.

Registration Day was like a circus and the end of the world combined. The new cadets, with their hairstyles still intact, had more than a few things in common with concentration camp inmates. They arrived, wide-eyed and terrified, in lines of buses and were shorn, poked, yelled at, given numbers and uniforms, then marched away into oblivion, like Hamelin's children following the Pied Piper.

After five weeks in Beast Barracks getting Cadet Basic Training – which would winnow out a hundred or so who just couldn't take it – and four grueling years that would winnow out a few hundred more, the same Pied Piper might eventually lead them onto the killing fields of Afghanistan or Iraq, or wherever else it was decided they should go by whoever happened to be occupying the White House that year.

Holliday had seen them come and seen them go and for years before that he'd seen them die in places the family and friends of the new cadets could never even imagine. The pomp and circumstance and hypotheticals of West Point would give way to blood and brains and severed limbs and all the other realities of armed conflict that never made it onto the evening news, let alone the pages of *The Howitzer*, the West Point yearbook. Proof of that, dating back to 1782 in the form of a soldier named Dominick Trant, lay in the old cemetery just along the way on Washington Road.

But that was over now. Ten months ago, following his Uncle Henry's death, had found Doc Holliday following the trail of a Crusader's sword that led him and his cousin Peggy Blackstock halfway round the world and to a secret that had changed his life forever: a Templar treasure hoard that now lay securely hidden in an ancient castle in the south of France, the Chateau de Ravanche.

Now he was hostage to that treasure, bound as a steward to its awe-inspiring secret. For months he had wrestled with his obligations and finally realized that in good conscience he could no longer spend his time teaching history; it was time to live it. He had handed in his resignation to the superintendent and agreed to finish out the year. Now the year was done.

Holliday reached the edge of the Plain and turned down Washington Road. He went past Quarters 100, the old Federal-style house occupied by the superintendent, and headed onto Professor's Row. His own house was the smallest on the treelined avenue, a two-bedroom Craftsman bungalow built in the 1920s, all oak paneling, stained glass, twenties furniture and polished hardwood floors. Married quarters, even though he'd been a widower for more than ten years now, but when he signed on at West Point after Kabul and the idiotic accident that had taken his eye, the little house had been the only accommodation suitable to his rank.

Holliday fumbled with his keys, managed to unlock the front door and let himself into the dark house. As usual, just for a second, some small part of his heart and mind imagined that Amy would be there and a second later he'd feel the soft sweep of sadness as he realized that she wasn't. It had been a long time, almost ten years now, but some pain just didn't go away no matter what the philosophers said.

He tossed the keys into the little dish on the sideboard that Peggy had made for him when she was twelve and headed down the hall to the kitchen. He switched on the gas beneath a pot of cowboy coffee he always kept on the stove, then went to the bedroom and stripped off his uniform. Even tipsy he made sure he hung it neatly in the closet beside his Ranger Class A's and then slipped into jeans and a T-shirt. He went back to the kitchen, poured himself a mug of the bitter brew and carried it to the small living room, a book-lined rectangle with a short couch and a few comfortable old chairs arranged around a green-tiled Craftsman fireplace complete with the original Mother Oak keystone.

Outside it was fully dark now and Holliday felt a chill in the room. He laid the fire, lit it and dropped down into one of the armchairs, sipping his coffee and watching as the flames caught in the kindling and licked up into the larger logs. In ten minutes the fire was burning brightly and a circle of warmth was expanding into the room, the evening chill dissolving in the face of the cheerful blaze.

Holliday's glance drifted up to the object hanging over the fireplace mantel on two pegs, glittering almost sensually in the dancing light: the Templar sword that he and Peggy had found in a secret compartment in Uncle Henry's house in northwestern New York. The sword that had started it all, thirty-one inches of patterned Damascus steel, its hilt wrapped in gold wire, the wire coded with its remarkable message. A sword that had once belonged to a Crusader knight named Guillaume de Gisors seven hundred years in the past. A sword once possessed by both Benito Mussolini and Adolf Hitler. Twin to the sword that Holliday had used to kill a man less than a year ago. The deadly weapon hanging above the fireplace was *Hesperios*, the Sword of the West.

Before he and Peggy had embarked on their long journey of discovery almost a year ago, Holliday's attitude toward history had been absolute. Facts and dates and the timelines of events were literally written in stone as well as textbooks. Words like 'unqualified,' 'unassailable,' 'irrevocable' and 'immutable' were all part of his historical vocabulary.

But now, things had changed. A view of history could be upset as easily as a placid pond by a tossed pebble or a simple act of birth. Or, in Holliday's case, a sword.

Discovering *Hesperios* in Uncle Henry's house in Fredonia had altered not only his own history but others' as well. If he hadn't found it, good people and bad he'd never known would still be alive, some dead now by his own hand. Uncle Henry's past had changed as well as Holliday uncovered the circumstances and secrets that led to the sword being in his possession.

His understanding of Templar history had also changed. Once upon a time he'd taught his students at the Point that the ancient brotherhood was no more than an interesting footnote in the chronicles of medieval times, a group that had seen a ragged assembly of less than a dozen unemployed knights transform themselves from *routier* highwaymen on the Pilgrim Road to Jerusalem into an economic force that spread itself over thirteenth-century Europe like a cloud.

He'd also taught his cadet students that all of that had come crashing down in a single day, Friday, October 13, 1307, as Philip of France and Pope Clement's order for the arrest of all Templars in France and the confiscation of their property and wealth was carried out.

Every other country in Europe soon followed suit, seeing an easy way to rid themselves of crippling royal debt to Templar banks. According to accepted history the Templars had simply disappeared, erased from history, a brief phenomenon that had come and gone. Holliday had taught all that as fact. And he'd been totally wrong.

On that particular day in 1307 King Philip's bailiffs cut off a thousand Templar heads, but Philip forgot that there were also a thousand Templar tails. The knights, or at least most of them, were gone, but the accountants, many of them Cistercian monks, survived. By the end of World War II Germany was a rubble-strewn wasteland, but when the smoke cleared it was the same men running the trains, policing the streets and teaching the children. In the United States, presidents came and went every few years like a revolving door, but the bureaucrats remained. So it was with the Templars.

Long before King Philip sent out his edict, the lower echelons of the Templar Order saw the potential for disaster and took steps to avoid it. Deeds and testaments were quietly rewritten, titles to properties changed and notes in hand for enormous sums were transferred to supposedly innocent hands in distant places, far from the clutches of Philip and his English cousins. It was no accident that the man who invented double-entry bookkeeping was a monk. The concept of keeping two sets of books wasn't far behind.

When Philip arrested the Templars he confiscated their visible wealth but their *invisible* wealth had long since been spirited away. As Jacques de Molai, the last official Grand Master of the Templars, said shortly before he was burned at the stake in 1314: 'The best way to keep a secret is to forget that it exists.' And that was precisely what the Templars did.

For the better part of seven hundred years, under scores of different names and identities, the Templars' hidden assets had grown to almost unbelievable proportions, doubling and redoubling over time, diversifying into every walk and facet of everyday life in virtually all the nations of the earth.

Consolidated into a single force, the power of that much wealth would be almost overwhelming, capable of toppling governments with ease. Forged into a mighty hammer the influence of the Templar fortune was capable of doing enormous good or unspeakable evil. It was the key to the kingdom of heaven or to the burning gates of hell.

And the key lay in the small, blood-spattered notebook now locked in a desk drawer in Lieutenant Colonel John Holliday's study. The notebook was the gift of an ex-priest named Helder Rodrigues, dying in Holliday's arms on the island of Corvo in the distant Azores.

The gift came with a codicil, however: use it wisely, use it well or use it not at all. The Templar treasure Rodrigues had revealed to Holliday and Peggy that day in the furious rain had been great enough; the secret revealed within the bloody notebook was a million times greater. The neo-Nazi Axel Kellerman had forfeited his life for it, run through by *Aos*, Sword of the East. The anonymous assassin from the Vatican's *Sodalitium Pianum* had died for it on the narrow midnight streets of Jerusalem.

All of which lay behind Holliday's decision to leave West Point. He knew the menace inherent in the notebook from Rodrigues wasn't over and there was no way he was going to imperil the cadets or anyone else at the Point; if there was danger ahead, it would be his alone.

Holliday dozed, warmed by the fire, then fell into a dreamless sleep. When he awoke it was almost dawn, the first pink light creeping up over the trees along Gee's Point and the Hudson River. The fire had burned to cold ashes in the grate and Holliday's joints ached after a night of sitting up in the chair. Something had awakened him. A sound. He blinked and raised his wrist, checking the old Royal Air Force Rolex he'd inherited from his Uncle Henry. Ten to six. Too early for reveille by forty minutes.

He levered himself out of the armchair and crossed the room to his front window. There was a blue Academy Taxi from Highland Falls idling on the street in front of the house. A figure climbed out of the taxi and started up the walk. He carried only a flight bag for luggage.

Holliday recognized the handsome dark-haired man immediately. It was Rafi Wanounou, the Israeli archaeologist he and Peggy had befriended in Jerusalem. From this distance he looked fit and well, and the only evidence of the savage beating he'd taken on their behalf in Jerusalem was a slight limp. The expression on his face, however, was grim. He climbed the steps, favoring his right leg. Holliday went to the front door and threw it open.

'Rafi,' he said. 'This is a surprise. What on earth are you doing here?'

'She's gone,' the archaeologist said. 'They've taken Peggy.'

He just wanted a decent book to read ...

Not too much to ask, is it? It was in 1935 when Allen Lane, Managing Director of Bodley Head Publishers, stood on a platform at Exeter railway station looking for something good to read on his journey back to London. His choice was limited to popular magazines and poor-quality paperbacks – the same choice faced every day by the vast majority of readers, few of whom could afford hardbacks. Lane's disappointment and subsequent anger at the range of books generally available led him to found a company – and change the world.

'We believed in the existence in this country of a vast reading public for intelligent books at a low price, and staked everything on it'
Sir Allen Lane, 1902–1970, founder of Penguin Books

The quality paperback had arrived – and not just in bookshops. Lane was adamant that his Penguins should appear in chain stores and tobacconists, and should cost no more than a packet of cigarettes.

Reading habits (and cigarette prices) have changed since 1935, but Penguin still believes in publishing the best books for everybody to enjoy. We still believe that good design costs no more than bad design, and we still believe that quality books published passionately and responsibly make the world a better place.

So wherever you see the little bird – whether it's on a piece of prize-winning literary fiction or a celebrity autobiography, political tour de force or historical masterpiece, a serial-killer thriller, reference book, world classic or a piece of pure escapism – you can bet that it represents the very best that the genre has to offer.

Whatever you like to read – trust Penguin.